ALSO BY ELIZABETH BYRNE

The Grave Keepers

BOOK,
BEAST,
AND
CROW

BOOK, BEAST, AND CROW

ELIZABETH BYRNE

Quill Tree Books
An Imprint of HarperCollinsPublishers

Quill Tree Books is an imprint of HarperCollins Publishers.

Library of Congress Control Number: 2023937039
ISBN 978-0-06-248478-9

Typography by Laura Mock
23 24 25 26 27 LBC 5 4 3 2 1
First Edition

For Mike and for Gilbert

CHAPTER 1

OLIVIA CRANKED THE heat and rolled down the windows so the crisp wind whipped our hair into our faces. "I still don't understand why we had to do this at lunch," I said, but she couldn't hear me. She peeled back the foil from a leftover burrito, took a huge bite, then returned it to the cup holder. I sat in the passenger seat, my shoulder-length hair mixing with my bangs and blinding me behind my glasses. My best friend, Olivia, had recently shaved the left side of her head, as if preparing for exactly this moment, driving through the early afternoon in her parents' old Volvo, in the town we grew up in—were almost *done* growing up in—a town so small it was permanently lost in the crisscrossing train lines of central New Jersey.

"It's a little chilly," I shouted.

"You mispronounced 'fucking *freezing*,'" Olivia yelled back. "Ha!" She raised the windows a few inches and turned down the charging guitars of whatever artist the algorithm had thrown at us.

"Tell me again why this couldn't wait until after school?" I said.

"There's an info session about the track meet on Saturday. I can't miss it. Plus"—she took another bite—"it'll only take five minutes."

"You're lucky it's your birthday," I said to my reflection as I fixed my bangs in the mirror. "I just don't want to be late for the field trip."

Olivia slammed on the brakes. "Wait, we have a field trip? Today?" Her face broke into a grin, then softened when she saw the panic written all over mine. "Sorry, I was just kidding. I know we're going to clean up that stream, or whatever, for bio. I haven't forgotten."

I massaged my neck where my seat belt had dug into it. "We will definitely miss it if we get rear-ended." I checked the traffic in the side mirror, but the street behind us was empty.

"Don't even sweat it, Anna. We have plenty of time." Olivia sped up. A hot-pink button glinted on the zipper of her jacket. It said **Put a Gate in the Wall and Call Me in the Morning.** It was scratched and faded, like she'd been wearing it for years, which she had.

The Wall was one of three things that Hartwood was famous for, all of them weird and unexplainable, especially for the suburbs. The Wall penned in the Great Swamp, which sat at the center of our town like a bull's-eye. Olivia pressed the car faster as the road curved through the woods and met up with the Wall. It towered above us—Twenty feet high? Thirty?—parallel to the road, about fifteen feet from the asphalt. My neck hurt after a few seconds of staring at the rusty barbed wire running along the top. This section of it—minus the barbed wire—was original, comprised of the old stone blocks erected centuries ago. For most of its perimeter, the grass beside the Wall was a moat of empty cans, plastic bags, the occasional solitary flip-flop. But in one specific section, the grass was almost entirely gone, walked over, dug up, and planted with the offerings of Hartwood townspeople for, I dunno, ever? It was one of those things you took as a given, until some point in middle school when you realized that maybe most towns *don't* have a public altar. Maybe some kids *don't* leave small tokens before the first day of school, or the morning of the SATs, or at the start of the spring track season to ensure a personal record in the 800 meters.

But whatever, we did.

The second thing our town was known for was the Ladies of Hartwood.

Set into the Wall, watching over all the offerings, was a weathered, chipped carving of four women sitting side by side on a bench. They wore toga-type dresses and braid crowns, and most of their faces had broken off long ago, but you could still make out individual toes on their bare feet. We learned about them in elementary school and studied photos of each lady and what she was holding: a bird, a large urn spilling water, a cat

3

or possibly a dog (I was Team Cat), and something that looked like a book but that we were told was a basket. No one was sure where the carving had come from or how it ended up being used as a building block instead of on display in some old-fashioned sculptor's studio. Hence, the benign worship, the practice of leaving offerings for the four mysterious and yet clearly powerful women. The ground at their feet became an altar.

Olivia and her mom, Bonnie, visited the altar at the Wall weekly, replenishing the goat milk or duck eggs or whatever was specific to that time of year. Bonnie Tiffin, in addition to being my mom's best friend since kindergarten, was an orthodox Waltar-goer, down to the marble mortar and pestle that she used to grind walnut shells before scattering them over the dirt. But offerings could be anything, really, as long as they were given with pure intentions. That day, in the reusable shopping bag sitting at my feet, we had brought: wallet-sized copies of our senior pictures, tied together with friendship bracelet string; a thimble's worth of vodka—that Olivia had swiped from her parents' bar cart—in a mason jar; a used round-trip ticket from Hartwood to New York Penn Station; and two carefully folded pages of loose-leaf paper with Olivia's personal requests to the Ladies of Hartwood.

The Volvo pulled off to the side of the road, as if it knew the way, which it practically did. We had done an offering like this every birthday since we were twelve, a sort of friendship pact. It made me a little nauseous to think that this might be the last time we'd be together on her birthday.

Olivia used her mom's gardening trowel to dig a small hole

and we took turns nestling our offerings inside. I poured the vodka on top of it all with a flourish. "Take these offerings," Olivia said, "and remember us kindly throughout the year."

"We are Olivia Tiffin, birthday girl, and Anna Kellogg, BFF," I said, "just to be clear."

I stepped forward to help Olivia fill in the hole, but she stopped me. "Wait, I almost forgot." She fished around in her jacket pocket and tossed a single wrapped condom on top of our vodka-soaked offerings.

"Don't you think that would do more good if you kept it and, I dunno, used it?" I asked, my foot poised to kick the pile of dirt back into place.

"It's symbolic," Olivia said. "For good health, for good times, for us all. You're welcome."

"You sure you won't need it?"

"If I keep it, I won't need it. That's how these things work."

"Ironclad logic," I said.

"Just bury it already!" We started kicking dirt over the pile of hopes for our last semester of high school.

I stamped down the dirt and smoothed the edges. I didn't want anyone to get an accidental peek, even though that was a major Waltar taboo. As I surveyed our work, a bright green tendril of ivy, curling through a crack in the Wall, caught my eye. "It's not even spring yet." I let my eyes wander up the limestone slabs. "Is winter disappearing, too?" When I turned back, Olivia was gone.

I looked over at the car—no sign of her. My stomach did a swan dive. "Olivia?" I spun around, straining to hear my friend scream, imagining a trail of enormous paw prints leading to a den littered with mangled skeletons. "Olivia!"

The third, and more infamous, thing Hartwood was known for was the beast.

"Over here!" Olivia's head emerged from a hole in the Wall about ten yards up the road. "Look what I found." The way she said it made it sound like something she'd just stumbled upon, instead of something she'd walked out of the way to see and ducked down into the dirt to crawl through.

At this point, you may be asking yourself, *What is the deal with this Wall? Why the need for a Wall at all?*

The Wall surrounded the Great Swamp Wildlife Refuge because the beast lived in the swamp. Most people would have moved far, far away after the first dozen or so gruesome attacks in the early 1700s, but not Hartwoodsfolk. We stubbornly stayed put, and if it meant losing our animals or our lives, well, that was a price worth paying. We decided to wall in the swamp at the town's center, to keep the beast in its place and—hopefully—keep the town safer. As time wore on, roads and train tracks and everything skirted it like it was the mouth of a volcano.

And the kicker was: the Wall didn't really work. Maybe at first it helped, but it had been Swiss cheese for so long that it was now more symbol than system. There hadn't been a full-blown attack for over a decade—a fact I reminded myself of, over and over, as I walked—but Hartwood schools still taught students how to defend themselves in the event of "a wild animal encounter," how to administer first aid to humans and pets,

6

and the general street smarts of having a town beast: avoid Dumpsters at dawn and dusk. Don't use bird feeders. Keep your dog on a leash at all times and your pepper spray handy.

Every few years, there would be a beast sighting, and our town would flood with *Weird New Jersey* fanboys hoping for a glimpse of what was basically an urban legend. Ironically, the thing that was the biggest threat to Hartwood's existence had become the foundation of the town's biggest industry: spooky, mystical shit of all varieties. Sure, we had a post office and a dry cleaner, but we also had four psychics, two mediums, three occult shops, and one herbalist who catered to offerings for the Waltar (but also carried the widest selection of Hartwood beast merch). The town itself seemed to produce strange everyday occurrences. For instance, Hartwood had more lottery winners per capita than any other town in the state, and more unsolved house fires, too. And of course, we had more than our fair share of things going *bump* in the night. Trash cans were found mangled and empty, a quarter mile away from where they should've been. Large animal tracks turned up in the snow at the playground near the elementary school. And lost pet flyers plastered telephone poles and the town's Facebook page.

Pretty much since we were in seventh grade, there'd been a debate going on in the town between people who wanted to open the Great Swamp to the public—people who wanted more green space and opportunities for ecological education—and others who wanted to keep it locked up tight, for obvious reasons. They had competing bumper stickers that said, "Tear Down This Wall!" and "Good Fences Make Good Neighbors."

Somehow in the last year, the Wall-openers had pulled into the lead. We'd grown up in a town permanently prepared for attack, and it was like people *wanted* to be on high alert. They needed that extra little shot of adrenaline with their coffee in the morning. We heard the beast howl in reply to the train whistles every night and felt comfort from the familiar chill running down our collective spine.

Because of their work for the Parks Department and Historical Society, respectively, my mom and Olivia's mom were on the town committee in charge of the "gate question." At first, that meant weekly open forums so they could gather the bottomless feedback from the public. But then, about a year ago, the town put it to a vote to decide once and for all: gate or no gate. People stood in groups at the main intersection of town, holding signs for or against. Flyers spewed out of mailboxes. At the time, I didn't feel invested in it; it was above my pay grade. I was just tired of the issue and ready for it to be over. Olivia, for her part, sported an assortment of pro-gate paraphernalia; a sticker on the back of her phone simply had a cartoon of a smiling gate on it. Her mother was a leader of the anti-gate movement (my mother was with her in spirit, but working for the town prevented her from taking a public stance). Olivia thought her mom was being ridiculous. They fought about it for weeks before the vote. Olivia tried to convince her mom that everything was safe now, they all needed to move on, but it was like yelling into a cave. All she heard was her own voice. She didn't hear how scared her mom still was.

The vote finally happened just before the holidays and now

it was official: we were getting a gate. A massive slice had been taken out of the Wall right outside Town Hall, with columns erected to hold the new gate that would be opened with much fanfare in the spring.

"Here," Olivia said suddenly, and I almost jumped out of my skin. I'd nearly walked right by her. The hole looked just like another piece of uninterrupted Wall in shadow. But it was big enough for an adult to squat down and duck through, or for a large animal, such as a dog, to come and go easily.

"Come on," Olivia said, and disappeared inside the Wall.

"Whoa, whoa, whoa." I put up my hands. "I know you're pro-swamp access, but this is a little premature, don't you think?" Normally, no matter what we were doing, I stood beside Olivia like a disco ball, reflecting the light from my friend, just happy to be there. But that day, more than anything, I wished that an older version of myself would step through the looking glass and tell me exactly what to expect, right down to the littlest surprise, so that I wouldn't have to go through life wondering, *Is this right? Am I doing this right?* Which was my general default setting, and always prevented me from enjoying things until they were almost at an end. Like high school. Or forays into a beast-infested swamp.

Olivia laughed. "The pond isn't far from here. I know you know that."

I grumbled and folded my arms. "How dare you use my fourth-grade, award-winning, built-to-scale model of the Wall and the Great Swamp against me."

"Let's just take a look." I checked my watch and she said,

"Quickly! A quick look."

"The bus leaves in forty minutes."

"Oh man, we have even more time than I thought we did." When I didn't move, she said, "How much longer are we going to be able to do dumb shit like this before we're too old for it?"

"Isn't that what college is for?" I asked. "Doing dumb shit before we're too old?"

"You're talking about *Booksmart*-dumb shit. Experimenting, carpe-ing diems, pledging whatevers. What I'm talking about is celebrating a lifelong friendship that only has a few more months before—"

"Before what?" I demanded. "Our friendship expires on graduation day?"

Olivia sighed. "All I'm saying is: I want to enjoy every minute I have left in Hartwood. Specifically, with you." Her speech clicked on a teeny tiny lighter in my chest, even in spite of the rising tide of anxiety.

"You're bumming me out," I said, "and pumping me up at the same time."

Olivia smiled, knowing she'd won.

My heart pounded as I ducked through the crumbling seam. By the time I'd stood up, Olivia was walking straight ahead on a clear footpath into the swamp, not even waiting for me. I glanced left and right, left and right, ready for terror, then jogged ahead to keep up.

Over the years, dozens of mysterious disappearances were chalked up to the beast. About ten years earlier, a kid from the cross-country team, Chris Rowan, had gone for a long run down the county road that runs through the swamp. After two days of searching, only his left sneaker was found, with his severed foot still in it. It was the cautionary tale we all grew up with, recounted by well-meaning adults with a mixture of shock and relief. It had happened to someone else, to some other family. Chris's name went up on the memorial in the town park—a busted fountain with a large brass plaque listing the names of people who'd gone missing over the years. It was meant to help us remember them, but once the ceremony was over, it had the opposite effect. We all went back to littering and leaving our windows open at night. We'd all survived the culling. We were safe for a little bit longer.

A very old sign, bent and weather-beaten, was nailed high up onto a pine: **NO DUMPING $500 FINE**. "Tiff," I said, "have you been here before?" *And didn't tell me?* Olivia was more likely to know her way around the East Village than to know her way through the Great Swamp. Or so I thought.

"No, I just looked on Google maps." She raised her phone in one hand.

"Huh," I said, not believing her spontaneity for one second. I looked around me. *So, this is what the inside of the Wall looks like.* Pretty typical suburban woods, looking a little starved, sounding a little too quiet. I stepped on something brittle, which turned out to be a mini-bottle of cinnamon-flavored whiskey. "You know what these woods would be great for?"

"What?" Olivia said.

"Dumping a body. Or, you know, dragging a poor, innocent runner off the road and enjoying your meal in peace."

11

Olivia said something in reply, but it was drowned out by the dial tone I heard as the air pressure changed and my ears popped. The trees started flickering, flashing from skinny gray trunks to massive ancient trees, as if parts of *Lord of the Rings* had been spliced into my regular life reel. I squeezed my eyes shut, propped my glasses on my head, and dug my knuckles in. My heart was beginning to race again. *Come on, Anna, don't have an episode now.* I took deep, shuddering breaths, like my therapist had taught me.

Olivia didn't say a word. I felt her hand on my shoulder, then her puffy-coated arms squeezing me to her. I felt the uneven ground below my feet, felt my hands pressed into my face against her collarbone. I smelled the coconut oil that she used as lotion. I kept breathing.

I pulled away just enough to slide my glasses hesitantly into place. The trees slowed and then stilled, and everything stayed the same size, thank the gods.

"All good?" Olivia asked.

I shoved both hands into my coat pockets, to try to get them to stop shaking. "Yeah, I'm okay." I kept my breathing deep and even, just in case, and looked around me for evidence of one of those massive trees. We resumed our walk to the pond, Olivia with one arm around my shoulders. Just off the trail, hidden under a cluster of impressively large ferns, I thought I saw . . . speckled eggs. Big ones, like you might see at the drugstore during Easter, full of jelly beans. I blinked and they came into focus: just a collection of pale mushrooms with egg-like caps. I took off my glasses and cleaned them on the hem of my dress.

We walked in silence for a while, and Olivia strayed a few steps ahead. From time to time, I heard a dry crack as she stepped on a twig. Trees swayed before I felt the breeze, like they were moving on their own (again), gossiping about us behind their hands. Birds called around us, invisibly. Something sounded different, though. The birdsong wasn't the usual repetitive nonsense that people imitate with stupid onomatopoeia—there was movement to this song, a melody and harmony and bass line. "Do you hear—" I started to ask, just as a moth flitted by, trailing an alto solo. I told myself to shut up and—

Something cold and wet slapped me in the face. "Eeeuuggh!" I shrieked and stumbled back a few steps, releasing the branch I'd stepped on, which had snapped up like a cartoon rake and flung a soggy handful of mud right at my head. I took my ruined glasses off and clawed at my eyes. It smelled so, so bad—dirty diapers and rot and food well past its sell-by date, all blended into a nice facial mask that would ignite a glorious breakout, I was sure. "Ew, ew, ew," I chanted under my breath, trying not to gag as I smeared muck and grass clumps through my hair, desperate to get it off me.

Olivia rushed up. "What is it? Oh—" She paused for the briefest instant, then burst out laughing.

I felt myself shrink the tiniest bit. "Shut up," I grumbled, and scooped the remaining mud out of my eye socket. Grit clung to my lashes. "I'm so glad I remembered my sense of adventure today."

"But not your sense of humor." Olivia wiped away a tear. "Come on, you can wash off in the pond."

13

Up ahead, sunlight glinted on water. The trees grew right up to the water's edge, lots of raggedy pines with short, blunt needles. That's why we were only a stone's throw away when Olivia stopped short and pointed to the woman sitting with her back to a tree and her legs in the water, hunched and scrubbing a mound of cloth against a rock. The sun was on the other side of the pond, backlighting her long hair trailing in the water and making her look like a moving weeping willow. I gasped softly and the woman turned.

Three crows were nestled on her shoulders, tucked into her hair, and for a second, I couldn't tell if they were real. But when they saw us, they screeched and broke free in a fury of wings, sending her hair flying. The huge birds circled her for a second, then settled on branches above her head. Her eyes grew wide as she took us in.

She was *old*. Old like a glacier is old. Her eyebrows were wild, fuzzy creatures. Long wiry hairs sprouted from her chin. Her nose was partially mashed into her face, flattened on one side like she'd fallen asleep on it centuries ago, and her cheeks were soft and sunken where teeth used to be. All of this on its own was bizarre enough, but have I mentioned that she was topless? The woman's boobs hung almost to the water, drooping like stretched pizza dough. Not only was she sitting with her legs in a January pond, but she didn't have a stitch of clothing between her back and the winter breeze.

Olivia moved closer to me, brushing up against my arm.

The woman slowly passed her wet clothes from one hand to the other, watching us. *That water must be so cold,* I thought.

Finally, she said, "Ye're a bit early this time, yeah?"

I had no idea how to respond. I quickly averted my eyes to the pond to be polite.

"Yeah, no—I'm sorry," Olivia stammered. "We didn't mean to, um. We didn't know anyone would be here."

"I didn't know I would be here myself." Even her voice sounded worn. "Here for a swim, then?"

"No," Olivia and I said at the same time.

"It's a good day for it. This water is fecking freezing." The lady slapped the pond with her wet clothes, and Olivia and I jumped. "Fed by an underground spring, ye know." She paused and when we didn't reply, she slowly went back to her washing.

I gingerly stepped through the dirt toward the boulders poking out of the water, feeling like I needed to do something to give us a purpose for being there. I began ladling handfuls of water onto my glasses, which momentarily made them worse, and I heard the woman take a sharp breath. She was staring at me as if I'd done something utterly shocking by sticking my hands into the same pond she was washing in.

The woman said, irritated, "If ye're going to ask me, ye'd better get on with it."

"Sorry," I said, "ask you . . . what?"

At that moment the birds dropped their symphonic harmonizing, cranked the volume to eleven, and shrieked and yammered like an alarm. One crow swooped down between me and the old woman.

"Oh," the woman said irritably, looking up at the sky. "Pipe down. This shirt doesn't belong to them."

15

You mean that isn't your shirt? I thought but didn't ask.

I glanced back at Olivia, who was standing very straight, shoulders squared, like she was gathering courage to walk into a job interview. She opened her mouth, then shut it. Took a breath but didn't speak. The birds quieted a bit, but the crows still chirped insistent, random interjections as though a predator were nearby.

The woman turned back to us. Her gaze rested on Olivia. "Ye're meant to ask me whatever your heart desires. Most people are interested in the future—fame, glory, true love."

"You grant wishes?" I asked, thinking, *Holy shit, the offerings might actually work.*

"Not quite. I have knowledge, some of which I can share." She returned to kneading the clothes against the rock. "Ye didn't sneak up on me and suckle from my breast, so strictly speaking I owe ye nothing, but I'm not in favor of the traditional assault, so let's compromise. I'll answer ye one question each."

Olivia looked stone serious. It was everything I could do not to shout, *Suckle from your breast?!*

Olivia looked at me when she asked, "Do you know when I will die?"

The old woman clicked her tongue. "Yes, I know when ye will die, but is that your question? Ye have to ask, *When will I die?* The phrasing matters."

"But how do you know?" she asked politely enough, but my toes curled out of embarrassment on her behalf. "Where did you get the *knowledge* you said you have?"

The old woman sighed dramatically. "I have always had this

knowledge. Or I guess I should say the knowledge has always had me."

"Are you from around here?" Olivia asked.

The old woman looked at her, puzzled. "I am *of* here," she said, and the saucy, silent *obviously* hung in the air.

"We've never seen you around town, that's all," I said, attempting to be a participant rather than a gawking bystander. I stood up, my glasses in my hand, and the woman seemed to visibly relax. "I'm Anna." I waited a beat, but when she didn't reciprocate, I said, "What's your name?"

Another few seconds passed. "No one has ever asked me," she said cryptically, as if that might be the reason why she had no name. She collected herself, threw one long boob over her shoulder, and said, "Now here's how this is going to work." She plopped the wet clothes onto their rock and stood in the water to face us. A soaking wet skirt hung past her knees in the water. "One at a time, ye ask me a question about *ye*, not me. All right?"

We nodded.

Water dripped from the ends of her hair as she waited for one of us to speak. I felt colder just watching her. "I can't think of one," I said to Olivia.

"Too many, more like." The woman gave a honking laugh, and for the first time I noticed her one long tooth protruding from her upper gums like a fang.

"I have a question," Olivia blurted.

The old woman raised her eyebrows, waiting.

"Will I be happy next year, in college?" she asked in a timid voice. I felt my mouth open as I looked at my friend—my confident, successful, competitive friend, who, of anyone I knew, was destined to get to college and explode in fireworks of happiness and success. But she was worried about it?

The woman moved her jaw a bit, as if chewing on her tongue. "Next year and college are two different things. When ye get to college, yes, ye will be content."

Olivia didn't reply, probably just as flipping stumped as I was. *Next year and college are two different things* echoed in my head.

"Anna, is it?" The old woman quirked her head, like she knew that wasn't true. "Have ye thought of one?"

"I wanted to ask," I began. My face felt too exposed, so I put on my glasses. Water dribbled down my nose.

I could feel the old woman's curiosity like a force field. When I looked her in the eye, I could feel her thoughts pushing back at me. She had as many questions about us as we did about her. Her chin hair twitched as she bit her lip with her single snaggletooth. The crow in the tree above the washerwoman shook out its wings and resettled.

"What's going to happen to us?" I rushed in one breath. The woman's attention dimmed, then came rushing back.

Of course, I meant something along the lines of Olivia's question: next year, college, moving away, friendships, but what I really wanted to know was: What happens to your town when all its people—*your* people—leave you behind? What if the people were why you wanted to stay in the first place? I felt pathetic, but I would have followed Olivia around like a duckling for years more if given the chance, no question. No one else was as broken up at the thought of leaving Hartwood; generally, that's what the entire point of college *was* for most people. We lived in the "Born to Run" state, after all—a place Bruce Springsteen made famous by singing about how badly he wanted to *leave* it. The thought of going to college somewhere completely foreign and starting from friend-square-one made me nauseous to the point of dry heaving. I hadn't finished a single college application without talking myself out of it. *You have so much time,* I reassured myself on the actual day it was due.

I scanned the trees nervously.

The woman said, "It isn't often someone uses their question on another's behalf." She glanced down at the rock and the misshapen pile of cloth, then up into the sky, thinking.

I felt the familiar embrace of humiliation, but I didn't understand why.

"I don't remember it going this way before," she said to herself. Finally, the woman's eyes settled on me, and she said, "Some friends ye'll have to let go, or perish trying to save them."

No, I thought. *Not possible.*

She squinted at me. "Let me put it another way, then. Olivia won't be far," she continued, choosing her words carefully, "but out of reach. Ye may find her and never know it. Don't let grief cloud your sight. She'll come to ye, so keep your eyes open—*all* your eyes," she added, as if there might be eyes I'd forgotten about.

She nodded at me, so I said, "Thank you," even though her answer was about as much help as a Ouija board.

"I see ye have been marked by the swamp." She pointed at

her face, where the mud was drying on mine. "Don't wash it off."

"Okay," I said, thinking, *Yeah, right, lady.*

"How'd ye get in, anyway? Not Beltane yet, is it? No, I'd know." She glanced up at the crows.

"How'd we get into the swamp?" I asked, when what I really wanted to know was, How did she know Olivia's name?

"The swamp"—she snorted—"yes, let's call it that."

"We came in through a hole in the Wall." Olivia hooked her thumb over her shoulder. "We were leaving offerings at the Waltar—at the altar to the Ladies of Hartwood—and I just noticed this hole. . . ." She shrugged exaggeratedly, pretty much confirming my suspicion that all of this had been premeditated.

"Mmm-hrrph." The old woman made some sort of affirmative noise as she chewed on her lip. Her eyes moved to me and I felt a pressure—like a sinus headache building steadily—and somehow, I understood that it was her mind pressing too close, trying to get in. *Ye shouldn't be here—it isn't time yet,* she said urgently. I heard the old woman's voice in my skull.

Instinctively, and because it hurt like hell, I put both hands over my head and bent into a crouch.

The Otherworld is dying; one way or t'other, they will kill us all slowly or at once. I can see both threads so clearly. I—I can't tell which. Her voice faltered. *Ye are marked in more ways than one, Anna Kellogg. The energies of the Otherworld are yours to conduct, if you can name them.*

I thought my head might burst into flames. Tears squeezed into my lashes.

We need you, Aine. Come back to us. Remember who you are.

Olivia knelt next to me and said, "Anna." And as suddenly as it came, the pressure let up. I gasped in relief and tipped onto all fours, suddenly self-conscious and blushing like crazy. An echo of an ache reverberated through my head. I pushed myself up, dusting off my knees as if I had just been crouching at my locker and not possessed by a shirtless old lady who did her laundry in a pond that was probably bacteria soup. I refused to look at her.

The old woman waited—I could feel her still watching me—then said matter-of-factly, "Well, the questions ha' been answered; I best be off, then. And so should ye," she added. "Leave now and don't come back until it's time." With that she scooped the bundle of clothes to her chest, turned, and dove into the pond.

I walked jerkily, hurrying then stopping then hurrying again, to the edge of the pond where the woman had been standing. The rock she'd been washing her clothes on was bone dry and sun-warmed to the touch. The water was still as glass. I watched for air bubbles. I scanned out to the middle of the pond where a rock rested like a jagged turtle shell, but I didn't go in after her. I didn't know how I could help her even if I did.

Olivia gazed out at the water with her mouth open. "That was amazing," she breathed.

"Shouldn't she have surfaced by now?" I asked, even though I was desperate to leave.

"I think she's gone," Olivia said. "In a good way."

In a good way, my butt, I thought as tiny starbursts of light popped in my periphery. "Please," I whimpered, "let's get out of here."

"Yeah," she said, "okay." Olivia followed, then stopped to glance back at the water once more. "Did you want to wash your face?"

"That's okay. I'll run to the bathroom before the bus leaves." I looked back, too, just to be sure, but the pond was motionless. There was no sign that the woman had ever been there. If I hadn't had a fellow witness, I would have convinced myself it was all in my head—another episode, another neurological firestorm, another suspected seizure and MRI in my future.

The three crows sat in the tree, watching us until we left.

I stared at the back of Olivia's head, her one long earring swinging in time to her step. *Olivia won't be far, but out of reach.*

I thought I knew what that meant, but in about an hour I'd find out how wrong I was.

CHAPTER 2

WHEN WE GOT in the car, my watch said that only twenty-five minutes had elapsed since our excursion into the swamp, but the car clock and our cell phones told a different story. Olivia sped across town, and we barely made it back to school in time for the field trip. In the panic about being late, I forgot all about the mud mask I was wearing, that is until Olivia's twin brother, Alex, looked over the bus seat in front of us. "Have a good lunch?" he asked, smirking pointedly at the dirty half of my face.

"Bite me," I said at the same time that Olivia pushed his head down into his seat.

"I'm sorry you didn't get to wash that off," she said. "I didn't think we'd spent that much time there. Would hand sanitizer help?"

"It's okay." I combed my crunchy bangs. "I'll live." As the battered yellow bus drove us across town, I watched Alex through the gap between his seat and the window. He pulled out his phone and thumbed through content of some sort on his screen, but I couldn't see it. He spent so much time on Reddit and Instagram and who knows what else that his personality was basically forty percent internet. The muscles in his jaw twitched incessantly. Compared to his sister, Alex was skim-milk skin and dark, wild hair that always looked overgrown, no matter how recent the haircut. Where Olivia's features were broad and square, Alex's were delicate. His cheekbones, the architecture of his nose—he could've played an elf extra in *The Hobbit*. But my favorite thing about him, which I'd never, ever told anyone, was his in-between, not-quite-hazel, not-quite-brown eyes. They changed like a mood ring, sometimes leaning to green, other times shot through with spokes of gold. His eye color, and the fact that he was the only person whose eye contact I could hold for more than point-two seconds. The only person besides Olivia, of course.

We passed a large wooden sign with gold lettering: UNION COUNTY VOCATIONAL DEMONSTRATION FOREST. A minute later, firmly in the middle of nowhere, the bus pulled over beside a dingy creek that ran perpendicular to the road. Mr. Putterhut, our AP Bio teacher, handed each of us a stoppered test tube as we exited. "Try to space out your sample collecting from your friends'. It'll give us a better picture of the health of the stream."

I slid mine into my canvas bag, hoping it might break under

24

the weight of *The Complete Stories of Flannery O'Connor* and all the other detritus I carried around with me. I was feeling jittery, like the washerwoman might burst out of any body of water we went near, ready to crack my mind open like an egg. I hadn't told Olivia why I'd nearly collapsed at the pond, and she didn't question it. It was easier to chalk it up to one of my unexplainable episodes than to try to convince her I'd heard the washerwoman's voice in my head *and* I wasn't crazy. There were limits to every friendship.

We waited for the people ahead of us to disperse into the drainage ditch that Mr. Putterhut called a stream. "That's enough Game of Phones, thank you!" he shouted. "Keep it moving." He wasn't a bad teacher; he just had an unfortunate last name. You could tell he was teased for it a lot growing up—his face got all red whenever someone made an adjustment to his name and called him "Put-Put" or "P-hut" or, his least favorite, "Pooter-hooter." I wondered if he would be as stern and serious if he were named, I don't know, Mr. Brown. Mr. Smith. Basically any one-syllable name. A person's name shapes them, for better or for worse. Take it from me—the girl with the unpronounceable name. Aine. Would it have been so hard for my mom to write out *Anya* on my birth certificate instead of *Aine*? She's never been able to explain it—the need for the unpronounceable Irish spelling—so I decided in second grade that I was Anna and I never looked back. The washerwoman was the first person to call me Aine in years. She had an accent that I couldn't place, but I didn't think I could fully blame her calling me Aine on that. The creepy feeling followed me like a shadow.

25

Alex and his best friend, Lou, stood in front of us in deep discussion, oblivious to their surroundings, as usual. They'd been at work on some sort of complicated game that made it sound like they were writing *Game of Thrones* fan fiction. "I don't want the pantheon to get too big. It waters it down," I overheard Lou tell Alex.

"But a tri-part goddess of war is not too much to ask?" Alex goaded him.

"Oh, speaking of," Lou said excitedly, "I've been doing more research and I sketched out a possible scenario for the Morrígan. Can we meet on Saturday? I have guitar lessons on Friday." He smoothed his long, dyed-black forelock across his face. Lou Leishman lived with his grandparents in the next neighborhood over from me, Olivia, and Alex. As far as I knew, his dad had never been in the picture, much like mine, but I didn't know where his mom was. His grandparents, though, loved him so hard they practically asphyxiated him in hugs. I knew Lou never wanted to ask them for anything; if he could have paid rent without incurring the wrath of his grandma's wooden spoon, he would've been chipping in since sixth grade. I'd only been to his house once, when Lou had forgotten his phone and was taking forever to find it in his room. I wandered in from the car, and his grandma, who was wearing a pink rosebud-printed apron that matched her slippers, offered me pork roast, chicken soup, Stromboli, and cheesecake in the span of forty-five seconds. She was very sweet, but the insistence bordered on fairy-tale witch and made me nervous. If I started eating, would she ever let me stop? Finally, Lou pounded down the stairs, phone in hand, and nearly pushed me out the front door. Whether he didn't want me to see his house, or he didn't want his grandparents to see me, I couldn't be sure.

"I didn't know you took guitar lessons, Lou!" Olivia said with saccharine interest. Lou was to Alex as I was to Olivia, and through some transitive property of equality, Olivia treated him as if he were her actual brother, too.

He spun around, surprised to be overheard. "Excuse me, I'm *giving* the lessons. I'm being *paid*. I haven't taken lessons in years."

"Aw"—Olivia patted his arm—"my mistake."

"For the record," Alex said without turning, "I haven't taken lessons at all."

I strongly suspected that the only reason Alex hadn't taken guitar lessons was to be able to say he hadn't taken guitar lessons.

"Are you even a part of this conversation?" Olivia demanded.

"Not by choice," he said without taking his eyes from his phone. I couldn't tell you what Alex's problem was, now or ever.

Test tubes in hand, we trudged down into the gully of the creek. It ran into a sinister-looking drainpipe under the road that seemed to eat all light and warmth as well as the flowing water. I looked as far upstream as I could, checking for long, straggly gray hair, or a pile of wet clothes on a rock, but there was nothing but colorful flecks of litter and the stench of something rotten.

"I don't get any service up here," Olivia Harris said with a twinge of anxiety in her voice. (Our grade was lousy with

27

Olivias; there were three in our AP Bio class alone.)

"Hey," Jeremy Klopner practically shouted to no one in particular. "Seems like a prime place for a beast sighting, doesn't it?"

"Don't even *joke*," Olivia H. said.

"You need to carry much more than a cell phone if you want to survive an attack," Jeremy said with a snort. "That's why I'm getting my permit the minute I hit eighteen."

People fanned out along the creek, and no one replied. I cut my eyes to Olivia—*my* Olivia—but she was already looking at me, thinking the same thing: *As if we need another reason to avoid Jeremy for the rest of our lives.*

Jeremy was a Hartwood Beast conspiracy theorist, one of many. The legend of the beast drew tourists to our town every year to see the massive wall around the Great Swamp where he or she dwelled, like Nessy up in the loch. The trouble was that, unlike Nessy, the Hartwood Beast didn't respect boundaries. Most people who grew up in Hartwood accepted the legend the same way people who live in earthquake zones accept the occasional tremor. But some, like Jeremy, got defensive about it. He and his family were big into hunting. His social media feeds were plastered with pictures of him holding a rifle next to an animal corpse, the sun glinting off his braces. It was thanks to Jeremy that I knew you could start hunting at age ten in New Jersey. "First chance I get," Jeremy said to no one, because no one was interested, "I'm going into the swamp and I'm gonna bag that beast."

I stooped down and dipped the test tube into the water.

"How long do we have to do this?" I asked.

Olivia shrugged and checked her phone. "Anything is better than gym class, which is where we'd be right now if we weren't here."

"Point taken," I said, and Alex let out a sarcastic snort. I hadn't even seen him and Lou keeping pace with us on the opposite side of the stream. *WHAT'S SO FUNNY?* I wanted to ask him. *Share it with the class, why don't you?* But I knew the answer already. I spent more time with Alex than with my own mother, but it was accidental togetherness from hanging out with his twin sister, plus eating four-ish dinners a week with his family. I had my own toothbrush in the upstairs bathroom. We tolerated each other, like the faux siblings that we were, and Alex knew as well as I did that gym class was my own personal hell. Frisbees and kickballs and badminton rackets alike loved to hit me in the face.

As I picked my way over rocks onto higher ground, I pondered the washerwoman's prophecy. *Some friends ye'll have to let go. . . . Olivia will be out of reach. . . .* The red flags were there now that I was looking for them, lined up for years. I didn't want to be class VP to Olivia's P. I didn't want to join Model UN or Relay for Life. I didn't want to work at the Y summer camp with her. I didn't want to go to junior prom, especially not as the third wheel to her and her then-boyfriend, Julian. Olivia was destined for the senior superlatives, and I was not likely to even participate in the voting. And I know, it's not like my *not* doing these things prevented her from doing them. *Au contraire,* she excelled at them all, she just wanted me to enjoy them, too, and that was a pretty big ask. I finally saw the writing on the wall, as big as billboard graffiti: It was only a matter of time until Olivia found a new best friend, someone who shared her penchant for extracurriculars and typical teen socialization. She probably didn't even realize a friendship based on actual shared interests existed! But soon she'd find herself at a college filled with similarly high achievers and she'd be able to say, *I used to have this friend—she was weird.*

We came to a tree that bent way out over the water, blocking our path. I followed Olivia up into the woods to try to get around it. Prickers scratched my leggings. A bush with dusty wine-colored leaves shivered in the breeze. My nose itched to the point that my eyes were watering. Suddenly, a tightness grabbed me at the back of my neck, like a heavy magnet somehow pulling my head back. The purple leaves shuddered and shook. At the edges of my vision, the scene in front of me fractured into kaleidoscope pieces that threatened to close in and obscure everything in sight.

Not now, please don't happen now, I told my nervous system.

Walk away! a voice in my head commanded. The voice was older, confident. It wasn't mine. *Break the connection,* it said.

What connection? I thought, feeling around at the nape of my neck for an actual hook. I took a step, then another, and the blood moved around in my limbs and made its way to my head. My breath came rushing back—I hadn't even realized I was panic-panting. *It's working,* I told the voice, but it didn't reply. Out of the corner of my eye, I saw a few purple leaves lift off and flap into the afternoon, and a new jolt of adrenaline shot through my body. I rubbed my eyes and looked again. It wasn't my eyesight playing tricks on me: I watched as, gradually, the whole bush took flight. They weren't leaves; they were moths, tiny blood-colored moths.

Olivia was a little way ahead, talking with a few kids from class, Sierra Strobel and Bodhi Goodman-Wu. I was in no hurry to catch up just yet. In case I really did faint, I wanted to do it in privacy, thank you very much.

Olivia kept chatting with them, then turned toward me with a smile, but it fell right off her face when she saw me. "Anna!" She rushed to my side. Sierra and Bodhi did not.

Hoping no one could see the cold sweat on my face, I asked, "What?"

All three classmates were goggling at me, or at least, in my general vicinity. Bodhi's otherwise gorgeous face was slack in shock.

"Look." Olivia pointed straight above me. I tipped my head back, thinking, *Don't pass out, don't pass out.* A cloud of moths tumbled over itself, expanding and contracting, and expanding again as more and more moths joined. I'd seen birds do something like this, in big clouds in the sky, but I didn't know moths did it, too. I turned and looked behind me. A fluttering stream led back to the now bare bush, like living bread crumbs.

"Shouldn't those things be dead?" Bodhi asked. He and Sierra had moved closer, but still kept their distance. "It's January."

"I didn't do anything," I said stupidly. Moths were landing on me now. I could feel their eyelash feet in my hair.

31

"Ahh!" Bodhi yelled, and swatted one away from his face.

"Make it stop, Anna," Sierra said, backing away. "This is really gross."

I held my arms up; it was almost impossible to make out the corduroy beneath the tiny shifting bodies. "Get off," I said, and shook my sleeves. Some moths broke free, but most stayed put. "Get *off*." I stomped and shook my whole body.

Olivia took a step away from me. "Anna, what's going on?"

Bodhi scrambled after Sierra, scratching his neck uncomfortably. "Fuckin' weird, man," he muttered.

"What the hell?" Lou ran up, shaking water off his Vans. "Are those things real?" He pinched a moth off my coat.

Alex walked up, hands in his pockets. "Is this shit weird enough for you?" he asked Lou.

"What's that supposed to mean?" I asked as I shimmied under the moths.

By now the rest of my class had caught wind of the commotion and were crunching down the gravel shoulders of the stream.

"Come on," Olivia said. "Let's get away from—whatever this is."

Break the connection, I heard again. *Take control.* I lifted my head and the moths fell back. Olivia swatted at my bangs and ran her hand down the back of my coat, guiding me down the path, away from the crowd of observers.

Please leave me alone, I asked the moths. *Go back to whatever you were doing before.*

For a split second, the pressure in my ears changed and I

couldn't hear anything. The silence was more deafening than regular noise. Then, just as suddenly, I heard a rush of whispers, like fifty people whispering in my ears all at once. I couldn't make out anything they were saying. Goose bumps printed themselves up and down my arms. I put both hands over my ears, ducked my chin, and told myself over and over, *I am here in my body. I am here—alone—in my body.*

"Anna, what—" Alex started to say, but Olivia cut in.

"Don't follow us, okay?" She and I walked until we couldn't hear our class anymore, and until I couldn't hear the voices anymore. Distance from the site of an episode—or whatever that was—had never played into my recovery before, but hey, I'd take it. We finally came upon a boulder and instead of skirting around it, into the woods, Olivia helped me climb up and sit on the chilly stone. My coat and shoes were bug-free and ordinary once again. Olivia sat beside me in one fluid movement of her long legs. We sat hip-to-hip, the only way we could both fit.

"I'm sorry," I said. "That was embarrassing."

"Don't apologize! You didn't do anything wrong." Olivia picked at a loose flap of rubber on her sneaker. "Was that—would you call that an episode? Or was it something else?"

I bit the inside of my cheek. "It wasn't an episode, I don't think. Usually those are all in my head—I see or hear something that isn't really there, and my vision blinks out, or I get light-headed." I didn't mention the kaleidoscope vision that came on when I passed the moth bush. It was too much to explain, even to myself.

"Does it hurt?"

"You mean when I have an episode?"

She nodded.

"Not really." I shrugged. "Sometimes I get headaches afterward."

"Oh." Olivia seemed startled. "I didn't realize that was what caused—"

"It isn't. Only sometimes." Olivia was familiar with my semi-chronic migraines. "Don't worry, episodes don't happen that often. And this was just . . . strange. You saw what was happening before I did. And then Bodhi flipped out. . . ."

"What a dweeb, scared of bugs. He's the one who should be embarrassed."

I picked another piece of dried mud out of my hair. "Yeah, I guess everyone already knew I was a freak magnet for weirdness."

Olivia looked me in the eye. "When are you going to realize: that's why I like you."

Alex's voice echoed in my head: *Is this shit weird enough for you?*

What happens if I get better? I thought. *Will I be weird enough then?*

We slowly made our way back to the bus to wait out the rest of the field trip. Pete, the driver, leaned against the far side near the door, sneaking drags from his vape until it was time to go. "It smells like a gym sock in here," Olivia said as we slid down in our two-seater. The bus's cranking heater didn't bother me a bit; it smelled like freedom. I had never been so excited to get back to school, inside a dusty building where the only bugs were spiders in ceiling corners and the only old women were fully clothed.

"My battery is dead," Olivia H. complained as she walked past. "It was at ninety-six percent when we left."

"My phone's dead, too," someone else chimed in.

Not that I really cared, but I checked my phone out of curiosity. No sign of life. "Searching for service probably drained the batteries," Olivia said, looking at her own blank screen. She slipped her phone into the front pocket of her backpack.

After a few minutes, the bus was full. Mr. Putterhut counted heads and gave Pete a thumbs-up. The Demonstration Forest closed in on either side of us as the bus coasted down the twisting road.

Lou turned around in his seat. "Listen, I just want to offer, for your consideration—"

"No," Olivia said.

"You didn't even hear what I was going to say!" he sputtered.

"Mr. Leishman!" I craned my neck just enough to see Mr. Putterhut's red face aimed in our direction. "*Sit* in the seat, for crying out loud."

Lou closed his eyes and melted into a pool of teenaged angst in his seat. "Sorry, Put-hut," he called.

If I hadn't been straining to see the fury on Putterhut's face, I would never have seen the blur race across the street in front of the bus. I would have missed the long tail, like a panther's, stretched out behind it, just before I was thrown forward as the driver slammed on the brakes. Tires screeched and the bus swerved into the ditch beside the road, the centrifugal force hurling my forehead against the window. My teeth clattered from the bump as the front tires landed, then the back ones. People screamed, even the boys. I took a breath, but my voice caught in my throat and no sound came out. The bus rocked, spilling people into the aisle, then crashed into a tree with a sickening crunch. My face flew forward into the seat in front of me, then everything was still.

Mr. Putterhut got up first. "Is everyone all right? What happened? Pete, oh my god."

Everything moved in slow motion. People got up; they moaned, "What the hell?" Across the aisle, Bel Nguyen had a cut somewhere on her head and her hair was wet and matted. She started crying—wailing so loudly I almost didn't hear Mr. Putterhut declare, "Everyone off." He wrenched open the bus doors. Without saying a word, we shakily followed him outside into the tall grass about four feet below the road. The smell of burnt marshmallow was so strong it made me choke. The nose of the bus leaked steam and smoke, hissing like a pressure valve about to burst. We'd narrowly missed sideswiping the wooden sign that declared the woods in front of us the Union County Vocational Demonstration Forest. I wandered toward the back tires, Olivia and Lou and Alex and I in a tumbleweed of people.

Lou's nose was a blood faucet. He played it off like a tough guy, but when Alex looked away I could see the pain on his face. "Here," I said, and fished a cardigan out of my bag. "For your face."

"That's okay, it'll ruin it," Lou said. "Bloodstains are murder to get out." He laughed. "I crack myself up." He wiped the back of his hand over his mouth, and it came away with a rusty streak.

"It's okay," I told him. "I have others."

He smiled, his teeth bloody, too, and took the sweater.

The inside of Olivia's mouth was cut, where her teeth had ripped into it. Her lower lip was starting to balloon. My left brow bone ached, but the black eye wouldn't develop for several hours yet. *Is this what it feels like to be punched?* I remember thinking. *How do boxers do it?*

"Are you okay?" people all around us kept asking each other. They'd describe what they were feeling and then stop themselves. "Wait, are *you* okay?"

"What happened?" Olivia asked.

Pete, the driver, had a cut dribbling deep red down the side of his face and one shoulder was hunched at an odd angle. Mr. Putterhut limped from group to group. "Does anyone here have a working phone?" But of course, no one did.

Out in the grass, Bodhi hurried over behind a tree and puked.

It felt like minutes later that I registered Olivia's question. "Something ran in front of the bus," I said. "A mountain lion or something." A high-pitched drone gradually swelled in my ears.

"A mountain lion? In New Jersey?" Alex examined his left hand. The knuckles were rubbed raw.

I massaged my left ear. The droning kept on. "That's why he swerved. A really big animal."

"The beast," Alex said.

"Don't be a dick." Olivia prodded the inside of her cheek with her tongue.

37

Behind us, Bel was sitting on the ground leaning against the bus tire. Her best friend, Mary-Kate, was crouching in front of her. "Tell me a story, Bel," she said. "Come on, I know your head hurts, but you can't close your eyes like that." She pressed a maxi-pad to Bel's head.

"I'm being sincere," Alex said, and spat a glob of pink. He scanned the trees warily. "I think we just experienced a beast sighting."

Lou's voice was muffled by my sweater. I reached out and lifted the dangling part away from his mouth and he said again, "The beast doesn't come out in broad daylight."

"Yes, it does," Alex said. "Remember the accident on route 22 last month? Something ran across the highway at rush hour, right into the glare of the setting sun. Daylight. Just like this."

"I want to punch you so badly right now," Olivia said.

"No need." Alex actually looked pained for a second. "The bus window already took care of that."

A scream pierced the air.

"Get back on the bus!" someone shouted.

"Run!"

"What's—" Olivia began to ask, but people were stampeding blindly, fumbling into each other to get away from some invisible threat. And then—the blur was back.

It zigzagged from tree to tree, then broke into the open and raced around the bus, corralling us into a herd. I tried to follow it, to get a better look, but it ran too fast. The ground sprayed up under its feet, which sounded like a galloping horse. All I could make out was caramel-colored fur, a flash of white where its mouth opened, and a long panther tail whipping behind it. It charged around us on long, powerful legs. *Much too big to be a panther*, I thought in a daze.

Don't move, that firm, confident voice replied. *Don't move a muscle.*

"It's playing with us," Jeremy said, suddenly standing beside me. His glasses were in two pieces in his hands. He watched the animal race around us until his voice took on a deeper register. "He thinks he can play with us."

As if it heard him, the animal changed direction and darted through the group of us still standing outside. It sent Lou and Alex flying, and Olivia jumped out of the way. Dirt and grass hit me in the face as it passed by, and I could smell its earthy animal funk in the breeze. Jeremy was tensed but still next to me. *Don't move*, the voice told me, and my thoughts replied, *I couldn't even if I wanted to.*

The animal came back for a second pass. More people ran in a panic for the bus door. Backpacks lay abandoned in the trampled grass. Lou curled into a ball on the ground with his arms over his head and Alex was frozen where he'd fallen, half reclining on his elbows. Only Olivia was on her feet, ready to dodge again. The animal came back through and somehow—all I remember is that—it brought Olivia into its blur and carried her away. That's what it looked like. She was there one second, and then the next she was yanked off her feet and dragged like a kite into the trees.

That's when I found my voice and screamed.

CHAPTER 3

"NO!" ALEX SHOUTED, and scrambled to his feet.

Move! the firm voice commanded. *Go after her!* My legs sprang into action, and I found myself sprinting in Alex's wake. The cold shade of the Demonstration Forest was a shock. My thoughts pounced from *That kind of sounded like my mom's voice* to *There are no roads in a forest* to *It feels like it might snow.*

Alex and I crashed through the trees. I was totally unsurprised to find that Jeremy hadn't followed us. No one had. Leafless branches and pricker bushes grabbed at me as I did my best to trample them. "Olivia!" Alex shouted. "Olivia!" The animal was long gone. We couldn't even hear it anymore.

"Oliv—!" He tripped and fell hard—I heard it before I saw it.

"Alex." I stopped beside him and reached out to touch his shoulder, but he pushed up from the ground with dirt on his face, his legs still churning.

"I'm fine," he said. "Olivia!"

A snarl and the crack of a large branch breaking came from the left.

"Over there!" I cut diagonally through the trees, at that moment not caring if Alex was following, but at the same time certain that he was. The light was brighter up ahead, a clearing in the forest. A heap of clothes and hair lay on the ground. Even from half a football field away, I knew it was Olivia.

We flew through the woods. I hurdled a downed log without missing a step. I guess all those stories about feats of strength and agility in times of crises were true. Never in my life had I been so coordinated. Then just like that—

Wait, the voice commanded me, and I skidded to a stop. Alex nearly whooshed by, but I was able to grab him at the last minute and pull us both behind a tree. "What the hell? Let me go!" He windmilled his arms. He was stronger than he looked—but so was I. I leaned my entire weight against his momentum.

"Wait," I said, his jacket in my fist. My words came out in my voice, but it wasn't really me who said it. I think Alex understood because he stopped flailing and made himself small enough to fit in between me and the tree trunk. It occurred to me that he might have been as scared as I was. I peered around cautiously. "I can't see the beast. Can you?"

Alex breathed heavily. "There." He pointed quickly up at

41

the tree canopy. A long tail dropped from a branch out of sight and twitched like a ticking clock. It disappeared into the cross-hatched branches and reappeared four trees away, much closer to us. A leg descended to dangle beside it. It was muscular like a cougar's but it ended in a hoof, a heavy brick of a thing, sharply cloven, with greasy, dirty tufts of fur all around it. I wondered, as my mouth went completely dry, if the beast was putting on a show. Was he going to tease us with one body part at a time?

Olivia lay on the ground, her legs curled into a backward question mark, like she had been dropped without a care. Her left shoulder, facing us, was ripped and bleeding badly.

I looked back at the tree with the dangling leg, but the animal was nowhere to be seen. My eyes bulged out of my head, I was straining so hard to catch the tiniest glimpse of the long panther tail. How could we not hear it moving around above us on its clunky clodhoppers?

A sudden movement in the clearing made me jump, but it wasn't the beast. A woman materialized out of nowhere. She was much smaller than the washerwoman and younger, more like my mom's age, with bright red hair in a wild tangle down her back. She wore a heavy gray shawl crossed over her chest and tucked into a wide leather belt that cinched her waist. And she was barefoot. She blinked down at Olivia but made no move to help her.

"What the hell do you think you're doing?" she asked.

For a second, I thought she was talking to Olivia. Then the beast pounced from the tree it had been sitting in—a tree about twenty feet directly in front of us. It landed in a crouch, long tail flicking with irritation. "Holy mother," Alex murmured. The beast was so, so much bigger than I had fathomed, and not panther-like at all, except for the tail. I could feel the fear seeping out of my pores.

"Waiting for you," he replied in a jagged smoker's voice. "I got your message about the little field trip today." He snickered. "That was fun." *There really is a beast in Hartwood*, I thought. *And he talks.*

"I gave you an assignment. I told you to bring me the girl marked by my swarms."

My stomach threatened to empty its contents all over the back of Alex's jacket.

The beast moved closer to her, and his massive shoulder blades rolled with each step. He almost had the body of a bear, but with enormous shoulders and longer, powerful forelegs. I could see how he managed to climb up and down trees even with hooves: his front paws were wide as pizzas with terrifying claws that splayed his toes. "I did; she was surrounded by them," he said, and gestured toward Olivia.

The woman placed her bare foot against Olivia's cheek and turned my friend's face to the sky. The woman's toenails were long and filed to sharp points. I felt Alex's arms tense. The woman crouched down and put both hands into Olivia's hair, feeling around on her scalp.

The red-haired woman stood and pinched the bridge of her nose in frustration. "I'm sorry to have to tell you this," she said, not sounding sorry at all. "You brought the wrong girl."

His fur bristled up his back and fanned out in Wolverine points on his face. "This is the swarm girl," he insisted.

"I made it very simple. Only one girl out of the entire class." She spoke slowly; each word was a threat. I suddenly felt cold all over. Alex looked at me out of the corner of his eye, and I knew we were thinking the same thing. *Swarm girl.* Not Olivia. Me.

"I waited just like you told me to, and I saw it happen." His voice had a note of panic in it, and he lowered to the ground in a tight crouch.

"What am I supposed to do with her?" She motioned in the direction of my lifeless best friend.

"Her?" The beast seemed to consider the identity of Olivia for the first time. "I don't know. Nothing. Let me go back; I'll find the right girl."

The woman waved the idea away. "It's too late for that. The authorities will have been called since you made such a spectacle of yourself. And besides, you bit her—you drew blood from another human—and it isn't the new moon."

"But I did this at your bidding!" He was in full alarm mode now. "I wasn't hunting. I don't hunt. Well, only . . . "

"Only at the new moon. You know how this works." Together they looked down at Olivia. I felt Alex tense beside me. "What's done is done. I can't help you now. We're outside the bounds of the Liminal, so basically I get no service here."

"Let's go, then. Let's go back across the Liminal," the beast pleaded.

The woman shook her head slowly. "Too late for that, I'm afraid."

The beast growled low. "What's going to happen to me?"

"Your powers are linked to mine." She motioned with one hand as she spoke, and I noticed her nails were painted bubble-gum pink. "You help me make the transformation each time a new person comes to the Otherworld."

"So? What's different about this? Let's take her back and make her a new citizen."

The woman kept talking as if he hadn't interrupted. "You help me by giving some of your own power for each transformation. Outside the Liminal, your power is very finicky. It isn't strictly loyal to you. The new moon protects you, of course, insulates you from the blowback when you hunt, but it's, what?" She squinted up at the bright daytime sky. "Waxing gibbous already? It was your power that did the hunting today, not you. When you bit the wrong girl, your power abandoned you for another host." She looked down at Olivia again.

"Turn me back," the beast said. "Make me a crow again. I can do much more for you as a crow."

"It's too late," she repeated. "You transferred your powers to another. You're going to return to your original form."

"My original—but I'd be over a hundred—I couldn't go back to being human—I—" He seemed to finally catch on. "I can bring you the swarm girl as a crow," he pleaded. "Give me another chance."

A look of sheer exhaustion crossed her face. "I thought we had each other's back. Who else in the Otherworld can I even still talk to?" The woman started pacing around the clearing. She flung her arm toward the ground. "This sets me back weeks. I'll have to figure out another way, another messenger."

"Use me. I'm still—" and his voice closed off. His back legs started shaking violently and then gave out on him. He staggered toward the woman, dragging his back half. "You're doing this. Make it stop!"

She shook her head sadly. "I promise, I'm not."

His lifeless hooves left deep trenches in the dirt. "Please," he said, more panicked. "Stop, please. It hurts," and he let out a roar of anguish that sent goose bumps prickling over my entire body. I watched as his legs bent impossibly straight. His fur slid off one leg in clumps, revealing the smooth skin of a human calf and foot, while the rest of him remained the beast.

"I'm sorry, Dennis," she said. She actually seemed it this time.

The beast roared in response.

All I had time to think was, *Dennis?!* And in one movement, the beast lunged across the clearing. The woman disappeared so cleanly, I doubted she had ever been there. No puff of smoke, no crack of lightning—she was just gone. The beast roared again, and his front legs gave out. He lay alongside Olivia, completing the semicircle that her body made. His huge body heaved with every breath. The leg that had returned to human form looked so small.

We have to get to her, I told the stern voice in my head. But there was no response and no release. Alex took one step out from behind the tree, then froze.

Another woman stepped into the sunlight of the clearing. A young woman in a long gray dress with loose sleeves and a fitted wrap, like a cross between an evening gown and a trench coat. The woman had magnificent antlers sprouting from the top of her head and a few golden rings, like bangle bracelets, caught the light as they dangled from them. She rolled back one of her sleeves and looked at the dozen or so watches she wore up the entire length of her arm. "Shit," she said. "How am I always one minute late?"

Despite her young face, her hair was gray verging on white, and it swung in the air as she bent over Olivia. She reached out a hand and said something but didn't touch Olivia.

The woman turned to the beast as if she'd been expecting this, as if they'd planned to run into each other here. She knelt down beside him and checked his eyes, then stroked his head like a pet's. His breathing slowed. *What are you doing? I wanted to scream. He's not the one who needs your help!* She said something softly to the beast and gestured to Olivia. The beast, in response, opened its mouth all the way—the better to show off its forearm-length canines—and hissed. Alex slipped back behind the tree again.

The woman didn't appear at all scared. Like, not the least bit. Her posture was impeccable: shoulders back, chin lowered, antlers reaching for the sky. She kept her eyes trained on the beast, whose head was too big to fit in her lap even if she'd wanted it there. She kept talking, but I could only hear her when her face turned toward us.

"I need to know your name," she said.

"I don't answer to you," he growled.

"Your real name," she persisted, still smoothing the fur

down his head. "From your life before. I know you remember. All servants of the Swamp Witch get their memories back, right?" *Her voice sounds familiar,* I thought in a daze. "I'm trying to help you this time."

"Like I would ever speak my name aloud," he grunted through the pain, "where anyone could overhear."

"So whisper it." She crouched closer.

The massive cat opened his jaws again and hacked up a ball of phlegm. "You are not my master," he said, stronger this time.

"Go, then." The woman rose to her feet and pointed into the woods. "Go back to your master and see what she can do to save you." Her voice was *so* familiar, but I was too preoccupied with the dying predator in front of me to sift my memory for her. The beast raised his head with effort but said nothing. The antlered woman shouted, "Go!" and the ground reverberated with the force of her voice.

Startled, the beast ran off awkwardly on its lopsided feet, limping and tripping, desperate to get away from her.

She bent over Olivia again and held her palm flat above her. My heart pounded. Midair, she ran her hand from Olivia's shoulder, down her arm. Olivia stirred. The woman asked her a question. Olivia nodded and her whole body started to shake. *What is she doing to her?* I couldn't hear anything that was happening, but in a faraway corner of my mind I realized: Olivia's crying. The woman took one of the gold rings hanging from her antlers, held it in front of her mouth like a giant bubble wand, and blew through it, straight at Olivia's mauled shoulder. Olivia stilled, and her chest rose and fell in deep, shuddering breaths.

The woman replaced the ring on her headpiece.

When she stood up, she looked straight at Alex and me, and nodded. I gasped so hard I nearly choked. Then she turned and walked back into the trees, back to wherever and whenever she had come from.

Go, that voice said, and I knew the coast was clear. I let go of Alex's jacket, which I hadn't even realized was still in my death grip, and walked shakily to Olivia, understanding somehow that the need to rush and save her had passed. She'd be okay. I'd heard all that in the one-word command, *Go*.

The ground around her was completely covered in acorns. My shadow fell across Olivia's face and she flinched. "Hi," I said, crouching down beside her. "It's me. Are you okay?"

Her cheeks were muddy. Leaves and other forest debris were tangled all through her long hair. Tufts of white feathers bulged from the tear in her coat and her shoulder was a meaty mess, but it didn't look like it was actively bleeding. It was so red, though. The inside of Olivia's body was so red. She gave a small laugh and said, "I'll live." By some miracle, the beast's foot-long canines had wrapped around her arm and not punctured her rib cage. She was more or less whole.

"How do you feel?"

She closed her eyes. "Medium to terrible."

Alex appeared on her other side, took one look at his sister, said, "Goddamn," and stripped off his jacket, then his shirt. He wrapped the shirt around Olivia's shoulder, coat and all, and tied it tight.

She winced, but said, "Thank you."

"Where do you hurt?" he asked, and I almost laughed, but then I recognized the question from our first-aid training. He ran his hands over the back of her head, checking for injury.

"It's just my shoulder," she said.

"Can you stand?" he asked.

"I think so."

Alex slid his army jacket on, and we crouched on either side of Olivia. I put my hands under her armpit to help her up and racked my brain for something else that I might have in my bag that could help. Then I remembered that my bag was back at the bus.

Olivia's feet slid over the acorns. Alex caught her, looping his arm around her waist, carefully avoiding her injured shoulder. She breathed hard, like the effort to stand was almost too much for her. "You guys are trained paramedics, right?"

"No," I said, "sorry."

She sighed. "Shit."

"We're gonna get you back," Alex told her, "and there will be an ambulance, and they're gonna make you feel better, and then at the hospital they're gonna fix your shoulder, and everything is gonna be okay." He repeated this checklist as we walked Olivia back through the trees, like a mantra. I said nothing, even though my stomach dropped at the mention of an ambulance. *Don't remind Olivia about the dead cell phones. Someone could've run to make a call.*

We walked in silence for a few minutes, the only sounds coming from our awkward six-legged limping and Olivia's ragged breath. Then suddenly she said, "Did you guys see—" She held her breath as we helped her climb over a fallen tree. "No. It wasn't real; I must've been dreaming, or hallucinating, or something."

I looked at Alex, who was already looking at me, and he gave a minuscule shake of his head. His eyes flashed: *Don't say a word.*

He was right. We could tell her at a time when she wasn't in severe pain. And then I thought, *Should we have told the antler woman that the beast's name is Dennis?* and felt a twinge of guilt.

Not two minutes later, we heard snapping branches, and my internal organs all switched places, thinking it was the beast back for a second go. But then voices called, "Olivia! Anna! Alex!"

"Over here!" Alex called. "We've got her!"

The paramedics and their neon-orange stretcher crashed through fallen branches and right to us. *How did you know we were here?* I wanted to ask, but my mouth was glued shut with relief. Two dudes strapped Olivia onto the board, while the third paramedic looked in my and Alex's eyes with a penlight and squeezed down both our arms and legs to make sure we were whole. Her gloved hands felt strange on my skin, and when she ran them over my face, I grimaced. "Is it here? Does this hurt?" She pressed my left brow bone and a starburst of pain lit up my head.

"Ahh!" I yanked away instinctively. "I mean, yes."

"Same exact place as his," she said, and nodded to Alex. "You'll probably need a scan, too, just to check under the hood, make sure there's no internal bleeding."

This was actually the most pleasant part of the expedition, sitting on the forest floor chatting about internal bleeding. I felt the cape of responsibility lift from my shoulders and settle neatly on theirs. When everything was sorted with Olivia's arm, they hoisted her on the stretcher and kept up an ongoing conversation as we walked, probably to keep us alert and calm as much as anything else, but it was short-lived. As we approached the edge of the Demonstration Forest, I could hear commotion on the road; I figured it was more paramedics taking care of the others.

We walked out into the sun. Dozens of cell phones pointed our way, and the crowd of students and first responders holding them cheered. I raised my hand to block the sun and see what the heck was going on. And that's the picture that was on the front page of newspapers all over the country the next day. Olivia's feet on the stretcher, poking out from between the paramedics; Alex scowling straight at the cameras; and me with my arm up and a shadow across my face, looking in the direction of the bus, like *What?*

CHAPTER 4

TWO WEEKS LATER, after the worst of the media attention died down, Alex and I sat slumped at opposite ends of the couch. I hadn't been in the Tiffins' house since the attack, and it felt familiar and strange at the same time. In most respects it was a typical Monday night. We'd eaten some kind of lentil-and-sweet-potato stew, sitting around the kitchen island. This would ordinarily be when we settled in for several sitcom episodes that had aired before we were born. Except this Monday, Welcome Home balloons were tied to a knob on a kitchen cabinet. Olivia was upstairs sleeping in her own bed. And a pair of crows had followed me from my house to the Tiffins', where they perched on the peak of the roof.

Olivia and Alex lived in the oldest house in Hartwood,

which had been in their family for generations. Their property stretched into the woods across the street, including a creek that we played in until middle school. While Lou and I and most other people in town lived in fifties-fab split-levels, one after the other, all the same, the Tiffins lived in a rambling old maze of rooms that had floorboards wider than my laptop and a fireplace in almost every room. I could stand on my toes and touch the ceilings. In the kitchen, the fireplace was so big that I could walk into it without ducking my head. The living room had a deep, squishy sectional couch for us to lounge on while we watched TV, but the main focal point of the room was the mantel and the enormous built-in mirror above it.

"Bonnie, come sit," Alex's dad called down the hallway to his wife. "I'll get the dishes after." It was a rare occasion for Andy Tiffin to grace us with his presence. He traveled three weeks a month, and on the weeks he was technically home, he had business dinners in the city pretty much every night. I never totally understood what he did, except that it involved money and donors and sales figures. He hadn't taken time off since Olivia was injured, but he did fly straight home and proceed to take approximately one million calls on his cell phone as he paced through the house. He dressed like a TV lawyer. His pants were creased so sharply, they made me extra-quiet and jittery.

Bonnie didn't answer. She wasn't doing the dishes and Andy knew it. She was winding white string around a bunch of fresh thyme. I could just see her from my spot at the end of the couch. Two ears of dried corn waited on the counter with some strange purple fruit I couldn't identify. A box of matches, a package of tea lights, and a small wooden bowl rounded out the still life. She was collecting her offering. Bonnie had a little side business, helping agnostic townsfolk to leave offerings at the Waltar, like a broker between the four Ladies of Hartwood and regular old humans. There was always some sort of offering accumulating on their counter any given day, but this day, I had a feeling it was her own.

I swiveled my eyeballs to Alex, who chewed on his cuticle with determination, seemingly oblivious to the polite argument happening in front of him. He scrolled through dozens of shows on Netflix, then Hulu. Lois the beagle waddled over and put two paws on the cushion beside me. I helped her climb up. She sat with her front half on my lap, the better to lick the hem of my dress. Alex switched to the cable box and began surfing the channels, volume muted. He paused when a shot of our town center came up on the screen. It quickly shifted to close-ups of the bagel shop with its **Jersey Strong** sign in the window. Everything looked smaller and older on TV. A map appeared, and red dots marked the spots where people had been attacked in the last several years—two dots in the central part of the state; one just over the state line in Pennsylvania; and one a bit farther north, just above the center of the state's S curve.

No one else seemed to notice the news story. Andy kept craning his neck to catch a glimpse of his wife in the kitchen. I read the closed captioning as we all sat in silence: "Tonight, we're joined by research zoologist Dr. Lisa Vorstein of Princeton University. Dr. Vorstein, welcome to the program."

"I don't know why she insists on doing this," Andy said, gesturing in Bonnie's direction.

Alex sniffed before he replied, "Yes, you do."

Bonnie took a glass bottle of raw milk from the fridge and tucked it into a canvas bag beside the ears of corn. Alex's dad, no longer able to stand it, strode into the kitchen and began clattering silverware and dishes as he loaded the dishwasher.

"Investigators can agree that an animal was behind the attack on January fifth," the journalist said, "but that seems to be where the agreement ends and differences begin."

"Change the channel," I said, but he ignored me. More text flashed on the screen as the scientist replied: "The paw prints, claw markings, and teeth imprints do not line up with any animal we know about."

"And the witness accounts—have they given you any leads?" the journalist inquired.

"Both adults present offered vastly different descriptions of the attack. Most of the students were sheltering on or near the bus and didn't have a clear enough view of the scene to provide much information, but I believe they have all been interviewed."

I shifted nervously and Lois let out a *hrumph*. The police had interviewed us, especially me and Alex, and I'd told them everything I could remember, as embarrassing as it was to say "saber-toothed tiger" out loud. I told them about the red-haired woman evaporating into thin air, and the second woman, the one with antlers, waking Olivia enough to let her walk out of the forest. (The paramedics couldn't explain how she was mobile with such low blood pressure, but I knew that the antler lady had everything to do with it.) The police had decided not to believe me—I could tell from the way their attention wandered after I finished describing the beast. My eyes cut over to Alex, who was slouched so his head rested on the back of the couch. I never asked him what version of events he'd told the police, and he didn't ask me. We'd all signed some invisible agreement to focus on Olivia's recovery and not speak of the attack.

The voices from the kitchen grew louder. I heard Bonnie say, "Andy—" in a way that was a complete thought and also a warning.

The dishwasher clicked shut, and it was suddenly quiet in the house. "Please don't bring that there tonight," Andy said to Bonnie. When she didn't reply, he added, "Just wait until morning at least."

"If we stopped arguing about it, I could be back already," Bonnie said evenly.

"My daughter is upstairs"—Andy lowered his voice to a furious whisper—"recovering from an attack that nearly killed her."

Lois yawned and rolled onto her back. I scratched her belly at the same time Alex reached out and his fingers grazed the back of my hand. We both flinched away.

"Sorry," he muttered.

The scientist on TV touched her glasses. "I understand why people are afraid, and why their imaginations might run away with them, but from my point of view, people have lived alongside dangerous, even deadly, animals for millennia and still do today. In India, for instance, leopards are still predators of livestock, and being a shepherd is a very dangerous job. I'm—what I'm trying to say . . ." She trailed off and the closed-captions stopped for a moment. "I study large predators, primarily extinct ones. I think this kind of fear goes beyond legends, or memory, or witness accounts, or news coverage. I think it's programmed into our DNA. We have evolved successfully—we are here today—because our ancestors knew when to be afraid."

The stairs creaked and I jumped, startling Lois. Alex and I whipped our heads around to see Olivia's bare feet descending. We both stood at the same time and looked awkwardly at one another, like we'd been sitting next to each other and never realized. I grinned like an idiot. Olivia was up! We could watch *Who's the Boss?* like in the good old days! I was ready to give her the whole couch to stretch out on, and the remote, and anything else she needed or had a passing interest in.

She rounded the banister at the bottom of the stairs looking like she'd just woken up. Her hair was tangled and half covering her face. One sleeve of her hoodie hung limp, with her injured arm tucked up inside in a sling. She blinked and looked around the living room.

"Hey!" I called, but she just turned toward the voices in the kitchen and shuffled down the hall. "Rude," I said sarcastically, but Alex didn't laugh. He followed Olivia. I followed him.

The voices stopped, and Andy said brightly, "Honey, you're up!"

I stood in the kitchen doorway, thinking that Olivia would grab something to drink and return to the living room. Bonnie and Andy wore matching expressions of happy shock. Olivia, on the other hand, didn't seem to see them at all. She went straight for the sliding glass doors on to the deck.

"Olivia?" Bonnie called. "The door is locked." Her daughter didn't reply. She just tried again and again to open the door, which jammed against the latch.

Lois waddled into the kitchen from the couch and wiggled up to Olivia for a scratch. She whined and danced around on her long nails, but Olivia just kept slamming the door against its lock.

Andy went to her side. "Honey, what are you doing?"

"She's sleepwalking," Alex said, and took her by the good shoulder. "C'mon, Olivia, let's go back upstairs." He managed to turn Olivia—whose eyes were open, I checked—and guided her out of the kitchen. Olivia brushed by me and walked down the hall like a zombie until she got to the front door, then she tried that exit as well. "Also locked," he said. "Come on, up the stairs we go."

It took a minute, but then Bonnie went back to rummaging in her canvas bag of offerings.

"What the hell was that?" Andy asked, more upset than I'd ever seen him.

"She's on really strong meds right now," Bonnie said, "that have a mile-long side-effects list. I'll ask her doctor about it in the morning."

Suddenly, the air in the kitchen felt very private and I didn't want to be there anymore. "Thank you for dinner," I said vaguely in the direction of the adults as I crossed to the sliding glass door into the backyard and successfully unlocked it.

"You shouldn't walk home by yourself," Andy said. "Alex will walk you."

"I'm fine, really. I do it all the time." *You can watch me on the security camera if you're so worried,* I thought but didn't say.

"Even so, I'd feel better if you had a buddy." He looked pointedly at Bonnie.

But then Alex would have to walk back by *him*self. *Is this because I'm a girl?*

"Alex!" Andy yelled.

Alex yelled from upstairs, "What?"

"Come down here. I'm not having a conversation with you like this!" Andy had no idea how many conversations in their house were conducted exactly like that.

A moment later, Alex slouched into the room. "What?"

"Is Liv okay?" his mom asked quickly, and he nodded.

"She's back in bed."

"That's good to hear," his dad said. "Walk Anna home, please. And don't shout from upstairs. Your sister needs to rest."

Alex's face flashed a giant question mark, and I could tell he was thinking, *Wait, is this a joke?* But then Bonnie said, "Alex, please?" and her tone said, *Just this once.*

"I have to find my shoes," he said, and disappeared into the basement, leaving me stranded by the sliding doors.

The adults continued to not-argue politely. "What's twelve hours? You can't wait twelve hours?" Andy asked Bonnie.

"It has to be done at a certain time. Evening is the start of day," Bonnie said cryptically.

60

Jesus, Alex, please hurry up. It was weird enough being in their house without Olivia around, but as the only kid in the room, I felt like an unwilling spy. "I'll wait right outside," I said, and slipped out into the glare of the deck's floodlight. No one even noticed.

"Be reasonable," Andy said as I slid the heavy glass door closed.

I cupped my hands around my eyes and tried to find the Big Dipper, but the sky was smeared with clouds, and I could hardly see past the 100-watt bulb that pointed out into the yard. Alone in the quiet, the weight of the evening crashed down on me. *Olivia won't be far, but out of reach.* Was this what the washerwoman was trying to warn me about? It had never felt more true.

The door behind me slid open and Alex stepped out.

Sorry, I wanted to say. *That was even too awkward for* me *to handle back there.* Instead, my heart beat entirely too fast. We hadn't been alone together since the Demonstration Forest. I expected the walk to be short and silent, so I nearly jumped when Alex said, "Did you tell the cops? About the beast, I mean."

"Um, sort of," I sputtered. "I tried to, at least. I was crying, kind of a lot." He didn't reply so I said, "Did you?"

He laughed under his breath. "Yeah, I did. They had their artist draw a sketch and asked me if it was accurate. It looked like a fucking Looney Tune. It was all a joke to them. So I told Olivia's doctor in the hospital. The doctor actually listened. He made a note on his clipboard. Then the next thing I knew,"

61

Alex said, "a nurse was taking me to some empty operating room where two *Mad Men*–looking guys questioned me for over an hour. There was no air in that room. I thought I was going to pass out." He rubbed a hand up the back of his neck.

"And your mom just let them take you away? She didn't go looking for you?"

"She was pretty distracted," was all Alex said. I didn't ask where his dad had been.

"What did they want to know? The Mad Men."

We were almost at the fence, near the border of tasteful hedges planted to cover up the eight-foot-high, reinforced metal border with motion-sensor spotlights along the top. Bonnie believed in the beast the way she believed in the Ladies and their Waltar, and she had the security to prove it. Alex waited until we were under the cover of the shadows, then dropped his voice. "They wanted to know everything about the beast: size, fur description, paw prints, roar sound, any distinguishing characteristics—"

I laughed; I couldn't help it.

"I know," Alex said. "Every single thing is a distinguishing characteristic. And the strangest part was . . ." He paused. "It's like—it's like they knew the answers to the questions before they asked them. It's like they were just testing me."

"Testing you," I repeated, and wrapped my arms around my body. "Did you learn anything from *them*?"

Alex stood a little straighter, startled, and the light from the back porch caught the hood of his red sweatshirt. "What?"

"I just mean, like, did they give anything away by asking

a really pointed question. Like, 'Did you see anything that might resemble a flamethrower?' would make me think that the beast could breathe fire. For example." We stood in the dark, very close to each other, I suddenly realized. I glanced up at the second-story windows, but all was dark. Alex ran a hand through his hair and, for that split second, I could smell his shampoo.

"I have to think about it. I was so stressed, I wasn't really paying attention, I guess."

Something landed on the fence with a *clang* and talons scratched at the metal. We both jumped. It was my crow bodyguard, eyes shiny in the floodlight.

"Jesus, that scared me," Alex blurted.

"I should go," I said, and moved toward the keypad lock on the gate. I didn't understand how the washerwoman and the beast attack and Olivia's sleepwalking all fit together, but my instincts were screaming that they did and, more than anything, I wanted to tell Alex. I paused and half turned. "Have you gotten to talk to Olivia since the attack? Like, one-on-one?"

"A little," he said more quietly. "She hasn't done much talking."

"Did you tell her?"

"About the Mad Men?"

"No, the—" My voice caught and I cleared my throat. "The beast. The two women. The whole thing."

"She hasn't asked, so I haven't told her. Have you?"

"I haven't even gotten the chance to speak to her until tonight, and I doubt she'll remember seeing me at all." I hated how whiny I sounded. "I've been texting her—not about any-thing serious—but she hasn't texted back."

"She will," he said. "One day."

"*One* day."

I turned to leave, but he grabbed my elbow in a surpris-ingly firm grip. "Anna, wait," he said, suddenly serious. "Don't tell her. Don't tell anyone. That's what I learned from the Mad Men. I thought it might help her doctors, might help them find a treatment, but it only meant that they put her through endless tests and kept me and my mom away. The truth doesn't help; it only makes everything worse. Okay?"

"Okay," I said. "I won't." He let go of my arm and my elbow felt warmer than the rest of my entire body.

"G'night," he said, and abruptly turned back for the house.

"Good night," I said, thinking, *Wait, I'm only halfway home.*

CHAPTER 5

I CUT ACROSS my yard, staring at my feet, with one hand cradling my elbow like I was injured. That was the most intense I'd ever seen Alex, and he was level orange on the best of days. A hollow ache settled in my stomach the closer I got to my house. *Why do all these things have to involve the one person I want to talk to about them?*

Olivia is not dead, I reminded myself.

It wasn't until I got to my back door that I noticed the light on in the kitchen and Brendan sitting at the window over the sink, glaring at me like I was trying to sneak in after curfew. Brendan was our cat, a Maine coon the size of a beagle, with smoke-gray fur and white tufts at his ears. He was pushing twenty, but we still found him sitting on the roof every now and again, having climbed the wisteria trellis up the side of the house. Had I left the light on? No, only the outdoor ones, like the filmy one I was standing under at that very moment, thumbing through my keys. Then I heard a heavy thump, like a chair falling over, and Brendan jumped down from the windowsill. My mom was home.

I came up the stairs to the kitchen, past her boots and one dropped glove. In the room ahead of me, a chair lay on its back, covered in piles of dark clothes and bags. Brendan's food dish had been overturned and his fish-shaped kibble was scattered across the floor. My mom was at the fridge, bent in half and obscured by the open door. "Shit." She stood up and closed the door with a bag of baby carrots in her hand. "I forgot to go to the store again."

"Mom?" I said.

She screamed and threw the bag of carrots over her shoulder. "Aine! Jesus, you scared me!"

"Sorry, I was trying to warn you." I snorted. "You jumped so high your glasses flipped!"

She righted them on her face and smoothed loose hairs back into her ponytail. She cracked only the tiniest smile.

She retrieved the carrots, and I pulled the kitchen chair upright. "Have you eaten?" she asked.

"Yeah, at the Tiffins'." Brendan walked in and lay on my feet in greeting.

"I'll just have popcorn," she decided. "How's Olivia?"

Alex's threatening advice still echoed in my head—*Don't tell her. Don't tell anyone*—and it made me feel like I was holding a canary in my mouth. "She's resting, on a lot of medication, still, so . . . "

My mom squeezed my arm, and I knew I didn't have to explain anything more. "Want to watch something?" she offered.

I didn't, really. But I felt guilty for not wanting to, so I said, "Sure," and decided to carry the canary for a little longer.

"Hey, that's my dinner," she said as I took another handful of popcorn from the bowl. The dog on *Frasier* was pulling some kind of stunt, and Brendan watched from the middle of the living room floor judgmentally.

"Give me a break," I told her. "I know you made enough for me." There were countless "mom" things that my mom would never go near: bake sales, homemade costumes, sporting events of any kind. But her popcorn—that was her secret, crowd-pleasing weapon. I had no idea what she put on it, some magical combination of garlic salt and dried herbs, but it turned popcorn into a meal.

"How was your day?" she asked, tipping back a handful. This was code for, *Did you have any episodes? Any headaches? Did you feel faint or pass out at any point?*

I never missed this conversation on nights that my mom worked late. In addition to her committee work with Bonnie, planning for the gate in the Wall, my mom worked for the town as a kind of Leslie Knope–park ranger combo. She managed the Demonstration Forest for the forestry students of the county vocational school and "monitored" the Great Swamp, one of the few people who actually had access to it. (When I built my scale model of the Wall and the swamp in fourth grade, my mom helped lay out the creek and the pond so I could be as accurate as possible.) She also had weird political responsibilities that popped up every now and then, hence the Wall committee. Thanks to budget cuts, she was doing three peoples' jobs for the low, low price of unpaid overtime. I didn't turn away from the TV when I said, "My day was fine."

We watched TV in silence for a few minutes.

Out of nowhere, she said, "I think it would be good for you to get away next year, make a fresh start."

A dart of dread lodged itself in my neck. "Since when?"

"Since the past few weeks." She paused to place a single popcorn kernel in her mouth. "Since the attack."

"I thought you weren't worried about the beast."

Her eyes flashed in my direction, then to Brendan, who was half turned around listening to our conversation. "That's not what I'm saying. I'm not worried for your safety. You're a smart kid; I trust you not to take risks. I've just been thinking: application deadlines are coming up."

Application deadlines are long gone, I thought but didn't say. The impressive Dr. Diana Kellogg was totally clueless.

My eyes felt heavy. I yawned. My mom moved the popcorn bowl so I could stretch out on the couch with my feet buried behind her back.

She opened her laptop and soft ticking filled the air. "You know, when you had your first episode, you were only one and a half?"

"Yeah, I was talking to Brendan in full sentences, even though I couldn't talk yet," I mumbled. *Can I nap?!*

"That wasn't the first," my mom said. "I haven't thought of this in years, but when you were about ten months, we were taking a walk on the trail around the Wall—"

"There isn't a trail around the Wall," I interrupted, suddenly wide awake. "It's all overgrown, to keep people away."

"Well, at the time, the town maintained a paved footpath around the Wall and people used it all the time to walk and jog. It was a nice two miles around."

"Is that where Chris Rowan was running when he disappeared?"

"Mm-hmm, that's why it's gone," she said, like an afterthought. "So, I was walking with you in the stroller. It was the middle of the day, no people were around, it was very quiet, and all of a sudden you shrieked. Your little body went rigid and your eyelids were fluttering. All I could see were the whites of your eyes. I tried to calm you, but all your limbs would flail and then stick straight out, and then flail again. I couldn't get the straps off your shoulders to lift you out. It was a nightmare. I felt totally helpless."

"That sounds like my first seizure, not my first episode." Oh yes, I'd had both, and other than the blinding two-day migraine that followed, seizures were preferable. They were explainable. Medical. I took a prescription for them, and we'd gotten them under control. It was illegal for me to drive a car while I took anticonvulsants, so I'd never gotten my license, but I didn't mind all that much. I liked walking. The episodes, on the other hand . . .

"As suddenly as it started, it stopped." I glanced over at my mom. She was looking off into the room as if she were seeing everything she was describing in real time. Brendan jumped silently onto the arm of the couch. "Your whole body relaxed and you opened your eyes, and when you saw me you smiled. You looked around and clapped, just delighted by whatever you saw, which was pretty normal for you—you were an easily delighted baby—but we were in the middle of nowhere, with no people around. I looked over my shoulder to see what you were looking at and a whole cast of animals was standing there. Squirrels, birds, rabbits, a couple deer, turkeys even. They were all standing together looking at us."

I felt something in the base of my skull, a pressure, like a hand turning my head to face something I didn't want to see. My eyelids closed involuntarily, and I could see them, the group of animals. The red of the cardinals and robins came through first, then the jagged antlers and long neck of the deer. It was hazy, but I could just make out the gray-blue heads of the turkeys and the small shapes that were rabbits, frozen and alert. Was I remembering, or was this the beginning of another episode? A cold sweat broke out all over my body. I remembered the advice of my childhood therapist—a woman with Professor Trelawney vibes in a nineties working-mom shell—and visualized a chilly wind blowing through my mind and clearing out every thought.

"They were beautiful," she said. "I mean, I see animals up close all the time at work, but the way they were gathered together, like a painting or a children's book. . . ." She trailed off.

"And you were just glad to see them. You clapped and giggled. I stood up—I had been crouching beside your stroller—and the deer bolted. The other animals scattered. It all evaporated so quickly, I couldn't be sure it had really happened."

"That is weird," I said, not even trying to keep the sarcasm out of my voice. As far as my episodes went, this was a cheery *Snow White* version, and possibly the only one my mom experienced more viscerally than I did. She was still spooked, sixteen years later. Meanwhile, I dealt with far darker interruptions to my sense of reality on an almost daily basis and she never really tried to understand them, so I stopped trying to explain.

There was a time, in fifth or sixth grade, when my episodes got worse. My therapist recommended group therapy to supplement our sessions, since so many of my episodes were brought on by social anxiety. It would be two birds with one stone: therapy and socializing. It was my absolute hell. The first week we split into pairs to interview each other and then introduce our partner to the group. I looked down at the worksheet to ask my partner what her favorite ice cream flavor was, and when I looked back up, the desks were flickering in my peripheral vision. Dark shapes solidified and I found myself in the middle of a forest, staring up at an ancient tree covered in twisting, dark green vines. A long slash opened down its trunk, peeling back the vines and oozing thick sap the color of blood. As a kid, my episodes mostly consisted of flashes of images, or sounds that would get louder and louder until they passed, like a speeding freight train. This was the first time I'd fully lost touch with my reality. The air smelled like s'mores. I could feel warm spots of sun on my arm. The tree loomed over me, still and foreboding. I said something, probably "Where am I?" and that sent the picture spinning away like a broken film reel. I woke up to hands on my face and a juice box straw being shoved into my mouth.

"I don't know what made me remember that," my mom said, yanking me back to the present. Soft clicking started again.

I could feel sleep coming like a tide pulling me under. "I remember that, too—I was there," said a raspy male voice, somewhere ahead of me in a dream. I couldn't open my eyes to see who was speaking.

CHAPTER 6

IT WAS FRIDAY night, typically my mom and Bonnie's night to sit on the Tiffins' deck taking tiny sips of single glasses of wine while Olivia and I were somewhere else in the house. It was a tradition dating back to second or third grade. This was the third Friday in a row that we would miss it. I'd just picked up my phone to order a pizza when it chimed with a text. A text from Olivia!

Come over.

I scrambled for my shoes and practically jumped down the stairs to the back door. A gray streak ran between my legs and into the yard.

"You missed her, too, huh?" I laughed into the dark. For a cat, Brendan had some very doglike qualities, one of which was that he tried to follow me everywhere. The only place I allowed him to tag along was the Tiffins' house.

When the metal gate in the fence closed behind us, I had a sudden thought: just because she could text didn't mean that Olivia was feeling better. She could still be in bed. She could still be unable to eat from the nausea. I hadn't seen or spoken to her since earlier that week when she tried to break out of her house in her sleep, and I had no idea what to expect. I chewed my lip as Brendan and I crossed the deck to the sliding doors. Through the glass, I could see Bonnie, my mom, and Olivia (!) standing around the kitchen island, talking. A small sack of cornmeal had spilled across the granite and Olivia was tracing her finger through the grains. Brendan darted ahead of me into the room as soon as I opened the door. "Hey!" Olivia said, and hurried over to give me a one-armed hug.

"I missed you so much!" I said in a tight voice. "How are you feeling?"

"Happy to be home," she said.

"The gate opening has been coming for over a year," my mom said to Bonnie, then turned to me. "Hi, sweetie, how was your day?" She turned back to Bonnie before I could reply. "The committee review was a nice stall tactic, but even what happened to Olivia hasn't changed public opinion."

Olivia raised her eyebrows and tipped her head in the direction of the stairs, code for *Let's get out of this pressure cooker.* "Want a seltzer?" she asked. I nodded.

"And there's no reasoning with her?" Bonnie asked.

Her? I wondered. They still had conversations as if we were small children who didn't count. Most of the time, that was to our advantage.

"No reasoning, compromising, bargaining, bribing—none of it," my mom said. "I guess I was naive enough to believe that we wouldn't let this happen again. And now it's happening on my watch."

Bonnie squeezed my mom's shoulder. "It's so much bigger than you. There's nothing more you could've done." Her voice got quiet. "People don't know what's good for them."

My mom didn't reply; she just peeled off the safety seal on a jar of cinnamon sticks and dropped them into the offering basket. Brendan leaped up onto the stool beside her and she scratched his chin hello.

Olivia handed me a seltzer from the fridge and took a step toward the hall.

"The town commerce committee is in everyone's pockets," Bonnie said, returning to their earlier conversation. "They've made it such a pro-Hartwood idea that most people are scared to disagree." For years, the commerce committee had campaigned for open access to "what could potentially be a great source of scientific education for our children." They won grants from the EPA and got attention for trying to revitalize a local ecosystem. The committee ran ads on TV. They posted pro-gate/pro-education banners on the sides of NJ Transit buses and the back page of the town paper. It quickly morphed into a countywide STEM issue, and if you were anti-gate, you basically preferred to live in the Dark Ages with a wall to keep out monsters, which—if it actually worked—sign me up.

I knew Bonnie had been stressing over the whole thing, even before Olivia's accident. Bonnie looked into the distance and said to herself, "It's made of iron, at least. That will keep them out." Then she added, "But only when it's closed."

Olivia's eyebrows knit in concern, and she gave me a look that said, *Them? Who's them?*

"There's already a gate," Bonnie went on, "a small one, and it's all you need, right?"

"Yeah, for rangers and maintenance staff," my mom replied. "It's fine."

"But this will be a huge gate that stands open, like a theme park entrance. I hate it."

"Did you get the zeppole stand for the gate opening at least?" my mom asked. "C'mon, we can still hate it while eating zeppoles."

Bonnie scoffed.

Olivia jerked her head toward the stairs again.

Bonnie's phone lit up and began vibrating across the countertop. She glanced at the face of it and answered, "Jean? Hey, how are you?" After a pause she said, "We can definitely take an offering over. For something like this, it sounds like you'd want, hmm, some nigella seeds, some sage . . ." She wandered out of the room, still talking.

Alex stuck his head in through the doorway from the garage. "Lou brought devil's food cupcakes. Hurry if you want one."

Lou's nana's cupcakes were legendary. Olivia rushed for the door and disappeared into the garage. "Bring me back one!" I yelled.

My mom gave Brendan one last ear scratch and headed to the dining room table, where a thousand-piece puzzle was waiting. Bonnie found her there. "I'm going to the Waltar first thing tomorrow if you want me to bring anything for you," she told her.

"Couldn't hurt," my mom replied.

I opened my seltzer and hoisted myself onto a stool beside Brendan, but he jumped down and led the way to the garage, as if he knew exactly what was happening. "She isn't bringing me one, is she?" I asked. He waited, ears perked.

Just as I got to the door, I heard Alex say to Olivia, "Where's the friendly ghost?"

I froze. Brendan stopped short and turned to look at me.

"That isn't funny," Olivia said.

Lou snorted. "Don't be an asshole."

"I'm not saying it to be mean," Alex said. "Wherever she is, she just blends in with the wallpaper. She hardly says a thing."

"Anna!" Lou yelled. "Get in here already!"

With my heart hammering at every pulse point, I slid into the garage, hoping that my face wasn't giving me away too badly.

"Hey." I gave a general wave to the room and sat in a lawn chair.

"Jeremy Klopner is having a party," Lou told me, since I'd missed the headline the first time around apparently. "Cupcake?" He pointed to a plastic container in the middle of the floor.

"Tonight?" I asked, already thinking of excuses not to go. I selected a cupcake and quickly returned to my seat.

"In two weeks!" he shrieked from his beanbag throne. "And he's already publicizing it."

"It's totally going to get busted," Olivia said. She sat on a wooden picnic bench beside a fifty-pound bag of dog food and rolled a skateboard back and forth under one foot. It made me nervous.

Across the garage, Alex sat on his amp, plucking mutely at the strings of his unplugged guitar. He shrugged. "I'll still go." A floor lamp stood beside the music stand that he had stolen from the band room at school. HHS was stenciled front and back on the black aluminum.

Lou went on. "Jeremy's family is moving to Silver Pines."

"Oh, never mind," Alex said. "A party up there will absolutely get busted." The Silver Pines neighborhood was built on a ridge overlooking town, the farthest you could get from the Wall without leaving town altogether. It's where the rich people lived.

Lou laughed. "No, no, no, the party is at their *old* house. When it's empty, but before the new people move in." Their old house was a split-level, exactly like mine and Lou's houses, near our old elementary school.

I was too nervous to eat, so I held the cupcake in both hands like I was trapped under its weight. I thought longingly of the heated comfort of Olivia's house. "Can we go inside?" I said, but no one heard me. Across the garage, Olivia folded one leg under her chin, but it didn't fit well with her sling, so she just crossed her legs and slouched. The three weeks of school she'd missed seemed twice as long. I wondered if her shoulder still hurt sometimes, even with the medicine. Her dark hair hung in a curtain over her right eye. I tried to get her attention, to mouth *Let's get out of here*, but she was staring at the concrete floor.

These are my favorite people in the whole world, I thought, *and less than one year from now we'll have to just give this up, all for the sake of college.* It didn't feel like a new beginning, it felt like starting over, right back at kindergarten, except this time you had to have a brand, an ambition, an identity from high school that you could pack up and bring to college, to say, This Is Who I Am—or—This Is Not Who I Am Anymore.

But what if, I worried, *what if all my answers to those things are just: my friends?*

I'd zoned way out, sliding down the spiral of my future depression. I was staring at Alex without focusing, without even realizing it. When he caught me staring, he stared right back without smiling, just holding my gaze until I felt my ears getting hot. I glanced quickly at Olivia, who looked away fast, but not fast enough.

All of a sudden, miracle of miracles, the garage door rumbled open like the Cave of Wonders. "Goddamn it, Mom!" Alex shouted. "We're in here!" A gust of cold air rolled in and canceled out all the warmth we'd built up. Then the power went out with an abruptness that sounded like a pop. The squares of light from the dining room windows were missing along the driveway, the streetlight was out, and the house across the street had disappeared in darkness. Everything was suddenly quiet, even the dogs, like the moment Dorothy's house lands in

Oz and the twister has stopped and everything is still, and she looks up and says, "Oh."

The lights had gone out, but electricity flooded the air. I felt it crawling over my skin in jagged waves of static; stray hairs lifted from my bangs. My eyes bugged out in the dark, like I could voluntarily widen my pupils. "Weird," Lou said. "It's not storming."

Something was stalking through the neighborhood. I felt the ripples as it moved.

"Does anyone else feel that?" Olivia asked. I could tell from the location of their voices that we'd all jumped to our feet, as if losing power meant we'd need to run.

"Yes," I said quickly. *This can't be an episode, not if everyone else is experiencing this, too.*

Brendan prowled out into the driveway. My attention followed him, searching for the source of the disturbance. *Do not pass out,* I commanded myself. I took deep, even breaths and bent my knees slightly.

"Maybe a transformer exploded," Alex said softly.

"Wouldn't we have heard it, though?" Lou asked.

We stood there shivering. One by one, the neighborhood dogs started up—first Ollie down on the corner, then Dobby across the street. The disruption moved like a busted game of telephone until only Dobby was left belting out the final sentence. He barked triumphantly, then cut himself off with a yelp of pain. *His owner dragging him inside,* I hoped, even as the hairs on my neck stood up.

A new howl broke through the night, loud enough that I

flinched. Whatever had made it did not sound like a neighbor-hood dog, and it didn't fit with the faraway sounds we attributed to the beast when something would answer the train whistles in the dark. It was much closer. It sounded almost human.

"Shut the garage door," Olivia said. She turned her phone flashlight on and slid the beam around the floor.

"We can't, the power's out," Alex reminded her.

We stood there, waiting for another howl, willing the power to return, and I suddenly had the most intense feeling of being watched, like someone was pointing night-vision binoculars straight at us from the end of the driveway while we squirmed. I heard someone kick the plastic cupcake bin.

Olivia bumped into my abandoned lawn chair, sending my seltzer can rolling down the driveway. It sounded like an explosion in the tense stillness.

"Well," Lou grumbled. "I guess—"

"Shut up," I blurted.

"What?"

"Shhhh," I hissed. "Something is out there."

"Anna, you're scaring me," Alex said, kind of joking, but lacking follow-through.

"Don't move," I said.

Brendan stalked back and forth, his hackles raised.

Lou's Buick was parked at the end of the driveway, dark like everything else. Suddenly, the front doors opened and two women stepped out, talking and laughing with each other as if they'd driven over in their own car. They wore long cloaks and no shoes.

"Holy shit," I breathed.

"What? Is something there?" Alex asked.

"You can't see them?" The car doors slammed. "Or hear them?"

"No," Alex and Lou said at the same time.

Somehow, in total darkness, the women's eyes caught the light and glinted brilliant yellow. "You really can't see?" They met each other in front of the car and stood face-to-face, whispering.

"We've established that we can't see—whatever it is that you're seeing," Lou said. "Why are we even still standing here?" He tripped on a cord as he scrambled to the door. Behind me, I heard Alex fumbling after him. One of them knocked down the music stand.

"Go, go, go," Alex said, pushing past me. For a heartbeat I thought he was grabbing for me in a panic, but no. He was just hightailing it inside, the picture of chivalrous bravery.

The women broke into laughter again and one bent over to clutch the other. Chills ran along my shoulders and down my back as all the blood in my body rushed to my vital organs.

"Is that real?" Olivia said, suddenly beside me, and I jumped out of my skin.

"You can see them, too? Really?"

"Yeah, for some reason I can see really well in the dark." I reached out and took Olivia's hand. "Who are they?" The air crackled with electricity; my ears filled with pressure that muffled everything around me.

The women suddenly quieted and stood straighter. They

turned to face us slowly, standing side by side, holding hands, and something changed. I became aware of time like it was a physical thing. It was like time slowed so much that you could touch it, bend it. By then every part of them glowed—eyes, clothes, hands, feet. Their hair and cloaks swirled dramatically around them like they were standing in a slow-mo tornado. One woman had hair like spilled ink, so dark you couldn't see where it ended and the night began. The other woman I had seen before, but this time her white hair radiated light like a million burning filaments, illuminating the outline of her antlers rising above her head. Bangle bracelets glinted from the prongs, just as they had in the Demonstration Forest. "What are you doing here?" I asked the woman with antlers. I didn't like the idea of her just dropping by.

"Do you know them?" Olivia whispered.

"No." I laughed nervously. "How would I?"

My eyes moved back and forth between the two women, but they were like paintings. Their eyes stayed on me, unblinking, and I instinctively knew that Olivia saw them staring directly at her, too. They spoke slowly and in perfect unison, without moving their mouths. "There are eyes on this house. You are not alone here." Their voices radiated through my skeleton. I felt each syllable vibrating my solar plexus. Olivia squeezed my hand.

"You don't know what you call to, what risk you've taken, coming into the Otherworld. You could've been the ones to break the cycle, but it's too late for that now. Those who have seen the Otherworld can never truly leave it.

"The clock is ticking. Soon, Olivia, you will be lost. You are now bound to the Otherworld, like those who came before you, who willingly and unwillingly gave their lives."

That pulled me up short. *Hold on, gave their lives? What are we talking about here?*

The woman with inky hair tipped her head back and released a wail. This time, no dogs responded.

In the echoing silence that followed, one voice spoke in my head, the one I'd heard in the Demonstration Forest, and I knew it was the woman with antlers speaking: *You bear the stamp of time, Anna Kellogg. The Otherworld recognizes you. We have been waiting for your return, but first you need to FIND YOUR BOOK.*

The last three words echoed like thunder. "What book?" I said out loud. Olivia looked at me, startled, then snapped back to the two women. "Why are you here? This doesn't make any sense!" Last time the antler lady showed up, it was after the beast had attacked and dragged my friend into some alternate reality in the woods. This time, though, we were at home, just minding our business, and the uncanny came knocking.

We will meet again, at the prescribed time. I'll try not to be late. Don't forget: keep your eyes open—all of them. You need to find your book before she does.

"*She* who? What are you *talking* about?" I shouted down the driveway.

Your book will have the answers. You can trust yourself.

All of a sudden, something thwacked me in the chest, and I took a sharp breath, like I had just surfaced in a pool. The amp popped and squeaked behind us and the lights came back on, blindingly bright. Gasping for breath, I shielded my eyes to squint out into the driveway. "Wait!" I called, but I knew they were gone, even though Lou's car sat there as enormous and dull as ever. The air felt like air again and sounds rushed back in—cars passing on the next street, a plane overhead, taking off from Newark. Brendan sat down in the driveway, staring intently at the place where the two glowing ladies had just been.

Olivia let go of my hand and backed a few steps into the garage. She pressed her free hand over her mouth, like she was trying to keep herself from screaming. She whispered through her fingers, "She's watching the house."

"Who? What were they talking about?" I sputtered thoughts as they came: "What did we call to? What cycle? And I haven't misplaced any book!"

Olivia looked petrified. Her eyes flicked back and forth across the ground as if something might jump out at her at any moment.

I moved in front of her with my hands out to calm her, like she was a spooked horse. "I heard what they said about 'eyes on the house.' But we're safe. It's okay. You're *not* lost and you never will be. We're here—in Hartwood. We're safe." She didn't look at me. That wasn't what was bothering her. "Did they say something else, just to you, at the end?"

Olivia's wild eyes swiveled to me. "You didn't hear that part?"

"I heard only one of them, at the end." I looked away. "She said my full name. She said I need to find my book."

"What book?"

"Exactly what I want to know." I paused to recall the exact

words. "She said, 'find your book before she does,' and she said something like: Keep your eyes open, all of them." *Why did that sound so familiar?* I nudged my glasses up my freezing nose.

Olivia gazed off into space again, with a look of concentration like she was doing math in her head. Brendan circled around my legs, then darted off into the night.

"Did the other lady say something to you, in your head?" I asked as serenely as I could manage. I knew in my heart of hearts that she had, and I knew that Olivia knew that I knew. She was madly weighing the pros and cons of telling me the truth.

Finally, she said, barely above a whisper, "What am I going to do?"

I put my arm around her shoulders and led her back into the house because I didn't know how to answer her.

The boys had made it no farther than the kitchen. "What was that?" Lou said. "Did you see anything, for real?" He saw Olivia's face and reined it in. "You okay?"

Alex caught my eye, and I shook my head the tiniest bit. It wasn't the beast. "We tried to see out the front windows," he said, "but nothing was there."

I glanced sideways at Olivia, who was rubbing her shoulder under the strap of her sling. "I thought I saw something," I said, "but who knows." I made a show of taking off my glasses to clean them on the hem of my skirt. *They didn't see the two glow-in-the-dark ladies standing barefoot in the driveway?* my mind screamed. *How is that even possible?* Part of me tightened with nerves, but another part of me wanted to spill the beans about the apparition very badly. Since Olivia had seen it, too, I wasn't the lone weirdo for a change, and it was thrilling. Also, I'd managed not to cower with my hands over my head, so all in all it was a successful episode—if that's what it was. I glanced sideways at Olivia, who leaned against the counter with her arm wrapped around her middle.

The sliding glass door to the deck squeaked open and Bonnie and my mom came in with empty wineglasses. Bonnie reached out to palm Alex's head, and he dodged her like a professional athlete.

"Well, at least the power's back now," Lou said, "so maybe let's close the garage door, huh?"

"The power went out?" my mom asked. She and Bonnie exchanged confused looks.

"We were sitting under the porch light that entire time," Bonnie said. She went out to the garage, as if there might be evidence of a power outage in there. "Alex, will you check the fuse box for me?"

"It wasn't a fuse, Mom," Alex said. "The power went out on the whole street."

"But—it didn't."

"It lasted, like, several minutes," Alex said. "The amp squeaked."

"We didn't hear anything," my mom said skeptically.

Bonnie narrowed her eyes. "Are you gaslighting us?"

"No!" Alex said. "Jesus."

We all stood looking at each other for a second in mute stubbornness, but then Lou went to the pantry to rummage for cheese crackers and the spell was broken. Bonnie took the wineglasses to the sink for a rinse and my mom started talking about some newsletter. Olivia slipped out of the kitchen and upstairs without saying a word. Alex and Lou headed for the basement and the role-playing game they were writing. "Did anyone reply to your post?" Lou asked.

"Only, like, two people," Alex replied. "They said nothing new. I still think multiple character sheets would be a hassle."

"But if you played as the Morrígan, wouldn't you be able to split into three and combine into one at will?"

"So, *four* character sheets?" Alex grumbled. The basement door closed behind them.

I headed for the front hallway, past the wall of photos. The same one always caught my eye: my mom, Bonnie, and their best friend, Maggie, all about eight years old, standing in the creek across the street, huge toothless grins on their faces. It was a picture that fascinated me as a child, both because it was evidence of my mom as a kid, and also because Maggie had died when they were in high school. I couldn't reconcile someone who looked so young and alive being . . . not. Now it freaked me out, how close I'd come to having my own version of that photo on the wall, of me and my childhood best friend.

In the front hallway, I turned up the stairs. I hadn't climbed to the second floor of the Tiffins' house in almost a month, longer than I'd ever been away since Olivia and I became friends, when we still had baby teeth. The past three weeks without her had been torturously slow, as though time had limped along at half-speed. That first week after the attack, school was bonkers.

Rumors about Olivia's condition mutated from one day to the next. People who never seemed to consider Olivia a good friend before were crying in the nurse's office and leaving get-well notes taped to her locker door. Jeremy still talked about nothing but the beast; his determination to be the beast slayer was now set in stone. And probably worst of all, people avoided Alex like his worry was contagious and talking to him might invite an attack upon their own family.

Halfway down the hall, Olivia's door was open a crack and music leaked out. It sounded like an outer space opera. I tapped on the door. "Can I come in?"

"It's open," she called from the bed. She'd lain down and pulled all the covers around her like she was a burrito.

I climbed up by her feet and sat against the wall.

"Want some blanket?" Olivia started to unwrap her cocoon, but I stopped her.

"No, no, I'm fine. You stay."

"I got really cold in the garage for some reason." She stared at the ceiling. "I am so tired of weird shit happening to me."

"I get that."

"I want to be done already. Done with school, done with Hartwood. *Away.*"

"I get that, too," I said, but this time I didn't mean it.

"Monday is going to suck."

"Yeah, it might." I sighed. "But I'll be there. And Alex will be there. And Lou. We'll help you carry the suckiness."

Olivia snorted. "Ew. But thanks." She closed her eyes.

I took out my phone and sat scrolling at the end of the

bed, intending to let her rest, even though I desperately wanted to know what the glowing ladies had said to her, and what she thought it meant, and why the antlered woman from the Demonstration Forest had brought her friend to the Tiffins', and why her advice to keep my eyes open was the same as the washerwoman's by the pond. I jumped a little when Olivia said, "Anna? Don't tell anyone about, you know, earlier. Okay?"

"Of course," I said. "Don't worry."

I googled everything I could think of relating to the Great Swamp and a washerwoman and Hartwood and the Other-world, but the closest I came to anything substantial was a long Wikipedia entry about Celtic mythology. I sat there until Olivia's breathing deepened. I heard Alex come up the stairs and close his door across the hall. When I finally slid off the bed and tiptoed out of Olivia's room, I wasn't thinking about the driveway or the pond or how those things lined up with an ancient oral tradition. I was wondering if Alex was still awake on the other side of the door.

CHAPTER 7

THE FIRST WEEK back at school was medium to terrible for Olivia, as she predicted. People were nice to her, especially the teachers, but in a way that made her feel worse, I could tell. AP Bio was particularly weird, since everyone had their own memory of the attack running through their minds at the sight of Olivia, and it was obvious. All week long, she was a little more guarded, a little more suspicious about people's friendliness. Even after her sling came off later in the week, which she said made her feel less like That Beast Girl, she was still quieter than normal. Some days she seemed like a shell of herself, like this placeholder Olivia was walking around, sitting in her seat in class and cheering on her relay team from the sidelines, while in reality she wasn't there at all.

Every night that week I had the same dream. It started with a scent—not quite smoke, not quite rot—the smell of something old burning, something geological or long dead.

I was driving with Olivia. Late at night. She slammed on the brakes. The headlights reflected off something I couldn't see clearly. A flash of bone. It happened in double-speed. Olivia's face was streaked with tears. Had we hit something with the car? The headlights came to rest on the Wall and the film slowed. Fog moved through the light, and I recognized where we were: the Waltar. The ground was pocked with buried offerings. Something stuck out of the ground at an odd angle. I couldn't make out what it was, but I couldn't get a better look at it, either. The picture was frozen, and I couldn't move.

Every night, I woke from the dream in a cold sweat. I wanted whatever was sticking out of the ground at the Waltar—I wanted it more than anything. It would be unspeakable to steal an offering that had been left by someone else. Offerings belonged to the Ladies of Hartwood. But if something wasn't fully buried, was it even an offering? Who did it belong to then? The curiosity ate away at me and grew stronger with every recurring dream.

I didn't get a chance to talk to Olivia about it—any of it—until that Saturday when we walked to the Founder's House downtown. Once or twice a year, Olivia's mom asked us to help her give the Historical Society's colonial-era house a deep cleaning, in exchange for volunteer hours we could put on our college applications, which, LOL. Applications had been due weeks ago.

Olivia was waiting in my driveway, wearing paint-spattered sweatpants from her last volunteer day with Habitat for Humanity.

"Sorry I'm late!" I hurried down the steps.

"It's okay," she called in her rusty morning voice. "Are you sure you're dressed to get dirty?"

I stopped and looked down at my standard black jeans and Converse sneakers. "What's wrong with what I'm wearing?"

"Nothing, it's just—you're wearing regular clothes. They might get gross."

I continued walking and yanked my yellow beret down over my head. "They can take it."

"If you say so." Olivia turned and fell into step beside me. "Sorry I couldn't drive us. My dad's car is in the shop and my parents took my brother to Pennsylvania for another round of college visits."

"Never apologize for not giving me a ride. I owe you nine thousand as it is." I kicked a rock and it skittered across a manhole cover. "Did Alex actually apply to all these schools they're visiting?"

"Are you kidding? Any acceptance letter that Alex gets should really be addressed to my mom. I hope she takes the rejections okay."

At the end of my street, we ducked under the metal barrier into the trees and cut down to walk along the creek, which was technically just a concrete-lined drainage ditch that occasionally attracted ducks. I thought about how the creek eventually ran into the swamp, right under the Wall near the center of town. I tried not to think about the washerwoman, but she was always in the corners of my mind, creeping after me like the crow whose shadow flashed over us as it flew from tree to tree. Olivia seemed like her old self, chattering on about her parents and Alex. I wanted to hang on to the normalcy as long as possible, but in the last week I'd spent too many afternoons with empty-shell Olivia. I couldn't talk to that version of her. I needed to take this opportunity, Alex and his warning be damned.

Something the two glowing ladies said had shaken loose a memory that I'd kept locked away in the back of my mental sock drawer since about the fourth grade. Olivia had been there, too. I needed to ask her if what I'd convinced myself was true then: that it was a regular day, warped by the fear goggles that every nine-year-old wears from time to time. Nothing like the coordinated mental breakdown we'd had the week before.

"I have a random question for you," I began. "Do you remember, the summer before fourth grade—"

"Yes," Olivia said.

I looked across the creek at her and she was already locked on to my eyes.

"How did you know what I was going to say?"

"Because I've been thinking about it, too. Ever since that— vision—or whatever, in the driveway. Something they said reminded me."

"I am so relieved to hear you say that. I thought I was completely losing it. And I didn't want to bother you with it—you already have more than enough on your mind—"

"Anna." Olivia's tone was dead serious. "You of all people should not give me that shit."

"I know, I know." As reassuring as it was to hear Olivia say, basically, *I'm still me*, I couldn't shake this hollow, abandoned feeling I'd been carrying around all week. "It's just—it's not a happy memory."

"No, it isn't," she agreed. "What do you remember?"

I thought back to the late-summer day, when nine-year-old versions of Anna, Olivia, Alex, and Lou had ridden bikes to a neighborhood near Lou's house, to a part of the Wall that was falling apart—out of sight, out of mind. Lou had told us there was a gap and through the gap you could see a house *inside* the Wall. We didn't really believe him. He was full of stories, even then.

"I remember the house," I began. Lou had led us to the forgotten section of Wall, cracked and crumbling stone, hidden behind low-hanging branches. If we squinted through the trees into the swamp, we could see a structure, half caved-in, with small trees growing through the shattered first-floor windows. "You were so brave about it. Lou was the one who wanted to see the house, but you were the one who led us through the gap in the Wall. I was peeing my pants."

"I was peeing my pants, too," Olivia said. "And it's not like we made it very far."

"Things get a little murky for me after that."

Olivia was quiet.

"I remember the door opened, but it couldn't have," I said.

"I remember that, too," Olivia replied.

"That's why we tried to run. But there was a woman standing right behind us, out of nowhere. She grabbed Alex so none of us could run, like she knew if she caught one of us, she caught us all."

"And," Olivia cut in, "she said something like, 'It's good of you to drop by, but you're too early. Come back when this one is lost and you need to find her.'" Olivia paused. "And she pointed at me."

"Yeah," I said, vividly remembering the woman's wild red hair. "I've never ridden my bike faster than I did when we left that afternoon."

Olivia chuckled. "We peeled out of there, that's for sure."

"I haven't thought about that day in a really, really long time. Not until you made me go into the swamp."

"Same," Olivia said. "And then last week, during the blackout. Everyone keeps telling us the same thing—the washerwoman, the two phantoms in my driveway."

"What else did the glowing ladies say?" I asked a little eagerly. "The part that was just for you. Can you tell me?"

She looked down and began chipping her nail polish. It was only when she dropped into silence that she and Alex really seemed like twins. Their silences were three-dimensional. If she could just look me in the eye, I would know if she was okay.

Instead she said, "I wish I knew what they meant by 'lost.'"

I took a lunging step across the water and hugged Olivia around her middle. "Haven't lost you yet."

Olivia hugged me back with her good arm, just a quick

squeeze. She was still rattled, still stuck in the creepy house in the woods.

Before we got to the Founder's House, I said, "Can I ask you one more thing?"

"Shoot."

"Do you remember anything from the—from when you were . . . "

"From the attack?"

"Yeah. Well, from the forest. Right before we found you."

"I remember opening my eyes and not knowing where I was. But that's it, until you showed up." She smiled. "I've never been so glad to see someone in my entire life."

"Shucks," I said, feeling relieved that she didn't know the glowing woman with antlers was an old friend of ours, or that the red-haired woman had been there, too. The fewer memories of that day that she had to live with, the better.

"Why?"

"It's nothing, I've just been wondering." I kept my promise to Alex after all.

After the Founder's House morning, Olivia and I made a plan to meet up that night when the college tourists were back from Pennsylvania, and she had a car again. At ten o'clock Olivia texted, I'm outside—that good old reliable Olivia clockwork, driving around the corner to pick me up rather than asking me to cut through the backyard when she was ready to go. Little gestures like that made me ache a tiny bit.

"Hey," I said, sliding into the passenger seat. Olivia gave

me a closed-mouth smile. She seemed tired. Brendan watched us back out of the driveway from his perch on the front steps. Janet Jackson was playing, the weather was cool but not cold, and we were heading to the diner for midnight pudding—all signs pointed to a classic night, with just one little stop on the way.

"Olivia, I have a favor to ask. A tiny one. Can we take the long way and stop by the Waltar?" I'd been going back and forth about it all day—was it really a sign from the antler lady, telling me where to look for a book that might or might not be mine, or was it just a dream stuck on repeat? Would the dreams stop if I satisfied my hunger to see what was sticking out of the ground? I convinced myself that I needed to at least look. I didn't have to get out of the car, but I had to look.

"Um, okay," Olivia said. "What are you gonna leave?"

"It's not so much *that* as it is—" I could've told her the truth about the dreams and how I thought they connected to what the antler woman said to me in the driveway, but that would lend credit to the other things they said. I didn't want Olivia to think I believed their warning—that she was in danger. I didn't want to believe it myself. "I think I lost something the last time we were there," I lied pathetically. "I've looked everywhere and it's the last place I can think of." The last time we were there was the day of the attack. Olivia's hand tightened around the steering wheel. "But we can skip it; I should probably look in the daylight anyway."

"Can you take back something that's been left there?" a voice asked from the back seat.

"Jesus!" I whipped around and found Lou lounging across all three seats.

He grinned like the Cheshire Cat. "No, I'm Lou."

"What are you doing here?"

"The Doodles canceled on me. Their owners came back early from vacation, so they called off the party."

"Your dog-walking was canceled and then you magically ended up in Olivia's back seat?" I said, looking at Olivia but talking to Lou.

"Are you going pre-law?" he asked. "If not, you should consider it."

I hated how bitter I sounded, but there was absolutely nothing I could do to camouflage how suddenly embarrassed I was. "Being friends with you more than qualifies me for law school."

Olivia let out a small snort.

"I was hanging out with Alex," Lou explained, "and Olivia came in to get the car keys. 'Where are you off to?' says I. 'The diner,' says she. Alex didn't want to come—"

"Shame," I said sarcastically, and immediately blushed.

"But I was bored and getting hungry, so I upgraded my Tiffin. What did you lose? At the Waltar?"

My mind was a smooth, unbroken sheet of ice and responses slid right off it. Olivia turned onto Springfield Avenue toward the ice cream store. "It's nothing," I finally said. "Nothing important, it's just been bothering me."

"Oh, so, like, a glove?" Lou offered.

"Yeah," I said quickly. "I lost one of my gloves."

"Must be a pretty good glove if you need to look for it at ten p.m."

I turned to Olivia. "How did Alex's college visits go?"

Lights and bells flashed and clanged up ahead at the train tracks, and Olivia slowed to a stop. A New Jersey Transit train thundered past, its windows glowing yellow in the dusk. *Great*, I thought, *let's really stretch this awkwardness for all it's worth.*

Olivia sighed. "He just keeps saying he's not going to college, so probably that means UCC, or other community colleges. My parents are not about to let their only son *not* go to college."

Lou was quiet in the back seat.

"So," I said tentatively to Olivia. "What's your list, in the end? Besides Dartmouth." Olivia had been wearing Dartmouth gear for at least two years. She slept in an absolutely hideous pair of flannel pants that had the douchey Dartmouth crest on the hip like an afterthought. If she didn't get into Dartmouth, I wasn't sure what would happen to her. Babbling heartbreak? Spontaneous combustion?

"Here and there. Wake Forest, Colgate, Oberlin, Michigan, Reed." She held up a finger for each one and only stopped listing schools when she ran out of digits.

"Reed? Where's that?"

"Portland. Oregon," she added, as if I needed clarification.

"Wow. Pretty far away." Suddenly, I felt very small sitting next to my friend and her big plans. We passed the Founder's House, solitary in its spotlight. It looked so fragile, like a gingerbread house held together with nothing but frosting.

I turned back to Olivia. "Nothing in New York? I sort of

always thought we'd end up in the city together." The reason I thought that was because we'd talked about it since middle school, a "college years" spinoff. The two of us would share an apartment with a teeny tiny bathroom and an even tinier kitchen, scrape by on two-dollar slices and happy hour drinks, go to classes, maybe at the same school, maybe not, and just be together, our own little satellite Hartwood.

"Aww," Olivia said fondly. "Remember how we planned our entire apartment? Wow, I haven't thought of that in ages. I think I'm looking for more of a campus experience, though."

Well.

"Where are you applying, Anna?" Lou asked. I turned around to throw him a look, but he was genuinely asking.

"Um," I sputtered. "Probably Rutgers, TCNJ. Maybe Montclair. Who knows?"

"Shouldn't you?" Lou said.

"Where are *you* applying?"

"If I even go, it'll be in-state only. And only if I can get the New Jersey scholarship for boys raised by their grandparents because their mom is MIA."

"Ah," Olivia said. "That old chestnut."

Houses and their well-lit driveways smeared by in the window as we passed, packed closer and closer together as we got to the center of town. The measly park in front of Town Hall looked forgotten and sad. The fountain, which in my memory had never worked, was backlit unflatteringly. In this small segment of town, the Wall was on display. Town Hall and its park had been built right next to this most imposing part of the barrier, which had actual parapets along the top, like we lived inside a medieval fortress. Except now, a construction site interrupted the Wall where the gate would be in a couple months.

A police cruiser idled with its headlights off in the Friendly's parking lot. "Down!" Olivia commanded and I crouched as fast as I could. My seat belt locked so I had to slide down in my seat really fast, effectively giving myself a wedgie. Lou stayed seated, waved.

"It's not eleven yet," I grumbled with my chin jammed up against my chest.

Olivia waited until the road curved and the cop was out of sight before she said, "Okay, all clear. I just don't want to draw attention."

As I resituated myself, Olivia asked, "In our apartment, can we have a jar of olives in the fridge for my midnight cravings?"

"Obviously," I replied evenly, trying not to betray how happy it made me that she could still play the Dream Apartment game.

"And maybe also some of those little cheeses in the red wax."

"Is this a hypothetical refrigerator, or are you really getting an apartment?" Lou asked. When no one answered, he said, "Hypothetical Refrigerator is a good band name."

Olivia turned up the volume of the radio. We drove with all the windows down and heat full-blast on our feet. In the wind, our hair moved under its own laws of physics, and I thought of the two women in the driveway, whose hair bloomed and swirled of its own accord. Safe in the car, the memory lost its sharp edges, and I could think about it without agonizing over what it meant. In the side mirror, I saw Lou stick his hand out the window and roller coaster it up and down in the car's slipstream.

Slowly, the houses and apartment complexes became sparser, and thick clumps of trees and bushes filled in the empty spaces along the road. The dark stretched between streetlights. The speed limit climbed to fifty and Olivia pressed the car faster. The woods deepened on either side of us. Olivia's headlights swept over a carved wooden sign posted beside the Wall: **Great Swamp Wildlife Refuge, Hartwood, New Jersey.** The Wall beside us made a long, horizontal arc, one side of a vaguely rounded square. We were almost at the Waltar.

Olivia said something that I didn't catch. I turned the music down a bit. "What?"

"Oh, I— It's nothing, it's stupid, never mind." She waved her hand like she was clearing the air of smoke.

"Nothing is stupid," Lou said. "Tell us."

"Oh." Olivia seemed surprised, like she didn't realize he could hear her from the back seat. "It's something that Anna asked me earlier today. I never answered her."

"Intrigue," Lou said.

"You guys are going to think I'm crazy." Olivia bit her lip. It seemed like she was ready to burst with the secret, and still she held it back. "A couple weeks ago," she said hesitantly, "I started having these really vivid dreams. I'll be in the woods, trying to find something. Or I'm eating a huge feast at a long table like a Mad Hatter's tea party. The dreams never make any sense, but then I'll wake up and find mud all over my clothes and hands and feet, like I'd been sleepwalking outside all night long. In one dream, I met a lady with bright red hair." She paused, and when I looked at her, she was looking at me. "She needed help getting her cat out of a tree. I climbed the tree and carried it down, which I never would've had the guts to do in real life—and it didn't even seem like she cared about the cat!" In a smaller voice she said, "She was testing me. When I woke up, I had all these scrapes and scratches on my arms and legs. Her cat clawed me pretty good."

"Oh, Tiff," I said.

"But anyway"—Olivia rushed on—"in the dream, the lady was so grateful. She took me back to her house for tea and biscuits with jam. The most amazing raspberry jam I'd ever tasted. There were flower petals in it. I remember because they were in the corners of my mouth when I woke up and I tasted it. I thought it was dried drool." I rolled up my window, suddenly cold. She took a breath and gripped the steering wheel with both hands. "The red-haired lady has turned up in my dreams a lot since then, but now when I wake up, I can't hold on to what I've dreamed. It's like—blackout. I just see her and, the next thing I know, it's morning and I have leaves and shit in my hair and—a few times now"—she paused to chew her lip again—"there's been blood on me that isn't mine."

No one replied. We were probably all thinking the same thing: *If not her blood, then whose? And how did it get there?*

Olivia glanced over at me. "I think she's the one who's watching the house—the lady. It must be her. I don't know how."

"Whoa, whoa, wait," Lou said. "You're leaving things out. How do you know someone is watching your house?"

"Anna," Olivia said, "you tell." She kept her eyes squarely on the road, which curved, long and languidly, up and over a small rise. I took a deep breath, trying to find where to begin, but I never got to; on the other side of the hill, Olivia let out a short "Ah!" and slammed on her brakes. My seat belt locked for a second time as I jerked forward to a stop. Lou yelled in the back seat, whether from the shock of the abrupt stop, or the animal standing in the middle of the road, I couldn't tell.

CHAPTER 8

HUGE DARK EYES watched us, unblinking in the glare of the headlights; above them white-tipped antlers perched like multi-storied chandeliers on his head. This was no run-of-the-mill white-tailed deer that I was used to seeing grazing on the soccer field during first period. The stag was prehistorically big.

Olivia hit the power button on the stereo and the night noises of the swamp broke over us in a wave. She put the car in park and reached over to grab my wrist. I knew we were both searching the dark behind the stag for two barefoot women.

"Holy shit," Lou murmured.

The creature didn't move. Moths swooped in and out of the headlights' beams. The deer snorted and its breath came out in a fog. For a moment we just stared at each other—six eyes against two—and then I heard a door catch release. Olivia released my arm and slowly climbed out of the driver's seat, never taking her eyes off the buck.

"Olivia, what are you doing?" Lou whispered from the back seat.

I looked back at the stag and he hadn't moved, so I unbuckled and followed Olivia out onto the road.

"Hey," Olivia said softly. She rounded the car slowly and came to a stop in front of the left headlight. "Are you okay?"

The stag blinked slowly and dropped his head a bit. Even dipped, his face was well above eye level. For the first time in my life, I saw how antlers were meant to be weapons. Soft pattering came from the trees to my right, and I looked over as two crows landed in the same tree. A third joined them, closer to us this time, landing on the branch that reached across the road, just above my head.

"Olivia, I think we should get back in the car." I didn't feel any of the electricity I had the last time someone unexpected had shown up, but I didn't want to wait around for a second run-in.

"I think he needs help." Olivia stretched her arm out to the stag, palm up. "I won't hurt you," she whispered. I glanced over my shoulder and saw Lou clutching the headrest of the passenger seat, staring out the front window with his mouth open.

The stag let out a whine of pain, the kind of sound I thought only small animals made when they were snatched by claws. Its breath huffed out in cloudbursts. I couldn't look away.

The stag took a step closer to us, but his leg gave out and he collapsed, toppling forward onto the pavement in a deafening clatter of antlers and hooves. Olivia and I stumbled back behind the safety of the car, and in the direct spotlight we saw the stag's antlers weren't white-tipped at all. They shone with blood and something more—something slimy and silvery dripped in gluey strands. The thick, dark fur at his neck was torn and matted with gore. I clapped my hand to my nose and mouth as the smell of blood and animal warmth rolled across the pavement.

The beast, I shrieked in my head. *The beast did this.* My eyes bugged out, straining for any sign of life in the trees, swiveling from one side of the road to the other. Lou burst out of the car and rushed around to get a better look. "Holy shit, holy shit," he said under his breath. We all edged closer, but I couldn't keep my eyes on the poor stag. The beast was somewhere close by. This was the moment we'd been trained for in assemblies since kindergarten: make yourself big, be ready with your pepper spray, speak in a deep, booming voice. We'd gotten a pass last time—barely. This time we would get it right and no one would get hurt. But my central nervous system was unresponsive, my lungs could hold only sips of air, and my pepper spray was in my bag in the car.

"Is it dead?" Lou asked.

"No," Olivia murmured, "it's still breathing."

"Guys, we need to get out of here." I looked up into the branches and gasped. The tree limbs above us were lined with crows, at least fifty, easily. Had they multiplied, or come in so stealthily that I hadn't even noticed? Which answer was less scary?

I abandoned my friends and the stag and started back to the car when I noticed something glinting in the bare dirt alongside us, between the road and the Wall. The ground was rough with filled-in holes, and just a few paces in, something stuck out vertically. I lunged for it before I could change my mind and scrambled back into my seat. The car dashboard glowed like the control panel of a spaceship. The time read 10:14. I stared at the book in my hands. A twisting, vine-y wreath was embossed on the cover in gold. I shoved it into my bag, hoping it wasn't the reason we were about to find ourselves in another encounter with the Hartwood Beast.

Lou started back for the car but paused when Olivia didn't follow. He stood by the driver's door, trapped between retreating and staying. Through the windshield I saw Olivia's head disappear behind the nose of the car as she kneeled down beside the buck.

"Olivia, come on!" I craned in my seat to watch. For every second that Olivia didn't touch the deer or move any closer, I felt more and more sure that I was the one keeping her safe, as if her movements were determined by my thoughts. I wanted to scan every inch of darkness for a predator. I felt like I was listening with my skin. A breeze curled through the windows with the scent of burning rot and wet earth. It filled my nose with cold air. My hands, bunched in nervous fists on my lap, sprang open in shock.

It was the scent from my dream—the dream was happening right then. Every night, I'd gasp awake thinking we'd been in a car accident. The dream always felt so real, like a memory

I couldn't place; instead, it was a memory of something that hadn't happened yet. Until now.

I opened my list of favorites and hit the first name. Chills ran up and down my back. "Mom," I said when she answered. "We're on the swamp road. There's a deer—I can't tell if it's still alive."

"Stay in the car," she said, as if she could see me. "I'll be right there."

It was such a welcome relief to be told what to do, to obediently sit at the edge of the passenger seat, bracing myself against the dashboard so I could peer out at my brave, reckless friend comforting a dying deer.

Olivia was in a crouch, shuffling closer and closer to the deer. She pointed to his neck and said something, as if there were another person who had just gotten there and needed to be filled in. I searched the headlight beams, followed Olivia's gaze to whoever it was she was talking to, but Lou was behind her, next to the car, and she was addressing thin air. I leaned over to the side window to check if the crows were still there. They were. Of course, they were. After a pause, Olivia shook her head and said something else. My scalp prickled. *Faster, get here faster*, I willed my mom.

Lou got into the back seat. "What is she doing?" he said to himself.

"Could you hear what she was saying?" I asked.

"Not all of it, but I did hear her say something about—"

"What?"

"A thin place? I swear that's what she said. 'If you fall into a thin place, it feeds on you?' she asked someone, but I don't know who she was asking. How the fuck can a place *feed*?"

Headlights lit the car's interior and someone screeched to a stop behind us. My mom ran to the open driver's window. "Are you okay?" Her eyes darted around the car.

"We're fine. I'm fine." But it felt good to be asked.

Someone hurried up behind her, just footsteps in the dark until I recognized the silhouette. Bonnie glanced in the car and said, "Olivia? Where's Olivia?"

I pointed in front of the car. Without asking another question, she hurried to Olivia and put her hand on her back, guiding her to stand. When my mom saw Olivia and the stag, her eyes bulged for a split second before returning to her professional face. Bonnie asked something and Olivia shook her head. When her face caught the light, I could see that Olivia was crying. She stood protectively over the deer while my mom walked a circle around the Museum of Natural History diorama come to life. Bonnie didn't stray from Olivia's side, but her gaze was fixed on the stag.

A minute later, a squad car pulled up, flashing blue and blinding white. We got out of the car, now brave enough to stand in the street with the added light and people. Olivia shivered and kept her arms crossed in front of her like she'd just been rescued from a sinking ship. I wanted one of those aluminum foil blankets to wrap around her. She didn't say a word. When we climbed back in the car, Olivia's face was dry, but her eyes and nose were red and swollen. She made a slow K-turn and started back toward town. I half expected Bonnie to insist on driving us all home, but she seemed to have taken Olivia's place watching over the animal.

"Are you okay to drive?" I asked, as if I could offer to drive instead. She gave one small nod.

As we were leaving, I saw my mom squatting next to the stag, taking pictures with her phone. She had one latex glove on, and she used that hand to lift the deer's lips to take pictures of its gums. About half a mile down the road, we passed two dark vans speeding in the opposite direction. Hartwood Animal Control stood out in white letters on the cab doors.

That's when the noise started. First a couple crows, then slowly rising to a cacophony as they all joined in, growing louder and angrier.

"Shut the windows!" I yelled. The last pane of glass rolled into place just as the swarm overtook the car. I tensed, waiting for the Hitchcock reenactors to force us off the road, but they merely skated over the car like a tidal wave, thumping the windows and roof with their wings and trailing their warning cries. Olivia jerked to a stop until they passed, scores of them, flying in such tight formation they moved like a single organism. When the noise faded, Olivia let her foot off the brake slowly.

My ears rang.

"I fucking hate birds," Lou said.

"What *was* that?" I exploded. "Not just the birds, *all* of that."

"Honestly, what the *fuck*," Lou agreed. "Did you see the gash in its neck? It looked like it was smoldering, or like the gash was growing. I don't know how it was still walking around like that."

Olivia took a ragged breath. She was crying again.

"Tiff," I asked gently, "who were you talking to?"

A car passed with its brights on, and Olivia winced in the glare. She waited a beat too long before she said, "You only saw the deer?"

"Yeah," we said in unison.

"No one," Olivia answered. She cleared her throat and said with more conviction, "There was no one there besides me." Her hand was shaking as she brought it to her mouth and began to gnaw her thumbnail.

I took her hand away and held on to it. "It's okay. It was nothing, just a deer. We're all okay. Don't bite your nails."

She let go of my hand to grip the steering wheel as she bit the nails of her other hand. "No one was there," she said again, but this time it sounded like she was convincing herself.

"We won't tell anyone," I said as gently as possible. "Cross our hearts, right?" I looked over my shoulder.

"Cross my heart," Lou said, more solemn than I'd ever seen him.

Olivia blinked rapidly and wiped her cheeks. I waited, thinking she would spill eventually. I knew I shouldn't push her, but it was obvious to everyone—including Olivia—that she was lying through her orthodontically-straightened teeth. I was not going to let this one go. "You can tell us," I prompted. "Who else was there?"

"I told you: no one. I was talking to myself."

It was quiet for a second, then Lou asked, "Are we still going to the diner?"

"I don't really feel like eating right now," Olivia said.

Maybe it was just too real a reminder—the flashing lights, the trees around us, her mom's worried face. Maybe she just needed reassuring: she was okay. We were all okay. "Hey, you know what? Why don't you guys come over?" I said. "We can light some sage or pull some tarot cards. Or just watch a movie." *Or interrogate Olivia.*

Olivia shook her head sharply. "I just really want to go home."

I turned toward the window. My face crumpled, but I covered it, quick as I could. *If you fall into a thin place, it feeds on you.* I had no idea what that meant, but I understood how a place could devour a person. Hartwood was a ravenous place to grow up.

CHAPTER 9

OLIVIA DROPPED ME off at home, her way of underlining *this concludes our evening, good night.* My mom had rushed out so fast, she left most of the lights on, which I was glad for. I didn't want to be in the dark any longer that night.

I pounded up the stairs, Brendan hot on my heels. "This had better be worth it," I said, swinging my bag off my shoulder and onto my desk chair. I reached up and clicked on the lamp. Everything in my room was just as I'd left it: bed made; the contents of my hamper in a pile beside my hamper; framed photo of me and Olivia at middle school graduation gathering dust on my dresser. Except now there was also a heavy, leatherbound book lying on my desk with a twisting gold wreath stamped on its cover. "You better have some answers. You're the reason for tonight."

The book did not reply.

Brendan leaped onto my desk and immediately flopped down onto the book, contorting himself flirtatiously so that I would scratch his belly; then I realized he was actually just fawning over the book. He rubbed his cheek against the corner and curled his paws around the binding.

"What's with you?" I lifted him off the book. "Let's see if this thing can tell us anything about what happened tonight."

The spine was scarred with deep scratches and nicks and, upon closer inspection, the whole thing looked a bit worse for wear. I don't know what I expected when I opened the cover, but I definitely didn't expect to find paper so thick and mulchy, it looked almost homemade. The book practically had twigs and bark sticking out of it. I turned another page, and another, all of them blank—no title page, not even a scribble. "I put Olivia through all that just to get a blank book?" Heat began building behind my eyes. Brendan settled in my lap, where he sat facing the book, waiting for me to continue.

"I should just go to bed." I picked it up to shove it back into my bag and, instantly, a jolt shot through my arms. The leather cover grew slightly warm to the touch, like it was waking up. It felt alive—it felt like skin. I heard the energy coming off it, like the high-pitched frequency of a stereo left on after the record has stopped playing, but I couldn't tell if I was hearing it in the air or through the contact with my body. The smell of old smoke flooded my senses.

I let it drop onto the desk and lie there inconspicuously while all ten of my fingers bugged out in jazz hands.

Find your book, the glowing lady had said, *before she does.*

But this book wasn't mine.

The cover sprang open as soon as I put my fingertip to the edge and, out of nowhere, a gold hoop, perfectly round and smooth, tumbled into the center of the book, as if the binding had spit it out. Forgetting to be afraid, I turned it over in my hands and tapped it against the desk. It was real, all right—a gold bracelet, just large enough to slide over my hand and dangle from my wrist. Up close, I could see that the surface was ever-so-slightly dimpled, like it had been hammered into its shape. Brendan sniffed it, then sneezed. It reminded me of the hoops I'd seen dangling from the mystery woman's antlers. Those were tools as much as jewelry to her, and this couldn't be—it couldn't be.

The bracelet clattered against my watch. I scrunched my hand to slide it off, but it wouldn't budge. "This"—I struggled to slip it over my thumb joint—"is not"—I pressed until my skin went completely white—"funny." I clamped the bracelet between my knees and pulled until my whole hand was red and swollen.

Panting slightly, I gave up, closed the book, and sat back. "How do I undo this?" I asked it. In the light from my lamp, the wreath on the cover took on shadows that made it seem deeper than it was. I lightly touched a finger to part of the interwoven design. Nothing happened. I pressed harder, tracing one strand as it wound through the others. A current of electricity zipped around all the tendons in my hand. I jerked away instinctively, but my fingers still twitched, vibrating, like the current hadn't died yet. Brendan touched his nose to my bangle and jerked back like it had shocked him.

"Something is waking up," I told him. "I don't think it's just the beast. We've had attacks before; people have gone missing. It feels different now, though, don't you think?"

I pressed my palm into the center of the wreath, ready for a vision to flare up, or the book to spring open and belch out a diamond ring. But nothing happened. I picked up the book with both hands, shook it a little. It rattled, as if it had contents sliding around inside.

"It's not a Magic 8 Ball, you know," a raspy voice said.

I froze. "Who's there?" But the house was silent around me.

I shook it again. Same rattling. I rubbed my eye under my glasses, and out of the corner of the eye that was still open and able to see, the book was gone. Both eyes flew open. A large wooden box sat where the book had just been, with ornate vines, leaves, and four little feet, like those old-fashioned bathtubs, whittled into the lid. Dirt was packed into the carved surface. The catch was a piece of hammered brass with thousands of tiny pinpricks worked into scrolling designs. It fit over a loop that a scary-looking brass needle, the size of a porcupine quill, threaded through, keeping everything shut tight. I gently slid the needle out and lifted the lid. My bangle clattered against the wood. Dark shadows came into my periphery and my vision diminished to a narrow keyhole.

I took a breath, but before I could scream, my room disappeared in a clap, and everything was silent.

My pupils refocused suddenly in a bright, open space—saturated blue sky, a fringe of trees. I looked around me, prepared to get light-headed and stumble at any moment, but my footing was fine. Good thing, too, because I was standing in a crowd of people in the town square. Early morning shadows stretched across the green. The air felt cool and fresh like spring. In front of us loomed the Wall, as weather-beaten and gross as ever. To our right, every window in the brick Town Hall reflected the morning sun like mirrors. To our left, trees grew where my favorite boba teahouse should have been, and just beyond, the downtown stores began with a Sergio's Pharmacy, which was actually a UPS store, as far as I could remember. People filled the streets around the town square, right up to the Wall. Behind me, the gazebo overflowed with people trying to get a better look at something.

"Excuse me," I said, cutting between bodies and ducking under shoulders as I tried to get closer to the front. People moved aside to let me pass, but no one looked at me. They shifted just as I approached, or suddenly turned away to cough, giving me a way through. It was like no one even saw me. There was no chatter or laughing. No one was happy to be there. I climbed up on one of the benches that ran in a ring around the edge of the park, next to two little kids who were being held there by their parents. I glanced furtively around me, still not sure that I was truly invisible and not wanting to be rude. A man to my right with a comb-over and three pens in his shirt pocket lifted his huge glasses to dab his wet eyes with a handkerchief. A couple just behind him had their arms around each other's waists—he was in a blue jacket, steely-faced, and she was in a long floral skirt, standing a bit awkwardly with her kitten heels sunk into the grass. What year was this?

I felt sweaty and cold at the same time. I scanned farther up Main Street, which was closed to traffic, and forced myself not to panic. Police cars parked at an angle in the intersection with their lights rotating red and blue—huge, square-nosed police cars like in *The Goonies*. Beyond that, the street was blocked by a pair of enormous dump trucks, the telltale orange of Hartwood's Parks Department. I looked down Main Street in the opposite direction and it was the same setup, except a backhoe was involved. At the edge of the crowd, I caught a glimpse of someone who looked a lot like a younger version of my math teacher, but then people shifted and I lost her. My breathing sped up, my nervous system strongly recommending *flight*, but where could I go? The book had thrown me back in time to gods knew when.

"Okay, let's begin," a man's voice said over a crackly loudspeaker. "Thank you all for being here to honor the sacrifice nobly made by Margaret Theresa Mossfield."

I didn't like the sound of that.

"Margaret, you do us the honor, today, of sacrificing yourself to the swamp, that we may live in continued peace. You join the ranks of heroes and heroines who came before you, and like them, your name will live on in the Book of Names. We will never forget you."

The voices of the glowing ladies echoed in my memory . . .

like those who came before you, who willingly and unwillingly gave their lives.

My stomach plummeted. The man carried on, reading from a script. "We open the door to your new life and close the door on your old. May you find peace and grace, wherever the road may take you."

The temperature of the crowd was ice cold. Everyone was somber as funeral-goers. I stood taller, trying to pick out Margaret. A line of chairs faced the audience to the left of the speaker's podium: a man with a cane in a bright blue jacket, a younger man in tweed with shined shoes that glinted in the sun, a woman in a crisp dress with her ankles crossed, and a girl, not much older than me. Her brown hair was pulled back in two barrettes and her face looked drawn on. No expression registered, not even as people came up to give her gifts and goodbye hugs. A small suitcase lay open in front of her, and people placed gloves, socks, tinfoil-wrapped lumps that I could only assume were food, flowers, even a small stuffed animal. That's when I realized: she was attending her own memorial service.

A few people wiped away tears as they returned from leaving tokens in the suitcase, but the last two people to go were the only people who seemed to understand the weight of the occasion. Two girls walked up, one in a bright green puffy vest, the other sobbing over something in her arms. She laid a photo album in the suitcase and then both girls hugged Margaret where she sat in the chair. When Margaret didn't return the tears, the crying girl broke away and hurried off. The girl in the green vest hesitated, then gave Margaret a quick kiss on the cheek before disappearing back into the crowd. Margaret wiped her cheek, but she didn't say a thing.

Besides the two girls, everyone was freakishly calm, including Margaret's parents, who I figured out were the man and woman seated in the row beside her when the yahoo with the mic said, "And we thank Paula and Peter Mossfield, who themselves are sacrificing their only daughter for the greater good of the village of Hartwood. Your contribution to the safety and longevity of Hartwood will also live on in history. And now, we say our goodbyes."

Margaret and her parents stood up and hugged fiercely for a long, long time, not moving, not sobbing, just holding on. I heard a few sniffles—the parents to my left, who were holding their kids on the bench.

I turned back to the Wall and gasped. There was a door, a normal-sized door in the massive face of the Wall, and it was open. The man with the blue jacket and cane who'd been sitting on the stage stood hunched on one side of the doorway. The MC stood on the other side. *One of them must be the mayor.* "Margaret," the MC called, "it's time now."

Margaret and her parents unlocked their hug and straightened. She and her mom looked at each other a moment, while her dad bent down to close the suitcase. It was a handheld suitcase, powder blue. He clicked it shut and it sounded like he'd pulled back the hammers on a pair of pistols. I wondered if they'd bought the suitcase just for today. Margaret took the handle and walked toward the door. The MC shook her hand briskly, but the man with the cane was gentler. He folded her hand in both of his and said something very quietly so only Margaret could hear. She nodded and stepped into the doorway, then stopped and looked over her shoulder. Her face was still expressionless, but I felt like shrinking into my collar. I didn't want her to see me standing there, participating in her death. Her gaze moved around the crowd like she was looking for someone, or trying to freeze the moment in her memory, then she looked one last time at her parents, gave a little wave, and walked into the swamp.

"Maggie!" her mom wailed, finally breaking down. Her husband held her, and she sobbed into her hands, turning into his chest to hide her face even more. The MC quickly shut the door on the swamp. The door was studded with square-headed nails that held bands of black metal across the head and foot. Two men in coveralls walked up with a long heavy chain that they crisscrossed over the door, looping it from one hook in the Wall to another with ease and expertise. I knew it was an anti-beast precaution, but in the moment, it had the ridiculous effect of looking like they were locking Margaret in, like she was the threat.

I wondered when they'd closed in the doorway. In the present Hartwood—or my present, at least—the Wall had no door. It was one smooth expanse in this part of town, the only stretch that was maintained for form as much as function. At some point, they'd covered over the evidence.

"Thank you all for being here," the MC said, and shoved the microphone back on to its stand with deafening feedback.

People around me started to shift. Someone in the crowd shouted, "This isn't right!"

Another voice, farther away, yelled, "End the sacrifices!"

Others joined in with shouts of agreement.

The parents beside me picked up their kids and left, while the crowd that remained surged forward. Angry demands of "No more!" and "End the sacrifices!" came from a hundred mouths at once.

I looked frantically for an exit, not just from the mob in the town square but from this moment in time when Hartwood residents were effectively fed to the beast. I craned my neck, searching for an Exit sign or a shimmering portal—any wrinkle in time I could grab to get home. Someone tapped me on the arm. "Excuse me, you dropped this," and handed me the box. It was one of Margaret's friends, the stoic one in the green vest, standing beside the bench.

"Oh, thanks," I said automatically, but when I met her eyes, I was looking into the face of a young Bonnie Tiffin. I somehow knew it with certainty. Her gaze hit me like a slap, and I lost my balance. I felt a tremor, like an earthquake, and the horizon tilted sharply. I threw my arms out and, in the next breath, my foot slid off the bench and I was held in that agonizing instant where I was filled with the mortifying, time-stopping thought, *Oh shit, I'm falling*.

When I hit the ground, it hurt less than I expected. I was on a carpet, not the packed dirt of the town park, back in my room, lying on the floor with the box on my chest. My heart was racing, like I'd run there instead of dropping through space and time. I stood shakily, slid the box onto my desk—making sure it was closed and latched—and looked around my beautiful, beautiful room. The joy only lasted a second. My head pounded and my stomach hurt like I'd been gut-punched. I quickly sat down before I passed out.

Brendan walked up and nosed my hand, then climbed into my lap.

"What year was that?" I asked the box. "When did they cover up the door in the Wall? Why have I never heard about these sacrifices before? Did they always sacrifice kids, or could it be anyone?" Her mom had called her Maggie. The other girl, the one sobbing beside the girl in the green vest, it had to have been my mom. I knew her friend had died when they were teenagers. I had no idea she had been sacrificed by the town.

The box said nothing.

For a few minutes, I just sat on the floor with Brendan, thinking about Maggie, her barrettes and suitcase, and what her first night in the swamp must've been like. Did she die of exposure, or hunger? Did the beast go after her the way he'd gone after Olivia? Maybe people threw bundles of food over the Wall to her, I thought hopefully, before I realized that what I was really thinking about was what *I* would do. If that were Olivia, I wouldn't leave it at a photo album tucked into a suitcase. We would find a way to communicate, even if it was tin cans on string. We would not let something as pointless as a Wall or a sacrifice come between us.

What had Bonnie and my mom done?

Across the room, the long brass talon slid out of the clasp on the box and clattered onto my desk. A sharp wooden creak made Brendan jump and the lid popped open of its own accord.

CHAPTER 10

WHEN I WAS certain I wasn't going to faint or puke if I stood, I shuffled back to my desk, with Brendan half perched on my shoulder, and looked down into the innocent-seeming box.

A suitcase handle, powder blue, lay in the otherwise empty compartment.

I shut the lid. I did not want to deal with this anymore. I wanted to sleep. I hoped Olivia was asleep. I wondered what Alex was doing right then. A soft vacuum sound, like a drain suddenly opening, came from the box. "Did you just swallow the handle?"

I lifted the lid slowly, in case some rare bird flew out of it. But the box was empty. Then I noticed that the bottom panel of wood had turned to glass and through the glass I could see a table, but not the table that was my desk.

"I'm going to touch this now, for real," I told the box. "Please don't Portkey me."

I picked up the box with both hands, held it open in front of my face, glass facing out, and turned in place. It was like looking into a bizarrely misshapen telescope. As I looked around my room, I saw the low-tide debris of Alex's room—clothes, decimated dog toys, empty seltzer cans—as if Alex's room were superimposed over my own. The box had heard my thoughts. It was going to actually show me what Alex was doing right that moment.

Anna, I thought, *this is the creepiest thing you have ever done.*

I hadn't been in Alex's room since I was probably nine or ten. He was fiercely private, which was rather understandable considering that Olivia and I were slightly bully-ish to him toward the end of elementary school. Olivia hit a growth spurt ahead of her brother and we all handled it about as well as you would expect. If the box was showing me the truth, Alex's room hadn't changed at all. His old twin bed—tucked into the corner where my bookcase stood—had the same cloud-print sheets I remembered from his pillowcase at TV-room sleepovers. I pointed the box down at my feet and laughed in surprise. I was standing on a Hot Wheels rug with little streets and houses and trees. Just as I remembered.

I scanned around the room, following the box like a scuba diver follows their camera. Other than the half-eaten apple on the bedside table, there was no sign of Alex. "Okay," I said to the book-box, "let's see what you can do." Through the glass, I watched my hand close around Alex's doorknob and open the door onto the Tiffins' upstairs hallway.

I moved slowly down my own hallway, past the bathroom (Olivia's room) and to the top of the stairs. The Tiffins lived in a rambling old house with a long, steep staircase. I lived in a split-level with about five stairs dividing each floor. I wasn't sure how this was going to work. I took the first step carefully and, through the glass, it seemed like I had walked down three steps. I took another step and another three railing posts slid by. I could see over the railing now, into the living room on the other side of the front entryway.

I heard a low voice coming from the living room, a monotone chanting, like someone casting a spell. Instinctively, I dropped down, hidden by the banister, even though I was pretty sure no one could see me. It wasn't like my disembodied face floated through the Tiffins' house while my body remained in my own. Or at least that's what I hoped.

The living room lights were dimmed. The deep voice sounded like it belonged to someone talking in their sleep, mumbling low and trancelike. Peeking through the banister, I saw someone move in front of the fireplace—Olivia, inches from the huge mirror over the mantel. Was she sleepwalking again? She was looking into her own eyes. Her mouth didn't move—but her reflection's did. Mirror Olivia chanted with her chin slightly raised and her eyes closed. A prickle of fear walked across my scalp.

Olivia's head fell forward. Mirror Olivia kept talking.

I needed to get closer. I'd never paid much attention to the mantelpiece before. It was a built-in mirror, like an elaborate altarpiece, all carved dark wood, curling columns leading up to a canopy of branches and leaves. It was pretty, but also over the top in a Gatsby kind of way, and it didn't really fit with the rest of the Tiffins' furniture. It must've been original to the house.

I stood up on my staircase and walked the last couple steps down to the Tiffins' entryway, tiptoeing like I was sneaking out. Every muscle in my body strained to help her, but short of dropping the book and running to her house, there wasn't anything I could do. You're not supposed to wake a sleepwalker. Maybe that also applied to a mirror-talker? The possibility of getting caught seemed completely real, even as I bumped into an armchair in my own living room. Olivia and her reflection didn't notice.

The chanting stopped. Olivia's reflection opened her eyes. "On Beltane, the gate will open and the door will close behind you forever. You, my darling pumpernickel," the voice said with creepy intimacy, "my dearest mushroom soup, you will become part of our family, officially. But you needn't leave behind all your treasures, all your friends and family in *that* world—pack them up and bring them! The Otherworld can house us all. Bring them with you to your new home."

My mouth went dry. The Otherworld. The glowing ladies' warning. Olivia: *bound to the Otherworld, like those who came before . . . who willingly and unwillingly gave their lives.*

I understood what that meant now.

". . . new home," Olivia repeated, slowly and clearly. I moved right next to her, so close I could've lifted her chin and moved her hair out of her face. I desperately wanted to. I needed to know if her own eyes were opened or closed.

Mirror Olivia cooed, "Your place is set at the table of time, dearest." It turned my stomach so much to see a strange voice coming out of Olivia's reflection, I had to look away. As I lowered the box for a breath of normal air in my own living room, I caught the toe of a sneaker off to the right. I scrambled to get the box back in place and turned toward the front window, where the couch was in the Tiffins' house. Sitting at the far end was Alex, forearms resting on his knees, watching his sister talk to someone not herself in the mirror.

Thank the gods, thank every single one of them, I thought. *Olivia isn't alone.*

"Bring your brother," the mirror said in a more commanding tone that sounded suddenly familiar. Alex's spine straightened. "Twins have a powerful connection, and it wouldn't be right to sever it." She spoke with the same self-assured cadence as she had in the Demonstration Forest. Olivia's face was in the mirror, but I knew the red-haired woman was on the other side of it somehow. "Remember: Beltane is the key. Bring your brother to my house on Beltane and we'll dine together under the twin moons."

Olivia lifted her head slowly and opened her eyes.

Suddenly, the lights raised to ordinary brightness. Olivia cleared her throat and stepped back from the mirror, tossing her hair over her shoulder. Her reflection did the same. "What was I going to get?" she said to herself. Rubbing one eye, she walked through the living room toward the kitchen at the back of the house, looking every inch the normal Olivia that I knew and loved. She didn't even notice Alex.

When we heard the fridge door slam, Alex got up from his spot on the couch and walked toward the mirror. I followed. He waved his hand in front of the glass and a reflected Alex hand waved back. "Hello?" he said. We waited for a reply, but only Alex's pinched face peered at us. He sighed, "What the fuck is Beltane?" and headed for the hallway. I watched him leave in the mirror.

She's watching the house, Olivia had said. I thought that meant from the outside, like a paparazzi stakeout. I'd never considered she was watching from within.

From the hallway beside the stairs, Alex glanced back at the mirror. "Anna?" he said.

I dropped the box and the lid slammed shut.

He saw me! My face in the mirror! I panicked. *I need to explain.* For a split second I hesitated—do I go over in person, or—? I picked up the box and opened the lid. *Now's my chance to see if the audio works on this thing.*

Folded paper burst out like accordion snakes. "No, no, no." I rummaged through to the bottom and my fingers scraped along wood grain. "Come *on!*" I dumped out the paper and held up the box, the bottom of which was, once again, solid wood.

For a full minute, I sat on the living room rug, staring at the empty box. The mirror voice echoed in my head. I needed to get to Olivia. I needed to explain to Alex, but how could I possibly justify spying on them in the middle of the night with a crummy wooden box formerly known as a book?

Brendan moved directly in front of me and lowered himself into a loaf. His eye contact was unbreaking. "What?" I asked. "It's past midnight; I'm not going to feed you." His tail flicked. Suddenly, a sharp bolt of pain burst through my left eye socket. My hand instinctively went to my forehead. It felt like fireworks had gone off behind my eyeball. Usually, migraines only came after a seizure and I hadn't had one in years, not since we found the right medication. Was the book-box giving me seizures now? For a second it made for a more appealing explanation than any alternative.

I scooped the curling parchment into my arms and grabbed the box, intending to shove it all under my bed and sleep off the headache before it got worse. Brendan followed me up the stairs, mute but insistent at the same time. When I dumped everything onto my desk, he instantly leaped up and climbed inside the box.

"You better not pee in there," I warned him.

"Moi?" he howled. *"Moi?"*

I pitched face-forward onto my bed and pulled up the covers.

For a moment it was quiet, then I heard him batting the parchment. The sound of paper crinkling made my head pound. The cat was walking over the snakes of parchment, carefully spreading them out. He paused and studied one section before moving on to the next.

"Are you reading?" I asked him, and he jumped as if caught.

"Mrow," he said, and made a chortling noise in his throat, pleased with himself.

"Listen," I said, dragging myself out of bed with my covers wrapped around me like a cape. "This—contraption—has caused enough trouble for one night, okay? I've seen one of Santa's reindeer drop dead; I've been kidnapped through time; my best friend may be possessed; and for the love of the gods, I just want to go to sleep so I can figure out—wait, what is . . ." Brendan had spread out the parchment enough for me to see that it had a substantial middle section. It was all connected, like a sun with random rays branching off here and there.

The parchment draped over the side of my desk. It crackled stiffly as I smoothed it. It was a map, hand-drawn in deep emerald ink, with tiny pictures next to the names of monuments and locations. My gaze landed on a beehive-shaped structure at the bottom of a stair-stepped waterfall with an arrow pointing to the low entrance, the same place the water flowed in. All around it were reeds and cattails and clumps of other swampy foliage drawn in the same green ink. In curling writing, someone had written, *Grotto of the Oracle.* I quickly realized that every segment of parchment that branched off the larger center was a close-up of the area adjacent to it. And at the very top, in heavy block letters that looked as though it had taken a whole bottle of ink to fill in, the map declared: THE OTHERWORLD. Then below, in slightly smaller but no less sinister lettering: TO ENTER, YOU MUST REMAIN. TO REMAIN, YOU NEED ONLY ENTER.

"I can't deal with you right now," I told the map as I massaged my temple. I remembered the look of confusion on Alex's face as he said, "Anna?" and I wanted to fold my arms and legs into accordion pleats and close myself into the box. "One world is more than enough trouble; I don't need another."

I carried Brendan to my bed and dumped him onto the comforter. It was impossible to refold the different arms of the map to fit together correctly, so I shoved everything into my backpack, parchment and box alike, and crawled into bed.

With my eyes starting to close from the migraine, I turned to Google. Searches brought up more questions than answers. Wikipedia listed different versions of Otherworlds in ancient cultures around the globe. *Merriam-Webster* defined "otherworld" as "a world beyond death or beyond present reality," which made the pit in my stomach deepen. I searched Margaret Mossfield and found listings for twenty-nine M. Mossfields, nothing for a Margaret or Maggie, or a Paula or Peter. A trickle of doubt dripped into my thoughts. The town square had felt as real as the near-accident on the swamp road—hadn't it?

Had I really seen into the Tiffins' living room, I wondered as I drifted into a fitful sleep, or was that just what the box wanted me to see?

CHAPTER 11

THE NEXT MORNING, I woke with a start. My headache was gone, but the events of the night before seemed like they'd just happened. I threw the covers off and onto Brendan, who dozed near my knees. "Olivia needs to see this map," I told him.

Brendan ran ahead, scaled the dogwood tree, and jumped to the other side of the fence. I punched in the code to the gate between our backyards and looked up at the red eye of the security camera before stepping through and pulling the heavy door closed behind me. A crow sailed through the bright sky. Olivia hadn't returned any of my texts, not even the bubble tea emoji. I worried she was mad at me for making her drive to the Waltar the night before. I worried I was annoying her. I worried she was still upset about the dying stag, or that she had woken up somewhere other than her bed and couldn't find her way home. I worried about her.

Brendan waited for me at the sliding deck door. I let him in and looked up to see Alex sitting at the kitchen island in his red hoodie with an impressive case of bedhead and puffy, sleep-punched eyes.

"It was massive," Lou was saying, standing at the stove moving a spatula through a frying pan full of scrambled eggs, his back to the kitchen. "I mean, I've never seen a moose up close, but it had to be at least as big." A carton of speckled brown and blue eggshell halves lay open on the counter beside him.

I stood there for a beat too long.

Alex opened his mouth the smallest bit and then said, "Hi?"

Lou spun around. "Anna, thank god. Will you back me up about the deer last night? Tough guy over here won't believe me."

"I never said I didn't believe you," Alex retorted.

"You haven't said a word. Are you not surprised or something?" He raised his chin at me. "What did your mom find out?" His voice became serious. "I really want to know. What did she say?"

"Oh, I haven't seen her to ask," I said, feeling dumb. Instinctively, I reached for my phone to tell my mom I was next door. I hadn't even noticed if her car was gone or if she was asleep. "I left in a hurry."

"Huh," Lou said, obviously disappointed. He returned to

the eggs. "These'll be done soon. You want some?"

Brendan leaped up onto the counter to examine the egg carton.

"Sure," I said, and glanced around what I could see of the downstairs. "Where's your mom?"

"Out." Alex shrugged. "My dad's in Montreal or something. Olivia is upstairs if you want her." Listening to him talk gave me a reason to look at him. He seemed completely unfazed, not like someone who was holding back questions about having seen my disembodied reflection in their living room mirror.

"There's enough for her, too." Lou plunked four slices of bread in the toaster and pressed the lever. "Tell her to come down. She can weigh in on last night, too." He smoothed his hair across his forehead, took a box of sea salt from the spice rack, and sprinkled a pinch over the frying pan.

"How often do you come over here and cook?" I asked. He seemed completely comfortable moving around this kitchen that didn't belong to him.

"From time to time," he said, then pointed at me. "This will be ready in ninety seconds. Go get Olivia."

I tried to catch Alex's eye, but he was on his phone, so I wandered out of the kitchen, texting Olivia as I went. Are you upstairs? Can I come say hi? I hit send and looked up, right into the mirror over the fireplace in the living room. I froze, waiting for it to move or turn on. I was still in my coat. I looked like a potato with legs. I waited and waited, but nothing happened. I was alone.

I trudged up the stairs to Olivia's bedroom door, knocked softly, and pushed it open. "Tiff?"

"Yeah?" She was sitting at her desk with her closed laptop in front of her.

"Hey, Lou is making eggs." I cut myself off. Her window was wide open and the mini-blinds lifted in the freezing cold breeze. Sheet music had blown off her music stand and scattered all over the floor. I crossed the room and shut the window, gathering up the pages of the violin part in "Jupiter," which she was learning for orchestra, even though she still couldn't hold her violin for very long.

"Thanks," she said, "I just ate. I'm gonna get to that Latin homework now."

I stood there, passing a strange feeling back and forth between my hands. It was Olivia's room, but only on the surface. It felt sanitized, cleaned to the point of lifelessness. Fifteen Timothée Chalamets flashed their dimples at me from the collage beside her bed, and I didn't trust them, not one bit. "Your room is very clean."

"Thanks," she said again.

"How are you?"

"Oh, fine, just tired. You?" Her eyes did look tired, but more than that. Dulled.

Olivia's bed was made, not a single hair on her pillowcase, but the sound of a muffled gong came from its depths. "Are you going to get that?" I asked, recognizing the sound of her phone's alert.

"You can." She shrugged. I moved aside Olivia's stuffed panda bear and the throw pillow with *Resist* cross-stitched in a fancy Victorian font, and there was her cell phone, glowing with the reminder of the text I'd sent two minutes ago. A perfect tiny acorn lay on the sheets beside it. Instantly, I remembered the Demonstration Forest, the acorns blanketing the ground beneath Olivia. Seeing one now felt like a threat. I pocketed it before she could see.

"Here you go," I said, and handed her the phone.

She took it from me without even a glance at the screen and said, "Thanks," then turned back to her Latin notebook.

A low static filled my ears. Slowly, I turned in place. The stereo was still on, but no record was playing. A Beths album waited on the turntable. Olivia would never leave one of her children exposed to the elements like that, not even to duck out for a quick run.

I pushed the power button on the stereo and replaced *Future Me Hates Me* in its sleeve, its sleeve in its album, its album in its plastic protective cover, and returned it to its alphabetically assigned space. "We'll be downstairs if you want to hang out."

"Okay, see ya," she said in a faraway voice.

As I reached the bottom of the stairs, I heard Lou say, "I didn't want to ask her without including you."

"Aww," Alex said. "Sweet of you."

I rounded the corner into the kitchen and when Lou saw me he paused. "Does Olivia want food?"

"She . . . already ate." I sat gingerly on a stool at the island.

"So, she's not coming down?" Lou asked.

"No," I said. "She's doing Latin homework. With the window open."

Alex looked down at Brendan, who was curled in his lap. "I didn't hear her get up."

"She didn't seem like herself." Anxiety prickled up and down my back.

"Maybe it's better that she's not here." Lou put the fourth plate back in the cupboard and forged ahead. "I've been thinking. Ever since, you know, the attack—Olivia has seemed off, hasn't she?"

Alex came to life. "Wouldn't you be?" he demanded.

"No, yeah, of course. But I mean, not *because* of the attack. There's something going on *now*. She started to tell us last night. Do you know anything?"

Alex shook his head, and I knew—the box had shown me—that he was lying.

"She was going to tell us more when we almost hit the stag." He put plates of buttered toast and fluffy scrambled eggs in front of us and dragged a stool around the island for himself. "Actually"—he handed me a fork—"she said for you to tell the backstory."

I felt Alex's warning radiating from his slouching body: *Don't tell anyone.* Too late. We were all in the story now. I took a breath. "Weird things have been happening since before the attack." I started with the washerwoman at the pond and relayed the meeting with as much detail as I could remember, as if it were a dream that might fade the longer I stayed awake. Alex listened with undivided attention. I kept glancing up from staring at my hands and being startled; each time he was looking me dead in the eyes, stone-cold serious. I spilled my guts about everything that had happened—the two glowing ladies in the driveway (Alex gave no sign of recognizing the woman with antlers from our time in the Demonstration Forest), the time-traveling vision the box had thrown me into, and seeing Olivia talking to herself in the mirror.

"Last night, like, late?" Alex asked, and I knew what he was really asking.

I nodded and waited for him to ask more, but that seemed to be all the confirmation he needed. I kept going. I told them how I went back and forth between wanting to get to the bottom of things but also desperately wanting everything to go back to the way it was before the field trip. Before the questions at the pond, and Olivia's senior photo posted all over Hartwood Beast fan sites. Before anyone was watching any house, when books were just books, and the gate in the Wall was a new idea, not a one-way door to a sacrifice.

I didn't pause or give them a chance to ask questions until I got to the present morning. "And now Olivia is there but not really—" The moment I stopped talking, feathers bristled in my line of vision, no matter where I looked. "I have a bad feeling about it. She's so distant, it's like someone else is in her skin."

The kitchen was silent, then the fridge clicked on with a drone. "Anna Kellogg," Alex said with amusement, "is that what your voice sounds like?"

I felt the temperature rising in my cheeks. He said it in the same tone as when he asked, *Where's the friendly ghost?*

"What did the clothes look like?" Lou asked. "The ones the banshee had."

"The what?" Alex and I said at the same time.

"The washerwoman at the pond, you nerds."

"They were all in a pile"—I shrugged—"so I couldn't tell if they were a shirt or a dress or what."

"What color were they?"

"Maybe black? I'm not sure. They were dark because they were wet. After everything I just told you, I did not expect your first question to be about the clothes."

"Hmmm," Lou said, crossing to the sink to rinse his plate.

"Lou," I said, fiddling nervously with my bracelet. "Please talk to me. I feel like I'm losing my mind here."

As he was drying his hands, he said, "I think you and Olivia saw a banshee. She washes the clothes of someone who is bound to die soon. So yeah, it kind of matters what the clothes looked like in case we could tell who they belonged to."

"That isn't funny." I thought of how close Olivia came to dying that very day and felt myself shrink. "I only told you because I thought you'd believe me."

"I do believe you, you lunatic! I'm being serious." I watched Lou, waiting for him to crack up and give himself away, but he threw the wadded paper towel at the garbage can, missed, and huffed across the room to pick it up. He was being serious.

"How do you know? About the banshee," I asked.

"You mean why should *you* believe *me*?" Lou said.

I sighed, then nodded.

"You know why." He smoothed his hair across his forehead. "I *like* all that myths-and-legends crap, okay? I subscribe to 'Lore.' I read every *Game of Thrones* message board. I have an *Encyclopedia of Fairies* and a *Dictionary of Imaginary Places*. Alex and I have been writing a game inspired by Celtic mythology for almost a year now. Do I need to go on? I find this shit com*pelling*. I like the idea that some regular Joe Schmoe could be plucked from obscurity and told he's a wizard or given some monumental task that gives total meaning to his life. I like—I like stories that have the possibility for weirdness, where people have to prove themselves worthy, or wrestle with fate, and, yeah." He took a breath. "I was there at the bus. I saw Olivia get taken. What more proof do we need that this shit is real?"

It took me a second to identify the warm feeling spreading through my chest, it had been so long since I'd felt it. Reassurance. Comfort. I didn't have to carry it all on my own. I sat down and took a bite of eggs and *damn* if they weren't the lightest, mouth-melting-est eggs I'd ever had. It occurred to me that maybe those eggs had been intended for a Waltar offering. I hoped Bonnie wouldn't miss them.

Lou looked at me and said, "I wanted Olivia to be here for it, too, but oh well. Do you remember the time in third or fourth grade—"

"Yes." I set down my fork. Lou and Alex both froze mid-bite. "I know what you're going to say and yes. I remember everything. Olivia does, too. I asked her about it . . . yesterday? Oh god, that was only yesterday." I turned to Alex. "Do you remember?"

His eyes darted cagily from his plate to the window and back again. "Some of it. Not a lot."

"Just the fact that you can say that means you know what

we're talking about. Come on, you remember," Lou said.

Alex let out a sigh-laugh.

"Don't be an asshole," I said. "It doesn't matter that we were little kids; that really happened. That creepy woman and that creepy, rotting house. And only your mom believed us. She helped us bring an offering to the Waltar for protection afterwards. I know you remember."

I heard Lou's voice reply, but I lost my grip on what he was saying. A ribbon of pain unspooled behind my eyes, and I closed them instinctively. I pushed my glasses up onto my head and pinched the bridge of my nose with two fingers. "I think I'm getting a migraine." The sharp tang of rubbing alcohol hit my nose and I thought, *No, no, no,* as the kitchen broke into puzzle pieces and collapsed around me.

Fluttering heart-shaped leaves. A flash of thick cream-colored fur that bristled and rolled under massive shoulder blades, fur like a bear's pelt, but also—feathers? Long, barred feathers sprouted just above the shoulder blades and stretched out of sight. A crow cawed distantly, but I couldn't tell if that was in real life or in my head.

I heard water lapping at rock, a heavy *whooshing* sound, like massive wings muscling through the air. For a split second I saw—just a snapshot, a still of the scene. A woman standing inside the front door of the rotting house in the swamp. Ivy grew up over the staircase behind her. A basket on the floor was full of acorns. She held her arms out, gathering us together. "The table is set!"

I looked past her into the house. Someone was tied up on

145

the floor in the next room. Panic swelled and my adrenal glands went *pew-pew-pew*! I had to get out of there. The vision pulled me closer; I smelled something burning, then the dusty warmth of an animal.

Soft fur met my cheek.

Lou put a hand on my shoulder and my eyelids wrenched themselves open. He placed my glasses on the counter in front of me; they must've fallen to the floor. "You okay?" he said. "Your eyes went"—he rolled his eyeballs back and fluttered his eyelids open—"for a second there."

I blinked until Brendan's face came into focus, inches away from my own. I took my breaths as slowly and deeply as I could manage, trying to feel the ground beneath my sneakers as he nuzzled me with concern. "What did you put in these eggs?"

Lou snorted and returned to his seat. He said something to Alex, and Alex replied, but I wasn't listening. I wanted to slide off my seat like a pile of slime and just melt through the floorboards. I massaged my temples, then stopped because it was painful to touch a new breakout developing there. I reached down and pulled my backpack onto my lap, under the strict supervision of Brendan, who seemed to think I was going to pass out any minute. "I'm okay," I told him.

Without warning, I dumped the contents of my backpack onto the kitchen island. Pens and Jolly Ranchers and bobby pins scattered everywhere. The box landed with a crinkly *clunk*, along with the tangled mess of a map. "This is the book I stole."

Alex raised his eyebrows.

"From the Waltar," I added. Brendan pawed at a scrap of parchment. "I brought it over to show Olivia, but I don't think she's . . . in the right place just now."

"Anna," Lou said gently, "that's a box and a pile of paper. Books are usually"—he clasped his hands together—"some sort of combination of the two."

"It *was* a book, at first. It turned into a box last night, after I got home."

Lou leaned on his forearms over the island and his hair swung into his face. "Let's see this alleged book." He peeled back the tentacles of parchment and smoothed out the center so that THE OTHERWORLD arced across the top, facing him. "It's a *map*."

Alex came around the island to stand beside Lou. "You said that the two glowing ladies said, 'Get the book before she does.'" Alex recited the words I'd heard in the driveway that night. "But how is this a book? And who's 'she'?"

"I have a theory," I said. "I think it's the red-haired woman from the day of the attack. And—"

"And the rotting house in the swamp." Lou nodded. "I had the same thought."

Alex grabbed a loose pencil from the detritus on the counter and used it to lift folds of the map. "Do you remember what the woman with antlers called her, in the woods after the attack?" he asked.

I hadn't until he asked. "The Swamp Witch."

"The *Swamp Witch*," Lou said with gusto. "It fits." He leaned precariously over the counter to read the tiny handwriting cramped on to a ray of paper that branched off the top right of the map. He read out loud:

Beware the waters, seek high ground
Beware the crow's nest, time surrounds
Spend too long & you'll be gone
Get out before the day is done

Lou squinted at the map with one hand on his stubbly chin and another holding his hair out of his eyes. He straightened up. "I can't find any crow's nest. Do you see it?" He bent closer and checked every branching piece of parchment, too.

"Dude, at least carry your glasses with you," Alex said.

"You shut your mouth. I do not need glasses."

Alex looked for a second and declared, "The crow's nest is definitely not on here, unless it was in one of these spots that got singed." He poked his finger through a hole and left a heat smudge on the granite.

"Look," Alex said. "Two ladies and an elk." I leaned around Lou to see where Alex was pointing. Two women, one with antlers, both with long hair and bare feet poking out of their robes, sat on either side of a jagged tree stump. The head of an elk, just like the one we almost ran over, was drawn directly over it. *Elk's Well*, it said underneath. I hadn't noticed it before. I looked up at him in surprise and he was already nodding. "The two glowing ladies, right?"

"Ohhhhh shit," said Lou. He leaned close and I followed his gaze to the small beehive-shaped structure at the bottom of the waterfall. I hadn't noticed the label before. "Look, look, look, it says, 'Grotto of the Oracle.' I bet this is where we'd find the banshee."

Alex squinted at the parchment. "It also says, 'Beware: Surety brings ruin.'" I followed Alex's finger to the faded words that were upside down under the grotto. The warning circled the entire drawing, but *beware* was faded, like someone had tried to rub it off.

Brendan walked across the countertop and leaned his weight against me. As I ran my hand along his spine, all the way down his tail, I took in the entire map; for the first time, really let myself get lost in the minuscule labels and bizarre landscape. This was not a map with any sort of key, or compass rose, or scale for calculating distance. It looked like one of those maps that had *HERE BE DRAGONS* in places that hadn't been explored yet. Two roads made a meandering *X* across the map, stretching from one corner to another. One endpoint, I noticed, lined up with something called Port Sacrifice. Narrow paths forked off the main roads and led to places like Medusa Head Falls (accompanied by a small drawing of a waterfall) and the Sterling Diner (an actual sixties-looking, chrome-bedecked diner in the middle of all this medieval-seeming stuff).

"I was hoping Olivia would come down by now," I said, dread building as the words came out of my mouth. I wanted her to see the map, to examine it with the same level of interest and seriousness that the boys were and tell me without a doubt that she had no memory of any of these places. That it had nothing to do with her blackout dreams or the scrapes on her legs or the giant stag from the night before.

Alex tapped the map. "This is the source of the weirdness," he said, seeming to read my mind. "All these things are coming from the Otherworld—the banshee"—he let the pencil fall like a drumbeat on the Oracle's stone hut—"the two ladies, and the stag. It's all come out of the Otherworld to terrorize you and my sister, just like the beast."

His mouth opened as he realized what he'd said, and he looked right at me.

Like the beast.

I looked again. The rough circular outline, the boundary around the edges, not just decoration but an actual edifice: the Wall. "This is a map of the Great Swamp," I said. "The Great Swamp is the Otherworld."

"Or vice versa," Lou said. "The Otherworld is in the swamp."

"That's gotta be it." Alex threw his pencil down. "The swamp is a palimpsest for the world the map shows."

I didn't say anything. I knew he would explain if given—

"A palimpsest is when the original picture or text or whatever is erased and something new written over the top."

"I know what a palimpsest is," I muttered.

"Like world layers. Or parallel universes," Lou said.

I thought back to the afternoon at the pond. We went through the Wall, but I didn't remember any doorway or portal or anything to differentiate Hartwood from the swamp. There was nothing out of the ordinary until the washerwoman—the banshee—herself. So, had we been in the Otherworld? Or had she fallen out of the Otherworld and into the Great Swamp?

Alex pushed off the counter and stood up straight. "If this is where it's all coming from, this is where the answers will be."

"Okay," I said. "What do we do now?" The cat clock on the wall swiveled its eyeballs back and forth.

As he carefully folded the map, Lou said, "We do exactly what she said we would: we go find the Swamp Witch in her falling-down house. But this time, we go through the swamp."

CHAPTER 12

"DO YOU THINK we need to carry it in the box?" Lou whispered. "Probably not, right? I'll put it inside my jacket to keep it safe."

"No, definitely take the box, too," Alex said. "Keep it all together."

Lou's jean jacket hung open and he pulled his car keys and a knit cap out of his pocket. I looked at the dark green wool a beat too long and got a flash of his nana knitting it in the light of the television.

Brendan jumped to the ground and stalked back and forth in front of the door. "You can't come this time," I told him. "But you can stay here with Olivia . . . if you want."

"What did the Swamp Witch say again?" Alex asked. "Do

you remember *exactly*?"

"She told us, 'Come back when this one is lost and you need to find her.'" I suddenly got so cold my teeth started chattering. I grabbed my bracelet for something to hold on to. "And she pointed at Olivia."

"And we trust her?" Alex asked.

"Shit, no," Lou said. "But what other option do we have? Tell your parents? Go to the police?"

"No," Alex said. "Those are not options."

Lou shrugged. "We can deny it, or choose not to believe it, but that's where we have to start: the Swamp Witch. And you're sure we shouldn't bring Olivia?"

Alex looked at me and I shook my head. "She's not herself. We have to find out why."

We climbed into Lou's maroon Buick, which he and no one else called the "Lou-ick." I hastily brushed the pile of cassette tapes from the seat to the floor, expecting to be chastised for my poor passenger etiquette, but Lou was nervous and hustling, as much as Lou ever hustled. "They put in a new fence near the rotting house," Lou told us as he drove. "I guess it was too tempting for kids to try to climb the fence and investigate."

"Or too easy for the Swamp Witch to get out," Alex said from the back seat.

"I know a different way in," I said.

Lou parked near the Waltar and I led them through the hole that Olivia had found.

We had barely passed into the thicket of brambles and vines that crowded the pine trees when Lou whispered, "Does it feel warmer in here?" It did, but I didn't say so because across the path, faintly gleaming in the thick shade of the trees, stood a tall iron gate. It was free-standing, connected to nothing but posts on either side of the trail.

"I don't remember this being here," I said, walking up to it.

The gate hinged on two stone columns topped by sculpted busts of screaming human heads, frozen in terror. Both columns were covered almost entirely by vines. It gave the impression that the gate was growing out of the ground itself. I could feel a faint heat coming off the iron like a radiator.

The two doors met in the middle of the gate with a large brass handle in the shape of pterodactyl talons, or some other enormous raptor. The gates were clearly way more for show than for function; there was enough room to slide underneath easily, even if it was too high to scale. Plus, it was entirely possible to just cut through the trees and walk around it. At the top, each door ended in a vicious spike. It gave the distinct impression that those stone heads belonged to traitors.

Let's forget it, I willed one of them to say. *Let's just go home and wait for Olivia there.*

A crow swooped in and landed on one of the stone gargoyles. It looked right at me and cawed, sharp and loud.

Lou approached the gate with a hand out. "It feels like it's on, like it's vibrating—*ah!* It shocked me." He held one hand in the other. I caught a faint whiff of singed hair. "I didn't even touch it!" He shook out his hand and slowly backed away.

"Can't we go around it?" Alex asked. "It's just woods on both sides, we can—" He stepped off the path and yelped. His leg went rigid, and he staggered back on to the path.

"Shocked you, huh?" Lou nodded.

Alex picked up a stick and chucked it angrily at the gate. Instead of clanging off, it sailed through the seemingly solid iron and broke into a fluttering, stumbling bat. Its wings sounded like faint handclaps beating against its small brown body. It turned in the air a few times before getting its bearings and flying up into the trees.

Alex turned to us with his mouth open.

"Do that again," Lou said.

Alex threw another stick, which arced through the lower part of the gate and hit the ground as a bug-eyed, long-fingered toad, who sat there blinking as if woken up from a dream about being a stick.

"Hah!" Lou shouted. He picked up a stick and threw it at the gate and it burst into flames, scaring the toad, who leaped into the weeds and out of sight. Lou's stick burned a brilliant bright green, then went out with a curl of noxious-looking smoke. "This gate hates me. Anna, you try."

"I think we should look at the map," I said. "I didn't see a gate, but maybe it tells us a password. . . ." I wrestled the box out of my bag.

"I took a picture before we left. Here, let me help." Alex put his hand out for the box and a possessive jealousy flared up out of nowhere. I shifted the box to my other arm and gave him the cold shoulder.

"What the junk is your problem?" he spat.

"O-kay, whoa," Lou said in a placating-dad tone. "Alex, you look at the pic. Anna, humor me and put down the box for one second so you can throw a damn stick."

I planted the box on the ground. The gate loomed over me like a bully who'd slapped the books out of my hands. Alex's voice rang in my head. *What the junk is your problem?* Oh, if I had a quarter for every time someone asked me what my problem was, or what my damage was, or slowly and sarcastically said, "Are you okay?"

I searched for a stick and blinked rapidly until the mists cleared. "I wish Olivia was here. She's so much better at this stuff than I am."

"Yeah," Alex said, and it hit me like a dart. "But from what you told us, it sounds like you do okay."

"Hey," Lou said. I looked up and he was holding out a small branch. "Throw this sucker. Do it."

Up until that point I really hadn't wanted to. Throwing, catching, dodging, dribbling—anything we may have done in gym made my insides turn to water and go sloshing about. I was so uncoordinated, sometimes I marveled at myself for ever having been in marching band. Playing music and walking at the same time is no stroll in the park. As I was thinking all this, my hand closed around the dry bark, and before I realized what I was doing, I was standing a few paces from the gate. *It doesn't matter. None of this matters. Only Olivia matters now.* My mind wiped clean, I chucked the stick as hard as I could.

CRACK.

It hit the talons of the raptor's claw with a shocking sound, right where they curled around the lock. The claw recoiled, toes curling into a tight fist, and the gate doors parted with a rusty creak. The ivy retreated from the ironwork, each tendril slithering to the side like they were being wound onto the support posts. A faint indigo glow burned along the edges of the iron, growing stronger, like a neon light warming up.

Lou and Alex rushed forward. "Are you *kidding* me?" Alex exclaimed.

"How did you know—?" Lou sputtered.

"I didn't. I didn't at all." My arm was still poised in mid-throw. I didn't know whether to be more shocked that I'd made contact with the lock or that the doors had parted like I'd said the magic words.

Alex took a few stop-and-start steps toward the gate as if a giant magnet were drawing him against his will, but he skidded to a stop when a hairy cannonball dropped from one of the columns and lopsidedly rolled to a stop, facing us in the middle of the path on the opposite side of the parted gate doors.

"Well done," a deep voice droned. "I would clap if I had hands."

CHAPTER 13

IT WAS A head. A human head. With slicked-back greasy hair that was a darker shade of red than usual, mud in the lines of his face, a colossal strawberry-blond mustache, and a stump of a neck that presumably was attached to a body at some point. I frantically looked from column to column—one had a stone head, the other was empty. He contorted his face into every horrifying shape imaginable. "Right stiff," he muttered, and let out a huge yawn. He was so red-faced, he looked furious. If he weren't separated from the rest of his body, I would've guessed he'd died of a heart attack. His irises were electric blue, and all the brighter for the bloodshot whites that surrounded them.

Alex backed slowly to where we were standing. I couldn't stop staring at the rough, cauterized-looking skin around the bottom of the head's neck.

I started to back away, too, mostly to vom in private, but Alex grabbed my arm. "We can't leave now," he hissed. "We've gotta at least knock on her door."

"What door? Whose?"

Lou finally ventured, "The Swamp Witch?"

The head laughed a high, bubbly giggle that did not fit with his heavy brow or thick mustache that covered most of his mouth. I tried not to look too closely at the crust of old food and dried nose-drippings in it. "Good luck to you," he said, catching his breath. "That house moves around on its own."

"How do we know you're not just trying to turn us away?" Alex asked.

The head grew stern. "I have one loyalty: to the Otherworld. As long as you are not a threat to the Otherworld, you can go beat down that door until the crows come home to roost. If you can find it."

Lou opened his mouth a few times before he said, "The Otherworld? Is that . . . here?"

"You are on the doorstep of the Otherworld," the head said with pompous self-importance. The head raised his chin and said, "I am the Guardian. I have been enjoying two decades of retirement until this moment, so this better be worth waking me. Tell me: What purpose do you have in the Otherworld?"

"Our friend needs help," Lou said.

"Her name is Olivia. She looks like him, sort of"—I pointed at Alex—"but a little taller, with long brown hair and brown eyes." Alex held my eye contact with a furious suspicion that made me feel like he was walking through the rooms of my brain and flicking every lamp on.

"*Mmrph*, haven't seen her." The Guardian rustled his mustache. "Had she attempted to enter into the Otherworld, I would have been awakened."

"Oh, right," I said, feeling more crushed than I thought possible at that point.

"The Swamp Witch told us to come see her," Alex added.

"The Swamp Witch? When have you had business with the Swamp Witch?" the Guardian asked with deep skepticism.

"It was a long time ago," I said. "She has business with us, too, I think."

The Guardian studied me.

"We have a map," Lou said. "We can take it from here."

"Wait a second, what map? How did you get a map?" the Guardian demanded, somewhat defensively.

"I found it," I said, catching myself just before saying *in a book*, "but now it's . . ." I gestured at the box.

"I can't." The Guardian stretched his neck to see. "You have to bring it here."

I attempted to lift the box from the ground, but it stayed in place, superglued to the dirt. "I'm sorry," I chuckled, "it's not—" *Don't do this to me*, I thought, fumbling for a better grip. *In a second Alex will swoop in and make me look like an inept doofus.* "Come *on*." I heaved as hard as I could, lifting with my legs and all. The box came up with a ripping, popping sound and I staggered back a couple steps, clutching it to my chest. Each foot of the box trailed scraggly, warlocky roots, packed with clumps of dirt. Disturbed roly-polies scrambled to get back underground.

"Any day now," the Guardian droned.

I snapped out of my momentary confusion and hustled to the bodiless head. I crouched just in front of the gate, careful to keep the box balanced on my knees. "This was the map," I lied, "but it turned into a box and we're trying to get the Swamp Witch's help for our friend."

"Hmm," the Guardian said, as if I were describing the classic symptoms of a rare map disease. "All right, fine. I'll take you to the Swamp Witch," the head grumbled. "Grab that basket." He jerked his chin toward a tree to his right, where a shallow wicker basket was hanging off a broken branch.

"Do I just . . ." *walk through this electrified gate that shocked two of my friends?* Behind me, the boys were doing perfect imitations of *Petrificus Totalus.*

Useless, I thought, as I stepped straight through the indigo gate.

I expected to feel a buzz or some kind of soap bubble membrane as I passed through, but there was only air. On the other side, I turned and looked back at the boys, who were no closer to following than they'd been ten minutes ago.

"Are you okay?" Lou shouted, like we were separated by more than a few yards—maybe also a dimension or two.

I motioned impatiently. "Just come on."

I retrieved the Guardian's basket from the tree, and when I turned back to where he sat, it was like a lens had slid over my eyes. The world inside the gate clicked into focus. He sat (stood?) on a road, not a path. Under the pine needles and leaf mulch, white stone showed through in places. The trees were farther apart than they'd been a moment before, like they stepped aside to accommodate the road, and at the same time they were now gigantic—redwoods where maples had just been. Every few trees, a tarnished mirror hung from an iron hook that was slowly being absorbed into the bark. It also—it was warm. It felt like June, not January.

"When you're ready," the Guardian said.

"Sorry?" I snapped out of my goggling.

"That's my chariot," he said.

"Excuse me, what?"

He sighed. "I can roll and get around on my own if I need to, but it's"—he wrinkled and twitched his nose—"it's inefficient. We'll all get to the Swamp Witch much faster if you carry me in that basket."

The boys shuffled up behind me, Alex furiously whispering something I couldn't hear. "Okay." I put the basket on the ground. "How do we do this?"

"Just grab me by the hair. It's strong hair. All the men of my line had strong hair."

I reached slowly for the bodiless head. His hair felt disgusting. It was slicked back with hardened wax or animal fat or something equally gross that I didn't want to contemplate. When I lifted him into the air, the Guardian gave out a bone-rattling war cry and for a split second he looked exactly as he had when he was frozen in stone on top of the gate column. I jumped and almost lost my grip but was able to cover it up as an effort to angle him under the basket handle without bonking his nose.

He huffed a few breaths in the basket, like the yell had taken a lot out of him. The floridity of his face deepened to a nice plum hue. "Right," he blustered. "We have a lot of ground to cover. You'll need to maintain a decent clip." The basket came up to the bridge of the Guardian's significant nose. He could just see over the side. I waited. I didn't want to be the default caregiver. Alex shoved his hands deep in his pockets and Lou blinked into the sky. I picked up the surprisingly heavy basket. "Onward!" the Guardian crowed.

We walked in silence, down the stone road into the trees.

After fifteen or twenty minutes, a fat bead of sweat rolled down from my underwire and tickled my stomach. "How are you doing?" I said to Lou.

"Hot," Lou said. He looked exhausted and scared.

Alex was in his own world, impossible to read, his eyes roving from the trees to the road, then to the head I held in my hands.

Every two or three trees, a heavy nail stuck out from a tree trunk with a torn scrap of paper pinned beneath it. No trespassing signs, I figured, or no hunting. After a couple minutes, we came to a sheet that hadn't been torn off. It fluttered from a tree ten or twelve feet back from the road. I didn't realize I was turning toward it, trying to read the tight mass of text, until the Guardian said, "You—Alex. Retrieve that posting."

We all froze, probably thinking the same thing: *How does the Guardian know his name?* Alex went tromping into the undergrowth and ripped down the sheet, skimming it as he made his way back to us.

"Hold it up, let me see," the Guardian said. "All men of my rank are literate."

Alex frowned and held the page in front of the basket. It was handwritten in black ink, with splatters and splotches throughout, like whoever had written it was either in a rush or really mad. Across the top it said: *AGREEMENT BETWEEN THE TOWN OF HARTWOOD AND HER SACREDNESS, THE SWAMP WITCH, ON BEHALF OF THE OTHERWORLD.*

"Agreement with Hartwood?" Lou whispered.

A tight block of letters followed the all-caps header, so small and crammed together I couldn't really read them. But at the bottom, in bigger letters again, it concluded, *MADE WITHOUT CONSULTATION OR CONSENT OF THE CITIZENS OF THE OTHERWORLD.* It was underlined twice.

"Rip it up," the Guardian said. "It's rubbish; just tear it up and leave it. Onward." At his command, my legs started moving without my thinking about it. I fished frantically for a reason why we could keep it, or a trick to make it *seem* like we'd ripped it up.

Behind me, the sound of ripping paper came long and slow.

A few minutes later, a commotion reached us: voices, creaky wheels, dull *thunks*, someone shouting, "Hey, Woodpecker! How ya been?" The road curved and opened onto a bustling intersection shaped like an asterisk, six possible roads to go down, Robert Frost times three. I don't know what I expected to see, but it wasn't what we found. Around the diameter, wheel-less wooden wagons and stone huts were crawling with more animals than I'd ever seen outside a zoo. No, scratch that—more animals than I'd seen together in one place, including a zoo. One wagon, staffed by a raccoon and a couple twitchy squirrels, was piled high with what I initially thought was yard waste. As we passed, I heard the raccoon negotiating with a koala, who was clutching a nearby tree. "My price is six days a kilo, take it or leave it, dude." They were haggling over a wagon of acorns.

The stone huts were made out of massive blocks and broken shards. I peeked into the gaps in one shed as we walked by and saw a mole filing the nails of a badger in a barber's chair. Voices and snatches of conversation competed for my attention, but there were no people in sight, only animals. A sheep walked by chatting to, I assumed, the crab riding on its head.

At the center of the asterisk was an open square. A post with tarnished brass arrows pointed in six directions. I slowed down to read it, but the destinations were pictures: a waterfall, a lake with cattails, a diner. All from the map. *The places were real.* The map had been accurate, and the Guardian had told us the truth. We were in the Otherworld. It slowly dawned on me that we were the only humans present—complete humans, not just heads.

A loud rattling came out of the trees and a ram pushing a cart with his horns approached from the left. His cart looked homemade, basically a large wooden crate with four bicycle wheels, piled high with computer mice, power strips, and cords of all lengths and colors. A fox rode on top, curled up with its magnificent tail hiding all but its eyes. The ram's eyes quickly slid past us, like he'd decided to pretend we weren't even there. A low growl joined the rattling of the wheelbarrow. "Fox," the ram said with a warning.

"Onward, southeast," the Guardian said, startling me. His voice was so loud it vibrated the wicker.

"I don't know which way is southeast," I said. Clusters of talking animals brushed past, barely missing me. I was scared to move and step on someone.

"Turn right," he said.

Just as the ram was about to pass us, the fox sprang from the wheelbarrow and circled around behind his legs. "Fox," he said again, and the fox hissed—at us. Its eyes were locked on the basket in my hands.

"I'm surprised that you would even show your face," the fox said, and let out a yip. The fox lowered herself into a crouch, her dark muzzle parted and tongue throbbing with each guttural noise she made. On top of her head, two bloody scabs stood out from her orange fur. They reminded me of the Frankenstein monster's bolts but misplaced.

"Carry on," the Guardian commanded, but I couldn't move. I was in a standoff with a fox, who was talking to the head in my basket.

"Leave him go," the ram said. He stopped with the wheelbarrow pointing down the road that led to the diner. "He's not worth the time."

"Your place is on a pike, Guardian." The fox said *Guardian* like it was a rancid, bitter word she needed to spit out as quickly as possible. "You are not welcome here. Remember that." And with one more snarl, she slinked around to trot beside the wheelbarrow.

The Guardian didn't raise his voice, he merely replied, "Remembering is not a problem for me." He let that hang in the air a moment before he said, "I may not travel fast, but I have my memory, and it is bottomless." The fox stopped and turned slowly in place with her ears flattened against her head.

She didn't snarl or hiss. She wasn't threatening; it seemed she just wanted to recognize that what the Guardian had said was true. Whatever he meant about his memory, it clearly packed the knockout punch. But then—she perked up her ears and, for the first time, looked me straight in the eye.

Her whole body softened. Her fur smoothed down her back and she dropped to the ground with her mouth open slightly. Her head tilted to the side as she said to me, "My apologies, Aine. I didn't recognize you—I wasn't expecting . . ." She trailed off and lowered her head to her paws. The clearing was suddenly very quiet.

"It's okay," I said reflexively.

For a very long moment, no one moved or said anything, then slowly, animals began dipping their heads. The squirrels on the compost heap brought their little hands to their chests; the sheep lowered itself onto its front knees, and the crab slid right off its perch.

A raccoon approached nervously and said, "It is an honor." I noticed two small scabs on his head, just like the fox had.

"Thanks." I gave a little wave and backed away from the curtseying animals. "Good to see you, too." I stumbled toward a stand on the far side of the square and pretended to be very occupied with browsing at a table of what looked like objects washed up on the beach at high tide. A mouse skittered around the wares.

Alex came up next to me. "Have you been here before?" he asked with accusation in his tone.

"No, Alex. I don't know what that was about any more than you do." I felt painfully aware of every inch of my body. I'd never wanted to disappear more, and for me, that was saying something.

Alex sighed. "Do you really think this is where Olivia comes at night?" he asked quietly.

"I can't tell," I said. I looked for a flash of insight, but none would come.

The mouse stopped and sat up. "Listen," he said, "I know this guy is showing you around," he motioned to the Guardian, "but he's basically a crow. The crows work for the Swamp Witch. They are not your friends. Never trust a crow. Get me?"

I thought of the crows lining the branches above the fallen stag and a shiver ran up my back. It seemed ludicrous that we would ever be in the position to trust a crow, but then again, the warning was coming from a mouse.

"It's not the crows you need to worry about," the Guardian said in a low voice.

Everyone's eyes shifted nervously in the fog of awkwardness. The mouse disappeared over the side of the table.

The Guardian twitched his nose and rustled his mustache. "Heave-ho," he said impatiently, "that's enough standing around."

Alex left to find Lou before I could hand off the basket. My fingers were cramped in a permanent curl around the handle. Human heads are not light. I started to turn away from the table. That's when I saw her.

CHAPTER 14

LONG DARK HAIR, tucked behind one ear, her favorite extra-long earring glinting against her neck. Olivia looked up at me from her senior portrait, beside which was the friendship bracelet string we used to tie it to mine, even though *my* wallet-sized photo was nowhere to be seen.

"How did this get here?" I grabbed the picture and held it up to the Guardian's nose.

He blustered, "What? Hmm?" obviously caught off guard.

"This was part of an offering. I was there. It belongs at the Waltar—how did it end up—wait, is it for sale?" I looked around, realizing for the first time what I was actually looking at. "Is this entire table full of people's offerings? To *buy*?"

"You would rather they just rot in the ground?" the Guardian asked.

I quickly scanned the dirty objects for anything else familiar, then turned the basket so he wouldn't see me slip the picture into my pocket.

Alex and Lou fell into step with us as we left the bustling square. "What was all that about?" Lou demanded as soon as we had some privacy from the crowd. "Why do people"—he tried to find a better word, but couldn't—"why do people here know you?"

"I don't know," I told him. "It's not important right now. We need to start asking around about Olivia." Lou blinked a hundred times a minute. "There are answers here, I know it. Look what I found," I said, and flashed Olivia's picture for everyone but the Guardian to see.

"Where did you get that?" Alex reached for it, but I jerked away.

"It was for sale in the market. We gave our senior pictures as offerings—me and Olivia. And somehow her picture ended up here."

Alex clenched his jaw.

"That can't be a coincidence, can it? That only Olivia's picture is here?" Lou asked.

"Turn *right*," the Guardian commanded. My legs robot-walked to the right.

After a few moments of silence, with more distance between

us and the talking-animal town, I asked, "Why did some of the animals have scabs on their heads?" They seemed painful and it bothered me.

The Guardian shifted in his basket to cast a look at the three of us. "Is this how you learn what you already know?" he asked me. An amused frown crossed his face. "I suppose it had to begin somewhere. Didn't think I would be present for it."

"That doesn't answer my question. And why would I ask what I already know?"

"Why indeed."

We passed a rusted purple mailbox with a tarnished metal crow on the side. "Do you get mail?" Lou asked.

"Don't be ridiculous," the Guardian scoffed. "The mail stopped running a century ago." I glanced back at the mailbox and a squirrel with tiny goat horns paused before it disappeared through a rusty hole in the side.

"What happened a century ago?" Alex asked.

The Guardian let out a sigh of disgust. "The decline and fall. Energy shortages. Great depression. Population collapse, etcetera, and so on." He was trying to sound bored, but it came off edgy and nervous, like telling the truth about the mail would ignite a long fuse and blow everything to smithereens.

Maybe, I realized with a cold dawning awareness, *there really is a reason to have a gate in the Wall. Maybe Olivia's right—maybe there's a whole neighboring town we never even—*

"What was all that about remembering?" I asked. "With the fox."

"What?" the Guardian said brusquely, but I knew he'd

heard me. "It's nothing—it was unsportsmanlike for me to have said that."

"Does she have amnesia?"

The Guardian grumbled and sniffed disgustingly. "You could say that. A sort of amnesia."

I thought of Olivia's blackouts, her verbal paralysis in the car when she tried to tell us what had been happening to her. A sort of amnesia. "I don't know what you're trying to say. Whatever I'm supposed to already know, I don't, so just tell me."

I half expected the Guardian to snap at me with some command that put me in my place as his chauffeur, but instead he replied matter-of-factly, "In order to become a citizen of the Otherworld, you must give up your memories."

"Memories of what?" Alex asked.

"Whatever came before—your life, your name."

"Came before, like reincarnation?" I asked, very confused.

"It's a fair trade," the Guardian said, dodging my question again. "The Otherworld offers so much more. Time without end in a summer without end. A fresh start, a chance to be a totally new individual. It's tempting to many." He twitched his mustache and sniffed.

"You say it like it's an option for a retirement home," Alex said.

I felt goose bumps rising along my arms and desperately wanted to drop the basket, pick up my skirts, and run as fast as I could toward the nearest exit, find Olivia, grab her hand, and keep running. But there were no exit signs or eject buttons. The box rattled in my bag with every step.

"How do citizens lose their memories?" Alex said.

The Guardian's mouth barely moved as he spoke. "There is a transformation. You get a new life, and she gets the security of knowing that you belong only to the Otherworld. There will be no pining for your past life because you cannot remember it." He paused. "She takes them; she takes your memories."

"She?" I asked.

"Hmm, the Swamp Witch," he mumbled. "I thought you knew, given that you have business with her. She rules over the Otherworld and all its people, or did you not pick up on that?"

I just needed to hear him say it. I needed confirmation.

"Your past life," Lou said. "Like, you die before you come here. This is the afterlife?"

"*An* afterlife," the Guardian corrected.

"There's more than one possible afterlife?" I asked.

With a note of surprise, the Guardian said, "Why would there be only one?"

No one spoke for a while after that. I concentrated on breathing and not losing myself in the whirlpool of panicky thoughts swirling in my brain. The road unfurled over small rises and into dry-mud ditches, around and between enormous trees so wide their bark looked like it was splitting, trying to keep everything inside. Could all of this really fit within the bounds of the Wall? I tried to keep a map of the swamp in my mind's eye as we walked, but the physical limitations seemed impossible to translate.

"Here," I said to Lou, "hold this for a bit," and shoved the Guardian's basket face-first into his stomach.

"Turn me about," he grumbled to his new servant.

I walked a few paces ahead and I heard Lou ask, "So, were you always just a head, or . . . ?"

"*No,* I wasn't always just a head. I was a warrior, from an ancient line of warriors, in a world that existed long before this one was born."

"Wow," said Lou, genuinely impressed. "How did you end up in this world, then?"

"It was a storm for the ages. The rain thrashed us for days, in darkness so thick we couldn't find land. Wind came up and blew my men straight off the ship as if they were straw. But not me. I rode the ship straight into the pit of the sea itself and when it broke the surface of the water again, I was here."

"Did anyone else make it?"

"I was the only soul left on the ship."

"So, is this your afterlife?" Lou asked.

After a pause, the Guardian said, "Walk on," and we continued on in silence.

We walked for maybe ten minutes, keeping to the stone road. I caught Alex checking his phone and flipped out internally. *What text is so important he has to read it right this minute? We're in the middle of the* Otherworld *for Pete's sake—does he even get service?* But then I caught a glimpse and it was a photo—the picture of the map that he'd taken back in the kitchen. He was following our route on the map like a good little Goonie.

The Guardian shifted ever-so-slightly so he could side-eye me over the edge of the basket. "How old are you now, Aine?"

"I'm seventeen," I said, more meekly than I intended. "Why?"

"It's starting," the Guardian said almost to himself. "Or it's already begun. These time loops," he grunted, "they get me all turned around. Plus, being living stone for a few dozen years, it's easy to lose track."

"What's your name?" I asked.

"I told you, I'm the Guardian," he said, all business. "Names are dangerous and meaningless around here, so everyone pretty much goes by whatever they are. Squirrel. Deer. Rabbit. Or, as in my case, their title."

So that was Fox, I thought, but didn't say.

"That sounds confusing," Lou said. "Aren't there, like, thirty thousand Rabbits?"

"What was your name from before, from the old world?" I asked as casually as I could.

The wicker basket creaked as the Guardian swiveled to me again. "That's the only thing I don't remember. It's been an age since names were *not* dangerous and *did* have meaning. That time has come and gone."

"So, I would be Human?" Lou asked.

The Guardian thought a moment. "Or Boy, I guess. For now."

The way he added "for now" made my fingers play with each other nervously.

"How come Anna gets to be Aine and I'm 'Boy'?"

"What do you mean 'dangerous and meaningless'? Isn't that kind of an oxymoron?" I asked, and Alex let out a sigh.

"Not if one is the result of the other," the head droned. "I really—I need to explain this to *you*?"

He didn't say it meanly. I think it was actually meant as a sort of compliment. "Names became meaningless because they were dangerous? Why were they dangerous?" I pressed.

"This isn't an appropriate discussion," the Guardian said gruffly. "I'm beginning to regret telling you anything." Like an ornery GPS, he directed us down various paths that curved off the road. The farther we got into the leafy, mossy, mulchy wood, the more I missed the reliability of that straight, paved way. I also tripped a lot more; I was glad Lou was responsible for the basket. Scorched-looking ferns swished around my knees. Eventually, we came to a pathetic-looking brook, shallow and ringed with noxious slime. A wooden footbridge that looked like it had seen one too many floods, and a long time ago at that, stretched over the marshy water. "Halt," the Guardian said, and we all abruptly and awkwardly halted just before the bridge. "This is as far as I go."

"You're not coming with us?" Alex asked. "Shit. I knew it."

"I have some business to take care of before I calcify again. Leave me on the bridge, if you would."

Lou hesitated.

"In the center, come on now, have the courage to walk onto a bloody bridge," the Guardian said.

"Thanks, uh, thanks for your help, I guess," Lou said as he inched out to the middle of the rickety bridge and darted back to solid ground.

"Yeah, thanks for leading us on a wild-goose chase," Alex spat.

The Guardian squirmed around in his basket. "Listen well," he said. "First and most importantly, you must leave before dark. Second, do not eat or drink. Anything. Mushrooms, marshmallows, raindrops—nothing."

"Marshmallows?" I asked.

"From the marsh," the Guardian said.

"What happens if, let's say, we eat something by accident?" Lou asked.

"Don't do it, all right? It's not worth it. That's the taboo that I'm setting you. Heed my warning."

"Okay, okay," Lou mumbled.

"Third," the head continued, "leave before dark."

"You already said that," Alex mumbled.

"So then do it, Boy," the Guardian barked.

"Why are you warning us about all this stuff?" Alex asked, undeterred. "I thought your job was to protect the Otherworld, not its visitors."

The Guardian looked as stern and stony as he had perched on top of the gate. "I protect it by protecting you. There is a delicate balance to maintain, a boundary to preserve."

"And now what?" I asked. "We're just supposed to find our own way out of the maze?"

"Follow the brook upstream to the waterfall. A stone grotto is at the bottom. You won't get lost; just *follow the water*," he said in a strange voice, like it was a secret code for the *real* thing we should do.

"We're not looking for a stone grotto." I began to panic. "We're looking for the Swamp Witch's house. The rotting one."

"Her house changes, remember? Just *follow the water* in and back out again. And whatever you do," he said somberly, "make sure you leave before dark. You aren't meant to stay yet. Farewell." He turned to face away from the direction we were going in.

I looked at Lou. "Yet?"

He raised his eyebrows. "If you linger, you shall stay," he said in a creepy voice, quoting the map. Lou stepped into the undergrowth and down the gentle slope to the brook and I followed.

"Whoa, whoa, whoa," said Alex behind us. "You're just going to go along with what he told us?"

"I mean, what choice do we have?" Lou smoothed his hair across his forehead.

"I don't like this," Alex muttered.

I sighed. "Me either. But we've come this far. We'll ask the Swamp Witch about Olivia. Then we'll go help her. We're almost done."

"I don't know, I just—can we trust that talking head?"

"He was probably, like, some kind of queen's guard for the swamp," Lou said.

"Exactly," Alex said. "Who is he loyal to? And don't say the Otherworld."

"The mouse told us he worked for the Swamp Witch. We're trying to get to the Swamp Witch. And anyway, why do you care?" I asked, thinking about Olivia, and Margaret Mossfield, and also the return of a gate in the Wall. Lou kept quiet.

Just then, a crow cut over us silently, following the brook. I turned to watch it fly out of sight. I hadn't gone anywhere without a crow chaperone in so long, I needed to see it go. Alex walked around me, not even giving the sky a second glance. As the crow approached the bridge, it dropped lower and swooped with its talons extended. "What the—?" It took a few heaves of its wings, but the crow was airborne again, this time with the basket handle clutched in both claws. The Guardian had found his Uber.

Suddenly, Alex's paranoia didn't seem so unwarranted. I turned to catch up and almost collided with him. He saw the airlift, too. We locked eyes until I could feel the blood rising in my neck. I brushed by him.

After a few minutes, we reached a shallow pool of greenish water. Tucked into the side of the cliff, where the waterfall met the pool, was a small stone hut. The Guardian hadn't lied about that.

I thought to myself, *grotto*, like it was a vocab word in a new language, having never seen a grotto before. It seemed like a man-made cave, stones of all shapes and sizes layered together into a short, squat beehive. Water lapped at the mouth of the grotto. Muddy, marshy grasses surrounded the hut, just like on the map. We gingerly made our way around the rocky edge of the pool, and I felt freezing-cold water seep into the vent holes in the side of my sneakers.

"Hello?" Lou called through the opening. "Anyone home? We've come to pay our respects to the Swamp Witch." A breeze rolled through the trees and sent the reeds and cattails whispering.

"I don't like this," Alex said again. Chiseled roughly into

the stones over the opening, it read, SURETY LEADS TO RUIN.

"Come on," Lou said. "We're just doing what she told us to." He ducked his head into the low opening. "Hello? Do you mind if we come in?" He didn't wait for an answer before crouching and disappearing into the dark.

"Well, shit," Alex said, and ducked down to follow.

I was about to go next when I noticed a movement in the murky marsh water around the side of the hut. Something below the water began moving toward me, fanning ripples growing closer and closer. I heaved my bag into my arms, ducked under the stone opening, and fell into the safety of the grotto, crash-landing on Alex.

"Sorry," I gasped, attempting to regain my footing and some dignity. My bag fell to the stone floor with a deafening clatter that echoed around the stone room, and my eyes roved upward.

A hole in the ceiling emitted a shaft of light on to a deep-looking pool of water. The grotto was much bigger than it appeared from the outside, and as my eyes adjusted, I realized we were standing on a platform, not far from the edge of the water. And all around the platform where we stood: bones. Human bones. Everywhere.

CHAPTER 15

THE JAGGED STONEWORK made scores of small alcoves up and down the walls. In each one, candle stubs flickered and dripped wax over body parts in various states of decomposition. Skull shards and human legs trailing skin, rib bones, and what looked like a pyramid of lidless eyeballs. The smell was incredible, and not in a good way.

"What is a grotto for again?" I pulled my shirt up over my face. Any moment, I expected a hand to spring to life and crawl across the floor toward me.

"I think we were supposed to bring an offering," Alex said.

"You have a spare body part you want to leave?" I asked.

"There's always your last baby tooth, I guess." Alex reflexively put a hand to his cheek.

Lou shook his head. "Feel how cold it is in here? These things are in storage."

Water sounds echoed. Every sound echoed. Alex and Lou stood a few paces closer to the pool, squinting into the dusky water.

"Hello?" Lou said again. "We've come to ask—we need your help." He shifted his weight nervously from foot to foot.

There was no reply, just the steady trickle of water into the pool.

"There's no one here," Alex said. "Let's just go."

Something broke the surface of the water on the far side of the cave: a quiet pulsing, like the sound of gentle strokes splitting a still pond.

A human head with only the eyes above the water floated toward us slowly. A long train of hair fanned out on the water like a ratty fishing net, tangled and trailing detritus. *Mermaid*, was my first thought, because who else swims with their breathing parts below the water? The closer it came to the light, the less human it looked. The skin of its forehead was so smooth it looked like rubber, and its eyebrows were a wild species unto themselves, curly and growing in two impressive crescents over enormous wide-set eyes.

About four feet from the edge, the swimmer rose slowly from the water until only her head and bare shoulders were exposed. Water ran from her hair continuously, as though it was producing water, not shedding it. She was beautiful in the most terrifying and familiar way. Her features looked almost too big for her face: huge eyes, razor-sharp cheekbones, and teeth so long and sharp, her mouth was perpetually open like she was about to speak, or chomp. She was decades younger than when I'd seen her last, but I recognized her, even without the pile of wet clothes. She lifted her chin to regard us for a moment before saying, "Who be ye?"

Lou stammered, "Uh, we're—I am—my name is Lou—Louis—and this is Alex"—who'd retreated to stand behind me and Lou, once things started to get interesting—"and this is—"

"Anna," the woman replied. "We've met."

The boys' heads snapped around. "Who *are* you?" Lou asked me.

I ignored him. "We met at the pond, right?" I said. "Are you the washerwoman—the Banshee?"

The Banshee nodded. "That would be me—another me, another time. I'm glad to see you used the front door this time." She smiled with a mouth full of weapons.

"And you're younger now, but you remember?" I asked.

"Time doesn't move in a straight line for me. Loops, digressions, dead ends. I can see it all at once, so it gets a little . . ." She scrunched up her angular face and still looked beautiful. "Muddled. I've been confined to water for going on four hundred years now. So, what business today?"

"We, um"—I didn't want to be rude, but—"we were actually looking for the Swamp Witch. Not that we're not happy to see you. I told them about you." I gestured to the boys.

The Banshee looked genuinely confused, like she was searching her memory but coming up short. "What did ye want with the Swamp Witch?"

184

"She told us to come back when Olivia, who you met," I blurted, as though the information had been yanked from me. "She was bitten by the beast and ever since—"

"Have you seen her since the pond?" Alex cut in. "She's been sleepwalking, and someone is spamming her in the living room mirror, trying to get her to come here."

"To the Otherworld," Lou added. "We don't know what's been happening to her. She doesn't remember. We think the Swamp Witch is behind it."

The Banshee gave a small nod. "So I see."

The second I let my attention drift away from the present, I felt my head wrapped in cotton, lights and sounds dulled, and something reaching out and into my thoughts, pressing, hunting for a soft spot. The bracelet unstuck from my skin, shifted on my wrist, and pulled me out of the threatening fog. I stumbled back a few steps. "You told me that I'd lose Olivia." My pulse pounded in my ears. "But you didn't mean as a friend—"

"I seem to have been right on at least one account." The Banshee smiled and her face softened enough that I could see where time would set in—a sketch of wrinkles she was still accumulating.

"My sister," Alex pressed. "Have you seen her recently?" He glanced nervously to the bones nearest him.

"I haven't seen Olivia since that day last week."

"Last week?" I asked. "It was almost a month ago."

"Mm-hmm," she agreed. "Same thing, when ye account for the time difference." She tilted her head the slightest bit, toward the bones, and said to Alex, "None of these were given willingly; they cannot be considered offerings." As if she could read his mind's concern about coming empty-handed.

The muscles at Alex's temples jumped. "That doesn't make me feel better."

"These . . . parts . . . are merely here for safekeeping. Until they are needed again. They seemed to think I wouldn't mind, as I'm not home all that often." She gave a one-shoulder shrug. "And how did ye find my grotto?" Her eyeballs swiveled over to me. Water dripped from her lashes and ran down her neck to pool in the hollows of her collarbones. "The Guardian brought ye, did he?"

We nodded—or Lou and I did. Alex stood like a palace guard, mute and unmoving. He'd shoved his hands deep into his pockets.

She narrowed her eyes. "Cheeky brute. When did he say he'd last been woken?"

"He didn't say exactly," I told her. "I think he said he'd been in retirement for a couple of decades."

"Retirement indeed. And did he tell ye that he works for the Swamp Witch?"

"We . . . picked up on that," I said.

The Banshee's forehead wrinkled. "He has a strange sense of humor, and duty. He probably thinks it'll tickle my sister that he made ye my problem instead of hers."

"Ohhh no, no, no." Lou started to pace.

"You're her *sister*?" Alex exploded. "Come on." He grabbed Lou and pushed him toward the entrance. "We aren't safe here.

For all we know, the Swamp Witch is luring Olivia with her help."

"I promise ye, even if my sister is involved with Olivia, I haven't had any part in it. Siblings share many things," the Banshee said, "but at the end of the day, they are each their own person. Wouldn't ye say so, Alex?"

He paused, then let Lou go.

"The Swamp Witch and I are not of the same mind about"—she paused—"well, almost everything. I take it ye have met her?"

"I think so," I said. "We were kids, a long time ago. She wears a sweater crossed over her chest like—" I made a big *X*.

The Banshee's face smoothed in recognition.

"She said to come back when Olivia was lost," I continued, "and she's not technically missing, but she's also not . . . there . . . sometimes."

"I think the Swamp Witch spoke to Olivia through our mirror at home," Alex said. "But she looked like Olivia's reflection."

The Banshee's long arms moved slowly below the surface. "She changes form at will—young, old, bird, wolf."

"Wolf?" Lou repeated under his breath.

"She was there when the beast attacked. We only saw her from a distance," Alex added.

In a more serious tone, the Banshee said, "The beast and the Otherworld are like her children, and she is a vicious mother on their behalf. She takes great pains to secure what's dear to her."

"Olivia wasn't threatening the Otherworld," Alex began,

and the Banshee held up a long-fingered hand.

"To be sure. But her beast . . . she has always doted on her beast."

"The beast attacked Olivia, not the other way around," Alex said with barely contained rage.

"And yet only one of them is still living," the Banshee said evenly. "Did the Guardian tell ye how he met his now master?"

"No," Lou ventured. "Just how he came here from another world."

"Yes, he's fond of that story, but it isn't the whole thing. The Swamp Witch took the Guardian's head ages ago, after he tried to overthrow her. Not how I would've handled it, but it isn't for me to advise. She's the eldest. My point is, she isn't afraid to face a warrior as a warrior. She always wins."

"A crow picked up the Guardian after we left him on the bridge." My stomach dropped as everything the Banshee was saying clicked into place. "He's going to tell her everything."

The Banshee glided to the edge of the pool and hooked her elbows over the side. One long forearm rested on top of the other and her nails looked like jagged bits of shell pressed into dead flesh.

The boys looked at each other, deeply confused.

"Should I—?" said Alex.

"Should we—?" said Lou.

"But then—" said Alex.

"So let's—" said Lou.

"If we—" said Alex.

"And I—" said Lou.

"But then—" said Alex.

"So let's—" This continued, mind-numbingly. I pinched Lou and he didn't react.

"Anna," said the Banshee, and motioned me closer. When she saw the worry on my face she said, "Ah, never mind them. They're fine; I'm just keeping them busy. Come." She motioned me forward again and I crouched where I stood, not an inch closer.

Beside me, the conversation started over again like a broken record.

"Should I—?"

"Should we—?"

"Ye know how this part works," she said. "Ask what ye wish to know."

"We told you. My friend Olivia—she's broken. Lost. She was bitten by the beast and nearly died. She's been haunted—watched—ever since."

"That does sound like my sister," she replied. "The Swamp Witch works in many media, but her two favorites are mirrors and fear. Her weakness is her memory. She relies on her crows and her beast to be her memory for her."

"I need to know how to help Olivia. Where is she when she's sleepwalking? Is she okay? How can I break whatever spell she's under . . . if that's what it is?"

Instead of answering, the Banshee went rigid, a look of terror on her face. Her head tipped back in the water, and she let out a blood-chilling scream.

"Wait!" I wanted to grab her by the shoulders and shake

her. "What's Olivia in danger of? I don't understand how I can help her if—" Her paralyzed face slipped slowly underwater. "Come back!" I rushed forward. The Samuel Beckett play continued beside me. "You need to fix my friends!"

"But then—"

"So let's—"

"Lou!" I shouted into his ear. "Tell me you can hear me."

"If we—"

"And I—"

"Alex," I begged, so close to his face I could've kissed him. "Please hear me. Please stop." He stared blankly ahead, looking right through me.

Behind me, something burst from the water with a huge splash, grunting and snarling and thrashing so hard that waves lapped up onto the stone where we stood. "Anna," the Banshee gasped. Tears—not water, I could tell—leaked from her eyes uncontrollably. She cleared her throat and caught her breath. "Olivia is in the thrall of a powerful—creature," she whispered, "who will bend Olivia's destiny to buttress her own." The Banshee chewed her lip for a second, then said, "Olivia is on borrowed time, until the first day of summer. For today, and every day until Beltane, ye will find her at home when ye return. After that, the deal goes through and the door closes."

The glowing purple gate with the crow's foot lock. The chains they crisscrossed the door with after Maggie went through. Olivia would be on one side, and I would be on the other. "You mean the deal between the Swamp Witch and Hartwood? We saw a poster, or notice, but I didn't understand what it meant."

"Should I—?"

"Should we—?"

"Can you make them stop?" I asked, and the boys fell silent.

The Banshee took haggard breaths. "I can see the strands of her future—yours, too. They intertwine with that of the Otherworld and all beings here. Which is to say, me, as well." She sighed, exhausted. "I'm not supposed to influence the future. But time is a circle and history is our destiny. Look to the past for answers. I cannot say more than that." She sniffled disgustingly and wiped her nose on her wrist. "The new day is almost here. Ye must get home or ye'll be utterly useless."

"I'm not leaving yet. I still don't see why or how the Otherworld has anything to do with us—*aaah!*" The last thing I saw was the Banshee's lips drawn back and her teeth parted in a hiss. She rose from the pond, grabbed my hands, and plunged them into the water. My vision split—blinding light, then numbing dark, and I heard voices, so many low, pleading voices speaking directly in my head.

A heart-wrenching wail. "Maggie!"

"The ancients are disappearing. Stag is dead."

"Fox lost her antlers; many of his followers have. They're grieving."

Someone tapped me on the shoulder. "You dropped this."

I opened my eyes; no one was there. I was in the grotto, but it was dry. The waterfall from the stream had been dammed, the whole place drained of water, and a foul-smelling little fire burned below the skylight. Smoke gathered under the domed ceiling.

A man in a khaki-colored windbreaker sat hunched over a huge tome in his lap, examining the page with a penlight. Another person squatted down in the dry basin and took a travel-sized test tube out of his pocket.

I knew that this wasn't one of my snapshot visions; the Banshee had sent me somewhere, just as the book had.

The first man tore a page from the book spread across his knees. I walked a few steps closer to him to confirm what I knew in my gut: he was holding my book, the one that had shapeshifted into a box. How it ended up in the Banshee's grotto, in the hands of this guy, I had no idea. He was older, grayer, but I recognized him as the MC from Margaret Moss-field's memorial service. "That doesn't belong to you," I said, but my voice didn't make a sound.

"Hey," the man with the test tube said. He was younger and seemed like the deputy in the situation. "We're supposed to be collecting samples."

"I know," the other man replied. "That's what I'm doing." He stared the deputy down as he crumpled the page.

The deputy rushed over. "You're destroying an artifact," he stuttered. "That needs to be cataloged. At least let me photograph it."

"You have your job," the first man said, "and I have mine. Just focus on your chemistry set and let me work." He threw the page onto the fire burning at my feet. The deputy retreated to the other side of the grotto, shaking his head.

The page opened in the heat and the flames turned green as they ate through the parchment and ink. Before it was entirely consumed, I made out the heading written across the top of the page:

THE BOOK OF NAMES

And below it was a single name:

Olivia Grace Tiffin _____ *May 1, 2024*

The Book of Names. The record of sacrifices. People who willingly and unwillingly gave their lives. Olivia. A date barely three months in the future.

My heart seized. The two glowing ladies had warned us. I staggered backward. *Breathe,* I told myself. *Deep breaths.* But I couldn't. My hand pressed to my sternum, and I was about to start dry-heaving when the whole scene folded in half, fresh air curled around me, and I was back in the watery grotto. I landed hard, cold stone under my hands. Her name, and the fire burning around it, was all I could see.

Water trickled into the pool where the Banshee rested her chin on her forearms and waited for me to say something.

"I know that book. I have it and it's right here." I pointed to the wooden box, poking innocently out of the top of my bag. "It used to be a book, but it changed last night." I coughed a deep rattling bark. That smoke was wretched. "But you're telling me that it will change back. That I'll somehow lose it. That Olivia's name will get written in." My hand found the bracelet on my opposite wrist. "May first is Beltane, isn't it? The town is starting the sacrifices again."

"It won't look the same, but—" She stopped herself. "The Otherworld is dying, and the Swamp Witch grows desperate."

"Those people didn't look like Otherworlders to me. They

looked like regular old pencil pushers, like my mom's coworkers. I know one of them works for the town."

The Banshee kept her level gaze on me. "Who is sponsoring the gate in the Wall?"

Goose bumps broke out over my entire body.

"It isn't just the Swamp Witch who will benefit, make no mistake. The town is as desperate as she is to secure the Liminal."

"The what?"

She closed her eyes, like she'd given something away that she meant to keep. Very quietly, she said, "The swamp can't contain the Otherworld any longer." She glanced over her shoulder, like someone might be listening. "The thin places in the Liminal are multiplying. Ye saw what happened to Elk."

"The Liminal did that to him? I thought the beast—"

"No, no, the beast could never take down a god. Elk fell through a thin place in the Liminal and it—consumed him. It burned through him like acid."

"If you fall into a thin place, it feeds on you," I remembered. Lou had said the gash on the stag's neck was growing or burning. I'd smelled it.

"Ye and Olivia found me at the pond by wandering through a thin place, and I don't rightly know how ye're still in one piece. The sacrifices were a temporary fix, a temporary source of energy for the Liminal. My sister thinks that they will work again, but even if they do, people will still go missing. They will fall through and be taken by the Otherworld. And if they aren't enough—if the Liminal reaches a tipping point . . ." She shook her head. "Ye can't stop the reaction once it starts. Ye have nuclear weapons in your world, yeah? It would look something like that. There would be nothing left."

I pinched the bridge of my nose. "I just want Olivia to be okay."

"Ye must act. Now. For Olivia, for ye, for the Otherworld. To save one, you must save all three."

"I'm *trying*," I said. "Can you at least tell me where to start?"

"I'm not supposed to influence the outcome—"

"And yet here you are, sending me on a field trip into the future and giving me all this background on the Liminal." A light bulb went off. "Are you actually warning me, or setting things in motion?"

"Ye sound like my sister," she muttered.

"Can you give me some kind of *clue* about how to save Olivia? And myself and the Otherworld, if I have to?"

"I'm not able to say," she said pointedly, "but . . . I do love a good puzzle." One long finger pointed to the wooden box. She pushed off the side and glided in a strong yet effortless backstroke across the pond.

"That's it? Seriously, no words of advice?"

"Solve the puzzle. But first, get out before dark," and she dove out of sight.

CHAPTER 16

"WAIT!" I YELLED, and my voice echoed around the grotto. "What about the boys?" What would I tell Bonnie when I returned her short-circuited son to her? What would I tell Lou's nana?

A voice made me jump. "Should I—*ugggh*, why can't I say a complete sentence?!" Lou shouted. "Oh."

"What the hell just happened?" Alex said, wiping spit from the corner of his mouth. "That was like being trapped on an M. C. Escher staircase."

"Where's the Banshee?" Lou rubbed his arms and his shoulders crept up to his ears. "Are you guys suddenly freezing cold, too?"

Alex yanked off his red hooded sweatshirt and handed it to

Lou, then said urgently to me, "Where did she go?"

I looked across the grotto. "She's gone. I'll tell you what happened, but listen, I think we really need to go home. Like now." The shaft of sunlight was gone from the roof. "The Guardian said we need to get out before dark and the Banshee just said the same thing, so c'mon." I hoisted my bag and splashed through the exit. Sure enough, the shadows were stretched long in the setting sun.

Alex consulted the photo of the map on his phone. "If we just head straight for the Wall, we can climb a tree and get over, or follow it around to a place we can get through. I think."

"The Guardian said to follow the water," I said. Both boys just looked at me. "Oh right, I forgot—traitorous. Not to be trusted."

Alex squinted at his phone as he zoomed in on the map. "Nothing is to scale, and I have no idea how far it is."

"Sounds promising," Lou said. "Let's go." Alex took off at a jog, following the stream to a road. Lou and I followed without complaint. We startled a herd of deer, who went leaping into the trees. Alex veered away from the road and led us into the woods. Immediately, something was different. We made more noise, of course, considering I was carrying a wooden box full of what I now suspected were puzzle pieces and Lou had all the grace of a charging moose, but we weren't the source of the change. The air felt different; I could taste it—a burning smell, like a chemistry classroom. Quiet sounds were amplified, and loud sounds weren't there at all. No birdcalls, no cawing crows. A breeze went through the trees and sent the leaves crashing.

Two squirrels circled a tree trunk and the first one turned to meet the other with a headbutt you could hear. Tiny goat horns sprouted from their foreheads. A truly enormous rabbit, bigger than a cat, tore the curled heads off a bunch of dead stalks and regarded us coolly as we passed. Bone-white antlers, like miniature versions of a deer's, dwarfed its long ears.

I kept seeing Olivia's name in calligraphy beside her sacrifice date.

A fat crow with gray on its shoulders and belly swooped so close to us I felt the slipstream of its wings. It landed on top of a mirror hanging from a tree up ahead, and I hadn't realized until that moment but it was strange to see a crow on her own. As I passed beneath her, she lifted off gracefully, following the path in the same direction we were headed. She didn't caw, or even stare, but I knew that we were what she was following, not the path. The crow made a low croaking sound in her throat and swooped.

A loud *crack* made us all jump and look behind us. For a split second I cowered, expecting a falling tree, then the sound of more splintering branches reached us. "Wait." Alex grabbed my arm so Lou could catch up. It came again, faster. *Crack-crack-crack.*

"Something is following us," Lou huffed. That's when we started to run.

The crow swerved through trees, under and over branches, while we did the same, more clumsily, on the ground. Stealth was not possible. I stumbled through brambles that caught my tights in their grabby fingers, scratched my face on serrated leaves. The crashing kept up, following our pathetic struggle. Lou tripped and fell, twice, stepping on fallen logs that crumbled beneath him. The first time Alex helped him up; the second time, Lou's legs kept moving even when his whole body was on the ground. It felt like the swamp was trying to slow us down, like we were perfectly capable of running through the woods, but then some force said, *Let's see what she does with this* . . . and tripped me.

I crunched through jagged, dried mud, my eyes darting wildly between the crow and where I was about to step, all the while thinking, *The beast doesn't crash through the woods. The beast sneaks up on people, attacks without warning. It can't be the beast chasing us. It can't.* When I stole a glance behind me, there was nothing to see but trees.

"This way!" Alex made a hard right at a statue of a satyr with no head.

The crow flew straight to the Wall, to a part that, by the grace of the Ladies of Hartwood, had a gap about as wide as a pizza box that we could squeeze our way through. Lou went first. Just as I was turning sideways, I glanced back and saw Alex standing there facing the woods, waiting.

"Alex!" I screamed. The crashing stopped. Eyes watched us; I felt it.

A digital click and flash broke through the dusk and spooked us all; whatever had been following us went bounding back through the woods, the noise growing fainter as it disappeared. Alex held up his phone and continued snapping pictures. "It's too dark. Shit."

I grabbed Alex by the back of his shirt and pulled him to the Wall. Safely on the other side, I lit into him. "What were you thinking?" I was furious. "What if the flash scared it and it charged us?"

Alex continued fiddling with his phone. "That wasn't Olivia's beast—I mean, the one that attacked her."

I hated the sound of "Olivia's beast," but I knew what he meant, and it made me cold all over. The beast had singled her out, but he had been wrong. The Swamp Witch had wanted me.

"Are you saying there's a second beast out there?" Lou asked.

Alex glanced at me, then back at his phone. "Maybe. I don't know. I just wanted to see."

The sun was just meeting the horizon. The gray-flecked crow still sat on the top of the Wall, watching us.

"Jesus, let's go home," Lou said, rubbing his eyes. He looked up and stopped short. "Holy shit. It's my car."

That got Alex to look up from his phone. "Holy shit, it is. How did we end up back here?"

We shouldn't have been there, on that side of the swamp, on that side of town, but the Otherworld had spat us out exactly where we started.

I almost stopped walking, just sat down right where I was and refused to move. It was all too much. "Did you lead us here on purpose?" I asked the crow. "Did the Swamp Witch tell you to?"

She pulled herself up, still and magisterial, and with her head silhouetted against the pale sky, I could just make out two short horns protruding from the crown of her head.

"Thanks, I think." I waved up to the crow. We walked to Lou's car, and I collapsed in the back seat. My stomach growled for dinner. *I should tell them what the Banshee showed me.* But they didn't ask, and I didn't feel like reliving it. Not yet.

Lou pulled into the Tiffins' driveway and turned off the car. We all exited the car much faster than we normally would, suddenly wide awake. I speed walked to the kitchen door, holding myself back from breaking into a run. It was locked. Weird. I let myself in with the key Bonnie had given me in fifth grade, which had lived on my key ring alongside my own house key ever since. The house was still and empty. Behind me, the boys came in the door. "I'm gonna go check on Olivia," I told them.

"Do you actually think we're not coming with you?" Alex asked.

While the boys struggled to get their wet sneakers off, I stepped out of my shoes and tiptoed down the hallway, past the mirror in the living room, and up the stairs, holding my bag against my chest so the box didn't rattle.

How long have we been gone? Lou made breakfast; then the rigmarole with the map. So, we'd been out since let's say ten o'clock, found the gate, met the Guardian, trudged over to the grotto—but all that took maybe two hours. The visit with the Banshee was forty-five minutes, tops. It couldn't be that a whole day was gone.

I knocked on Olivia's bedroom door and turned the knob slowly, held my breath as I stuck my head into the dim room. It took a second for my eyes to adjust, but then—

I found her sitting at her desk again, hands limp in her lap, just staring at her reflection in her makeup mirror. My heart sunk. She was still gone. But then she looked up at me and her face relaxed into the person I knew. "Hey," she said, "sorry to scare you. I left school early, my mom picked me up. Are you mad?" I dropped my backpack and several metric tons of worry onto her bedroom floor.

I hugged her long and hard, eyes shut tight, happily drowning in the cloud of her perfume. "I have no idea what you're talking about," I said, and she laughed. "Of course I'm not mad. Are you feeling better?"

Olivia pulled away from our hug, unzipped her backpack, and piled textbooks on her desk. Her sleeve inched up her wrist and she tugged it back down quickly. "I just all of a sudden couldn't be there a second longer." She flipped her hair out of her face, and I noticed her side shave was shaggy and growing over her ears, like she was three weeks overdue for a haircut, when really, we'd just touched it up with the clippers last weekend. I pretended to need something at the bottom of my bag so my eyes could reabsorb some of the tears before she noticed. I hadn't realized how much I'd missed her.

"Olivia?" said Alex behind us.

"Alexander?" she replied, and he laughed.

"Hey!" Lou said. "All right!"

Brendan darted into the room and ran to me, sniffing my mud-splattered tights. "Were you watching for me?" I laughed.

"What is *up* with you guys?" Olivia asked, slightly amused. "Anna, you okay?"

"Yeah, I was just looking for my meds. I have a mega headache." It was the truth. That reprieve from my chronic headache in the Otherworld seemed to have strengthened the headache in the real world. I had no idea what time it was, but I also had a strong sense of time moving excruciatingly fast. I felt like I had eaten breakfast yesterday.

"Here." She grabbed her canvas bag from the floor and plopped it in my lap. "The bottle is in there somewhere. You left it at my house last week."

"Wait, last *week*?"

Olivia's face turned serious. "I *told* you it was there; I've just been forgetting to give it to you. Have you needed your medicine before now and you didn't tell me?"

"Oh, right," I lied. "No, I forgot. What day is it again?"

She softened and put her hand on my shoulder. "It's Friday, pal. You really are out of it."

I looked at the boys as casually as I could, but in my mind, I was screaming, *Friday? We jumped from Sunday to Friday?* I slid my phone out of my bag, expecting dozens of missed calls and texts from my mom, but there were no notifications.

"Last weekend—last Sunday—where were you first thing in the morning?" Alex asked.

Olivia wrinkled her forehead. "I was here. Where else would I be?"

"You weren't yourself, though," I said. "I came over to see you, after the whole thing with the deer the night before, but you just kind of sat here."

"You didn't want any of the eggs I made," Lou added.

Olivia turned back to her mirror and her voice came out monotone when she said, "Huh, I don't remember."

Lou, Alex, and I exchanged glances, but no one said anything more.

"I like your bracelet, Anna," Olivia said, looking at my reflection. "Is it new?"

My hand instinctively went to the bangle and tried for the millionth time to slide it over my hand. "Yeah, I can't get it off."

"How do you not remember?" Alex pressed his sister.

Olivia spun around in her chair. "Alex, I *don't know*." She took a breath and added, "It's a relief to hear I was home, to be honest."

The muscles in Alex's jawline clenched and unclenched.

"If today is Friday, that means tonight is Klopner's party," Lou seemed to remember out loud.

"Yeah . . . ," Olivia said slowly. "Don't you remember talking to him about it today in English class?"

"I, uh, yeah?" Lou yawned. "I need a nap."

"Were Alex and I in English, too?" I asked. My headache was beginning to make my eyes close.

"Yes. We *all* were in English class today," Olivia said. "Do *you* not remember?"

An awkward silence followed, during which I lay down on Olivia's bed, fully clothed in my filthy, ripped dress and tights. Brendan climbed onto my legs.

"Where did you all just come from?" Olivia asked.

Lou pulled his phone out of his pocket and stepped into the hall. "Hey, Nana. Just calling to check in. Didn't want you to worry."

"What's the last thing you remember?" I asked Alex. "From Hartwood."

"Driving to the Waltar with the box."

"Same. That was Sunday morning. I talked to you right before we left," I told Olivia. "You were right here, in the same spot, but you didn't seem like yourself."

"Okay, I already told you, I don't remember," she said.

"I know, that's what I'm saying! It's happened to us all. All week. Did we seem like ourselves?"

Olivia thought a second. "No, I guess you seemed a little distant."

"Distant, ha," Alex said. "Yeah, 'cause we weren't there."

"We were in the Otherworld," I told Olivia. "And that's where you've been, too."

Lou came back into the room. "My nana now thinks I'm up to something. Totally backfired."

"If I've been in the Otherworld," Olivia began, "that would explain why I don't remember things that happened here."

"Exactly," I said, feeling strange comfort at having some explanation.

"But you guys remember what happened to you in the Otherworld, right?"

We glanced at each other to confirm—yes. We remembered that cuckoo-bananas day.

"That's the thing," she said, crestfallen. "I don't remember the Otherworld at all. Only what those people in the driveway told us."

"Do you remember pieces?" I asked. "They don't have to fit together or make sense."

Time seemed to cyclone around us.

"I haven't been sleeping," she said. "It's hard to remember much these days."

"Not sleeping, like, at all?" I asked.

"Some nights, yeah." She ran a hand through her shaggy side-shave. "I feel really stupid saying this, but lately I've been so distracted. I haven't felt like myself in—I don't know how long."

"Olivia, do not ever feel stupid for being unable to describe physical or emotional feelings to *me*. I hold the record for number of fainting spells during a single school day." I turned and held up a spread palm, all five fingers. "I better get a plaque in the trophy case." Olivia gave me a half-smile.

She took a pillow and held it against her stomach. "I've been feeling kind of . . . possessed. Hearing this voice and, like, sometimes, I can't trust myself to go to bed in my room and wake up in the same place."

My eyes darted to her mirror.

"What kind of voice?" Alex asked. "Saying what?"

"An older woman, but not as old as the one we saw at the pond," Olivia said to me, "and not with her accent. I never remember what she says, just the sound of her voice. She's watching the house," Olivia said matter-of-factly, and I felt the hairs on the back of my neck stand up.

"Have you talked to anyone?" Lou asked. "Like an adult, I mean. Like your parents or a doctor?"

"No, I haven't really said much of anything until now. It doesn't happen every night. It's not predictable, or in any kind of pattern—but I still wake up sometimes with leaves and shit in my hair, and my hands are filthy, my knees are scraped, and I don't know how I got that way. Still. It's been weeks." Her eyes grew shiny. "My mom would have a fit if I told her. She'd drag me to the Waltar even more than usual. My dad would send me to a doctor, but after—" She gestured to her shoulder. "I just . . . need a break from doctors. They wanted to do tests on me."

"Who, the hospital?" Alex demanded.

Olivia nodded. "They wanted to try to treat my shoulder with a new medicine they'd developed, like an antidote. But it was totally experimental, and my parents said no."

"Why would you need an antidote, though?" Lou asked. "Was the bite poisonous?"

Olivia shrugged her left arm out of its sleeve and pulled her sweatshirt up around her neck.

"Oh my god," I cried. I couldn't help it.

A shiny, deep purple scar twisted around the top half of Olivia's arm, from the end of her collarbone down to her inner elbow. The edges were tinged a bright green, like she was turning into the Wicked Witch of the West. If it weren't for her hand, sitting normally at the end of her arm with three faded friendship bracelets bunched around her wrist, the whole appendage would have looked entirely fake. "I have to keep putting ointment on it," Olivia said. "It won't properly heal on its own. No one knows why."

"I had no idea," I whispered. That should have been my arm; Olivia's wound was meant for me. It looked so painful, like her body was fighting an invasion.

Olivia shivered. "It's cold," she said, and pulled her sweatshirt back on.

"Okay," I said, "no parents, no doctors. That leaves it up to us. What are we going to do?" Olivia looked up at me, slightly stunned. "We can take care of this. I know—" My voice caught and I swallowed. "I know we can." I was speaking on the borrowed confidence of adrenaline and fear. "You can sleep at my house, or I can sleep here. We can set up a recording— don't your parents have security cameras out front? We could look—"

Olivia's face crumpled and she nodded. "I did look at them, once," she managed to say after a few breaths. "It just showed me walking down the driveway around one in the morning. I don't know how I got back. They erase every day at noon unless something happens and you download the footage. I keep waiting for my parents to find it, but they never look."

I reached for the tissue box on her desk and handed her one.

"Why didn't you tell me sooner?" Alex asked. "I've been right across the hall this whole time."

"What could you have done?" She sniffed.

"I could've stopped you! Or gone with you."

A look of panic crossed her face. "Alex, no. I don't think that's a good idea. If I don't go, she'll . . ."

"She told us all to come back, remember?" Lou said gently. "We were invited."

Olivia dropped her voice. "And you dill-holes went without me."

"We were worried about you!" I sputtered. "You were like some Olivia clone, going through the motions of being you."

"Yeah." Lou's eyes got big. "What would've happened if we brought your clone to the same place as your actual self?" Olivia rolled her eyes.

"That's it," Alex declared. "We're taking shifts. We're not leaving you alone to wander off to the Otherworld."

"Ex*cuse* me?" Olivia said.

"Kellogg, you're on the first watch," Alex said, then to Lou, "Can we order pizza or something?"

"I do not need babysitting." Olivia seethed.

"I'm starving," Lou agreed, and the boys left the room discussing topping options.

"You'd better get enough for us!" I called after them.

"Are you kidding me?" Olivia fumed. "You agree with them?"

"I'm just worried about you." I rubbed my eyes. "And I need a shower."

"So, go take a shower."

"I don't think I'm supposed to."

Olivia threw up her hands. "I don't need a babysitter!"

"I'm not your babysitter. I'm your buddy. Where you go, I go."

A sinister grin spread across her face. "So, if I wanted to go to Jeremy's party?"

"You wouldn't."

"Better take that shower, Anna."

"Brendan, you take the first watch." I stood up reluctantly, but when I looked down, my tights were clean and whole, my feet dry and warm, and my dress betrayed no sign of having been dragged through the mud. I stumbled to the mirror. "What are you doing?" Olivia laughed. No scratches on my face. No dried river silt under my fingernails.

"It does make you feel crazy, the Otherworld," I said.

"Yeah, I don't need you to tell me that part of it."

CHAPTER 17

OLIVIA AND I were getting out plates and glasses when the boys came through the kitchen door, both talking at once.

"Are you saying it's like a Hodor scenario?" Lou asked.

"No, nothing warged into our minds—" Alex replied, tossing his keys on the counter.

"No, I mean, something punched through time."

Olivia and I exchanged a weary glance. Whenever they talked about the RPG they were writing, it was like they broke into a dialect we couldn't understand. Brendan asked to be let outside and I opened the door for him.

"Something punched through time so we could be in two places at once?" Alex asked and my ears perked up. "Maybe."

Lou put the small stack of pizza boxes on the island.

"Were you talking about us?" Olivia asked.

"No," Alex said unconvincingly. He sat down next to me and began piling slices on his plate. "So, okay, for all intents and purposes, we were in school this past week, but really, we were in the Otherworld. Mystery one. Then add to that we were only in the Otherworld for a few hours, but a week went by in Hartwood." He sounded nervous, like he was giving a presentation to the class. "I'm trying to figure out how that could be."

"He was on Wikipedia while I drove, paid, and returned with our dinner," Lou grumbled.

"And what did you find out?" I asked, taking a huge bite from the first slice I saw.

Alex sighed and relaxed a bit. "Nothing that I really understand. There's one theory—the multiverse theory—that says there are basically, like, infinite worlds and infinite timelines with infinite possibilities."

Lou tossed his hair out of his eyes. "You mean even though we're high school students in New Jersey in this universe and timeline, there is an equal likelihood that we are also elderly people in the same nursing home in Montana? Or different people from different countries who never ever meet?"

"I don't like that universe and timeline," Olivia said.

Alex spoke with his mouth full. "No, I think it's more like, we could've gone to the Otherworld, or we could've had a regular Sunday, like turn left or turn right. And in the multiverse, they would say both things happened. But in our universe, both things happened as well."

"So we, like, split into two people on two different time-lines?" I asked.

Alex shrugged. "I have no idea. Could be."

"What's the word for parallel versions of ourselves?" Lou asked. "Like a twin? Or—not a twin. A doppelganger?"

"How would they know how to be you convincingly, though?" Olivia asked. "If you knew you were in the Otherworld and not Hartwood, wouldn't your doppelgangers know that they were somewhere other than where they'd normally be?"

"I don't think so," Alex said. "I think it's like they were still part of us, but like an echo."

"It sounds enough like you," Olivia said, "that no one would think twice."

"And you can't remember what your echo experienced," I said.

"Echoes have no memories," Lou said.

"How is it that sometimes I have no memory of Hart-wood or the Otherworld?" Olivia asked. "Am I an echo in both places?"

"I think the Swamp Witch is blotting out your memory of the Otherworld," I said, "but I'm not sure why. She does memory magic—she wipes the memory of everyone who lives there."

Olivia almost spit out her soda. "Everyone who *lives there*?"

"We'll tell you everything you need to know," Lou said. "Consider us your memory."

Olivia listened without interruption for what felt like an hour. The pizza dwindled. I think it was more like forty minutes, but it included all the important highlights: the map in the book-box, the Guardian, the younger version of the Banshee, all the way up to the crashing that pursued us to the Wall. I watched her for a reaction, but all she did was pull her hair over one shoulder and begin braiding absentmindedly.

"So, that's why we can't let you be by yourself," Alex concluded. "Too much could go wrong. There's another beast that we didn't even know about, and the Swamp Witch is bad enough on her own."

"Mm-hmm, yeah, I see," Olivia said, a little too agreeably. "Well!" She threw her hair behind her back and slapped her thighs. "I don't know about you all, but it's Friday night. I'm going to a party."

"No, no, no, please," I begged. The guillotine of swamp-induced jet lag glinted over my head, which ached so badly I almost wanted Robespierre to cut the rope and get it over with.

"Put your money where your mouth is, Kellogg," Olivia said.

"This wasn't my idea!" I looked at Alex and Lou. "Can you just go and I'll stay here, in case . . . ?"

"In case what?" Lou snorted.

"No way," Alex said. "We're all going."

Ten minutes later, we were all in Lou's car, three of us varying degrees of exhausted, and one of us vacillating wildly between glee at making us go to a party and raw anger at being forced to travel with bodyguards. Olivia and Alex bickered in the back seat like the siblings that they were.

"I can't believe we're actually going to a party at Jeremy Klopner's," I whined.

"Bizarre things are normal now, Anna," Lou replied.

"No, I mean, after everything today—or tonight, or this week—we now have to go have fun. Forced fun."

"I'm just glad for the distraction," Lou admitted. "I'm glad everyone is okay." The car thudded over the railroad tracks.

"Me too," I said. The seat belt alarm started dinging and Lou muttered under his breath as he pulled the strap across his body. A few houses still had Christmas lights up, even though the calendar was flipping toward March. As we approached downtown, the streetlights all had lit snowflakes hanging from them. A banner stretched across the road, announcing the Gate Opening! May 1st! At the town green, the Wall was a construction site, cordoned off by neon sawhorses and various unidentifiable machinery. Scaffolding scaled the Wall, all wrapped in canvas like a mummy. "Looks like the gate is— almost an actual gate," I said.

"I didn't care much about it before," Lou admitted, "but after today, I'm not sure it's such a good idea."

"Drop it, Alex!" Olivia yelled.

"Fine!" he shouted, and the back seat was quiet.

"I've been having strange experiences for so long," I said to Lou, "I never expect anyone else to even believe me, much less experience them, too. It's nice to not be the only one for a change."

"You're rubbing off on me, Kellogg. Next thing you know, our cycles will be synched." He put his blinker on a full block before the turn. "What did you and the Banshee talk about while Alex and I were—" He ran his index finger over his lips and made a babbling sound.

"Nothing good," I said, wishing Lou would let it go for tonight, but knowing he wouldn't.

"Go on," he prompted.

"Yeah, I'd like to hear this, too," Alex piped up.

"A long time ago, and for a long time"—I cleared my throat—"Hartwood sacrificed someone to the swamp every spring."

Lou swerved to the shoulder and put the car in park. He turned to face me in his seat. "Sacrificed? Like a blood ritual?"

"Not quite so violent. They just chose someone at random, I guess, to go into the swamp and never come back. There used to be a door, almost exactly where they're putting the new one, and they would send the person through and lock it behind them." I was scared to look into the back seat. It was too quiet. "It happened every May first. They kept track of the sacrifices in the Book of Names, which you know better as a box."

Lou looked out the window for a moment, then put his blinker on and pulled back onto the road. "Is that why they're putting a gate in the Wall?" he asked quietly. "Is that what the Banshee said?"

"She said"—I had to make myself say it—"she said that Olivia would be the first, if we don't figure out how to secure the Liminal." I turned around to look at her, but she was staring resolutely out the window.

"Well, fuck that," Lou said, and I laughed.

"What does that even mean?" Alex asked. "The Liminal."

"The Banshee wasn't exactly forthcoming. She just said that the swamp can't hold the Otherworld much longer and the

216

thin places in the Liminal are multiplying. She said the elk fell through a thin place and that's what killed him."

"Jesus," Lou said. "What difference would sacrifices make?"

"I'm not sure. I think they're supposed to help the Liminal hang on for a while longer. She said the town wanted to secure the Liminal as much as the Swamp Witch did."

"Google it," Lou demanded. "*Liminal.* Google it."

Almost immediately, Alex read, "Liminal, adjective. *Merriam-Webster* says it means, 'of, relating to, or situated at a sensory threshold.'"

"Threshold," Lou said, "like a boundary. The swamp can't hold the Otherworld, but maybe that's not totally accurate. . . . Maybe it's the Liminal that holds the Otherworld inside the swamp. It separates the Otherworld from Hartwood."

"That makes sense!" I said. "The elk ended up on the road, outside the Otherworld and the swamp both. That's how he got injured—he fell through a thin place."

"If you fall through a thin place, it feeds on you," Olivia said eerily.

"And we passed through the Liminal when we went through the Guardian's gate," Lou added. "But that must've been like a portal or doorway or something. We had the Guardian to make it legit."

At the mention of a doorway, I pictured Olivia disappearing behind the Wall like Margaret Mossfield and my stomach twisted. "Nothing is going to happen to you," I told her. "The Banshee pretty much said that we have the ability to stop it. And we will."

She gave me a small smile, then turned back to the window. If I hadn't been with her the entire time, I would've sworn it was her shadow self sitting in the back seat.

Lou parked around the corner from Jeremy's house. Olivia immediately got out and Alex had to scramble to keep up with her. Lou took his time, so I did, too.

"What would Alex do without Olivia?" I asked as we crunched through gravel in the gutter.

"I don't know, but I bet that's the question fueling his 'twenty-four-seven Olivia-Watch' plan."

A tiny night-light went on in my brain. "Oh."

"And who knows? It might be the reason why he's failing three classes right now. Conscientious objection to the upcoming fork in the road."

"Alex is failing?" I blurted.

Lou sighed. "Man, I don't think I was supposed to share that."

"How could he be failing? School is a breeze for him. He can sleep through classes and still do better on tests than I do."

"I know, it's infuriating."

I felt for my bracelet through my coat sleeve. "There's one other thing I found out that I haven't told anyone."

"Go on," Lou prompted.

"You know how my mom and Bonnie had a friend who died in high school? Maggie?"

"Oh, shit," Lou said. "The beast?"

"Not exactly. She was sacrificed by the town. I need to ask

my mom about it before I tell . . ."

"I get you." Lou elbowed me. "I'll keep it to myself."

The porch light by the driveway door was blindingly bright. Olivia, and therefore Alex, were waiting for us and we walked into the kitchen together.

"Anna! Welcome!" Jeremy jogged over and gave me a hug that I returned with a one-handed tap on his shoulder. As soon as Jeremy pulled away and moved on to high-five-handshake Alex and slap him on the back, I checked the time on my phone: 9:16. "I do not want to stay past ten thirty," I told Olivia as she passed me.

She smiled over her shoulder and said, "Too bad. You stay as long as I want you to." Then, as though she felt guilty, she added, "You can do it! I believe in you!" Like magic, she walked up to a group of people and blended right in to the party. She did look more relaxed. I felt miserable.

I took a can of nothing and slunk through the kitchen into the dining room, trying to follow Olivia, but not in a Secret Service kind of way. The house was the same floorplan as mine, a creepy double that looked like it had been bugged by the FBI. Cameras the size of mini-flashlights pointed out from the corners. *I hope those are no longer functional*, I thought as I nervously adjusted my bracelet. The rooms were mostly empty, except for a weirdly textured pink couch in the living room and a card table in the kitchen.

Olivia stood talking to Bodhi and Chris Salib. "I'm pretty sure the marching band is playing at the gate opening," I overheard Chris say. "It's becoming a whole thing." I thought about joining their conversation, but instead, I collapsed onto the couch. There wasn't a bit of give to the cushions. I doubted anyone had ever sat on the couch before that night. Lou and Alex stood in the dining room, talking. Lou hit his head on the chandelier.

"He-hey," Jeremy shouted. "Leave that alone, okay?" He rushed to the front door, where a few underclassmen I didn't know were testing out an elaborate peephole that looked like the periscope of a submarine. Music came from speakers in the ceiling and then suddenly got very loud. I sat up with a gasp.

Where was I? I checked my watch, but it read 3:25. I hadn't changed it since we returned to the Hartwood time zone. Disoriented from sleep, I turned back to where Olivia had been, but Bodhi and Chris were on their own. An acid pit began eating my stomach as I pushed myself up to look for her.

I shouldered through the crowd, texting Olivia as I went. My phone read 9:57. Where were Lou and Alex? A dull headache led me to two enormous zits coming up in my hair, roughly where my bangs started. They felt bigger than any zits I'd ever had in my life, and they killed. I said a little prayer of thanks that no one could see them, though at that rate, I'd have to start wearing a hat. "Lou!" I reached between people and grabbed the back of his shirt. It was so loud, he had to read my lips. "Have you seen Olivia?"

He shook his head. "I'll look upstairs." He pointed toward the front door. I gave a thumbs-up and I continued making my way to the kitchen. Because I was craning to see over the shoulders of everyone around me, I bumped into Mary-Kate

Jorgenson and Bel Nguyen, physically bumped into them as they were coming out of the kitchen doorway.

"Oh hey, sorry," Bel shouted, holding an unopened beer.

"Have you seen Olivia?" I yelled back.

They glanced at each other and shook their heads.

"If you see Olivia, will you tell her I'm looking for her?"

"Sure," Mary-Kate said as Bel pulled her onto the dance floor that had erupted behind me.

I ducked into the kitchen, which was now as crowded as a train station, and stood on my toes to see better. When had so many people gotten there? I perked up at the sound of Olivia's name.

"She's a total attention whore, dude. It's obvious what happened. She got all disoriented from the bus crash and wandered off into the woods. The end." I glanced over to the card table where three boys from my grade were sitting around a game of quarters.

"But she was in the hospital for weeks," another one replied. "They don't keep people in the hospital because they got disoriented for five minutes."

"Ever heard of a mental hospital, Cooper?"

"He tries not to think about it. The memories are too painful." The boys laughed.

My eyes started getting hot. I wanted to casually walk over and slam each of their heads into the table. Instead, I dialed Olivia's number and it rang through to her voice mail. "Hey, it's Olivia." I hung up. I sniffled loud and disgustingly. Where are you?? I texted her.

I knocked on the door nearest me, thinking it was another bathroom, but it was the stairs to the basement. The lights were on. "Olivia?" I called. "Anyone down here?"

Two steps down, the basement smell folded around me, subterranean mildew and damp. All basements are creepy, the way all squares are rectangles. Not all creepy things are basements, but all basements are creepy. The stairs creaked and groaned to announce my presence, but no one upstairs could hear me. The empty house had nothing to absorb sound, so the music crashed around at twice the volume. It felt so good to be out of that energy, all those competing voices and body sprays.

I checked my phone. Still no word from Olivia. Have you seen O? I texted Alex and Lou.

As soon as I reached the bottom of the stairs, I gasped. Every inch of the basement was covered in weapons—I'm talking gun racks lining the walls, metal storage lockers labeled with specific ammunition, vests hanging from pipes, camouflage hats, the whole nine yards. With my pointer stabbing the air, I counted thirty-seven wall-mounted guns. I suddenly felt very cold. I'd never seen a gun in real life before.

I walked slowly around the island of neatly labeled lockers in the middle of the basement. ARROWS said one, and I looked along the wall until I found the contraption that most resembled a crossbow. I opened the MISC. locker, which seemed to have bear spray, some animal whistles, and traps. They looked exactly the same as they did in cartoons.

"Anna, hey! There you are." Jeremy came down the stairs behind me, shouting as usual. "You can't be down here, okay?"

He laughed. "Come back upstairs."

"This is really something." I played dumb and interested, but it wasn't much of an act.

He rubbed the back of his skinny neck. "My dad's a big hunter. He travels for it, competes. It's a lot, I know. My mom hates it."

"Is all this stuff going to your new house, or . . . ?"

"My dad's building a special storage bunker for it. He would never get rid of his guns, they're like his children." He smiled self-consciously. "Like his pets, I mean. He's been practicing for the gate opening; he's convinced the beast will go on a rampage. Like the only thing that's been preventing that all this time is the Wall."

I swallowed. "That's very Gaston of him."

Jeremy laughed, actually getting my joke. "Yeah," he said. "The gate opening should be pretty fun, anyway. I heard there's gonna be a street fair all the way down Main. You gonna go?"

"Probably not," I said, then immediately felt bad and tried to smooth it over with, "So, you're not big into hunting?"

He shrugged one shoulder. "I like parts of it. Getting up early, sitting in the woods and being quiet for hours. It's kind of peaceful. But that's . . . not the point."

"Have you ever killed anything?" I'd seen pictures of him posing with dead deer and huge fish dangling on hooks, but that didn't necessarily mean that was all his doing. I rather doubted he had anything to do with it at all.

Jeremy looked up at me and I could tell he was trying to gauge my interest, to weigh how much he should brag. But then he told the truth. "Yeah," he said, "I have. Not really by choice." He rubbed the back of his neck again.

I closed the locker, which had been standing open beside me conspicuously ever since Jeremy caught me. "Have you seen Olivia?"

Jeremy suddenly stood up straight and looked at something behind me, but when I spun around, nothing was there. I turned back and his eyes had glazed over, welling with tears that somehow stayed in place. He grabbed my wrist so hard the bracelet dug into my arm.

"Let go of me." I tried to shake him off, but his grip was too strong. A heavy dampness curled around my ankles, and I smelled pine and dirt and an earthy animal scent.

"Anna," he said, but it was a woman's voice that came out of his mouth. The light bulb flickered and dimmed.

"You talked to me in the Demonstration Forest, when Olivia was attacked." I recognized the voice—the same confident, commanding voice, the one that had told me to stay put behind the tree. She sounded much less confident now. She sounded desperate.

"Oh, good, you can hear me!" the voice said, through Jeremy's mouth. Jeremy's eyes were filled with water, but he didn't blink. "I've been trying to reach you for weeks."

"Why didn't you just show up in the dead of night again? What's with all this cloak-and-dagger shit?" I tried to pull away again, but his grip was unbreakable. "Do you work for the Swamp Witch, too?"

"Anna, c'mon," the voice admonished.

"Then why are you bothering me? Do you know where Olivia is? I'm getting so sick of uninvited guests."

"Oh, I just wanted to say hey, see how things were, you know, check in."

"Are you serious?"

"No!" Jeremy's expressionless face got creepier and creepier the more the voice spoke. "I'm trying to help you, you dork. It's taking longer than usual for you to figure this out. The Liminal grows thin."

"I *know*," I said. "What am I supposed to do about it?"

Jeremy paused and swallowed, like being a human microphone was making him thirsty. "The Liminal needs a tremendous amount of energy to hold space between Hartwood and the Otherworld. You must return to the Otherworld and reset the balance. It's the only way."

"Return?" I asked. "But I was just there and it didn't make a difference." The light bulb flickered, brightening then dimming again.

"First you have to find their names. Bring them back with you. Feed them to the Liminal and unite the four Ladies of Hartwood. It's the only way to save Olivia, to preserve Hartwood and all the people on either side of the Wall."

"Names like from the Book of Names?"

"Ugh, Anna, I can't hold your hand through this. I'm breaking enough space-time rules as it is. Just try following a hunch for once. You have the tools. Get to work."

The light bulb popped and returned to its normal wattage. Jeremy dropped my arm and shook his head. His eyes were red-rimmed, but otherwise tear-free. "Who are you looking for?" he asked in his normal voice.

I massaged my wrist and waited to make sure it was really one hundred percent Jeremy. The metal of my bracelet felt hot.

But then he snapped his fingers. "Oh, Olivia. Right. I'll help you look." He put his arm out. "After you."

I climbed the stairs shakily. If the Liminal was such a hungry thing, I didn't know how names would satisfy it. I angled through the crowd in the kitchen and craned my neck to scan the heads in the living room. Jeremy got roped into something at the keg; big help he was. I desperately wanted to leave.

"Hey," Alex said, appearing out of thin air with Lou right behind him. "Any sign of my sister?"

"No. She's not answering my texts. I'm going to leave to look for her."

"I'll go with you," Alex said. "Lou, you drive ahead and call us if you find her."

"You sure you don't just want to all stick together?" Lou asked.

"If she's on foot, she would've cut through the fields. You'll have to go the long way in the car."

"Okay, I'll take one last look here. Meet you at your place," Lou said.

I slipped out the door ahead of Alex, pulling on my jacket. The cold air hit me like a welcome slap in the face. Oxygen. Darkness. And rising over the trees like a leering snoop was the moon.

CHAPTER 18

I LURCHED THROUGH the dark, around the house to the driveway. Alex moved silently behind me. "This is all my fault," I said. "I fell asleep."

"It's not entirely your fault. I think Olivia was trying to give us the slip. Prove her point." After a second he said, "I'm still nervous."

"You're probably right," I said. "She's pranking us."

We followed the road as it curved downhill toward the train station and the lights of the shopping center in the middle of town.

"I bet she's home," I said. "If she's anywhere, it'll be there." He kicked an acorn. I checked my phone again. Still nothing.

Alex pulled the hood of his sweatshirt up. "I saw you and

Klopner coming up from the basement together," he said.

"It wasn't like that. Not even close." My nails dug into my palms.

Alex snorted. "Klopner's a good guy."

"Why do boys do that?"

"Do what?"

"Call each other by their last names?"

Alex shrugged. "You call my sister Tiff."

"That's a nickname."

"Oh, forgive me."

We crossed the train tracks and turned down a dim, empty street, passing squat brick warehouse-offices that used to be storage for the train line but now were cubicle cities for companies I'd never heard of. Thick stands of trees ran around three sides to separate each building from the tracks and each other.

Out of nowhere, Alex said, "Olivia always says how funny you are." He gave me one of his bulletproof stares, then broke into a smile and looked at the ground. "She also tells me to stay away from you." He kicked another rock. "She would not be pleased to see us walking home together."

"I seriously doubt she'd care." I sounded much more self-assured than I felt. "I thought you were the one who found me annoying. Like a friendly ghost," I said. The pavement glittered as we walked into and out of a streetlight beam.

"I don't really think that," he said. "I was just being a dick; it wasn't about you. To be totally honest, I like my family better when you're around." He paused. "I mean, it's like everyone is the best version of themselves. You make things easier."

I decided right then to believe him. But I still said, "So the silence and death glares are really just heartfelt appreciation? I've had it wrong all this time?"

He took a step sideways and bumped into me. I bumped him back to hide the fact that I was grinning like a dork.

We walked for a bit in silence, past the biggest building on a huge expanse of a manicured lawn. "I still don't understand why Olivia wants to keep us apart," I blurted. "Does she think I'll change my loyalties to another twin?"

"I don't think she's worried about *your* behavior."

My arms stopped swinging normally with each step. "She thinks you'll be mean to me?"

"Something like that."

"But you already are."

"I am not mean to you!" He actually seemed offended.

"You pretty much stop talking or laughing or having any fun at all when I walk into a room."

"I do not. Give me a break."

"Then 'what the junk is your problem,' Alex?" I quoted. "I thought you hated me."

"I don't, Anna." His voice was surprisingly soft. "I don't hate you."

"Okay then." It didn't make me feel better, this version of Alex. It made everything more unstable. It was like carrying a ticking time bomb in my pocket. We walked beneath a streetlight and back into the dark, our shadows rushing out ahead of us.

"Can I look in your bag?" he asked, moving around behind me to where it was slung across my back. "I stashed the notice that the Guardian made me rip up. I forgot until right now."

"Crafty," I said, genuinely surprised. He pulled out a crinkly handful and we stopped walking to look under my phone flashlight.

"Are those oak leaves?" I asked.

"I didn't put oak leaves in your bag," he said quickly.

"I know."

He spread them out in his hands, turned them over. Still oak leaves. "How is that even possible?"

The empty lot next to us seemed vast and jungle-ish in the dark. "Let's keep going," I said. Alex dropped the leaves into the street.

We were coming up on the perimeter of overgrown trees and brush. This patch seemed different from the others—more crowded, more sinister. It was so dark, the only thing I could make out clearly was the silhouette of bare branches against the moonlit sky. A twig snapped and startled me, but I covered it up, I hoped, by scratching my nose. Then three or four more branches snapped, and Alex grabbed my arm. "Whatthefuckwasthat?" he said in one breath. The tree-weeds twitched, and he dragged me into the middle of the street. My eyes bugged out of my skull, but I didn't see any better. "Should we run? Are we not supposed to? Shit, I should've paid attention in the assembly."

"I think"—my heart pounded so loud—"we need to back away and make ourselves big." I lifted my arms and Alex kept his hold on my wrist, like I was the winner in a boxing match. The bracelet slid up my arm. A few more crunches came from the slice of corporate woods beside us.

"Olivia?" I called. "Are you trying to scare us?"

A *hrumph* came out of the darkness like the sound a dog makes when it's grouchy, but more like if the dog were a lion. The wind came up at our backs and pushed all my hair into my face. The dead-ish weed patch shifted with creaks like a ghost ship and the snapping started again, this time faster.

"Okay, now we run." I took off down the street and Alex's fingers clawed my sleeve.

"This way!" Alex passed me and I saw his red sweatshirt streak off across the huge corporate lawn. I followed Alex into the next parking lot, out an entrance-only driveway, and across the avenue into our neighborhood.

We were told to stay out in the open, walk down the middle of the street if we felt scared. Stay where it was well lit. Don't run or risk provoking the predator. It all came back to me as Alex and I did the exact opposite of every recommendation.

I couldn't tell if we were being followed; at least there were no galloping footsteps in the distance. All I heard was my own ragged breath and the slapping of our sneakers as we ran up a driveway or across a patio. We cut through half a dozen yards, tripping floodlights left and right. Dogs barked, then more dogs barked in response. When we got to a yard with a fence hidden behind decorative bushes, we didn't know how to get out. We skittered back and forth across the yard until a man came out on the deck and bellowed, "Who's there?" Then we bolted back down the driveway, the way we'd come.

We went the long way after that, down the streets, across

front yards only. In the back of my mind, I couldn't stop thinking, *He should've caught us by now. What's he waiting for?* We reached the corner of my dead-end street and beelined for my house. At the garage, I punched in the code, and something caught my eye. A long, serpentine, dragon-type thing slithered across the moonlit sky. "What the hell is that?" I pointed.

"Shit, it can fly now?" Alex choked. "Or is that a new one?"

The moon was so bright, I could make out a ridge of bristling fur along the beast's spine. Every few twists, a pair of feet would drop down and gallop through the air.

The keypad lights turned off and I had to punch in the complete code again. I ducked under the shuddering garage door before it was even halfway up. "Come in," I told Alex, and he ducked under as well. I fumbled with my keys at the inside door. Part of me was shaky and sweaty from running three quarters of a mile in the middle of the night, but an equal part of me wanted to look back. I hit the garage door button and it rattled down again. "I guess we could've knocked on someone's door," I said as I stepped inside.

"People would've called the cops"—Alex gulped down a breath—"before they let us in."

I led the way upstairs to the kitchen. "Do you want a glass of water?"

"Yeah, uh." Alex felt his stomach with one hand. "Maybe just—" He held up two fingers an inch apart.

Brendan came slinking around the doorway from the dining room while I filled two mugs with water from the fridge dispenser.

Alex stood at the top of the stairs with very good posture. "Hello, cat," he said. I couldn't tell if he felt awkward because he was alone with me in my house at night, or because he was trying not to puke. With one eye on Alex, Brendan knelt to take a drink from his dish.

I collapsed into a kitchen chair, still in my jacket, and texted Olivia, We stopped at my house. We'll be over soon. I decided not to specify who "we" was. Then I texted Lou a heads-up about the sighting and breathed a sigh of relief that he had his car.

"You know how I heard a voice when we were in the Demonstration Forest, the woman with antlers?" I started.

"Yep, and she got out of Lou's car that night, somehow."

"Yes, well, I heard from her again tonight. In the basement at Jeremy's, which, by the way, was terrifying." Alex's eyebrows raised with interest. "Completely packed with guns, just there for the taking. Then Jeremy found me and he became, like, possessed. The woman with antlers used him as a two-way radio."

"Excuse me?"

I sighed. "I don't even know. It was only slightly more unnerving than actually talking to Jeremy himself."

"What did she say?"

"She said she'd been trying to reach me, that I'm taking longer than usual to figure this out."

Alex chuckled. "Terrific. Very reassuring."

I glanced out the dark window, as if I could see all the way to Olivia's house to check on her. "Then she warned me about the Liminal. She said to 'find their names' and 'feed them to the Liminal.'"

"Whose names?"

"Good question!" The zits in my hair throbbed, like stress was making them grow. "There's more."

"Oh, good."

"She told me to return to the Otherworld and 'restore the balance,' or something. It sounded like she meant return for good. Like I'm supposed to be there, not here." I didn't realize it until I said it out loud.

Alex was quiet for a minute.

I swallowed and made myself say, "Just like I was the one who was supposed to be taken by the beast."

"Hang on." Alex put his hand on the table. "What happened is no one's fault except that dumbass Dennis, okay? None of this was meant for anyone."

I nodded, but I was beginning to think that wasn't true.

"The Banshee also told you to solve the puzzle," Alex said. "Where's the box?"

"You want to do it right now?"

"Anna, if a puzzle is all it takes to get some answers—is it still in your bag?" He got up and turned on the light over the kitchen sink, then returned to his chair.

I reached down and lifted the box carefully onto the table. It seemed many times heavier than it had been a few minutes ago. "There had better be a puzzle in here," I told the box.

Just then, a sharp knocking at the kitchen window made us both jump.

CHAPTER 19

"WHAT WAS THAT?" The *rat-tat-tat* came again, more insistent, but I couldn't see anything with the light on. I hit the switch and caught the peaked profile of a blue jay sitting on the windowsill outside.

It let out a piercing shriek and I could see its breath uncurl from its beak like smoke.

A brand-new voice flooded my head, blocking out all senses and pressing on my skull from the inside. *I will always find you, Anna!* the voice taunted.

When I could open my eyes again, the blue jay was gone from the window, but our reflections there were different. Alex sat, staring at the window, while Brendan was in full defense mode, tail vertical, slightly crouched. And seated at the table beside Alex and behind Brendan was a woman with big red hair spilling over her charcoal cardigan. Her head cocked to the side like she was about to hit us with the punch line. She had a mischievous smile on her face to match.

"You must be Alex," the voice said through the mouth of the reflection in the window. "It's funny; for twins, you and your sister look nothing alike." In the window, she reached out and cupped his face. I saw him stiffen at the table in real life. She patted his cheek once and then gestured between me and Alex. "I saw you two yesterday, traipsing about in my swamp."

Oh, good, I thought. *The Swamp Witch is here.*

Alex said nothing, didn't even blink. She had us under some leg-locking spell. I was paralyzed with my hand still on the light switch. I fought to move, to somehow wrench myself free from the connection between the voice and my brain, but all I could move were my eyes. My muscles flexed involuntarily, and a small strand of spit dribbled over my lip. Alex felt it, too. I could tell from the pained expression on his face.

She turned from Alex to the box on the table, which was somehow, again, a book. "I haven't been this close to your book in half a millennium." Her hand passed palm-down over the cover, and it opened on the table in front of Alex. Each page rose and fell in an orderly waterfall. The Swamp Witch's reflection reached out to stroke the page. A stack of gold bangles climbed up her left forearm and, even though she was just a reflection, they made a rasping scratch across the tabletop. "Wherever did you hide it? All this time and you've been right under my nose," she chuckled. She could've been talking to the book or to me.

"This book first belonged to me, you know. And it knows its mummy, darling book." Brendan made a hacking sound, and the Swamp Witch slammed the book. "You've been borrowing this long enough. I'll make you a deal. I'm very good with deals, Anna, just ask your mother."

My mother? I thought, and then, *the names—I can't forget. The Banshee, the puzzle.* My thoughts raced and tripped over each other, and I knew that she could hear them all.

"Don't give it to her, Anna!" Alex shouted, momentarily breaking the binding spell in what looked like a full-bodied effort. His head jerked way back, as if he were about tip over backward in his chair. My eyes jumped to the window, and I saw the reflected Swamp Witch with a fistful of Alex's hair.

"You shut your piehole, Alexander Tiffin," she hissed. "You're more annoying than a mosquito, you know that? Always getting in the way." The Swamp Witch in the window leaned close to Alex's exposed neck and I swear it looked like she was about to take a bite.

Help! I thought, and Brendan roared to life. He snarled and leaped across the kitchen, straight onto the counter. With his face inches from the window, he arched his back and hissed and spit. All his hair stood on end.

"You have way overstepped your bounds here, pal," a raspy, attaboy voice said. "This house is protected. Get back to where you came from."

My muscles started to relax, and my hand dropped to my side. Alex slumped down in his chair, released from the shadow Swamp Witch's grip. I immediately wiped the drool from my chin before he could see. When I looked back at the window, the reflected Swamp Witch was fading into an empty chair and the blue jay was once again perched on the window ledge.

"Protected, hmm?" the voice returned, even more coldly this time, and my body seized up again. "Yes, you've done your duty to your family, well done. But know this, Anna Kellogg: I can take things that are precious to you, too. Has anything—or anyone—gone missing lately?" A deep, throaty laugh rumbled in my skull.

You, I thought and some of the stiffness broke in my joints. "You," I said aloud. I wrenched myself forward and staggered to face the window over the sink. "You sent the beast after us tonight," I told the blue jay. "You've been watching Olivia, drugging her, or sleepwalking her into the woods. You sent the beast after me that day in the Demonstration Forest, but it got her instead. It should be me." I paused as the guilt hit me like a blast to the chest. "You should be going after me, not Olivia. I'm the one with the book. Leave her alone." The last part came out a bit more like a sob than I had wanted it to.

Her laugh was full of mirth this time. "Think whatever you want! I know who and what I'm after. It's all happened before, and it'll happen again." The silence stretched for several seconds, and I thought she'd left, but then my fists curled in on themselves and the voice said, "I'll see you again soon, Anna."

"Get lost!" Brendan hissed, and lunged at the glass.

Reeent! The blue jay bounded off the windowsill, instantly disappearing into the dark.

My ears popped. Alex started coughing. Brendan removed his paws from the window and sat stiffly with his tail wrapped around his legs. He didn't take his eyes off the sky.

When I caught my breath, I said, "Did you hear—?" at the same time Alex said, "Was that—your cat talking?" he asked.

We both looked at the oversized gray cat with tufts at his ears. "Brendan?" I said. "I think you saved us."

"Well, somebody had to," he said, and turned his copper eyes on Alex.

"I was frozen," Alex said defensively. "We both were."

"Yeah, I know, so was I," Brendan said, turning back to the window with an unbroken gaze. "Some of us just try a little harder."

"I *did* try—"

"Brendan." I reached my hand out to scratch his ears, but it suddenly seemed condescending, inappropriate. What had that cat seen me do? How many times had he seen me undress? I braced myself against the counter and cleared my throat. "Have you always been able to talk?"

"All animals in the Otherworld can talk."

"I—we're not in the Otherworld." I looked at Alex. "Are we?"

"Yeah, I guess I should've said, all animals *from* the Otherworld can talk. Including me." I knew he wasn't, but Brendan sounded like he was chewing on a toothpick while he talked. "Listen, we need to get to Olivia."

"Oh my god, Olivia!" As I flew down the stairs to the back door, I heard Brendan yell at Alex, "Take the book!"

I sprinted across the yards, to the bright windows spilling light over the deck. I slid open the glass door to find Olivia and Lou sitting on stools at the kitchen island. "How do I know you want to hang out," Olivia was saying, "and you're not just babysitting me?"

"Hi," I huffed. "You're okay? Why didn't you text me?" Brendan and Alex burst in behind me.

"I'm fine! God! You all need to calm down." Olivia got a seltzer from the fridge and closed the door so hard the condiments rattled.

Brendan jumped up and sat himself in the middle of the island like an Egyptian statue.

"Well, in other news," I said.

"There's been a new development," Alex said.

"Uh-oh," Lou moaned. Olivia crossed her arms and leaned against the counter.

Alex and I looked at Brendan, who said, "Hey, Lou."

"WHAT!" Lou leaned forward so fast I thought he was going to collide with the cat.

Olivia's entire face opened like a flower. "You can *talk*?"

"I've always been able to talk," he said. "You aren't supposed to be able to hear me."

"A spirit guide." Lou hit the table with his fist. "It's about time!"

"How did you get here from the Otherworld?" I pressed. "Did you get lost or—?"

"I'm not *lost*." He sounded offended. "And I'm not your spirit guide, whatever that is."

"Yeah, we'll see about that," Lou muttered.

Brendan ignored him. "I *choose* to be here. I can come and go from the Otherworld any day of the year, not just the thin ones. Don't ask me why."

"Now there are thin *days,* too?" Alex pulled out his phone.

Brendan shifted on his front paws. "There are only two Thin Days a year: Beltane and Samhain."

"Beltane," Alex echoed. The alarm bells in my head started clanging.

"Samhain, like, Halloween?" Lou asked.

Brendan nodded. "Two days, equidistant from each other, when the boundary between Hartwood and the Otherworld softens. Those are the only days people can go back and forth. Otherwise, the door is closed."

"The Swamp Witch doesn't seem to have a problem going back and forth whenever she wants," Alex grumbled. "Or the one with antlers."

Olivia's face clouded with worry. "Or the one with long dark hair?"

Brendan blinked slowly. "Gods live by other rules."

"Gods!?" Lou shouted, at the same time that Olivia asked, "Does that mean you're a god?"

"No, no, no." Brendan shook his head. "I'm more of a glitch than a god."

"So, on Thin Days, everyone gets to be a god?" Lou asked.

"Not really," Brendan said, then added, "Sort of."

"But does that mean that the people"—I said it even though I meant *animals,* and even though I was talking to a cat—"who live in the Otherworld can't leave except on Thin Days? They're trapped there?"

"Yeah, but so are you. Trapped here, I mean. Does that bother you on a day-to-day basis? Do most people even notice? There's a reason people only see one world at a time. Sometimes it's hard to even handle that one. Crows are the only ones who can come and go," Brendan added. "Crows and the beast. And me."

"And that's why they work for the Swamp Witch," Alex said. "They're her spies. What about you?"

"I don't work for anyone, thanks," Brendan said. "And if you think she can't see things beyond the Wall in other ways, you are sadly mistaken."

"Olivia and I met the Banshee on the day of the attack, in the swamp," I said, and Olivia bit her lip. "It wasn't a Thin Day."

"I'm not an expert," Brendan hedged, "but I think that day was marked in other ways. The Swamp Witch and the beast crossed over, too, as you know."

"Maybe they forgot to lock the Liminal behind them," Lou said.

Alex took a water bottle and drank until the plastic crackled. "Why did she show up tonight? Is today marked in some way?"

Brendan's ears swiveled, like he was listening for something before he could answer.

Lou's eyes were big. "The Swamp Witch was here?"

Olivia stood motionless.

"She came to my kitchen window as a blue jay," I told them. "It was more mirror magic—she never came inside. Brendan scared her off. We're fine; we're safe." Olivia's shoulders dropped a fraction of an inch. "If anything, it's more *my* fault that she showed up tonight. I stole the book from the Waltar. I brought Alex and Lou and the book into the Otherworld. I am the common denominator in all of this." I picked at a hangnail on my thumb. "Maybe I should return it—the book." Everyone turned to look at me. "If I give it back to her, she won't come after us anymore, right? The Swamp Witch is after *this book* and she's using Olivia to get to it. I could bargain with her." I tore at the hangnail until I tasted blood. "Protection for Olivia in exchange for the book. She said she wanted to make a deal."

"Anna." Alex waited for me to look at him. "You cannot give her this book."

"For one thing"—Lou counted on his fingers—"the two glowing ladies told you to find your book before she does. For a second thing, it contains the Book of Names—"

"Which we need if we're going to fix the Liminal or whatever," Alex added.

"And third: it's your damn book, not hers."

I wanted to hear from Olivia, but she kept quiet.

"They don't have the internet in the Otherworld," Alex said. "This book is her internet. Everything she needs to know to get more power—the names the antler lady was talking about, and who knows what else—is in this book. We need to protect it as much as we need to protect my sister."

"Alex is right," Olivia said. "Not about protecting me, but about not giving it to her."

I sighed. "I was really looking for an eject button from this whole situation." But it made me feel better to have Olivia's vote just the same.

"This book has loyalties," Brendan told me. "I know it's shown itself to you."

"I wouldn't call it *loyal*," I said. "This book has its own agenda."

"It responds to you, doesn't it?" Alex asked.

"No—well, at first it did," I sputtered. "It's given me things, shown me things."

"Like?" Alex prodded.

"Like the inside of your house when I wasn't there," I told him in one breath. "I could look through the bottom of the box like a porthole. Whatever part of my house I was in, I saw that part of your house."

Olivia wrinkled her brow. "How do you know it was really my house you were seeing into and not, like, a superimposed Google Earth of my house?"

"I saw you, both of you," I said very quietly. "You were talking to your reflection in the mirror over the fireplace."

Olivia's face went slack, but Alex said, "I saw you, too. In the mirror."

I nodded. "And after that, the map appeared. Then the Banshee told me to solve the puzzle. But I'm not feeling so great about the Banshee right now."

"She's a victim of the Swamp Witch, too," Brendan said. "Her own sister confined her to water. She hasn't been on dry land in—"

"Four hundred years," I finished. "Yeah, she told me. I

didn't know the Swamp Witch did it, though."

Olivia retreated to lean against the far counter and crossed her arms again. I watched her stare at the floor. She kind of glazed over. Not just her eyes—her whole body retreated from the conversation, like a shell closing around her. Like she was disappearing right in front of me.

Brendan stopped pacing and sat in front of me. "There's a reason she goes by the Swamp Witch. That's not her real name, you know."

I sat up straighter.

"She and her sister gave up their names to found the Otherworld. It's a legend, but it's true."

"Gave them up, how?" Alex asked. "Like, quit using them?"

"More like sacrificed them. From what I can remember, they asked for powers in exchange for their names and buried them in the swamp. The Otherworld grew out of that offering."

"And that's why their powers are so linked to the Otherworld," Lou said. "The Swamp Witch and the Banshee both."

"Right. They made the Otherworld, but the Otherworld made them goddesses."

"Goddesses," Lou breathed. "So, it is the afterlife then."

"Life in the Otherworld is a *kind* of afterlife, I guess," Brendan said. "Once you cross over, you can't go back. That's why the Thin Days are such a big deal. It used to be that the Swamp Witch and the Banshee presided over the souls in the Otherworld together, along with a third sister."

"The Banshee never mentioned anything about another sister," I protested.

Brendan just blinked at me, then went on with his story. "When the Liminal started faulting, the Swamp Witch made a deal with Hartwood: a sacrifice a year in exchange for safety. The sisters didn't agree with her plan, plus they felt betrayed that she went ahead and did it without them. One sister left and was never seen or heard from again. The Banshee stuck around and fought, but eventually she lost, too."

"Is that when the Swamp Witch confined her to water?" Lou asked.

Brendan nodded. "A kind of Otherworld jail, especially for a goddess." He paused and said, "It was the splintering of the sisters that caused the real damage. They aren't meant to be apart. They are individual goddesses, but they also had the ability to combine their powers and merge to become an almighty goddess."

"Like when the Crystal Gems combine in *Steven Universe*?" I asked, trying to picture it.

"Or the Morrígan," Lou breathed. "Wild."

"They need each other," Brendan said, "for everything to work—their powers, the Otherworld. . . ."

"The Liminal?" Alex asked.

"Maybe," Brendan replied.

"Do gods have afterlives?" Lou wondered out loud.

"Okay, but hold on. You *can* cross over and go back," I said. "We just did, yesterday."

Brendan gave a single nod in acknowledgment. "You keep finding loopholes, wormholes. You have one foot in both worlds right now, but it won't always be so easy." His eyes moved to

Olivia. "That goes for all of you."

Olivia looked up, like she understood what he was really saying. "Why does the Otherworld need sacrifices?" she asked.

Brendan sighed. "I take it you met the Guardian when you were in the Otherworld?"

Three of us nodded. Olivia said dryly, "I've heard of him."

"He was a Viking, originally. He fell through a thin place and found himself in the Otherworld at the dawn of its existence. He became one of the ancients, the oldest beings to exist in the Otherworld, lesser gods than the sisters, but gods all the same. Elk was one. The Guardian was another. Around that time, the Liminal was beginning to show signs of weakening and the sisters were failing left and right to plug up the holes. The Guardian thought he had all the answers, started telling the Swamp Witch what to do, telling her he could bring people from his home and help populate the Otherworld, bring in more energy. He stepped on her toes one too many times. She dueled him, won, and cut off his head. She enchanted it to be living stone—a seeing stone—to keep an eye on everything that goes on in the Otherworld. Unless someone manages to open the gate, in which case he comes back to life." He gestured to us like *for example*. "His punishment is the oath he took to keep her realm safe. But what she never intended was that the loss of a god—a powerful conductor of Otherworld energy—would recharge the Liminal, thereby strengthening its protection of her home and her lifeblood, which are one and the same. He was the first sacrifice."

"Sacrifices strengthen the Liminal," Lou said, "which

Hartwood needs as much as the Otherworld." He shook his head. "That's messed up."

"I can't tell you the story from the Hartwood side," Brendan said. "I only know Otherworld history."

"I was told to 'find their names and feed them to the Liminal,'" I said. "Does that mean the Book of Names? The sacrificed people of Hartwood?"

"If they were sacrificed," Brendan said, seeming to think aloud, "I would think the Liminal would have been given their names already."

"Oh." I deflated. "That makes sense."

"What about the Swamp Witch and the Banshee?" Lou asked. "You said those aren't their real names."

"No one in the Otherworld knows their names. They guard them with everything they have. But if you can find out . . ."

"We can feed the names to the Liminal, exactly!" Lou practically shouted, then smoothed his hair across his forehead.

"But if the swamp has them already, wouldn't the Liminal, too?" Alex asked.

"No." Brendan shook his head. "You have to understand, the Liminal is its own entity. It grew on its own and exists *between* the Otherworld and Hartwood, a living boundary. It doesn't belong to one side or the other. It separates and insulates the two from one another."

"Okay, okay," Alex said. "So, all we need to do is find their names, give them to the Liminal, and Olivia is safe, once and for all?"

"Probably, yes," Brendan said. "But also: you would control

the sisters themselves. They and their powers would be at your mercy, which means—"

"Which means we would control the Otherworld," I finished for him. His eyes were the laser focus of a hunter's. He seemed hungry for the names himself. *We would control the Otherworld.* I turned the idea around in my mind. *Could we answer prayers made with offerings at the Waltar? Could we give Fox back her memories?* "But I don't want to control the Otherworld," I realized. "I just want my friend back."

Olivia blinked and looked at me, like what I'd said had woken her up.

"If you controlled the Swamp Witch, you would get Olivia back, no doubt about it," Brendan said.

"Any idea where we should look for the names of a couple ageless goddesses?" Lou asked Brendan.

"Would I still be a cat if I did?"

"It's a long shot," I said, "but I think I know where to start."

CHAPTER 20

I'D TOLD EVERYONE to meet back at the Tiffins' in the late morning, after at least eight hours of sleep, partly because we all needed it, but partly because I needed time. I had some more research to do.

The next morning, the sound of the shower running across the hall woke me from a deep sleep. Brendan had agreed to stay with Olivia overnight—the only babysitter she didn't resist. I pulled on a sweatshirt and wandered downstairs to wait for my mom.

Twenty minutes and a cup of tea later, she came into the kitchen in her Hartwood Parks Department sweatshirt with dripping hair. "You're up," she said, putting the kettle on. "How was your night last night?"

"It was—memorable," I said. "Hey, Mom? Can I talk to you about something?"

"Of course." She took a mug from the cabinet. "What's up?"

"Do you know who Margaret Mossfield was?"

She froze, a teabag poised over her cup.

Brendan had said he only knew the history of sacrifices from the Otherworld side. I needed to hear the Hartwood side. "Is it true that Hartwood used to sacrifice someone to the swamp every year?" I pressed.

"Not every year." She turned slowly. "I knew you'd ask me about this one day."

"Why didn't you tell me? Especially after the attack."

"I mean, if I was going to tell you, then after the attack was not the time. It's still hard to talk about." She let out a sound like a laugh but also a sob. "And it's been thirty years!"

I hadn't expected it to cut so deep. "Mom, it's okay, you don't have to—"

"No, it's important. It shaped my entire life." She sat at the table and tucked a strand of wet hair behind her ear. "Maggie was one of my best friends. She and Bonnie and I were insepa-rable. She and I grew up in the apartments by the train station, in the same building. They were the sisters I never had."

I remembered the framed photo on my mom's dresser, of her and two other little girls when they were eight or nine, with mouths stained red by Popsicles, the same girls in the photo on Bonnie's wall.

"You gave her a photo album to take with her," I said with-out thinking.

"How do you know that?"

"Bonnie told me," I lied. "She told me about Maggie. I'm so sorry, Mom."

Her body was rigid, her face creased with pain. "It's why I never wanted to leave. Why Bonnie and I always wanted to stay close to each other. We couldn't leave Maggie."

"I wouldn't be able to leave my friend, either." I stretched my hand across the table, palm up, and my mom took it with her own warm, dry hand. "There's more I need to ask you."

She nodded. "I'm okay, go ahead."

"When did the sacrifices start?"

"Pretty much when the town was founded, colonial era."

"Do you know why?"

She sighed. "The beast. It was to placate the beast, or so everyone hoped."

"Did the town keep a record of who was sacrificed? A list of names?"

"They did, but it was lost."

"Lost? When?"

"Not long after the sacrifices stopped. I wasn't working for the town yet, so I don't know what happened, but I would guess someone destroyed it. Destroyed the evidence."

"What made the sacrifices stop?"

"Public outcry. It was never popular, but for so long it felt necessary. I don't know what changed—maybe it was a generational shift, maybe the specter of the beast didn't loom so large anymore. Whatever the case, the town elected a mayor whose plan was to end the sacrifices and seal up the Wall, and no one's ever spoken of it again."

"When was that? When did the sacrifices stop?" I asked.

"After Maggie. She was the last one." The kettle started whistling and my mom got up to pour her tea.

"They're starting again, aren't they?" I asked. "That's what the gate is all about."

My mom set the kettle down on the stove with a *clang*. "I really hope not," she said. "I wish I could say for sure. The gate-opening 'street fair,' or whatever, sure reminds me of it. It's pretty tone deaf, to almost replicate the sacrifice ceremony just to open a gate for the first time."

"Will you tell me if anything changes? After Olivia . . . I need to know what's really going on."

"C'mere." She motioned for me to stand and wrapped me in a hug. "I'm so sorry to put you through something like . . . I never . . . I thought it was over."

"None of it is your fault," I said into her shoulder. "Not what happened to Maggie, or to Olivia."

She took a shuddering breath and cleared her throat. "I promise I will tell you if anything changes, and in the meantime, I'll do whatever I can to make sure it doesn't."

Later that morning, on the floor in Olivia's room, Lou took the box from my hands. "So, does this thing come with directions? Are *you* the directions?" he asked Brendan.

"Sorry, pal." Brendan presided over the room from the pillow pile on Olivia's bed. I could tell from the tilt of his ears that he was impatient for us to get the puzzle show on the road. He hadn't tried to talk me out of it, but it was clear he thought this was just a distraction from the Quest for Names.

Lou fumbled with the crowfoot clasp, pressing so hard his close-bitten nails turned white. "I can't get the stupid thing to . . ."

"Let Anna do it," Alex said from his perch on the bed.

Lou turned the box toward me. The crowfoot released its grip and curled into an empty fist at the slightest touch of my hand. I looked at Alex and thought, *How did you know that?* But he stared me down with a level gaze I couldn't break.

Olivia reached over and lifted the lid, revealing the pocked wooden interior and a lopsided pile of jagged stones. "*Are* these puzzle pieces?" Olivia upended the box on the rug.

"So I've been told," I said, tearing myself from Alex's tractor beam.

"I've never seen a puzzle like that," Lou said.

"Blah, blah, blah," Brendan droned. "Less conversation, more puzzling."

Lou leaned over and pawed through the pile. "These look kind of like—"

"Bones." Alex pushed himself upright. "Those are fucking bones."

We all retracted our hands at the same time.

"Are we supposed to reassemble a baby dinosaur or something?" Olivia lifted the empty box and shook it, then ran her hand along the seams and the underside of the lid. "No hidden compartment with directions. Could we Google it?"

"What would we Google?" Alex retorted. "Mystery

book-box bones puzzle?"

"If those are bones," Brendan said, "they are the cleanest bones I've ever seen. And they haven't been living bones in a very long time."

"The Banshee would give us a bone puzzle," Lou said. "Remember her grotto?"

I lifted a piece with two fingers. It was dry and bumpy, carved with lines down one side—short dashes in twos and threes that I couldn't read, but I somehow recognized as letters. "Do you know what this says?" I showed Brendan.

"I can't—I don't remember how to speak that language," he said. He looked like the words were stuck in his throat.

The bone had a uniquely shaped piece missing from each end, like a crochet hook for very particular yarn. I picked up another bone. It had similar scratches running down the length of it, but instead of hooks at the end, it had divots missing from one side of it, like Lincoln Logs. "I think," I said, fitting the first bone perpendicularly onto the second. "I think it's a 3D puzzle."

"Like Legos," Lou said. "Sick. I knew those ten thousand hours would come in handy one day."

I fanned out the pieces across the rug, dividing them up based on end hooks or side divots. Olivia saw the pattern and started doing the same. Lou ate from a bag of trail mix that he had clearly swiped from the pantry on his way upstairs and began casually sorting bones. Alex and Brendan just watched.

Olivia and I had the first layer built before Lou joined the section he'd assembled.

"This is not what I pictured when you said 'puzzle,'" Lou said, fitting a large bone, about what I'd imagined a turkey leg looked like, onto the platform of interconnected finger-sized bones below it.

"How is this supposed to explain how to repair the Liminal?" Alex grumbled. "And why are we trusting the Banshee when she's clearly on the same side as the Swamp Witch?"

"I'm with you on the puzzle question," Brendan said, "but the Banshee is not on her sister's side. Not by a long shot."

"What do you think these bones belonged to?" Lou asked.

Olivia and I looked at each other.

"I'd rather not think about it, thanks," I said.

Alex stretched out on his side and continued to oversee our work with great skepticism. "Probably bird bones," he said. "Necropolis Legos. Some dark-ass shit, Anna."

"These aren't *mine*," I shot back. "It's not like I bought this for fun."

"Yeah, but it *is* yours," Lou said lightly. "It responds to you. And you—"

"No, that goes like this." I took the bone from his hand and turned it on the diagonal. It fit into the structure with a neat *click*.

"As I was saying," Lou said and I blushed, "you understand it better than the rest of us."

"I may know how things fit," I said, "but I don't know what the hell this thing is, or why it's so important that we put it together."

"Well, that makes five of us," Brendan said.

The structure of bones looked like a hideous replica of the Colosseum, before it was a ruin. It was an oval-ish cylinder, about knee-high, made of layers of intertwined bones, and when you stepped back, certain bones gave the impression of columns rising about a foot from floor to top. The smallest bones made a subtle spiral pattern around the outside. The Banshee said that if I wanted to know how to save Olivia, I needed to solve the puzzle. The pile of unused bones was dwindling on the rug, but I wasn't any closer to understanding.

"You know what this kind of reminds me of?" Olivia asked. "The model of the walled-in swamp that you made in Mrs. Bivaletz's class." The one that had been sitting on top of my bookcase since the fourth grade.

"This is a puzzle of the Wall?" I said.

She shrugged. "Why not?"

I ran my hands over the last pieces, studying them, looking for a clue as to where they would fit.

"Jesus, Anna," Alex said. "What's in your hair?" He pointed to the top of my head, then to the top of his. "Here. There's something . . . there."

I knew he was talking about the two zit monsters, but I felt around in my hair, where my bangs began, as if I hadn't the foggiest. Brendan craned his neck to see. My fingers met two bumps, like marbles pressed into my skull. When I touched them, I felt the contact, but they were covered in soft baby hairs, not my skin. Around the edges, a bumpy scab outlined the separation between my scalp and these two invaders.

"Let me see," Olivia said. She took my head in her two hands and gently tipped my chin down so she could comb through my hair. I looked at my hands in my lap and noticed the blood on my fingers at the same time that Olivia said, "You're bleeding! Did you hit your head on something?"

"No." I would've felt much better if I had.

"Can I touch?" I nodded. "They're little fuzzy nubs," she narrated. "Kind of caramel-colored, lighter than your hair. They feel hard, though, like teeth. Do they hurt?"

"I've had a headache since January. Now I know why."

"Let me see," Lou said, shuffling over on his knees. He didn't touch my head—Olivia still had her hands in my hair, trying to part it so that she could see the root of the nubs more clearly.

"Those aren't teeth," Lou said after a minute. He pointed. "Look, they have rings around the base of them."

"The scabs?" I asked. It felt so strange to have two people examining a part of my body I couldn't see, but I guess that's all part of being a woman, right?

"They are kind of bloody," Lou said, "but they're not scabs. They look like the base of antlers. You know, like the cuticle of an antler?"

"I'm impressed you know what a cuticle is," I told him.

"I contain multitudes, Anna."

I felt Olivia's breath on my bangs as she leaned close. "Yeah, I see what you mean. Here." She grabbed her phone and snapped a few pictures, close-up and closer. "This is what they look like."

She handed the phone to me, showing a picture taken of them from afar. *Oh, that's not so bad.* To the touch, they felt like

Jurassic zits, just huge and offensive and impossible to look away from. In actuality, from this distance, they were pretty small—dime-sized—and unless you parted my hair, they blended into the whole mess. But as I scrolled to the close-up pictures Olivia had taken, they looked like parts of my skeleton trying to escape.

I clicked the phone off. Antlers? My heart pounded. "I'm fine. I'll show my mom when I get home. Let's just finish the puzzle, okay?"

"Can I touch them?" Lou asked.

"Get away." I pushed him, and he lost his balance and toppled over.

"All right, all right, sheesh." Lou smoothed his forelock and scooted back to his side of the rug.

"Pedicles," Alex said out of the blue.

"Cuticles," Lou said.

"No, the base of an antler—it's called a pedicle. Look." Alex handed his phone to Lou, who gasped a little, then cleared his throat.

"That is exactly what they look like," he breathed, and flipped through a series of photos. Brendan peered down over the edge of the bed. Alex looked at me and I knew we were both thinking the same thing: all those animals in the Otherworld, animals who don't normally have antlers at all. . . .

"Can we get back to the puzzle, you blockheads?" Olivia asked. "No one asked you to diagnose Anna's hair teeth."

"Ugh," I groaned. "Please don't call them that."

"Seriously, though." Lou passed the phone to me. "That is exactly what they look like."

Olivia leaned in to look over my shoulder. A slideshow of "antler growth and formation" took less than a minute to show 120 days of antler progression, the weirdest time-lapse I'd ever seen. We watched it once through, then I went back to the beginning. At Day 31 I hit pause; the deer had round, velvet-covered nubs like two jawbreaker halves on either side of his skull. You could see them more easily than mine because he didn't have bangs. I stared at them for a few seconds too long and Olivia moved back to the puzzle.

"Anna, you do the honors," she said, and held out what looked like a chicken bone. "It's the last one. I think it goes over here."

I handed the phone back to Lou and moved around the cylinder to where Olivia was. Brendan watched my every move, and I had a sudden pang of sympathy for the finches he left on the doormat in the spring. Olivia pointed to a subtle break in the pattern that seemed to be missing the tiny bone in my hand. I caught the hook at the end onto the bone above it and fitted it into place. The whole structure shuddered.

"What the actual hell?" Olivia said as the bones rattled softly, completely of their own accord.

"Ohhh, no," Lou said, backing into the corner.

"Anna, get back." Brendan leaped down from the bed and was between me and the bone sculpture in a blink.

The bones *click-click-clicked*, each piece fusing to the ones touching it in this strange, rippling wave of shivers. Like the gate, it began to glow, so softly indigo you could only really see it when you looked at it indirectly. Then you saw its aura.

The glow grew brighter and brighter until sparks shot off and a heavy electrical stench filled the room. A fog gathered in the negative space inside the puzzle. "Is it filling up?" I replied. The bones fused into one smooth skeleton with a spiral rotating around the outside; only the etched letters were left to differentiate one piece from the next. The indigo glow spread to the mist swirling in the belly of our mini-Colosseum and gathered into shapes: a push-broom mustache with eyebrows to match on a greasy face that looked right at me.

"Ahh!" I shouted, and suddenly found myself standing on Olivia's desk chair, as if I'd seen a mouse. As if that were a reasonable response to seeing a mouse.

"Wha-what—who—?" the face shouted back.

Brendan's fur stood on end and a low growl simmered in his throat.

"Who goes there? Show yourself." The face tipped as far back as his severed neck would allow and peered up at me through the open top of the puzzle. "I'll be damned," he said. "You figured it out. I owe Toad ten hours." The mist condensed into focus. "Is this thing on? Can you hear me? Blasted technology."

"Uh, yeah," said Lou. "Can you hear us?"

"Loud and clear." The Guardian picked something out of his teeth with his tongue. He grew more solidly 3D every second—was he really there, sitting in the middle of the bones? Was he slowly, slowly teleporting by dial-up?

Brendan remained locked at attention.

"How are we seeing you, some kind of magical video chat?"

Lou asked. He stuck his fingers into the spiral cage, and they disappeared into the fog swirling around the Guardian. He quickly pulled back. "Are you a ghost?"

The talking head laughed dryly. "Not yet. This is part of my guardian duties, on permanent watch day after day, decade after century, waiting for the right person to find this thing and turn it on. Bloody waste of a precious resource, if you ask me. Although"—he wrinkled his nose and shook out his mustache—"the watch has ended, so it seems." He glanced up at me again. "I didn't think this day would come, quite honestly. I'm glad it was you."

Lou turned his hand over and over, looking for damage that wasn't there.

"The right person?" I stepped off the desk chair and sat back down beside Olivia. Her eyes were wide and unblinking, and she'd sucked her lips in like she was trying to keep her teeth from jumping out of her mouth. I ran my hand down Brendan's back. "Are we the right people?"

The Guardian's forehead creases deepened. "You don't remember yet?"

Brendan turned to face me, as if the Guardian had said the secret password.

"How did you know to put the puzzle together?" the Guardian asked. "It's supposed to be rather a challenge."

"The Banshee, who you led us to, told us to solve the puzzle," I said impatiently, "which led us back to you. I mean, not to be rude, but. The Banshee told me that in order to understand how to save the Otherworld, we needed to complete the puzzle.

So, we did. So, now what?"

"*Hrrmm.*" He blinked rapidly, and his eyes darted to things off-camera that we couldn't see. "That's not how this is supposed to go. You retrieve the puzzle from the book. Well, first, you find the book, wake it up. Retrieve the puzzle. Figure it out. . . ." Finally, he sniffed and said, "The thing is, you're the one who's supposed to deliver a message to *me.*" He paused and squinted into the sky. "Time enough. But—you still don't remember? Anything?"

I threw my hands up. "No! And asking me if I remember, or why I don't remember, doesn't help, believe it or not." From the bed, Alex made a Jim Halpert face at me.

"Olivia!" The Guardian sounded surprised and very relieved. "I didn't see you there; this thing is still coming into focus. How've you been?"

Three human heads and one cat swiveled to Olivia, who looked petrified. "Fine," she said.

"I'm glad to see you; that makes me feel loads better about all of this. The Swamp Witch is treating you okay? You can tell me." His eyes danced to the corner, and he suppressed a smile. I couldn't tell if he was seeing something off-screen in his world, or if he was just nervously glancing at the bookcase. Was he alone?

Olivia fidgeted beside me. I started to ask how the Guardian knew her, but she cut in. "Yeah. All good." My mouth opened in a tiny *O.*

"Good," he said. "You tell me if—"

"Wait, wait. Hold on. The *Swamp Witch* is treating you

okay?" Alex sputtered.

Olivia threw him a look full of glass shards. "Not now, Alex."

"All this time you made it seem like you didn't know where or what you were doing," he said.

"And I didn't! Until now. Until we started putting this puzzle together. Things have been coming back to me."

"Have you been interning with the evil ruler of the Otherworld or something?" Alex asked.

"*Evil* is a little harsh," the Guardian said. "Strict? Misguided at times, maybe?"

"Evil works," Brendan said.

"Just forget it," Olivia shot back.

"Too late for that." Alex leaned so far off the bed I thought he was going to fall face-first into the puzzle. "Why did you throw out your prescription from the hospital?"

"You stopped taking your medicine?" I asked.

"I saw the pill bottle buried under old dryer sheets in the laundry room bin when I was taking the trash out. What are you doing?"

Olivia exploded. "Are you serious right now? What's your GPA, Alex? How did you do on the last quiz in calc?"

"Don't change the subject." The muscles in his jaw flickered. "Is your arm suddenly better? Where do you go at night? If you remember now, we deserve some answers."

"Alex, I said leave it—"

"I've kept your secret for weeks. I see it happening and I can't stop it. Maybe you can hide it from Mom and Dad, but I still see it. What the fuck is going on?"

"I keep your secret, too." Olivia's chest rose and fell. She was about to cry. I reached out and took her hand. A flood of images—light and wind and layered smells—filled my mind's eye. Holding her hand, both of us barefoot. Looking down on her injured shoulder through the metal ring of my bracelet. Planting the book in the dirt by the Waltar. Hugging her, burying my face in her thick fur.

I grabbed my bracelet. "I remember," I said quietly. "I remember!" Alex didn't move a muscle, but his eyes found mine like I knew they would. "I remember Elk."

The Guardian knew what I meant. He waited with his jaw set under his mustache.

"I remember him when he was alive. He was powerful, but it was almost like he didn't know it. He had an ease about him. He told a lot of dad jokes, but I don't think we knew to call them that." One side of the Guardian's mustache twitched in a smile. "He always put his cheek to mine when he said hello or goodbye." A sudden wave of grief washed over me. I saw his face again, when he was alive and scheming and—a person. He was a friend. I didn't know how we knew each other, but it also didn't matter, because in that moment I remembered him and lost him at the same time. I'd watched him die and didn't know him. He'd died alone.

No, I remembered. *Olivia was there with him.* I squeezed her hand, and she returned the pressure.

A new memory burst across the screen. "I remember the Banshee when she was young. We were friends, too." My free hand jumped up to cover my loose-cannon mouth. This stuff was flying out without my even knowing what I was saying. My mouth continued moving behind my fingers. "The Banshee wasn't confined to water then. She loved it—it was always her preferred element—but she could go to the market with me. We went for palm readings." A scent memory of perfume flooded my nose, floral and trailing, like the palm reader had just walked through the room.

Who cares? one part of me thought frantically. *Why does any of this matter?*

But it wasn't the substance that mattered; it was that it was the truth, solid, verifiable memories. It wasn't until I spoke it aloud that I realized it was true. All of it.

I couldn't stop. "We swam a lot together, me and the Banshee." A teeny light bulb went off in my temporal lobe. "You did, too," I told the Guardian. "We swam in the pond, but it was more like a lake then. It was deeper. How would I know that? But it was."

Lou raised an eyebrow at the Guardian. "You can swim?"

"Well, I can't drown."

I looked at Brendan. "And you! I remember—" I caught myself and the force of the words trying to burst out of me made my eyes water. If I spilled the beans about Brendan's double life, would I blow his cover? Would I buy myself a one-way ticket to the psych ward? I couldn't stop. "I remember you," I told him. "I remember the time we went to the pond and you transformed into a salmon. You thought it was so funny, but I was freaked out. I thought you'd died when you cast off your old skin like that." The puzzle pieces clicked together. "You did that just to scare me."

Brendan's eyes closed in delight. "Took you long enough."

"I remember—" The memory hit me like a gut punch and knocked the wind out of me. I remembered Olivia, but she wasn't Olivia. Her massive shoulders rolled under fur and feathers as she stalked, head lowered, into a clearing. Her snout opened to reveal a double jaw, two sets of Jurassic teeth and a long red tongue flicking spittle as she roared. My head swam in the memory, but it hadn't happened yet. I could feel the time difference like a long descent on a roller coaster. I listed to the right and Alex caught me.

"Are you okay?" he said.

"Olivia," I mumbled, as if I could warn her. "I saw you."

"Saw her what?" Brendan demanded.

The Guardian said uneasily, "Oh, this is my fault."

"What?" Alex prompted. "You saw her what? Where does she go?"

"You really want to know?" Olivia fumed. "I'll show you." And she lurched out of the room and down the stairs.

"This is all my fault," the Guardian said again. "You were only supposed to remember, not foresee."

CHAPTER 21

WHEN HER FOOTSTEPS faded, Brendan said, "What are you waiting for, you goons? Follow her."

Alex was the first out the door. He bounded down the stairs and rampaged through the first floor. "Olivia? Don't make us look for you. Where are you?"

Lou, Brendan, and I swarmed down the stairs in his frantic wake. In the kitchen I glanced out the window over the sink and saw my friend standing in the middle of the backyard, facing the house, in her bare feet. "She's outside!" I yelled.

The warm spring day was quickly cooling, and I felt unprotected without my jacket. I ran across the deck and into the grass and Olivia put her hands out. "Stop. Stay back."

I skidded to a stop. "Why?" The boys arrived, one on either

side of me, and Brendan at my feet.

"It usually takes a minute, but—" She doubled over and wretched like an invisible fist had walloped her in the stomach.

"Oh my god." I rushed to her, but her arm shot out and pushed me so hard I flew backward and slid across the grass. Brendan howled and darted forward to put himself between us.

"*Nnnrraaugh.*" Her voice warped the word *no* into a growl. Brendan froze.

Lou helped me up and kept holding on. We watched Olivia puke her guts all over the grass, heaving so hard she stumbled. When it seemed like she had nothing left, she still didn't stand up straight. Her back bulged under her sweatshirt and she yanked it over her head. Next came her long-sleeve T-shirt and her leggings, peeled off and scattered as she staggered, and I thought, *This is what people do when they're having a breakdown.* Her macerated arm was livid in the afternoon light. I wanted to wrap her in a blanket. She kept hunched with her back to us, hugging herself like she might throw up again at any moment, but something much worse came next.

Olivia's hair grew, longer and longer, faster and faster, until it draped her in a black cape and molded to every limb like a second skin. Splinters lifted on her neck and along her arms and stretched into feathers—massive tawny feathers dappled with cream and darker browns. Her neck, arms, and legs stretched too long for her body. The bones in her feet articulated into furry paws with talons at the end of each toe. Her hands froze in strained claws until her skin turned scaly, and as her fingers curled into crows' feet, she sank to all fours on the grass. Her

269

rib cage worked like a bellows; I could tell she was panting even with her back to us. After a minute, when her breathing slowed, a beautiful lynx face turned toward us on a long neck, and my heart galloped at every pulse point in my body.

"Olivia?" I said.

She made a small, strangled sound, *"Mmrrmph."* Her yellow eyes searched for something to focus on. She blinked like she was just waking up. She was beautiful and terrifying, but she didn't look like the terrifying creature I had seen in my vision a few minutes before. She was smaller, almost timidly curious about us. I wanted, more than anything, to comfort her.

"It's okay." I put my hand out toward her. "We're here." All I did was lift one foot in preparation for a step and she took off, straight into the air, wings pumping like oars and her awkwardly long body stretching ahead and behind. She serpentined over the neighborhood toward the swamp, just like the beast Alex and I had seen after Jeremy's disaster party. I looked at Alex, but he didn't take his eyes from the sky.

"We have to follow her," I said, and squirmed out of Lou's death grip.

"Where could she have gone?" Alex asked.

"Probably to the swamp," Lou said, "but I mean, she could be anywhere in the swamp. It's a big place. The Guardian might know, since he recognized her."

Alex was one step ahead of us, already at the back door. We sprinted across the lawn, through the house, and back to Olivia's room where the misty fog in the bone puzzle glowed an even stronger indigo than when we'd left. The Guardian sat there with his eyes on the door, as if waiting for us to return with the news. Brendan darted in behind us and began to circle the bone puzzle like an angry Patronus.

"If you don't tell us what the fuck is going on and what you've been doing to my sister—" Alex said.

"None of that was my doing," the Guardian said a little defensively.

"She turned—" I stopped to take a breath. "She turned into the beast."

"I know, I'm glad she finally told you."

"How long has this been happening?" Alex spat. His hands were in fists. The muscles in his jaw clenched and unclenched.

The Guardian sighed. "When the last beast died it—*wwrrrpp*." His face wrinkled left to right, like someone had physically zipped his lip. He met my eye, and I could tell he wasn't in control of his own mouth. Someone was listening. Someone was intervening.

"We don't need the whole story," I said. "We just want to find her."

"Tell us the truth!" Alex's voice cracked.

I glanced at him, mentally Morse-coded *BE COOL STOP*, then turned back to the Guardian. "She flew off. Where did she go?"

His mouth opened like normal and his whole face relaxed. He ran his tongue across his lower lip before he said, "You know where, Anna."

Brendan stopped pacing and looked at me like I might

morph into my own flying creature and take off after her on homing instinct alone.

Lou turned to me. "The gate. It's the only place to start."

"I'm driving," Alex said.

"You don't have time!" Brendan shouted at our backs. We whirled around. "I'll make you a portal, come on."

"You'll make us a portal?" Lou laughed. "What other secrets are you keeping under your tiny cat hat?"

"I told you I could come and go from the Otherworld at will. You never asked how." Brendan streaked past us, and I began to follow, but at the top of the steps, I remembered the box. *Don't go without it*, I somehow knew. In the hall outside Olivia's room, I heard the Guardian say, "It's done. I want out of it now, for good." A pause. "That wasn't the deal." It sounded like he was on the phone, but of course that was absurd. In the midst of everything happening at that moment, I drew the line at a severed head talking on a Bluetooth earpiece.

When I rounded the door, the Guardian was speaking into the corner of the room, but nothing was there. "Oh, Anna," the head said, startled. "Anna, is everything all right?"

I stepped toward the puzzle with a terrific windup—"Wait!" he yelped—and smashed my leg through the cylinder. I braced for an electric jolt, but the indigo neon flickered and went out as pieces snapped apart and flew across the room, just bones again. The talking head disappeared. A ringing in my ears that I hadn't noticed stopped. "Don't leave this here for someone to find," Brendan said behind me, so I shoveled the bones back into the box, not caring if they broke, slightly wishing they would. I snapped the lid shut and the crowfoot reached out and grabbed the latch completely on its own.

"I can't go with you," Brendan said. "To open a portal for long enough, I have to stay on one side."

"We'll be okay." I hit the light switch and hustled out the door. I kept seeing Olivia heaving, her back broadening like it was creating its own mass before my eyes. It looked so painful.

The boys stood awkwardly in the middle of the kitchen, Alex with his hands buried deep in his pockets and shoulders up to his ears. Lou saw me and said, "Why did you bring the box?"

"I don't really have a choice." I shoved it into my bag and regarded it like a particularly gross stain.

"Where are we going?" Alex demanded.

"The fence." Brendan darted through the sliding door onto the deck, which we'd left open. Olivia's clothes were strewn about the lawn like orphaned shoes you sometimes saw on the edge of the highway. I grabbed her sweatshirt and leggings and shoved them deep into my bag. Brendan led us to the back corner, most secluded by the hedges, and said, "Wait here." He leaped to the top of the fence and dropped out of sight.

"We could be halfway to the gate right now," Alex grumbled.

"This will be faster," Lou said. "Think of all the lights between here and the gate. And what if we get caught at the train tracks—"

"Okay, thank you." Alex popped his knuckles one after the other after the other.

Miraculously, Brendan appeared at the top of the fence

with a small branch in his mouth. "Here, move." He dropped to the ground and rammed the branch straight into the corner of the fence. Acorns popped off and scattered in the mulch. Light broke through the seam in the fence, like sun behind a window blind. "Stand back," Brendan said through gritted teeth. He drew the branch up, unzipping the fence, which gaped like torn metal. Brendan clawed his way up the fence, dragging the branch higher. "Whatever you do, don't touch the edges," he huffed with the effort. "Go! I can't hold it much longer!"

Alex ducked through first and disappeared, then Lou.

"Go!" Brendan yelled. Hugging my bag to my chest, I stepped through and turned back just in time to see my shadow-self walk through the gate in the fence, on her way to hold my spot in my house until I returned.

"Ah!" Lou yelped. "That thing was fucking hot! Damn," he said, putting his finger through a scorch hole in the shoulder of his T-shirt. The portal closed behind us, no sign at all of the fence or Brendan or the Tiffin backyard, just the faint smell of singed fur. The path ahead of us was white stone and the trees were suddenly gargantuan. Fungi everywhere, the hushing sound of wind through leaves the size of pillowcases, wafting burnt marshmallows, it all came flooding back and made the edges of my vision hazy. We'd stepped directly into the Otherworld.

Keep up with Alex was my only thought at that moment. He'd taken off into the trees, abandoning the road altogether. Lou and I were methodical and clunky, taking care to clear tree roots and leap over muddy parts, but Alex ran like Legolas, quick as a damn deer.

"Where are we going?" I yelled to him.

"The grotto," he shouted back.

The Banshee will know what to do, I thought with relief.

"This isn't the way," Lou yelled from far behind us.

He was right, I realized with a kick to my sternum. This wasn't the way the Guardian had taken us at all. Where was the market? Where was the asterisk, with all roads converging at the signpost? Alex followed a narrow path that cut straight through the trees, up embankments and down into steep gullies, through waist-high brambles and over decomposing logs. It was a path as the crow flies. How did he know where to go?

We came to a footbridge over a roaring creek. Alex slowed down and led us along the edge. The water surged, so much more than the faint trickle there'd been the last time. We came around a bend in the river and the small stone dome of the grotto appeared like a mirage, tucked in at the base of the waterfall, just as we'd left it. The water in the pool was murky. Something rust-colored swirled and bloomed between lily pads. *That right there is blood.* I looked up the waterfall, but it dribbled down the rock face as frothy white as ever. Goose bumps lifted all the little hairs along my arms. Alex splashed through the opening into the dark.

Together Lou and I ducked into the grotto, equally encumbered, Lou by his size and me by my stupid box. I stood up, my eyes adjusted to the dimness, and found Alex, bound and gagged at my feet. Long ivy vines wound around his wrists and ankles and pulled his mouth back at the corners. He made sounds like you hear when someone is gagged, but I understood what he was saying. I looked around and we weren't in the grotto at all. We were in the main room of a dilapidated old house with a view on to the chain-link Wall.

He was saying, "The Swamp Witch. It's a trap."

CHAPTER 22

"OH, LOVELY!" THE Swamp Witch clapped her hands. "The gang's all here." She stood at the center of the room, knit shawl crisscrossed tightly around her small frame and tucked into her belt. Her bright red hair spilled in a great mass down her back. Her feet were bare, dirt packed into every crease and wrinkle. They *shooshed* dryly across the floor as she came closer. Her skirt reached almost to her ankles, but her arms—surprisingly lean and strong looking—were sleeveless. Gold bangles climbed both forearms like gauntlets.

Olivia lay curled on the floor below a triple window that looked out on to the forest-backyard. Her tufted ears twitched, hearing faraway sounds we couldn't, and her chin rested on her massive bird claws, but her eyes stayed on me. *It's Olivia,*

I reminded myself as my heart rate kicked into fight-or-flight gear. *Your friend is in there.* Lou and I stood in front of an enormous fireplace—the identical twin to the one in the Tiffins' kitchen—that we apparently had just stepped out of. The walls and parts of the ceiling were covered in climbing vines just like the older parts of the Wall. Tendrils had made their way to the ceiling fan at the center of the huge room. Each fan blade bristled with heart-shaped leaves.

As I looked around, it became more familiar and more eerie. Instead of a granite-topped island, a long wooden table took up the center of the room. Where Bonnie's wall of photos was in Hartwood, the Swamp Witch had busily patterned wallpaper. The doors and windows were in the same places; even the floorboards had the same square nails in them. We were standing in the Tiffins' house, but in the Otherworld, it belonged to the Swamp Witch.

I frantically took this all in as Alex struggled against his bindings on the ground. *"Wun! Wun!"* he yelled.

"Don't be silly," the Swamp Witch said. "Make yourselves at home." She waved a gnarled hand toward the wall and ivy broke off with a snap. It wound itself around Lou's hand and yanked it behind his back.

"No!" I shouted. Lou was so petrified, all he could do was breathe more and more heavily. *Does he have asthma?* I racked my memory. *Why don't I know useful things about my friends?* I dug at the vines around his wrist, but that only made them tighter. His hand was turning red. "It's too tight," I told the Swamp Witch. "It's like a tourniquet. He'll lose his hand." Lou screamed and struggled as two more vines wrapped themselves around his ankles and face.

"He will not lose his hand," the Swamp Witch said wearily. "Much to my chagrin. I haven't made a deposit at the Banshee's bank in ages." She gave a push to the air with both hands and Lou sat down hard against the wall next to Alex.

My turn next, I realized. "I don't understand," I said out loud, thinking, *Stall, stall, stall*, "what we're doing here. What happened to the grotto?"

"Oh, the *Grotto of the Oracle*." Her laughter turned into a ragged cough; she hawked a phenomenal loogie and spat into the corner. Wiping her lower lip she said, "I take it you found the map."

"What map?"

"Uh-huh." She checked the fourth bracelet on her left arm, as if it were a wristwatch. "Let's give her a few more minutes. I'm nothing if not generous with time. Join me, Aine, won't you?" She pulled out a stool and gestured to one on the opposite side.

Cold sweat gathered in the underwire of my bra. I scooted the stool up to one of the three place settings, moving slowly, like I was approaching a wild animal, and awkwardly rested the box on my lap. Faded cloth napkins cradled stained silver that looked more like daggers than cutlery. A tarnished candelabra stood at the far head of the table with at least seven burning candles dripping wax onto the wood. By all indications, the Swamp Witch was prepared to serve a meal to her guests, but there was neither sign nor smell of food.

I didn't like her using my real name. Didn't like it one bit.

"Who else were you—are you expecting?" I asked. Somehow sitting at a dinner table elicited uncontrollable politeness.

"Three is a powerful number, to be sure," she said, checking a different bracelet. "Perhaps it's better that it's just yourself and me. But we'll wait. All the time in the world, have we," she singsonged. "So, tell me." She stopped futzing with her jewelry and folded her hands on the table edge. "When you look around, what do you see?"

"In this room?"

She nodded.

I didn't want to give her the satisfaction of knowing its double, so I said, "Dirt floor. Ivy on the walls and—" I gasped. As soon as I named it, the ivy melted into tapestries covering the wall on either side of the fireplace. The vines around the windows morphed into heavy drapes the color of deep jungle chlorophyll. Dark wallpaper unfolded along the walls as fast as my eyes could travel. I goggled around the room. The ceiling fan became a chandelier with two dozen burning tapers. The battered wood floor gleamed around the edges of a rug that I suddenly felt under my sneakers—the pelt of some giant, six-legged animal with fur as thick as a bear's. And the food! A fog of delectable goodness swabbed away the stench of mildew. Butter, onions, roasting meat, baking bread. My mouth watered involuntarily.

I didn't have to say a thing. The wily old Swamp Witch read it all over my face. "Ah-ha, so your sight is returning. Very interesting, Aine."

"Please call me—most people call me Anna. I prefer it."

"Choosing your own name is like choosing your own destiny."

"I don't believe in destiny." The sentence was pulled from my mouth like a tooth. "I believe in choice. Didn't you choose your name, Swamp Witch?"

The Swamp Witch turned her head to look at me with one mischievous eye. "I must say, I like this Anna Kellogg. You aren't at all what I expected."

"What did you expect?"

"From what your mother told me? Oh, a mousy little girl, very passive. Someone who, you take away her friends and then you can, *phtt*!" She flicked her finger. "Knock her right over." She smiled, revealing a mouth full of brown teeth. "But you have backbone."

"How do you know my mom?"

The Swamp Witch's face broke into a thousand craggy wrinkles. She chuckled and I smelled her nasty breath all the way across the table. "This is much more fun than I anticipated."

"How do you know my mom?" I asked again through gritted teeth. A new headache broke over my skull, from the crown of my head to my jaw and down the back of my neck.

"I inherited her," the Swamp Witch said, "your mother. Or, rather—she inherited me. I've always had a liaison in Hartwood." She said it with a French accent: *liaison*. "Your mother—"

"My mother works for the Parks Department," I blurted. "She works out of her truck, alone, which is how she likes it.

She doesn't have any liaisons, and she doesn't have anything to do with the Otherworld." A memory surfaced, of walking with the Guardian, catching the shape of a person moving through the ancient trees, not seeing a face or even the full figure, but somehow recognizing the hunch of the shoulders and the way she held her head, perpetually bent over whatever she was studying, even when she walked. Another memory that hadn't happened to me yet.

"Mmm, see, that's not *entirely* true." The Swamp Witch absentmindedly twirled her finger around a lock of hair on top of her head. "I've worked with your mother for years, even before you were born. I've grown quite fond of her, actually. I'll miss our dinners together."

A chill ran down my entire body, all the way to my feet. The table was set for three people. "She would've told me about you," I argued. "I asked her point-blank if things were changing—"

The Swamp Witch gave a cartoonish shrug—"Maybe she *forgot*"—and burst out laughing at her own joke.

My voice came out thickly. "Did you tell her what you did to Olivia?"

She glanced over her shoulder at the beast—Olivia—and gave a small shrug. "She knew the last beast, too."

The last beast, like they were elected officials, like they were expendable. I pushed the thought away. "What does she do for you? Smuggle you ingredients for your potions? Spy?"

The Swamp Witch's shrill peal of laughter rolled across the ceiling. "Spy? On whom? The town is run by a bunch of arse-licking eejits. Nothing they have I would ever need or want."

I knew that was a lie, but I just let her talk.

"And now they're putting a gate in the Wall." She smiled her hideous smile. "All the better to drive their heinous vans in and drum up tours for all the looky-loos obsessed with my pet. A *spy*," she scoffed. "I'll just have to look out my window."

I thought of the Jurassic vegetation, the giant fungi of every shape and color, the long-eared rabbits with their thin graceful antlers. They all seemed suddenly so vulnerable. "Your pet?"

She smiled at Olivia.

A black hole opened up inside my chest and began spaghettifying my organs one by one.

The Swamp Witch chuckled again. "And what they don't realize is that they will be giving much more than they get. Some will fall through a thin place without even realizing it"—I said nothing, so she went on—"and then it's only a matter of time before they return for good. You can't spend time in the Otherworld without it becoming part of you."

"To enter, you must remain. To remain, you need only enter," I recited from the map. "I thought you said the town didn't have anything you'd ever need or want."

"The Otherworld gets its power from the creatures who live here," she explained testily. "The ants, the trees, the bears, the algae—each one is like a battery walking around, charging and recharging the Otherworld itself. The bloody town council doesn't know a thing about sacrifice, what it takes to keep the sun moving across the sky each day. They think they understand the way energy moves in the Otherworld—the force of it, the physics—but—"

A knock came from the front door, and she said, "One moment." As soon as she was through the doorway into the hall, I rushed to Lou and Alex. The vines were so tight, I couldn't do anything to help them. *"Wun,"* Alex insisted again. "Go!"

I heard kids' voices. Lou, Alex, and I all strained to see past the Swamp Witch, who had her arms spread before the open front door, then suddenly disappeared. I caught a glimpse of a bike lying in the street on the other side of the broken Wall. There were four kids. One was wearing my favorite yellow shorts. My clear-framed glasses from fourth grade. The Swamp Witch's red hair appeared behind them, and they screamed. "Come back when this one is lost," we heard the Swamp Witch say, "and you need to find her."

The boys and I—our teenaged selves—looked at each other in disbelief.

The Swamp Witch closed the door with a heavy thud, as though she'd never left.

I scrambled back to my seat as she came in the room, rounded the table, and took her seat again. "It appears as though our last guest won't be joining us. Just as well."

"That was us, wasn't it?" I said.

"A version of you, yes. I told you you'd be back, didn't I?" She brushed her hair behind her shoulder. "The gate will bring new blood in," she said, as if our conversation hadn't just been interrupted by a visit from our nine-year-old selves. "So much faster than the old way. I thought you'd be pleased," she said with genuine bewilderment.

"You thought I'd be pleased that my friend is going to live

her life as a glorified tourist attraction for the benefit of the Otherworld? It was supposed to be me. Dennis was meant to bring me."

Her mouth was a thin line. "Yes. It was a bit of a mess at first. You and Olivia—your timelines are so tightly woven together, it was hard to distinguish you from a distance. You're both bound to the Otherworld now, plus two extras"—she jutted her chin toward Alex and Lou— "so it makes little difference. The ending will be similar enough."

My palm sweated against the wooden box.

"I hear a question that you're not asking," the Swamp Witch said teasingly. "Why you? Why you and *not* Olivia?" She smiled.

The question hit me in the gut. It had weighed me down for weeks. And now, sitting in the same room as the truth, I knew that whatever reason she gave would be a lie. She'd gotten what she wanted with Olivia—the only thing I could bet on was that she still wanted something from me. "I'll make you a deal," I said, and my voice cracked. "Let us all go home safely, and you can have the book. We won't bother you or your world ever again. We'll get out and stay out."

Alex yelled through his gag. *"Mnomnomno! Uh-uh!"*

"You need to let *all* of us go. That includes Olivia." My knuckles were bloodless around the box.

"I can let her go now," she said, gesturing at Olivia, "but she'll return. We'll just keep doing this over and over. But there is another way." She put her hand out. The box flew from my grip, straight up into the air, knocked against the edge of the table, flipped over, and landed softly in her open palms. Her face relaxed into pure affection, like I'd handed her a sleeping baby. She turned the box sideways and opened the lid like the cover of a book. Its spine crackled, leather and stitching once again. One arm held the book propped against her stomach while the other hand riffled through hundreds of pages that appeared where there had only been carved wood a moment ago.

"Now let us go. Olivia, too."

"Oh, you poor dear." The Swamp Witch's voice was still soft, but its vinegar was returning. "Olivia's not there anymore."

I looked at the beast—Olivia—lying on the floor like a well-trained dog. Her eyes blinked slowly, heavily, as if all this unscheduled commotion conflicted with her nap time. *She's lying*, I told myself. *Olivia is still in there. That* is *Olivia.* The Swamp Witch had her nose back in the book and wasn't paying us any attention, so she didn't see when the animal cut her yellow eyes to me and held my gaze with her slash-thin pupils, suddenly alert. She blinked once more, very purposefully, and all the tension in my neck melted. I sat up straight.

I see you. I'm here.

She was muted just like the Guardian had been in the puzzle, just like Alex and I had been in the kitchen. But I didn't need to hear her voice; her message came through loud and clear. "Turn her back," I demanded. "Now. You have the book, so you can do anything. Turn her back."

"That wasn't part of our deal, I'm afraid, seeing as it's impossible and all." Her fingers continued to leaf through the pages, running along lines of text. From what I could see over the edge of the table, it had turned into yet another book.

"Olivia doesn't deserve to be the beast. She's going to Dartmouth in the fall. She's the goddamn valedictorian of our class. She's going to be a journalist and we're going to live in an apartment with lace curtains and a cat named Pelican." We hadn't talked about any of that; it just spilled from my mouth with absolute certainty, like it had already happened and I was remembering the future.

"A cat named Pelican?" the Swamp Witch said. "Very unorthodox. And anyway"—the Swamp Witch waved her hand—"none of that is going to happen. You want to know what was in store for Olivia before she—?" The Swamp Witch made a *yikes!* face and hooked her thumb at the beast. "She wasn't going to get into Dartmouth. She'd go to Boston College and be moderately unhappy for four years, date the same boy from her freshman hall the entire time, and then take an entry-level, soul-sucking job at a startup in Vancouver just to get away from him after graduation. Another dull existence brought to you by privilege and dashed expectations."

"That would never happen," I said quietly.

"And you!" Her face lit up. "You've been pining for that boy"—she jabbed a sharp finger at Alex—"for most of your life, to the point where you're tethered to him like a selkie caught in a net. I've seen your dreams, such as they are. I've walked around in your subconscious long enough to know that you have given years to that particular dream, with zero return on investment." She reached into her shawl and produced a silver compact, a makeup mirror. She slid it between her fingers against the tabletop, waiting for me to ask.

"You have no idea what you're talking about." I tried to sound confident and offended, but my voice grew smaller with every word.

"You will stay home," she continued, "commute to college for a semester or two, thinking you have limitations—can't drive, can't decide on a major—and that your future has limitations, but the tight boundaries that you live within don't really exist." She pocketed the silver compact and turned back to the book, still looking for something.

I could feel Alex sitting behind me, could feel his eyes pressing. I tucked my hair behind my ear.

The Swamp Witch found what she'd been looking for and slapped the page. "I'll make you another deal. If I let Olivia go, turn her back and let her go home to her Boston College future, someone needs to stay in her place."

"Whuh-uhh!" Lou yelled.

The Swamp Witch kept her eyes locked on mine, doing some kind of furious mental calculus.

"Someone—meaning me," I finished.

She gave me such a predatory look, I could see the raptor lurking just below her skin.

"What would my future look like then?" I asked, and she smiled.

"I haven't had an apprentice in over a century," she mused. The Swamp Witch tapped her chin. "An apprentice might be important enough to take the place of a beast. You'd hold the same energy reserves, and I suppose there doesn't need to be a beast for people to come looking for one." The Swamp Witch drummed her fingers on the table. "I singled you out for a reason, Aine. You have great potential, abilities that seem like weakness only because you don't know how to use them. I can teach you. My sister can teach you."

"Mo-mo-mo!" Alex shouted.

"Can I have some time to think about it?" I asked, and she laughed.

"Sure! Take all the time you need, until Beltane." She returned to the book and flipped to another page.

More like an indentured servant, a voice said. Lou stopped struggling with his bindings.

Don't take the apprenticeship, another voice said in my head. *You have your own place here. She wants to keep you caged.* Suddenly very cold, I stood up from the table and walked around the room, feeling the Swamp Witch's eyes following me.

Who is speaking, please? I stopped to study the patterned wallpaper, which turned out to be three-dimensional, and not wallpaper at all. Moths, hundreds and hundreds of them, each with a small pearl-headed pin sticking them to the wall like some macabre diorama. Moths of every shape and size—with fuzzy antennae, or long-winged like tiny kites. Blue-gray and gray-white, tortoiseshell and sea-glass green. A moth the size of my palm had two spots like eyeballs looking out of its wings.

You know us, the voices said together. *You'll remember.*

I wandered around the room toward Olivia, who was firmly ignoring her captor and her antics.

You belong here, the voices said together. *That's why she's trying to keep you.*

Olivia's feathered side rose and fell slowly, and it was suddenly apparent to me how enormous her lungs must be. Her yellow eyes were open and alert. *It's still Olivia*, I told myself. *I'm still me.*

I crept down the room to face the windows looking out on the Wall and stopped directly over the beast. Olivia lifted her huge golden eyes to mine. *We're going to get you out of here*, I told her. *Do you hear me?*

I waited for her voice in my head. I waited.

Her long tail, which had been wrapped around her feet, flicked out and touched my hand. My fingers curled around her coarse fur, and I gave a reassuring squeeze. *She's still in there!* I could've shouted, but the relief crumbled as soon as I lifted my eyes.

Nightfall is the start of day, the voices chorused, *and if you linger, you shall stay.*

Out the window, two moons were rising over the treetops in the still-lit sky.

"Ah-ha, here it is." The Swamp Witch clicked her tongue then looked at me. "You keep thinking, Aine. The door is always open for you. Right now, though, I have a bit of cooking to get back to." She laid the book on the table. Her mouth moved as she read, her face inches from the page.

I glanced quickly at Lou and Alex and motioned toward the hall and the front door. They nodded.

"Come here, pet," the Swamp Witch said in a sickeningly sweet voice. Olivia rose on command and prowled to the table, her massive shoulders moving under all the feathers. "Up on the table, that's a good girl." The Swamp Witch patted the wood and Olivia leaped up smoothly and lay in a crouch. She turned her face into the Swamp Witch's chest for a scratch behind the ears and the woman bowed to press her forehead to Olivia's. A chill ran over my scalp. "Settle now, there you are." The Swamp Witch patted Olivia's head one more time as she rested her chin on her claws.

The Swamp Witch laid her book down beside Olivia and bustled around the table to where I stood beside the boys. All three of us tensed, ready to resist if she tried to stuff us into an oven for her dinner. She had a bemused little smile on her face, and she walked right up to Alex.

"You know, it's a shame it wasn't you." She cupped his face in one hand and he flinched away. "You have so much anger in you, I'd love to see what kind of beast that would make. But your twin—she has more magnetism than you, I suppose." The Swamp Witch tilted his chin so he had to look at her. I glanced at Olivia, who was licking her talons, her eyes flicking every now and then to the witch. "And yet, you come in handy," she said, and tore a handful of Alex's hair from the nape of his neck with her free hand.

"Arrhhh!" Alex screamed.

The Swamp Witch balled up the lock of hair and popped it into her mouth. She chewed, working it into her cheek. "And one more thing." She gripped Alex's face harder, and the vine-gag fell away. With one hand she forced his jaw open and stuck her other hand into the back of his mouth.

"What are you doing? Get away—!" I tried to raise my hand

and couldn't. My voice caught in my throat and I started choking.

"Ahhh! Ahh!" Alex squirmed and gagged, but her grip was so tight his head didn't budge. With a terrible sucking sound, a small molar came out, pinched in the Swamp Witch's fingers.

Alex was breathing hard, moaning and spitting blood. He lifted his face to say something, but his lips turned in on themselves and he started choking, too.

The Swamp Witch chewed her hairball, marveling at the tooth in the palm of her hand. She laughed softly and spat the hair onto the tooth, rolling it all together between her hands like a disgusting meatball. She shuffled back to Olivia's side, and I felt my muscles relax. I sucked air into my lungs like a surfacing deep-sea diver. Alex was catching his breath, too, just in time for vines to creep up over his shoulders and gag him again. He managed to say "What the f—" before they circled his face and pulled the corners of his mouth back in a Joker-y grimace. A thin dribble of blood leaked down his chin.

"Are you okay?" I whispered, too scared to make any obvious movements.

Alex nodded and wiped his chin on his shoulder.

The long side of the table faced the fireplace where I stood, the Swamp Witch and her book on one side of Olivia, me and the boys on the floor on the other side. The Swamp Witch was muttering again. I turned my face imperceptibly toward the boys. "It's getting dark. You have to go."

Lou whimpered and Alex shook his head slowly.

The Swamp Witch's voice rose suddenly. She was locked in some sort of trance. Her voice deepened and took on an echo that sounded like there were two witches speaking at the same time. "Feather and bone, fur and claw"—the Swamp Witch's hands rose over Olivia, holding their meatball made of Alex— "stretch and grow over one and all."

The candles guttered in their sconces on the wall. I felt a charge in the air, like an electrical storm you can see in the distance. The Swamp Witch's eyelids fluttered and all you could see were the whites of her eyes. "Form follows function, seize and twist. *What cannot be named does not exist.*"

Olivia let out a heart-wrenching wail. Her talons curled around the edge of the table and dug into the wood. She strained against an invisible force, arching her back and swinging her head.

"Aarrrghh!" Alex yelled through his bindings.

"Stop it! You're hurting her!" I screamed so loud my throat burned. I rushed to the table, hovering as close as Olivia's flailing would let me. "It's okay, it's okay," I told her as a wind came through the room and moved down the length of her body, disturbing feathers and fur alike. The Swamp Witch was locked into the spell, like a massive current was coursing through her. Her arms were rigid all the way down to her fingers and she shook under the strain.

I threw my arms around Olivia's long neck and wrestled her with my whole body. "Olivia, look at me. Keep your eyes open." Wide circles of white showed around her yellow irises. Her tufted ears pressed back against the sides of her head. She whimpered, obviously terrified. "Let her go!"

The Swamp Witch kept up her maniacal incantations over

Olivia's body and the wind swelled. "As is now shall always be. Nothing and everything is temporary." She raised her hands one last time, palms together, and plunged them deep beneath the skin, between Olivia's shoulder blades. Olivia screamed and threw back her head, knocking me to the ground. The Swamp Witch's hands were wrist-deep in her back, pinning her to the table like a butcher's knife. I stumbled, doubled over and dry heaving. With her eyes closed, the Swamp Witch felt for something in Olivia's anatomy.

The wind stopped suddenly, like a window slammed shut, and I looked up just in time to see the Swamp Witch's face relax as she mouthed, "Ah-ha." Slowly, not without care, the witch removed her blood-coated hands from around my best friend's spine.

Olivia's body tensed all over. Then, her shoulders moved—widened—growing apart from where the Swamp Witch had had her hands, and Olivia let out a wail. Her back paws scratched deep scars in the wood as her torso lengthened and her legs stretched. Just before her legs were about to slide off the table, Olivia lifted her head and roared, the thunderous warning of a wounded animal.

"Olivia!" I yelled.

Her snout elongated and her lips peeled back over long, crowded fangs. She gagged and opened her mouth wide. A second set of jaws, double-lined with razor teeth like a shark's, emerged from within the first, and a bloodred tongue, bigger than my entire arm, licked the air. Her yellow eyes suddenly looked like small afterthoughts in that enormous, dangerous face. She panted, exhausted.

The Swamp Witch made a quick sewing motion through the air to stitch Olivia's back together and that was the last straw. Her body shuddered and gave out. She fainted with a thud, her head lolling off the table.

For a moment the room was silent and perfectly still. *My face is wet*, I thought distantly. "What did you do to her?"

"It was time. I had to complete the transformation or she'd be in limbo, trapped between one identity and the other. It's enough to drive you mad."

"You mean you made her the beast, for good."

"No, not for good. All is reversible until Beltane, if you agree to take her place in time. But if not, then yes, this will be her final form." She wiped her hands on her skirt like a psychotic surgeon. "She's settling in nicely. She'll rest. She'll be able to talk again."

I burst around the table and pushed the Swamp Witch as hard as I could. "You *monster*." Both hands connected with her bony shoulders and sent her staggering back on her heels. She fell hard, smearing Olivia's blood across the floorboards. She'd toppled so easily, I didn't know what to do next. And then I saw the book lying beside Olivia.

I tore pages willy-nilly, one hand pinning it down, the other in full-on destruction mode, ripping the heavy paper from its stitching. "Never again! You will *never* do this to anyone again!" I screamed. The candles burned brighter. I kept tearing pages. In the corner where the boys sat, ivy slithered back across the ceiling in retreat. The animal-skin rug under my feet took a deep breath and I almost lost my balance.

The Swamp Witch wasn't interested in anything happening in the room; her face was frozen in horror at the sight of the tattered pages in my fist. She struggled to turn over onto her hands and knees, slipping on Olivia's blood, and stopped.

A dry popping sound, followed by a soft clatter, came from somewhere in the room. At first, I thought the popping noise was some weird reaction of the book, like a dying gasp. Then I realized the Swamp Witch was staring open-mouthed at the wall to my left. The moths, one by one, were coming back to life. They fluttered and strained their legs until the pearl-headed pins popped free from the wall and clattered to the floor, one after the other after the other. The air was filled with beating wings.

Anna! The voices closed in as the moths swirled around me. *You've got to get your friends out of here.*

"You wretched girl." The Swamp Witch seethed. Spittle flew from her lips as she huffed to her knees. "You will *never* be my apprentice." Her sweater-shawl had come undone and slipped off one shoulder. She moved to stand, deliberately and in pain, but her focus was on her shawl.

"Go!" I yelled. The boys raced for the hall. I dodged the witch, who was tucking the last end of her shawl into her belt like it was armor. I knew I should buy us time, but I couldn't, just couldn't bring myself to touch her again. I sped down the table, then turned back and grabbed the book. My book. In the doorway, I paused to look back at Olivia, her new bottlebrush tail tipped in blinding white. Don't ask me why—to tell her I'd be back? Or because I thought I'd never see her again?

The Swamp Witch raised her hand and the doorframe beside my head splintered.

I turned and the lights went out, even in the room behind me where Olivia lay. I stumbled down the hall and into the living room, straight to the mirror over the mantel. Following muscle memory I didn't know I had, I pressed the book to the glass and when it met its reflection it melted through. I hoped I'd be able to get it back when I needed it, but for now, at least, it was safe, and Olivia was safe from whatever else it could do to her.

"Anna? Where are you?" Lou called from outside.

My hip collided with a piece of furniture as I rushed out of the room. I fumbled for the doorknob, muscled open the heavy door, and threw myself down the front steps. It was still dark out, but the sky was turning pink. A pair of hands reached out and grabbed me and I screamed.

"Anna, Anna, it's me," Alex said. "It's okay. We're home."

"How?" I asked. There was no swamp, no Otherworld, just a dead-end street behind me, with a single wimpy streetlight that flickered and turned off. "Are you okay?" I asked him, and turned to Lou. "Are you okay?"

"Yeah, we're fine." Alex said it like it was a bad thing.

"Goddamn it," I wheezed. "Olivia's still there. How are we . . . ?" Adrenaline poured into my bloodstream.

"How's your tooth?" Lou asked Alex.

"Gone."

"Yeah, I mean, how's your mouth?"

297

"Sore. It's weird to have a hole in my jaw."

"Anna, I don't mean to freak you out," Lou said. "I think we're all feeling pretty vulnerable right now, but I need to tell you something."

"What, Lou?" If he was going to lay some kind of heart-to-heart confession on me after that near-death experience, I was going to give him a piece of my mind.

Instead, he said, "You have antlers. I can see them from here."

CHAPTER 23

MY HAND REACHED up and met two smooth bones protruding from my head where the nubs had been just hours before.
Hours in the swamp. Hours go faster there. I turned to look at my
shadow stretching on the grass in the early morning sun. They
were simple antlers, only one main branch curving gently toward
each other with a few barbs along the sides. They felt light, totally
and completely a part of my body, the same way my ears were. I
nodded my head, wiggled it sideways. They stayed firmly in place.

"Did I turn into a deer?" I asked dumbly.

"Only male deer have antlers," Alex pointed out. "Some
female sheep and goats have horns."

"Those aren't horns, though," Lou said. "They look like
jackelope antlers."

I casually brushed my hand across the back of my dress. *No tail, thank the gods.*

"We saw some jackelopes," Lou recalled with surprise. "On the way home from the grotto. Remember the giant rabbits with the antlers?"

"But there were also squirrels," Alex added, "with tiny horns like a goat."

"So, I have horns like a goat, too?" I was having trouble following.

"No, antlers," Lou said. "Distinctly antlers. What's on your head would look ridiculous on a goat."

"That's a relief," I said.

Alex broke the silence. "What are we going to tell my mom?"

Heat bubbled at the backs of my eyes, but I kept my voice steady. "Did you see what she did to Olivia?"

"Is that what the Guardian was talking about?" Lou asked. "The transformation? When people lose their memory of their past life?"

We stood in silence for a minute, probably all of us thinking the same thing: *Is Olivia gone? Did we just watch her die?* I thought of the smooth fur curving around her face the same way her hair did when she flipped it away from her side-shave. Her eyes were shot through with spokes of light and had vertical pupils like a cat's, but when she looked at me it was unmistakably Olivia, doing that infuriating thing where she would expect me to read her thoughts from a look. "We never should have left her," I said with a strangulating tightness in my throat.

300

"We have until Beltane," Lou said.

"I don't know what a Beltane even is," Alex said, "other than a Thin Day."

"Beltane, it's like May Day," Lou recited from his shockingly encyclopedic memory. "It's always May first. A pagan spring celebration. And Samhain is Halloween. Celtic holidays, celebrating the changing seasons."

"How do you know so much about Celtic holidays?" I asked.

Lou sighed. "Anna, I really hope one of these times it sinks into that antlered head of yours: I *like this stuff.* I read about it in my *Encyclopedia of Fairies.*"

"Can you tell me what I'm doing with antlers on my head, then?"

"Mmm, I have a theory."

"Can we get back to Beltane?" Alex asked.

"Brendan told us: Beltane is like Halloween," Lou said. "The membranes between worlds become semipermeable for a night and spirits can walk the land of the living again, or something like that. Beltane is the springtime version. Probably less death-y, but still porous."

"Membranes between worlds—like the Liminal. So, the Liminal becomes semipermeable on Beltane," I thought out loud. "More than it already is."

"Which means the town gate is pretty much a portal, at least for that one day," Lou finished for me. "Anyone who goes into the swamp would be going into the Otherworld."

"And after Beltane?" Alex asked.

"The door shuts again, until the next Thin Day." Lou

thought for a moment. "The Banshee said we need to save Olivia by Beltane. The Swamp Witch said she's not permanently the beast until Beltane."

"If we don't get her out by Beltane, her name gets written in the book," I added.

"What's today?"

I looked at my phone. "It's Wednesday," I said.

"Wednesday?" Lou practically shouted.

"And, um, two weeks in the future."

Alex laughed like, *I give up.*

"What's the date?" Lou demanded.

I checked my phone again. I didn't want to say it, so I held it up for them. "Wednesday, May 1" glowed into their faces. "Today is the Thin Day," I said. "Which may be why it was so easy for us to get home just now." The thought of one single day standing between Free Olivia and Captured Olivia made me want to sit down in the middle of the dark lawn and press my eyes to my knees.

Find their names and feed them to the Liminal. Only the book could cough up those names. "C'mon," I said, "we need Brendan."

Lou and Alex demanded a bathroom break, so I waited in the backyard, which was empty except for brown daffodils dying in clumps in the garden. The deck door burst open, and Lou emerged. His forelock stuck up at a crazy angle. "How come you always look fine after our excellent adventures in the Otherworld?" he mumbled.

Alex wandered out, in an undershirt, with his red sweatshirt

302

in one hand, mashing the heel of his other hand into his eye socket. I couldn't help watching his shoulders as he moved past me, the way the thin shirt stretched looked—nice—like maybe he did push-ups once in a while? What was wrong with me?

"We can make coffee at my house," I announced like a droid. "While we talk to Brendan."

We were nearly at the back door when I saw him. Brendan was sprawled across the doormat, covered in gluey, silvery ropes that matted his fur and made him look wet and so much smaller. I rushed to his side.

"Brendan, what happened? Can you hear me?" My hands wouldn't do what I told them. They kept closing in on him, then shrinking back in fear. "Talk to me, say something."

The boys ran up. When Lou saw Brendan, his eyes grew three sizes and he said, "Oh, Jesus," in the concerned tones of someone who recognized the silvery residue from the same gluey ropes that had taken down the stag.

"God, it stinks." Alex tucked his nose into the neck of his sweatshirt. "Like vinegar, or bleach. Is it acid?"

"It's the Liminal. It's burning him. I need to get it off. Can I touch him, you think?"

"I think of any of us, you can." Lou's eyes roved over my antlers.

I didn't need to be told twice. With both hands, I smoothed Brendan's fur from his face and down his back, pulling away the monstrous spider silk. The gluey ropes stretched, then popped, and clung to my hands and wrists until I wiped them roughly across the brick patio. I expected them to burn my skin, or at least tingle, but they just felt cold and slimy, and much heavier than it seemed possible. Mostly free from the glue trap, Brendan's breathing started to even out and deepen, but he still didn't open his eyes or respond. I stroked his face with the front of my knuckles, the only clean space on my hands. "We need to get him help."

"Look." Alex pointed to the discarded glue ropes. They shriveled and dried out like salted slugs, until they were nothing more than dead twigs scattered across the patio. "Where are we going to get help, an animal ER?"

"Take me to Bonnie," Brendan said hoarsely.

"My *mom*?"

"You're awake!" I shouted. I scooped up Brendan's limp body and tucked him against my chest. "Are you in pain?"

"What do you think?" he snarled. "Just get me to Bonnie."

Brendan's head was heavy on my arm; my thumb stroked his cheek as we sat in the kitchen, waiting for Alex, who went to find his mom. *Elk, Olivia, now Brendan.* I felt ready to dissolve. Sticky traces of the ropes still clung to his fur and my hands, as if it needed life to stay alive itself. The lonely whistle of an NJ Transit train passed through town, heading toward New York. I wondered where Olivia was and if she could hear it, too.

Bonnie strode into the room, tying her robe around her waist. "What's happened?" she asked.

"He opened a portal for us. I think the Liminal caught him." She took Brendan from my arms gently and whispered into his fur. Suddenly, my eyes were burning. I hoped he'd been somehow trapped in Otherworld time, that he hadn't been in pain like this for two weeks in Hartwood.

She laid him on the island and lifted one eyelid with her thumb. "Lou," she said, "take the mop bucket to the creek, rinse it out, and bring it back full." Alex swiveled his eyes to me, but Lou didn't hesitate.

"I'll go help him," Alex said, turning for the door.

"Alexander, I need you here. Get the rags from the bathroom cabinet, as many as you can find. Or any kind of brush."

Alex's shoulder grazed mine as he headed for the bathroom. I stood there awkwardly, waiting for my assignment, but Bonnie was bent over Brendan, checking each nail and toe. "What can I do?" I asked.

Her eyes roved over my antlers. "Stay close," she said. "I may need your bracelet." My hand went to it, as if it knew what to do. I wanted so badly to call my mom and tell her Brendan needed her, but it was May first. The gate opening. I knew she'd already be downtown, keeping her eye on everything, and she needed to be there more. *Nightfall is the start of day*, I remembered. It had been Beltane for twelve hours already.

Alex emerged from the bathroom with an armful of rags and old T-shirts. "I couldn't find any brushes." He dumped the dusty pile at the end of the island.

"Check the corner by the brooms," Bonnie told him without taking her eyes from Brendan.

Lou's struggling mass filled the doorway. "Sorry," he said, as water sloshed over the side of the mop bucket. "It's really hard to carry a full pail."

305

"Bring it here to me." Bonnie pointed at the floor beside her. Lou's grunting struggle jolted me awake and I rushed to help him steady the bucket. We made our way awkwardly across the room. A trickle of water dribbled over the edge of the bucket and down my wrist and I nearly let go. It felt like I'd taken a long, shirt-soaking drink on a mid-July afternoon. It felt like an oasis in the desert. It felt like the water had seeped from my skin directly into my bloodstream, like I had stepped on one of Mario's mushrooms and I was now twice my normal size. *What kind of nuclear runoff is in that creek?* It was everything I could do not to dunk my entire head when we set the bucket down.

Alex returned with a hand broom. Dust clumps and long hairs trailed from its bristles. "This is all I could find."

"Drop it in the bucket," Bonnie commanded.

Alex dropped it in without a moment's hesitation. I waited for the murky bloom across the surface, but the water stayed clear. Bonnie reached in and pulled out the brush, now good as new, bristles tidy and clean—even the rust was gone. She brushed Brendan gently, dipping the brush in the bucket as it clogged with silver gunk and going back over his fur again and again. The brush brought so much glue from Brendan's fur, even from places that looked clean. It had burned into him like acid.

"The stag was covered in this silvery Shelob thread, too," Lou said, gesturing at Brendan.

"It's not spiderweb, much more than that." Bonnie dipped her rag in the bucket and wrung it out. "I've only seen it once before, a situation like this. The creek water is the only thing that will separate the living membrane from a host."

I remembered the gluey ropes shriveling to dry sticks on the patio—they were dying.

Bonnie continued, scarily calm. "Brendan is an aficionado of portals; if the Liminal did this to him, it must be very volatile." She picked up a clean rag and began delicately drying Brendan's face and ears.

"Mom," Alex asked, "how do you know all this?"

"My mother taught me," she said simply. "And her mother taught her. It's part of the responsibility of living here. It's my job, I guess."

You were a salmon, I remembered telling Brendan. What other forms could he take? I watched his side with unblinking attention until the fur moved, almost imperceptibly, with his shallow breath. *This can't be your last. Cats have nine lives; it would be too ironic and that's not your style.* I needed a deeper understanding of who he was and what he could do. *What kind of ancient power lives within* you, *you weirdo?*

Without breaking from her rhythmic brushing, Bonnie asked, "Where is Olivia?"

The whole kitchen went quiet, except for the steady *drip-drip-drip* of water off the edge of the table. Alex pulled out a stool and slouched down across from his mom. "You know that legend about the Hartwood beast?"

"I'm familiar, yes," Bonnie said.

"Well, when it bit her, it turned her into . . . It's her—Olivia—she's the beast," he said.

The house seemed to take a sharp breath. Wood creaked and moaned as if wind had come tearing around the eaves, but when I looked outside, every tree, bush, and bramble was still.

"But Olivia's alive?" she asked. We nodded. "Thank the gods."

I hadn't realized the alternative had been so possible.

"What else do you know—?" I started to ask, but Alex cut me off.

"The Swamp Witch performed a spell on her last night, or sometime in the last few days. I'm worried she's not . . ." He tucked one string from his hoodie into the corner of his mouth and looked at the floor.

Bonnie reached across the island and Alex walked around to her. "She's okay," she said, pulling him in with both arms. "Olivia will be okay."

"How do you know?" he said into her shoulder.

"Diana and I have been worried about something like this happening our entire lives. We also knew there was pretty much nothing we could do to protect you kids. We've already been through it once—a version of it. When we were seventeen, our best friend, Maggie, was chosen as the sacrifice that year."

"Maggie from the picture?" Alex straightened up and looked at the photo on the wall. "You told us she died."

Bonnie let out a tired chuckle. "It was easier to explain death to my kids than to explain what their town had done to innocent people for generations."

"I'm sorry, Bonnie," I said. I'd been meaning to say it ever since my mom told me.

Bonnie gave a half-smile and her face fell into worry again. "Maggie didn't die. We've been in contact with her ever since she walked through that door in the Wall. Pen pals, kind of. Communicating through the Waltar, and on Thin Days, of course." She resumed cleaning my cat's wounds. "The citizens of the Otherworld are the animals, you must know that by now, right?"

I nodded.

"It's my favorite thing about the Otherworld," Lou admitted. "All those talking animals."

Bonnie looked up at the ceiling. "And you know how, up until recently, there's been a kind of pattern to the beast attacks?"

Lou said, "It happens, like, once every five or ten years. I don't know if I'd call that a pattern."

"Oh, it is. If you look back through the news clippings, it happens on the same day of the year. May first."

"Beltane," Lou and Alex said together.

"Just like the sacrifices," I murmured.

Bonnie shifted nervously, then straightened her back and looked at us one by one. "After the town officially ended sacrifices, the Swamp Witch took matters into her own hands and the town just looked the other way. Each and every single name on the memorial fountain—they weren't random victims. They were sacrificed to the Swamp Witch, who turned them into their animal form to give new life and energy to the Otherworld. They gave up their human lives and all memories of them, including their names."

Alex said, "Oh fuck," very quietly.

I couldn't take more than sips of air. Margaret Mossfield—Maggie—with her barrettes and her suitcase . . . chains crossed over the door . . . Fox without her memories . . . Olivia as someone other than herself, her voice without her thoughts behind it, without her humor, her memories.

"So, what you're saying is," Lou said, "all those animals that we saw—the goat and the koala and the squirrels with tiny horns—they're all people?"

Bonnie blinked slowly and I knew it was true.

"But if she was made to lose her memories," I said delicately, "how can Maggie still communicate with you?"

Bonnie smiled. "When the crows came to confiscate her belongings, Maggie was able to save a few small things—some photos, a ring, little things like that. She buried them. I found them the next day, at the Waltar. I'm not sure how, but the offerings we make end up on the other side of the Wall, and vice versa. Once we got in touch with her, we became a lifeline, of sorts. We've had to remind her who she is and where she comes from many, many times. Maybe one day it won't work anymore. Maybe the door to those memories only opens so many times. All I know is that your mom and I never gave up on her. We've been here for her every day since she left, and somehow, she's still there, too."

"The crows," Lou grumbled. "The Guardian told us they keep their memories."

"The crows are a different story," Bonnie said. "They were once people, too, but they were transformed millennia ago, long before the Otherworld needed new energy or sacrifices to hold the Liminal in place. Only the Swamp Witch can talk with them. She lets them keep their memories because—" She lifted one hand, palm-up.

"Because they're more useful to her that way," Alex finished.

"I saw a crow with horns," I said.

"Antlers are a show of resistance to the Swamp Witch," Bonnie explained. "They're a show of loyalty to someone else. Maggie grew horns after a few months—not by choice, it just happens for some people. Yours look nice, by the way." She nodded at my head.

"Thanks," I said, and reached up to prove to myself that they were there.

Alex spoke softly in a way that was scarier than yelling. "How are we going to get my sister back?" His face was nearly as red as his sweatshirt. "Olivia is hours away from being stuck in the Otherworld permanently."

All of a sudden, I could smell it: burnt hair and paper; the snapping, invisible energy field pulsing from the book. It smelled like something very old smoldering. I slid off my stool.

Behind me, Bonnie said, "You understand you have to be very, very careful around Olivia. She's probably confused right now, maybe a little unpredictable. If she were to bite you, it not only turns you into the beast—"

"It kills her, too," Alex said. "We know."

I followed the pull down the hall, straight to the mirror over the mantel. The book leaned halfway out of the glass, peeking through just like it had when it was semi-buried at the Waltar. I took it with both hands, and it came willingly. Holding it made me feel complete, like a lobe of my brain had been returned.

Looking in the mirror, I saw my antlers for the first time: kind of delicate, a light gray-brown that faded to a blanched bone color at the tips. Did the antlers make the decision for me, or was there always only one way to get Olivia back? Did I have any say in it at all? I held the book between my knees and twisted my hair into an improvised half-bun to hide the base of the antlers. Then I got the hell away from that mirror.

Back in the kitchen, my fingers twitched over the rough-smoothness of the cover. When my bracelet passed over the double-helix circle, an ouroboros took its place. The snake bared its fangs as it swallowed its own tail.

"Open it," Alex said, catching his breath.

The tome opened to the middle, the heavy pages of the beginning replaced by sheets so thin they were almost see-through. Across the top, it said:

THE BOOK OF NAMES

Down each page, two columns of names were written in elaborate cursive. Not scribbled signatures, but clear, purposeful documentation. A name, then a line across to a date.

Timothy James Cook_____1 May 1698
Rebecca Mary Williams _____1 May 1699

A new chunk of pages had been added at the back and the whole thing rebound. The dates were farther apart now.

Geraldine Berkley _____ *1 May 1870*
Matthew Charles Rolander III _____ *1 May 1876*

I flipped to the end.

Margaret Mossfield _____ *1 May 1989*

The book felt heavy in my hand. I moved my fingers along the spine to close it and felt something strange. Scratches in the leather. I closed the book and found a series of dots and dashes burned all the way down the spine. I'd seen it before, on the first night with the book, but I hadn't recognized it then. It looked like the pattern on the bones before we assembled the puzzle. Brendan had told me he couldn't remember how to speak the language.

I ran my thumb down the binding. *You have the tools*, the antlered woman had said. I thought she'd meant the book, but it wasn't much of a tool if I couldn't understand it.

Without removing my bracelet, I peered through it to examine the book. The dashes and dots didn't change, but suddenly, my brain understood them as letters. The bracelet had translated and the markings formed words. I couldn't speak the language, I didn't know what they meant, but then I realized—

Not words. *Names*. The sisters' names.

My head snapped up. I looked at Alex and Lou. "I'm ready."

Lou nodded. "Let's do this."

Bonnie dropped the rag into the bucket. "The green in front of Town Hall, that's where you need to be. That's where it always happens. I'll stay here with Brendan; he'll be okay. You go do what you need to do." She hugged Alex again, then Lou. When she beckoned, I walked around the island and hugged Bonnie in her bathrobe, something I hadn't done since I was about nine. She squeezed me tight and whispered, "Your antlers suit you, Anna. Tell Maggie hi for me."

CHAPTER 24

AS WE DROVE, I heard the echoes of an announcer's voice blaring through a rented sound system. Time felt like it was moving way too fast, like I was inside the Otherworld, watching the time speed by in Hartwood; I could feel the day slipping through my fingers. Lou parked on Main Street, and we ran toward the noise. Police cars blocked the intersection, and behind them, enormous Parks Department plows kept the rest of Main Street from view. We darted between the trucks, whose plows were taller than I was, and immediately the throbbing in my skull quieted down. We passed trumpet-shaped, tropical-looking flowers in the garden at the base of the Welcome to Hartwood sign. Their pink-and-orange bells were

315

so big I could've worn them as a hat to cover my new antlers. I considered it.

A breeze brought the subtle scent of burnt marshmallow with it. Two blocks of Main Street, directly in front of the town square, were closed to traffic and packed with face-painted kids and sno-cone–eating teenagers. Part of why it felt so crowded and manic was that it was so contained. The town square was bordered on one side by Town Hall, on the opposite side by trees and a row of stores, on the third side by Main Street and its crowds, and opposite that, the Wall ran parallel. We were in a town playpen. The orange Parks Department trucks parked at either end of the fair kept people from being able to see in without coming in. Police patrolled on foot and bike, keeping a tight perimeter on the event. Up ahead, I thought I saw my mom cut through the crowd, but I lost her as soon as I saw her.

"Take your hair down," said a faint, raspy voice. I looked into the bushes running along the sidewalk, but no one was there.

"What did you say?" Alex asked.

"Nothing, that wasn't me."

"Take your hair down," the voice said again, and this time I found the source: a crow, sitting on the wires above the street like a note on a staff.

"I—you mean me?" I pointed to my chest.

Even in stillness, the crow vibrated with potential energy. With each blink and tilt of her head I thought she was about to take off. Then I noticed tiny horns protruding from the feathers on her head. "You should take your hair down and show the Otherworld your antlers," she said again. "They're magnificent."

"Oh, uhh, thank you," I said.

"Maybe you should take your hair down," Lou said robotically.

"Okay," I said, and slid the bobby pins out of my camouflaging bun. "Hold this," I said to Alex, and piled the pins in his palm. "Hey, I noticed that you have horns yourself," I said to the crow. She sat a little taller. "Were you the one who helped us find our way out of the Otherworld?"

"I wish I could say it was me." She gave a little bow. "I'm honored to have met you, Aine."

It is no exaggeration to say my eyeballs nearly rolled out of their sockets and kept rolling, like that meatball on top of spaghetti all covered with cheese. The crow leaped into the air before I could ask her how she knew my given name—*had the Swamp Witch told her?* I turned to Lou and Alex, feeling extra exposed with my awkwardly curling post-bun hair and my antlers on display. "They look a little bigger," Alex said. "Are they still growing?"

That was not the comment I'd been hoping for.

"What?" he said. "They look good! Wait." He grabbed my hand and turned it faceup so he could pile the bobby pins in it. "These are yours." I was so startled by the touch I nearly flinched. Compared to my cold crab claws, his were warm and comforting. In a distant desert-scape of my mind, I had a thought: *I would like him to keep holding my hand.*

"Thanks," I blurted, and pulled my hand away, stuffing the

bobby pins into the front pocket of my bag.

"Hurry up." Lou waved us on.

I walked self-consciously, hyperaware of my antlers, but no one batted an eye. Food carts lined both sides of the street, churning out the scent of roasting meat. The crowd was an interesting mix of polo-shirt-wearing dads, moms in athleisure wear, and clusters of people in period dress from across the centuries of Hartwood: a couple guys in Revolutionary-era tights; a woman gliding through the crowd in a wide, sweeping skirt; a knot of people who seemed to represent each of the first five decades of the twentieth century. People in the last group smiled at me as we passed each other, or nodded, or both. I didn't recognize anyone. Actors, I assumed. The Historical Society had really gone all out.

"Just made it." Alex nodded across the green toward the Wall.

The new gate was about two stories high, shiny black wrought iron with bent spikes at the top curling in toward the swamp. A thick red ribbon stretched across, ready to be cut by what I assumed would be a preposterously large pair of scissors. And then I saw her: my mom, in her kelly green Parks Department shirt, directing people where to stand. Big lifeboat-type contraptions clung to the wall on either side of the gate, and from her waving and pointing, it seemed like she wanted two people stationed below each. Between the gate and Town Hall, a stage had been set up. Folding chairs led to a podium at the front right corner. A man holding an enormous roll of pink tickets shouted into the microphone. "The countdown begins, folks! The ribbon-cutting will take place in thirty minutes, so make sure you get your fifty-fifty raffle tickets before then." When I looked for my mom again, she was across the green chatting with the fire chief, who was standing very tall and wide in his dress uniform.

"I need to talk to my mom," I said.

"Anna, we don't have time!" Lou's forelock was damp with sweat.

"Dudes!" The voice cut through the noise of the crowd like a warning shot. Jeremy walked up with one arm raised fully in the air and the other hand cradling a gyro. "I thought I might catch you here," he said specifically to me, despite the fact that I was searching the crowd for my mom, who'd disappeared again. I waited for him to comment on my antlers, but he didn't seem to notice.

Jeremy cast an exaggerated glance over his shoulder. "Hoping for some fireworks when they open the gate?"

"Fireworks?" said Lou. "Not if we can help it."

"You know, a sighting. The beast," Jeremy said slowly, like he couldn't believe he had to spell it out for us. "First time in history the swamp has been opened up. Anything could happen. I'll be ready." He waggled his phone in our faces and then slid it back into his pocket. "I mean, isn't that why you're here, too?"

"We've all seen the beast before," I reminded him. "I'm not too eager to see it again."

"Oh, of course, of course," he said in a deep, sympathetic drone. "My bad, man," he said to Alex. "I didn't mean anything by it."

319

"It's cool. Hey, we have to meet our parents. We'll catch you later." Alex fist-bumped him.

"Sounds good, see you guys later. Bye, Anna."

"Bye, Jeremy," I said, trying not to sprint away from him.

When we were out of earshot, Lou chuckled. "He has it so bad for you."

"Leave her alone," Alex said.

"Anna!" a voice called, and my eyes darted through the crowd. "Congratulations on your antlers!"

"Who said that?" I whirled around but couldn't find the speaker.

"No shit, look at that," Lou said. "They finally fixed the fountain." Water tumbled down the central pedestal, from one birdbath-shaped level to the next. As my eyes followed the falling water, they landed on a head, peering over the edge of the lowest pool. Long fingers curled over the stone lip. I took off running.

"Anna, hold up!" Lou yelled, but I was already halfway across the green, running with my head down, following my antlers like a laser beam.

"You set us up!" I shouted at the fountain. "The puzzle was a trap! The Swamp Witch turned Olivia into the beast for good. She hurt her"—I sucked in a breath—"and Alex."

"I'm so sorry," she said, raising slightly. "Sometimes things have to get worse before they get better." Her eyes fell on the book under my arm.

"What happened to 'Siblings aren't always on the same

320

side,' huh?" Alex ran up with Lou right behind. "She pulled out my tooth!"

"I truly am sorry," the Banshee said. "Perhaps Anna can restore it for ye one day."

Alex and I exchanged a glance.

Lou fanned his shirt away from his chest. "Not to be rude, but how can you be here?"

"I'm tied to the Otherworld's bodies of water, remember?" the Banshee said, raising her head above the edge of the fountain, which was much deeper than an ordinary fountain. I took a step back in surprise. The Banshee had—what's the opposite of aged?—*youthed*. Her long hair was almost black. She looked about nineteen, but her voice sounded rich and worn. It was like seeing young Joni Mitchell speak with old Joni Mitchell's voice, which is also to say it was like time collapsing in on itself. Her spectacular eyebrows were once again dark and slightly curly. Her fingers were long and smooth, without any trace of algae. She smiled, revealing her trademark big teeth, but they were healthy human teeth, not pointed like the jaws of a bear trap.

Lou exclaimed, "But you're so young!"

"Time is slippery on Thin Days," she said.

"But—but backward?" Lou sputtered.

She shrugged. "Ye met me when I looked a different age, but only to ye. I'm all ages at once. I can move around in ways others can't, including through this chlorinated piss." She looked down and patted the water. "Just kidding, fountain, my love. Ye're gorgeous, ye know ye are."

"Right, but—" I looked around me. "We aren't in the

Otherworld right now, are we?" The Wall was distinctly ahead of us, with ribbon tied across the closed gate. But the trees around the edge of the park were bigger, I realized, like redwood-big. "Are we too late? Is the Liminal gone?"

"Oh, ye would know it if it were gone. We'd all be gone, too. It's Beltane, darling." She stood up to her full height, towering above me. Her dress was not much more than a blanket sewn together to fit her frame, and actually—I was almost certain—it was the same article of clothing that the washerwoman was wearing as a ratty skirt. "A Thin Day. The Wall comes down, as it were." When I didn't respond right away, she added, "Your antlers are lovely. How do ye feel?"

"I had a headache for a long time, but it's gone for right now."

"No, I mean, how do ye *feel*? Are ye feeling more? Are ye learning how to use them?"

"My antlers?"

"Yes."

Alex turned to look at me, mildly interested.

"What do I use them for?" A divining rod? A teeny tiny clothesline?

The Banshee laughed, and something in the timbre of her voice resonated with my very skeleton. "I'll teach ye! I used to have them myself." She parted her hair to show me the scabs. "They fell off around the time I took to the waters, so to speak. Some still have them out of loyalty to me"—she gave a sad little smile—"and to Elk. But yours are entirely your own. Ye owe no one your loyalty. The Swamp Witch may take offense at your antlers, but don't ye dare hide them, and don't back down. It isn't ye she's upset with. She has many wounds, none of which she tends to as she should." Her face became serious. "How is Olivia?"

"She's the beast, that's how she is," Alex said.

"Today is Beltane," she said with a hint of accusation. "Her time is almost up."

"Really? I had no idea." I absentmindedly reached up to scratch the base of one antler and immediately put my hand down.

"You don't need me to tell you what to do," the Banshee replied. "You will remember by doing," she said.

"I know what to do." I chewed my lip. Her real name burned on my tongue. Would it hurt her, feeding her secret to the Liminal?

"Ah-ha." Her eyebrows lifted.

"I don't want you to get hurt. You've only been trying to help us. We'll just tell the Liminal the Swamp Witch's name—"

"No, Anna." The Banshee grabbed my hands in both of hers. "All three or none. Individually, they mean nothing. Understand?"

"All *three*?" Lou repeated.

"But what will happen to you?" I asked.

"It won't hurt me a bit, all right?" She smiled. "It's one branch of my timeline that I haven't explored. Ye are giving me something totally new. What a gift."

A loud burbling came from the water over the Banshee's shoulder and a disgusting suction noise spat something up. It bobbed on the surface, blowing bubbles. The Banshee reached out and lifted the Guardian, sputtering and choking, onto the edge of the fountain, as if she'd been expecting him.

"What are *you* doing here?" I snarled.

"You son of a bitch." Alex lunged for the Guardian, but the Banshee was too quick. She snapped him up and tucked him under her arm like a football.

"Truce, truce," the Guardian said as water poured from his mustache. "I came to help."

"Yeah, like hell," Alex said. "You tricked us into going to the grotto—twice! Lured us right to the Swamp Witch. Why would we ever trust you again?"

"She wants the Liminal to snap," the Guardian blurted out. "That's what I came to tell you. The Swamp Witch—it was her plan all along. She thinks she can rebuild from the ashes, that she's preserved what can be preserved and the rest can be recast, but she's wrong. It will be irreversible. The end of the Other-world and then some."

"Atomic," the Banshee said under her breath.

"And you waited to tell us until now?" Alex demanded.

"I had no choice," the Guardian said. "Beltane is one of the only days I can speak freely."

A cold wind blew through the trees so fast it made eerie whistles and moans. The ribbon across the gate snapped and fluttered. Goose bumps prickled up and down my legs and I crossed my arms instinctively. At first, I thought the wind was causing the ripples in the fountain water, but when the wind stopped, the water kept pulsing. The Banshee looked down to where it swirled around her thighs, placed the Guardian on the edge of the basin, and submerged the fingers of both hands. Her eyes closed and her mouth opened in a silent scream.

It lasted a few seconds too long. She seemed frozen in pain, and I had to look away. The brass plaque listing the names of the beast's victims glinted in the sun.

She wrenched her hands from the water, gasped a breath, and opened her eyes, shaking. "A sacrifice will be made today, from Hartwood to the Otherworld. The Swamp Witch will write in the name of the sacrifice herself."

"Whose name?" Alex demanded.

"Shit, guys." Lou's eyes grew wide. "She's here. The Swamp Witch is here."

The Swamp Witch stood in the center of the empty stage, surveying. She looked so small and wiry, she could've been a child. Behind me, something splashed in the fountain. I turned around and the Banshee and the Guardian were gone.

"Big help they are," Alex said.

"What's she doing?" Lou asked. "Should we hide?"

Just then, a bright green shirt came around from behind the stage—my mom, ducking every few feet to check something under the risers. My heart fell down a flight of stairs, just seeing her alone up there, within striking distance of the Swamp Witch.

Jeremy materialized out of thin air beside me, eating baby-blue cotton candy out of a plastic bag. "What're you guys looking at?"

I followed his gaze to the stage, but she was gone. "Oh,

nothing," I said, with one hundred percent more nonchalance than I was feeling. "Just the gate."

"See those huge bags hanging along the Wall?" Jeremy nodded. "They're nets. To catch the beast." He started laughing. "Isn't that cute?"

"Anna, you need to go," Alex said under his breath. "I don't know what you're planning, but it can't happen here."

I scoured the faces of all the blissfully oblivious people making their way through the world. I had to wait until the last possible minute. "I need to find my mom first," I said, and then, "Ahh," as my ears filled with buzzing.

"You okay, Anna?" Jeremy asked.

Alex put a hand on my back, like I might pitch over at any second, and it knocked my focus back into place. "I think so." I caught my breath.

"Were you about to have an episode?" Jeremy asked. "Do you need some water or anything?"

"I'm fine," I said, even though I felt the complete opposite. Pieces of the view in front of me were flickering and shorting out. The gate in the Wall was open, then it was gone, just stone again. The man selling raffle tickets disappeared while counting change and a large iguana stood where he'd just been. Alex kept his hand on my back. "Something is happening," I told him. "Do you see my mom?"

A bloodcurdling roar broke over the town square and someone from the crowd shrieked. People pointed into the sky. "The beast!"

She flew over the Wall in a streak of feathers and fur and came to a galloping landing in the middle of the green.

People screamed and scattered. Olivia strutted and roared again, baring both rows of teeth and swinging her head. She moved cautiously toward the chairs set up in front of the stage.

"Now!" my mom shouted, running toward the stage. "Release the nets now!" Most of the volunteers had run when Olivia touched down, and the remaining two or three people struggled with the mechanism below the lifeboat-looking thing clinging to the Wall. Olivia watched my mom, the only person moving toward her, with interest. A net deployed with a loud bang and Olivia jumped forward. Half of the net stayed bunched up and the other half fell on the volunteers, who collapsed under its weight. A net on the other side of the gate burst open spontaneously, but no one had deployed it. The gate had begun to rattle. Indigo sparks flew into the trees and scorched the grass. The Liminal was shorting out.

Police officers leaped off their bikes and drew their weapons, yelling at the crowd to get back. My eyes darted from handgun to taser to tranquilizer gun. "Get back!" one motioned to us. "Move!"

We didn't move. "Olivia!" I screamed. "Remember who you are!"

Olivia roared again and I felt it in the soles of my feet. Stones broke free along the top of the Wall and dropped with sickening thuds.

The crowd churned. People started to run, smacking into

327

each other and shouting as they went. Olivia didn't know where to look. She huffed and turned slowly in a circle. Each step left a deep gash in the grass.

The police chief burst onto the green and began directing his officers to fan out and stop the advance. He held his gun with both hands.

By that time my mom had made it to the net and freed two of the volunteers, but one was still sprawled on the ground. She waved frantically. EMTs ran in a wide circle around Town Hall and along the Wall to stay out of sight for as long as possible. "Cover the medics!" the chief yelled.

Too much was happening. My consciousness pinged around my body like a pinball. *What do we do? What do we do?*

"Don't shoot. Use the tranquilizers," my mom panted into the microphone on the stage. "We need the animal alive."

"No!" I burst across the open lawn. "Get away from her! Don't hurt her!"

Olivia turned her yellow eyes on me and lowered her head. For the few seconds that I ran to her, time stretched to a thin strand and I thought a thousand thoughts at the same time: how much I'd missed Olivia, that we were going to make it, that I couldn't wait to hear her voice again, to hug her again, to share fries and a milkshake to dip them in, that it was almost summer, you could taste it, we were almost there.

But the strand snapped before I could make it to her. The sound of a gunshot echoed across the green. Behind me, everyone dropped to the ground. Olivia shuddered, then staggered, then she fell, too.

"Olivia!" I ran to her. Deep red ooze seeped out from the thick feathers at her shoulder and spit flew from her terrifying mouth as she heaved and moaned. "Olivia." I put my hand on her side. "It's me, it's Anna."

I looked out into the crowd, which was still cowering, and only one person was standing. Jeremy Klopner held his gun out in front of him like he couldn't believe what it had just done.

CHAPTER 25

I PRESSED MY face to her feathers and told her over and over, without knowing how, "I'll help you. You'll be okay." I suddenly felt myself surrounded, but when I looked up, they were the faces of Alex, Lou, and my mom, and they brought time with them. They dropped to their knees beside me and hugged Olivia, while outside our bubble everything moved at quarter-speed. The police scrambled slowly to find and disarm the person who'd shot the beast. A police officer jumped from the stage and took several seconds to land. The hinges on one side of the gate broke loose from the shuddering Wall and the wrought iron swung open, agonizingly slowly, as the EMTs ran with the volunteer on a stretcher. The red ribbon fluttered in slow-mo.

My mom laid her hand alongside Olivia's wound. "She's not safe here. She needs Otherworld energy."

I nodded. "We need to get her back into the swamp."

"But what if we get stuck?" Lou said. "What if the Thin Day ends and we don't know it?"

"You won't get stuck," I told him.

"I won't," Lou said, "but you will? What are you planning, Anna?"

"Anna, this is really risky," Alex said. "If you can't get back through—"

"I know what I'm doing. It's different this time." I turned to my mom. "It'll be different. It's my choice."

My mom understood. "But what if you forget?" Tears ran down her face.

"I could never forget you"—I hugged her hard—"or Hartwood, or my friends—any of it. This will always be my home, just as much as the Otherworld. I love you too much to give up a single memory."

She kissed my hair. Our glasses knocked into each other as I pulled away, too choked up to speak, and turned to Alex.

He still knelt beside Olivia. "I trust you, Anna." He sunk his hand into the deep fur behind Olivia's ear. "Tell us what to do."

Olivia stirred and opened her eyes. She turned her face a fraction of an inch, and I knew to press my forehead to hers. "Can you fly?" I asked. When I opened my eyes, she was already staring into them. She didn't say a word, but I knew her answer.

"She's gonna need room," I told them.

I didn't know what was keeping us in the time bubble, but I knew it would burst as soon as we moved. Our plan, if it worked, would get us as far as the gate. After that it was anyone's guess.

We all broke away from Olivia at the same time. Lou and Alex sprinted across the green, my mom and I for the gate. As soon as we did, the world around us clicked back into alignment and the noise hit me like a pillow to the face.

Lou ran to the stage and grabbed the microphone. He turned his back on the crowd, faced the Wall, and said, "My name is Louis Leishman and I'm here to make an offering."

Olivia got to her feet and jumped into the air. She veered to the left, clearly in pain, but righted herself in time to put several yards between herself and the ground. Tranquilizer darts arced below her. Lou watched Olivia twist through the air over the Wall and breathed a staticky sigh of relief.

Alex beelined for the fountain to see if it was still a portal to the center of the Otherworld. We didn't know how much time we'd have once we crossed the Liminal, so any shortcut would do.

"Okay," Lou said. "Here goes. I sleep with my baby blanket under my pillow. I got an eight hundred on the math section of the SAT. I've been saying that I don't want to go to prom, but it's a lie. I've always wanted to wear a tux." People paused and looked to the stage for a second, not at the disappearing beast, or the Liminal, which was glowing a deeper purple, fed by the secrets Lou offered it. "What else? Um. My nana still does all my laundry and folds my boxers and socks. I empty capsules of glucosamine into my grandparents' pudding cups because they won't take it otherwise."

I looked for Alex in the mayhem of the green and he was already running to me at the gate. The portal hadn't worked. We'd have to go after her on foot. Again. From the corner of my eye, I saw a figure keeping pace with me, a whited-out smudge of a person that disappeared when I looked directly at it.

A volunteer fought with a net near the gate and an arc flash hit him in the back. The Liminal had attached itself to him; it was feeding off him. Jolts of energy shot back and forth between his writhing body and the glowing Wall. Lou's offering wasn't enough. The Swamp Witch's true plan was finally falling into place.

"Now, Anna. It's time." My mom gave me one last hug and kissed my cheek. "I'll always be here." I took a few steps closer to the short-circuiting Wall with its gaping gate, as much as my fear would allow me. I didn't look back, but I knew that my mom was still standing right behind me.

"Hey, Liminal!" I shouted. "I have something for you!" I held the book in front of me with both hands, binding reaching for the swamp. It took all my strength to keep the spine perpendicular to the ground so that it could touch the Liminal before anything else. The book got heavier and heavier, growing in size the closer it came to the threshold. As the letters met the membrane, the attention of the Liminal seemed to shift, the indigo deepening around the gate right in front of me.

I took a breath and screamed each name as loudly as I could.

"The true name of the Swamp Witch is Macha!

"The true name of the Banshee is Badb!"

The Liminal swelled like a wave. Its glow dimmed, except for where it met the edges of the book, which smoked and smoldered so much that I let go. It stayed suspended in midair, and Alex let out a whoop, but it was too soon. Electricity surged. Sparks shot out and started small fires in the grass. "It didn't work," I said in shock. "The names weren't enough."

"The Banshee said we needed three names." Alex ducked as smoldering leaves fell around us.

"But there were only two written down!" I couldn't get the book back to check but I was sure. "There were *only two*!"

"We have to go, Anna." Alex shook me. "It's now or never."

I turned to look back at my mom.

"I'll be okay," she said. "Go on."

It felt like goodbye. I knew Alex felt it, too, because we both hesitated.

A crowd had gathered behind my mom, all the people in period costumes from across Hartwood's history. They weren't scared of the short-circuiting Liminal—they barely seemed to notice it. More than anything, they looked sad. They clustered together, watching us the way the crowd had watched Maggie.

"Go!" my mom yelled.

In the distance, Lou's voice had grown softer. "I worry that I won't live to see thirty. I worry that self-destruction is genetic. And . . . I've been in love with Olivia Tiffin since the second grade."

Alex grabbed my hand and we stumbled through the broken Wall and into the Otherworld.

The Liminal resisted slightly, and for the first time I felt the thin membrane between one place and the next, like soap stretched over a bubble wand. A film clung to my bangs and clothes even after we'd stepped through.

Behind us, the volunteer yelled in pain as the Liminal let him go, and we whirled around just in time to see him doubled over, gasping for breath, while my mom ran to help. The Liminal turned its attention back to the Wall, eating away at the stone and giving off a hot smell of burning plastic. Something crashed. This wasn't supposed to happen. The names were supposed to fix it.

All I could do was focus on the speck in the sky that was Olivia. I pictured the map in my mind. "She's heading for the market."

"Good, that isn't far." Alex hopscotched over jagged stones and fallen branches so gracefully, I couldn't keep up. Stone blocks shifted as I stepped on them. Wind came up and threw sand in my face. A tree fell across the path so close to me that it hit my heel as I darted forward, tripped, and did a full belly flop onto the ground. The breath left my lungs and forced tears from my eyes. And just like that, a rush of energy settled under my solar plexus. The ground was helping me up. It offered an apology.

Alex swooped down in front of me. "Are you okay? Jesus, that was close."

I touched a scrape on my cheekbone gingerly.

"Just a few minutes more, c'mon." He helped me to stand.

When we made it to the market at the asterisk, no one was there. Not Olivia. Not Fox. Not a soul. Doors to all the stone huts were pinned with CLOSED FOR BELTANE signs, towels hung over the windows. "Where is she?" Alex squinted into the sky.

"So you found my name?" a voice asked. The Swamp Witch stood beside the well.

Alex grabbed my arm and turned to run. "Wait." I pulled him back.

"Anna," he said. Even in that moment, with all the nonsense and danger, it still gave me a thrill to hear him say my name.

"You trust me, remember?" I murmured, and turned back to the Swamp Witch. "Yes, but it did nothing. The Liminal swallowed it and went back to its rampage, just as you wanted."

The Swamp Witch regarded me with a heaviness I'd never seen in her before. She looked defeated; she looked like she knew she was defeated. "It was supposed to work. It should've been enough to stop it."

"Wait, you *wanted* me to find your name? You and the Banshee both?" I felt Alex relax and he released his grip on my wrist.

"Of course not!" she said, sounding more like herself. "It was supposed to be a Liminal kill switch—a last possible resort should the end times arrive. I planted our names on your book centuries ago, not knowing if they would be found and hoping that there would be no need for them to begin with."

"You were ready to give up your power if it meant someone could save the Otherworld from the Liminal," I realized.

"Not at first! And not just *anyone*." She huffed. "You were the only one who'd be able to recognize the names. I was being practical." She threw her hair over her shoulder and stood straighter. "I knew that the Liminal had a life span. So, I made a plan. Then another plan. I tried everything I could think of—saving energy by limiting the Banshee's and my powers, generating energy by creating a beast. Nothing worked, at least not permanently. I had two options left: you and our names on the book, or back to square one. The first option was taking too long. Seventeen years in Otherworld time is an *age*. I couldn't just sit around twiddling my thumbs.

"I decided to start over. Do you understand what that means? I was ready to let go of thousands of years of creation so I could rebuild, this time with protection baked in. I thought if I forced the Liminal to short, I could control the reaction."

"The gate was the straw that broke the Liminal's back," I said, the pieces clicking into place.

She crossed her arms over her shawl. "So much for that. I can't control it. It's too far gone, too fast. I can feel it"—she looked down at her bare feet—"sucking the life out of this place. The kill switch didn't work. If the Liminal goes, the Otherworld is gone for good."

I was about to reply when a great whooshing rolled over the treetops and Olivia's massive wings brought her in for a landing. Her rib cage heaved from the effort and she half collapsed onto the ground. Alex rushed forward, but something made me pause. "Anna," the Swamp Witch said, but when I looked, she wasn't the one standing beside the well.

A younger woman in a long gray dress with loose sleeves. Gray hair verging on white. Head held high beneath a pair of magnificent, multi-branching antlers. Half a dozen silver bangles turned in the light. She leveled her gaze at me, and I walked to her as if drawn by a magnet.

"You helped Olivia that day in the Demonstration Forest," I said.

"I remember." She nodded. "And it seems like we're back at the beginning again." Her eyes moved to Olivia and Alex.

"Can you help her again? She's hurt, and if we don't change her back by nightfall—"

"I remember," she said again, "but it's not up to me this time. Here." She lifted a bracelet from her antlers and handed it to me. "It'll show you what to do. You've already done it, like you just said." She started to walk away, and I panicked.

"Wait, we need your help! Please!"

She turned just enough to say over her shoulder, "I know how much you hate to hear it, but you already know how to save her."

"Then why am I still scared?"

She turned to fully face me. "It is your choice, Anna. I know this whole time-loop thing can make it seem *fated* or whatever, and the Swamp Witch loves to take credit for anything that happens here, but it's your choice what happens next. Turn left or turn right."

"But what would happen to you if I made a different choice?

What if I . . . turn around? And save Olivia and we all go home?"

She smiled and shrugged. "I'd still be here somewhere, same as you."

"I don't want to be alone," I admitted. "You're always alone."

She laughed. "No, I'm not! It's just easier to portal jump solo, especially when I'm trying to keep the time difference in my head. I have great friends, just like you. My friends are my family, and my family is a big one. Olivia is still a major part of that. We don't have our apartment or a cat named Pelican, but we're still best friends. It was her idea to steal Lou's car that night."

The night the power went out. The black-haired woman who glowed. "That was Olivia with you in the driveway?"

"You'd be amazed how much *doesn't* really change."

We looked at each other a minute longer and I waited for the nudge. I wanted her to press her thoughts into my head, to see the fear that I couldn't explain and unpick it like a knot. But she just smiled again and pointed at the bracelet. "Remember to give that to your past self in the future, 'kay?" She gave a little wave—"Signing off"—turned and disappeared into thin air.

I gripped the new bracelet with both hands like a mini steering wheel.

"Anna!" Alex shouted. I snapped back to the present. He knelt by Olivia's side, pressing his hand into her wound. "She keeps passing out. She's in too much pain."

I ran over, knelt beside Alex, and did what I'd seen my future self do in the Demonstration Forest. I held the bangle up to my eye, then moved it outward until things came into focus. I saw through the layers of feathers and fur to where the bullet was lodged just below Olivia's shoulder. I saw the original wound from the attack, zigzagging down her arm like a flash of electricity. I saw the magic lump that the Swamp Witch had sewn onto her spine, glowing a sickly green. And beneath it all, I saw Olivia, curled up on her side deep in the belly of her beast skin, her face taut with pain.

The bullet wasn't the problem. I knew what I had to do.

I spoke through the bangle. "Olivia? I'm here. I'm gonna get you out."

The silver vibrated and moved my hand like the planchette on a Ouija board until it was positioned right over the place of the Swamp Witch's surgery. Threads of magic spooled out with that familiar indigo glow, connecting to every part of her beast anatomy, pulsing with a current. I looked deeper, to Olivia herself, and saw one thick strand wrapped around her injured arm. The magic was linking her form to the beast's.

"This is going to hurt," I warned her as I drew a bobby pin from my pocket.

"Just do it fast, Anna," Alex said. He held Olivia around the neck.

With both feet planted firmly on the ground, I placed the bangle on Olivia's back directly over the site of the magic implant and stabbed the pin between her feathers as hard as I could. Olivia's beast body screamed and thrashed. A jolt of electricity rocked me back and I almost lost my balance. Through the bangle, I watched the magic throb and fight. Threads tightened around Olivia's arm and more reached for her where she lay deep inside. The scariest thing was that she just stayed there. She didn't react at all to being swallowed by the invading spell.

My knowing faltered. Sweat made my glasses slip and my arms tingled like my nerves were catching fire.

"Somewhere there is a Future Olivia and a Future Anna," I said through gritted teeth. "Aine told me, so it must be real. This all . . . works out . . . *fine*."

I hooked the lump and yanked hard enough to snap the strands binding it to my friend. I withdrew the pin and the vile green mass of magic shriveled when it hit the air. I dropped it into the leaves, then blew through the bangle on to her wound. "Remember who you are, Olivia. Come back to us!"

A rush of voices, like a crashing wave, rose around us and I felt the ground shudder.

Alex cried, "Come on, Liv!"

"You can do it!"

The murmuring grew louder and the last of the day's sun slipped below the tree line.

All of a sudden, a groundswell of energy threw me and Alex across the clearing. The back of my head hit the ground hard, and I tasted dirt as my feet flew over my face. Alex must've scrambled to his hands and knees before I did because he shouted, "Olivia!" and I looked just in time to see her stagger, naked and in human form, into the middle of the asterisk. A circle of feathers fanned around her on the ground like a scorch mark. Her hair was down to her knees, ratty and tangled and matted with dirt and leaves. She took two staggering steps and collapsed.

Alex ran to her, casting off his sweatshirt and yanking his T-shirt over his head so he could put them on his sister. Her eyebrows were as overgrown as her hair, and her breath was truly foul, but she laughed when she saw me and returned my hug with her good arm. I pulled her hair out of the neck of the shirt and helped her into her leggings, which were still at the bottom of my bag. We all might or might not have been crying. I brushed her hair back from her face, held her hand, and basically didn't let her go for a long, long time.

"I saw you," she said. "Every time. I was watching. Making sure you were okay."

"Thank you." I sniffed. "At the time, though, you scared the shit out of me."

"Sorry." She laughed sheepishly. "It's hard to be graceful when you aren't used to having four legs. I'm sorry you lost your baby tooth because of me," she told her brother.

"That was not your fault," he said in a deeper voice than usual.

She glanced around anxiously. "Does the Swamp Witch know you're here?"

"Doesn't matter. Anna vanquished her," Alex said. "She won't bother you anymore."

She let out a long exhale and said, "Can we go home now?"

"I don't remember if there's a portal near here, do you?" Alex asked me.

I remembered what I already knew. "I've got you." I let go of Olivia to drag the new bangle in a straight line through the dirt. A faint indigo doorway appeared. "Shortcut."

Alex raised his eyebrows. "Well, well, well."

I went through the portal first, even though I knew it would get us back to the gate just fine. Drawing the portal was as simple as connect-the-dots. Olivia and then Alex stepped through behind me and the doorway sank back into the cracked stone road. The burning smell of the Liminal hit me before I saw it: sparking and raging, sending bursts of fire into the green. My mom, Bonnie, Lou, and Brendan stood on the other side. It seemed darker there, like night had already fallen. "Thank god!" Lou shouted when he saw us.

"You have to be fast!" Brendan called. "It's about to close! The Thin Day is almost over!"

"Take her." I pushed Alex forward as he helped Olivia through the gaping hole in the Wall. Bonnie ran to her children as soon as they were safe. Lou unzipped his hoodie and thrust it at Alex, then he hugged him hard. He took a step back and just watched Olivia as Bonnie and my mom fussed around her. *Since the second grade?* I shook my head. *Good old Lou.*

I dug my toes into the dirt as the Liminal sent out one final shower of sparks. Even though I knew I was where I belonged— and I had chosen it—I felt something in me break. Watching my friends way over there without me, a tiny voice in my head asked, *Who am I without them?*

My mom came as close to the broken Wall as she could. She knew I wasn't coming any farther.

I cleared my throat. "The true name of the Swamp Witch is Macha," I said again. "The true name of the Banshee is Badb."

Time softened and became pliable.

"And my name is Aine," I told the Liminal. "Together we are the Morrígan, a tripartite goddess more powerful than any one of us on our own. I'm leaving my old life and offer you this sacrifice to take the place of the beast, my friend Olivia. I promise to stay and restore the balance. As long as I'm here, the Otherworld won't need a beast, or another sacrifice, again."

The Liminal dimmed and stilled. My mom was crying again, but differently this time. Bonnie noticed first and raised her head from the group hug. I put up my hand as Olivia, Lou, and Alex, one by one, looked at me in confusion.

"Anna, no!" Olivia shouted, and stumbled up to the gate. "You have to hurry, come on!"

"Did you see my antlers?" I pointed to the top of my head. "I grew 'em myself."

"Anna," Alex said in panic. "What are you doing?"

"This is where I belong." I shrugged. "It took me long enough, but I think I finally figured that out."

"I knew you were up to something." Lou walked up to stand on the other side of my best friend. "You're too noble for your own good, Kellogg. But how are we still able to see you? Shouldn't the Liminal be closed by now?"

"It is closed, I think. But we've all been in the Otherworld so many times now, I think we're kind of immune to some of its glamour."

"So, we can see you like this anytime?" Olivia ran her arm under her nose.

"Anytime. And Brendan can bring me any messages or tell me when you want to meet."

"Yeah, we'll see about that," he said, just beside my feet. I hadn't even seen him cross back into the Otherworld, but there he was.

"But what about senior year?" Olivia pleaded. "Prom and graduation and the beach and our apartment?"

"Somewhere in the multiverse, there is some version of Olivia and Anna who are doing those things together right now," I said. "In this version, you just have to tell me about them. You know I hated all that social participation anyway."

Olivia laughed. "You really did."

"And anyway, I know for a fact that we have more shenanigans in our future. Remember the two glowing ladies?"

She nodded, then her mouth dropped open. "You're the one with antlers, and the one without antlers was *me*?"

"We saw ourselves." I laughed.

"I don't know if that makes it less scary or more."

I wanted to hug her so bad. "Our moms know how to keep in touch. They'll teach us, too."

"You know it, kiddo," Bonnie said, walking up to stand beside her daughter. "Thank you, Anna, times a billion. For everything."

I nodded and swallowed.

Olivia hugged herself with her good arm, shivering. It must've been cooler in Hartwood. Bonnie put her arm around Olivia and guided her into the Hartwood night. "I'll come see you every day," Olivia called. "I promise."

The boys lingered at the gate. "Shit piss fuck it all," Lou said finally. "I thought we'd done it." He brushed his forelock.

"We did do it, are you kidding me?" I was a little stunned that I had to spell it out. "Olivia is safe! She's herself again."

"No, you ding-dong," Lou said. "If one of us is still on the other side of the Wall, we have not succeeded."

A lump bubbled in my throat. "There will always be Thin Days, right? We'll see each other again."

He nodded at the ground. "Brendan, maybe you can work on a permanent portal. One that won't barbecue us when we use it."

"Yeah, we'll see about that," Brendan said again, but his sarcasm was soft.

"I'm really glad you have an *Encyclopedia of Fairies*, Lou. I'm glad you paid attention."

"You can borrow it sometime; you *definitely* need it more than me. I'll bury it at the Waltar for you."

"I'd like that." I nodded. "I'm gonna miss you, Lou."

"I'm gonna miss you, too, Anna Kellogg." He turned and moseyed away, hands deep in his pockets, but Alex stayed a moment longer.

"Alex," I said, and what I meant was, *I might miss you most of all.*

"Anna," he said, "or should I call you Aine?"

"Please don't. I still like Anna better."

"I like Anna, too," he said. "I'm sorry if I ever made you think otherwise."

I shook my head. "All in the past. We'll figure things out sooner on the next time loop."

He snorted, then glanced sideways at my mom. "I'll see you

soon. Use that magic box sometime, okay?"

I didn't understand at first, so I just said, "I will," as he walked away.

Alex looked back one last time, put his hood up, and smiled. "Goddamn it," I whispered, and Brendan laughed.

Then it was just my mom. "I guess we can't fight about who gets Brendan for the night, huh?" she said. "What am I gonna do in that big empty house without you guys?"

"Brendan can still spend the night with you! You have loads more nights than I do. The time difference is weird."

"Whatever you want," she said. "I love you, you marvelous person. Thank you for taking a detour to grow up with me."

"I love you too, but . . . what?"

"Brendan explained it to me earlier today. He'll fill you in."

"Well, whatever I find out, nothing will change the fact that I'll always be your kid, and you'll always be my mom. Thank you for letting me figure this out on my own."

My mom blew me a kiss and left. Then it was just me and Brendan.

The evening crept in around us. "Where do I live?" I asked him. "You've been holding out on me."

"It's kind of been my job for the last seventeen years, ya know? And anyway, my memory isn't what it was."

I scooped him up and scratched under his chin. "I'm partial to Brendan myself, but if you want me to, I'll call you Lugh."

His entire body relaxed, and he melted into my arms. "My name," he said. "I didn't know I'd lost it."

"You should really be more careful with your things," I said, and turned to walk into the swamp. The sun was still up. It was still Beltane in the Otherworld. I raised my head and almost jumped out of my skin. A small crowd had gathered on the stone road, blocking my way. People of all ages, in all kinds of dress. People—not animals—because it was still a Thin Day. A girl who looked about my age, with brown hair pulled back in two barrettes, stepped forward and put out her hand. "Welcome to the Otherworld," she said. "I'm Fox."

"Anna," I said. "Diana and Bonnie said to tell you hi."

CHAPTER 26

WE WERE LYING on my bed in my room in the Swamp Witch's house, which was Olivia's bedroom in Hartwood. It looked pretty bare without any personal artifacts—no Great Swamp diorama or Timothée Chalamet collage—but I had all the time in the world to rectify that. Brendan was letting me paint his claws a deep blue. "I still don't understand why you'd choose to stay a housecat when you can evolve into literally any animal you can dream up," I told him as I dabbed his last nail. "There." I blew on it. "All done."

"I would've thought you'd understand the appeal of blending in, Miss Human. Under the radar is a great place to be. Also, I can jump much higher than I would in my human body."

"I am getting kind of tired of all the looks I get anytime I step outside." Usually by now, a sacrificed person had turned into their animal form, all past memories and names kaput. Other than the Swamp Witch and the Banshee, I was the only human in the Otherworld. "Last time I was in the market, someone whispered that I was a long-lost sister to the witches, and the other person replied, 'No, she's one of the Ladies of Hartwood!'" I rolled my eyes.

Brendan studied his nails. "Aren't you, though?"

"A Lady of Hartwood?" I gaped at him. "Wouldn't I know it? And besides, there are four of them. If it's the Swamp Witch, the Banshee, and me, where's the last one?"

"The last one is also you," he said. "You in Hartwood, you in the Otherworld. You have full lives on both sides of the Liminal. You haven't realized that yet?"

"You live on both sides of the Liminal, too." I gave him a noogie and my bracelets jangled. I still hadn't gotten the hang of keeping the new bracelet balanced on my antlers. "Maybe you're the fourth Lady."

Brendan dodged out of reach and said, exasperated, "You were here first. Ask the Swamp Witch."

"I really look forward to the day that my memory returns in full so I can stop wondering if you're pulling my leg," I said.

"Would I do that?" he asked, fake-offended.

I made a mental note to ask the Swamp Witch at our next lesson. I still felt cagey around her, and never, ever called her by her real name. But to give her credit, she was doing her best to teach me the history of the Otherworld, which is to say, my history, too. I had no context for the issues that came up, like the diminishing water levels or unexplained gashes appearing on the oldest trees. I arrived at every lesson with a long list of questions and asked until her face started to turn the same color as her hair. She was more patient than Brendan, even considering her demotion from Otherworld ruler to metaphysical high school teacher, but the anger still simmered just beneath the surface. I slept with my door locked tight.

The Banshee was guiding me to use my antlers and bracelets to see through the layers of time. It was slow going, but it gave some credibility to the stories the Swamp Witch spun— that I was also a goddess, who had chosen to evolve into a new life and be born on the other side of the Wall. That's what my mom had meant about taking a detour to grow up with her, but how could it be something as brief and forgettable as a detour when my thoughts and feelings were still on the other side of the Wall? I desperately wanted to ask the antlered woman why I had done that seventeen years ago, and what I had hoped to figure out. But she wasn't here anymore, of course. I was the antlered woman now. Occasionally, I felt an old wonder creep into my thoughts: What would it be like to live a mortal life? What did it do to you to know it would one day . . . end? Those were the days I felt homesickness like an ache.

With the Liminal mended and the beast gone, the Banshee was freed from her water prison. I didn't know where things stood between her and her sister, but we all lived at the house together, like a very strange sitcom. Lou sent me all the research he'd done on the Morrígan for their game—printed off the internet and buried at the Waltar—and I still couldn't wrap my mind around how the three of us would one day unite into a single all-powerful goddess. I didn't even know if it was possible, considering the powered-down versions of Macha and Badb that I had created.

I hadn't been able to pack anything for move-in day, obviously, but Olivia and Bonnie made regular offerings at the Waltar with my name on them. Brendan brought them to me as soon as they arrived: Pop-Tarts, an array of nail polishes, a glasses-mending kit, a photo album, and most recently, a yearbook signed by literally every kid in our grade. I loved it—all of it—and I reminded myself of that often.

I had made a few new friends, like the crow I met at the gate opening, who introduced me to other horned crows. They told me about their shrine to Elk in the tallest oak in the forest. I couldn't see it, of course, since it was nested fifty feet in the air, but the first crow told me later, "Your picture is there, too. The small one, from school."

Brendan stalked to the door. "We should get going if we're supposed to meet Fox."

"I'll just draw us a portal when we get downstairs." Brendan had taught me the basics of portals within the Otherworld. He wouldn't even entertain the idea of a portal through the Liminal, which killed me.

"Is this how you develop your habit of always being late?" he asked testily.

"For the thousandth time: That. Was not. Me. That was her. I'm not going to just snap back into the old version of me that you used to know."

"Yeah, yeah," he grumbled. "Don't take forever."

"I won't." As soon as he was gone, I pulled the book from under my bed. It responded to me at the slightest touch now; I didn't even have to speak. The leather hardened to wood, and I opened the lid of the box. Through the glass bottom, I looked around my room but saw Olivia's. It was strewn with clothes but otherwise empty, so I wandered downstairs to the mirror over the fireplace. Alex was sitting on the couch. "Hey," I said.

He looked up in surprise. "Hey!" He came to the mirror so we stood face-to-face.

"How are you?"

"Good, good." Alex grinned. "Olivia got into Dartmouth finally. Act surprised when she tells you, okay?"

I laughed, too happy for Olivia and too happy to see my friend to care that he'd spilled beans that didn't belong to him. The Swamp Witch's prediction was wrong. She was wrong about me, too.

"We're having a party for her tonight. You should come." He motioned to the mirror, like that was a way to participate.

His invitation pressed on a bruise I'd been trying to ignore. "I'd love to, but—this isn't the same. And it's not anywhere close to another Thin Day and—"

"It's a lot harder to be on this side of the time divide, you know. You've only been gone, what, like a week in Otherworld time?"

"Ten days," I said. "I mean, give or take."

"It's already June here. Finals are next week."

"Finals." It echoed like a word I used to know in another

language. My entire face felt puffy.

"I'm not graduating," he said with an embarrassed smile. "I have to retake a couple classes over the summer, then I'm going to see if I can start classes at the county college in January."

"High school diplomas are overrated," I joked. "Sorry you won't get to walk at graduation, though."

"That's okay. It's one day. At least now I know I'll be here for the next year."

"A year, huh? That *is* good to know." I wanted to climb through the box, through the mirror, and tackle him to the floor. "Hey, I have to go meet Maggie right now, but if I get back in time for Olivia's party, I'll—make an appearance."

Alex snorted. "Great. See you then." He put up a hand and I closed the box.

A little while later, after Maggie and I had lunch at the diner, I stood in the brambles behind the Swamp Witch's house—my house—and opened the box one more time. Through the lit windows I watched Bonnie move around the kitchen, smiling and talking and pulling serving utensils from drawers. My mom poured drinks. She looked healthy, her smile genuine. Olivia, Lou, and Alex sat at the kitchen island, which was covered in white boxes. Bonnie had bought out the bakery. Andy Tiffin walked in and kissed Olivia so hard on the top of the head that she bobbed. I could tell, even from that far away, that Olivia had redone her side-shave and gotten her eyebrows threaded. She looked radiantly happy.

Alex was in his red sweatshirt, despite the warm June

night. So predictable. A sudden wave of jealousy swept my feet out from under me, and I wanted to know each and every person that he'd spent time with since we last saw each other. I wanted names and agendas in order of most fun to least. I wanted a footnote for every time Alex thought of me, and for how long.

I wanted that from all of them—my friends. I wanted proof that life went on without me. I wanted to see it in writing.

Alex kept looking over his shoulder at the hall to the living room, waiting for a signal from the mirror.

Before I knew it, I was walking up the Tiffins' deck steps, though I was still in my yard in the Otherworld. My heart beat harder. *Why am I nervous?* Through the box, I watched my hand close around the door handle to the Tiffins' house. I crossed the threshold into the Swamp Witch's house and saw my feet standing on the Tiffins' doormat. For a second, I let myself hold the box up to my empty kitchen and take in the faces of all the people I loved most, as if we were in the same room. When I couldn't stand it any longer, I walked down the Tiffins' hallway to the living room mirror and—"Anna!"—just like that, I was home.

ACKNOWLEDGMENTS

Thank you to everyone who read this book in one of its messy, monstrous drafts, answered out-of-the-blue Latin questions, or helped me talk through ideas, especially Genevieve Abravanel, Adam Cogbill, Christy Crutchfield, Kristen Evans, Lauren Goodman, Michael Gulden, Emily Houk, Khaled Khlifi, Juliette Langer, Andy McAlpine, Oliver Oparowski, Sean Rosenberg, and Alison Strobel. And biggest thanks go to Alyssa Miele and Seth Fishman, for your endless patience and reassurance.

Thank you to everyone at Quill Tree Books and Harper-Collins who helped make this project a reality, especially Sean Cavanaugh, Audrey Diestelkamp, Jon Howard, Rosanne Lauer, Lauren Levite, Laura Mock, Gwen Morton, Vanessa Nuttry, and Monique Vescia. And thank you to Jack Gernert for all your behind-the-scenes work.

To the Franklin & Marshall Writers House, the MFA Program of Western New England University, and the students of

New Providence High School—thank you for inspiring me and inviting me into your writing communities.

A few books were really helpful in guiding me through this story, including: *On Monsters: An Unnatural History of Our Worst Fears* by Stephen T. Asma; *An Encyclopedia of Fairies: Hobgoblins, Brownies, Bogies, and Other Supernatural Creatures* by Katharine Briggs; *Celtic Mythology: Tales of Gods, Goddesses, and Heroes* by Philip Freeman; *The Bog People: Iron-Age Man Preserved* by P.V. Glob; *A Brief History of Time* by Stephen Hawking; *The Red-Haired Girl from the Bog: The Landscape of Celtic Myth and Spirit* by Patricia Monaghan; *Animals Strike Curious Poses* by Elena Passarello; *Monster of God: The Man-Eating Predator in the Jungles of History and the Mind* by David Quammen; and *The Morrigan: Celtic Goddess of Magick and Might* by Courtney Weber. The Deer Ecology and Management Lab at Mississippi State University provided valuable information about antler growth. You can visit them at msudeer.msstate.edu.

The sculpture of the four women in the Wall was inspired by a sculpture of four mother goddesses that I saw in the Museum of London in 2018. It dates back to the third century and no one knows exactly who they are. Thanks to Leanna Oen for that marvelous trip, and thanks to Adelia Pope for reminding me that writing was a worthy use of my time.

I thought I was writing a book about a monster, but it turns out I was writing a book about friends. Thank you to my friends. Who would I be without you? Thank you to Lena Gaudette for all your time and care. Thank you to Colleen, Kevin, and Amy Byrne for your doubtless belief that I could write a book, and all your love and support. And thank you to Val for hours of company beside my desk chair.

And all my love and heartfelt thanks go to Mike and Gil, for sharing me with the Otherworld for so long.

BE SURE TO CHECK OUT
ELIZABETH BYRNE'S DEBUT NOVEL

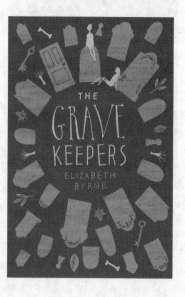

"At times deeply atmospheric and darkly haunting, *The Grave Keepers* takes us on a spine-tingling journey into a world much like our own, where more lies beneath than above."
—**MINDY McGINNIS**, Edgar Award–winning author

"A lyrical and gorgeously uncanny coming-of-age story of incantatory power."
—**KELLY LINK**, Hugo and Nebula Award–winning author

"Gothic surrealism as everlasting as a ghost's kiss blends with coming-of-age angst for the modern age."
—*KIRKUS REVIEWS*

Photo by Mike Wall

ELIZABETH BYRNE

grew up in New Jersey and holds an MFA from the University of Massachusetts, Amherst. She is the author of two novels for young adults, *The Grave Keepers* and *Book, Beast, and Crow*. She has tasted a glacier in Iceland, worked on the seventeenth floor of the Flatiron Building, and hiked among sheep in the Faroe Islands, but her favorite thing to do is grow flowers in her backyard. Liz lives with her husband and son in Northampton, Massachusetts. To learn more, visit her online at elizabethbyrne.net.